THE ROSEWATER INSURRECTION

WITHDRAWN FROM STOCK

PRAISE FOR *ROSEWATER*

"A magnificent tour de force, skilfully written and full of original and disturbing ideas"
Adrian Tchaikovsky, author of *Children of Time*

"A sharply satirical, ingenious thriller about an alien invasion that's disturbingly familiar. Tade Thompson has built a fascinating world that will suck you in and keep you guessing. This book will eat you alive, and you'll like it"
Annalee Newitz

"Quite simply one of the best books I have read for quite some time"
SFCrowsnest

"Mesmerising. There are echoes of *Neuromancer* and *Arrival* in here, but this astonishing debut is beholden to no one"
M. R. Carey, author of *The Girl With All the Gifts*

"Smart. Gripping. Fabulous!"
Ann Leckie, author of *Ancillary Justice*

"A fiercely weird, breathtaking biopunk tale of alien invasion, *Rosewater* is ambitious and smart and very, very cool"
Tasha Suri, author of *Empire of Sand*

"Inventive and creepy"
Ozy.com

"Part thriller, part mystery ... reminiscent at times of both Roger Zelazny and Nnedi Okorafor, *Rosewater* is the hardboiled, Nigerian alien invasion story you always wanted"
Lavie Tidhar

"One of the most imaginative alien invasion scenarios I have come across"
Aliette de Bodard, Nebula and BSFA award-winning author

By Tade Thompson

Rosewater
The Rosewater Insurrection

THE ROSEWATER INSURRECTION

TADE THOMPSON

www.orbitbooks.net

ORBIT

First published in Great Britain in 2019 by Orbit

1 3 5 7 9 10 8 6 4 2

Copyright © 2019 by Tade Thompson

Excerpt from *Blackfish City* by Sam J. Miller
Copyright © 2018 by Sam J. Miller

A CIP catalogue record for this book
is available from the British Library.

ISBN 978-0-356-51137-5

Typeset in Sabon by M Rules
Printed and bound in Great Britain by
Clays Ltd, Elcograf S.p.A.

Papers used by Orbit are from well-managed forests
and other responsible sources.

MIX
Paper from
responsible sources
FSC® C104740

Orbit
An imprint of
Little, Brown Book Group
Carmelite House
50 Victoria Embankment
London EC4Y 0DZ

An Hachette UK Company
www.hachette.co.uk

www.orbitbooks.net

For Cillian,
Who just wandered in

Prelude

Camp Rosewater, 2055

Eric

I am not an assassin.

I'd like that to be clear, yet I am cleaning my gun as I start this telling, having already stripped and cleaned my rifle, with the intention of killing a man. Orders.

For most Africans, the explosive discovery of a meteor-borne alien in London and its growth underground meant little. Our lives didn't change much. We peddled a more interesting variety of conspiracy theory, but that was it. A cup of rice was still expensive.

Even when we lost North America, China and Russia jostled to fill in the power and economic vacuum. A cup of rice became even more expensive.

But now it's here, in Nigeria, and that means, for me at least, extrajudicial murder.

I wait outside the command tent, broadcasting white noise like I've been trained. My boots are dirty from the mud I've had to wade through. Even now, standing to attention, I'm about an inch deep, and I squish when I move. There is a muffled argument from within, a man and a woman, the woman's voice more assured and familiar to me. There is a rustle and a man either charges or is thrown out. He stumbles, regains his balance. He pulls at his shirt tails to straighten them. He is like me, lean, light on his feet, with hair just growing out of the recruits' buzz cut. But, like me, he's broadcasting white noise, and he discovers my mind almost at the same time I do his, which is impressive because he is still emotional from the argument. We make eye contact.

He nods in greeting. "Did Danladi train you?" he asks.

"Motherfucking Danladi," I say.

"He's the only one worth a damn," he says.

Behind him, the dome glows, then crackles, starting with the ganglion. It's windy, but recent rains mean there is no real dust. Camp Rosewater exists in two modes: dust storm or mud bath. We both get a whiff of the open sewer. I feel him probing at my mind, inquisitive, just on the border of politeness. I can tell that he is stronger than me, and I slam down all my defences.

His expression does not change, but he offers a hand. "Kaaro," he says.

"Eric," I say.

"At ease, Eric. Where are you from?"

"Lagos and Jo'burg." No matter how short I keep my hair, people know that half of me isn't black. Some try to take advantage because they see this as a marker of privilege.

"Well, Eric-from-Lagos-and-Jo'burg, be careful. She is in fine form."

He heads out into the twilight and is soon lost in the crowd outside the barrier. I'm still wondering about him when she calls me in.

I don't know what to call her, so I just say, "Ma'am." She

does not introduce herself, but she is the leader of Section Forty-five. S45 is not a government department you've heard of. They report directly to the president, they handle the unusual with a cadre of agents who are unsung, and people like me are either employed as their predators or hunted down as prey. They started out saving fake witches from fundamentalist churches, but are now responsible for all alien phenomena. She's new in position, but acts like she was born into it. Her pupils and irises are black like coal, and it's hard to maintain the gaze, so I avert my eyes. Inside the tent is cool and dry. I am now in my socks because she insists on footwear staying outside. Her bodyguard is stocky and stays two paces behind, hands clasped together in front of his jacket, holding his tie.

"Do you know why you're here?" she asks.

"I was told to report."

She smiles, but her lips don't part and her eyes remain the same. "I need you to neutralise a problem."

She wears her wealth like a sidearm, like Europeans used to wear swords, obvious, obtrusive, a reminder of station to the observer, deliberately gaudy, especially distinctive in Camp Rosewater, especially effective against less fortunate subordinates. Like me.

I do not know what she means. "Problem, ma'am?"

"Do you know Jack Jacques?"

"No, ma'am."

"Do you know anyone in Rosewater?"

"No, ma'am. I came straight from Basic. Before that, I was in Lagos."

No thoughts coming from her. I have been warned of this. The higher-ups have a form of protection.

She says, "Jack Jacques is a troublemaker. Most people

3

think he is a joke, but I can see where he is going. He has to be stopped. The president wants him stopped."

I think she means for me to arrest him, and I nod with enthusiasm. I am keen to prove my worth to S45. I will follow orders to the letter because it's my first assignment. Her bodyguard steps forward and shows me my orders, complete with presidential seal, a document that requires both my handprint and proximity to my implant for unlocking.

The first thing I see is a smooth, unlined face, a black man, looking straight at the camera, a hint of a smile about the eyes, but not quite, the way a child suppresses laughter for a passport picture. Jack Jacques appears to be in his late twenties and is handsome, just shy of effeminate because of his hard jaw. His lips are thick, but to me belong on a woman's face.

"I'll leave you to familiarise yourself with the details," says my leader. "Don't let me down."

She and her bodyguard exit one end of the tent, while I go back the way I came.

Where is your issued weapon?

In my billet.

Surrender it to the quartermaster. You can't use official hardware for this detail. Can you get a gun?

I don't think I'll need to discharge a weapon.

... Eric, what do you think this assignment entails?

I can arrest him without—

"Arrest"?

She said—

Unless you mean cardiac arrest, I think you need to read your orders more carefully.

*

Not a lot is known about Jack Jacques. The name is thought to be an alias. He appeared in Camp Rosewater almost a month after the alien dome emerged. The first record is an arrest by army boys. No charge. Seems he was a loudmouth. Poor documentation. A line of text saying he refused to identify himself for twenty-four hours. Reading in between, I think he may have been tortured. After his release, pamphlets begin to appear all around the dome, cheap, black-and-white productions on poor quality paper.

> How long must we endure an existence that the rest of Nigeria, and the world, has left behind since the pre-antibiotic era? We call on the Federal Government to provide housing, public transportation, roads, modern sewage systems and, above all else, potable water.
>
> Jack Jacques

This is accompanied by a poor reproduction of a photo of Jacques in an ill-fitting suit.

Here he is as signatory to a petition banning the consumption of alien flora or fauna. Here is a statement from an informant about a gathering of troublemakers and leftists. She says Jacques was there, but nothing specific about his contribution.

No address, no known associates.

I have never killed before, but my employers think I have, which is why I've been tapped for this assignment. When S45 wants you, they find ways of questioning your close friends. I know who snitched. Except, it can't be snitching when there's nothing to snitch about. When I was fifteen my family experienced a home invasion which ended with one of the robbers dead, skull crushed. The police report says I caved his head in with a paperweight, but my sister killed him accidentally, her intention being to stun. My sister has a history, so we agreed as a family that I should wear the jacket.

I am shaving my head with a blade attached to a comb. My crew cut will identify me as military, so I'm getting rid of it. My mirror dangles on a string tied to a crossbar in the tent. It sways gently, and I move with it to keep up with my reflection, weaving like a boxer. When I finish, I change my clothes and step out to the camp.

It's busy like you wouldn't believe. About four in the afternoon and the vultures are swooping down on the market areas, eating the hollowed-out carcasses left by butchers. Camp Rosewater is basically shanties hugging the alien dome all the way around, except where the electric pylons, the ganglia, project as towers of alien neural tissue. It is a mess of tents, wooden shacks, corrugated iron improvisations and lean-tos. There is a barter-based economy mixed with the regular Nigerian naira. The camp grows daily as people arrive from ... everywhere. New people simply stake out land at the periphery and build. There are one or two new concrete structures – churches, mosques, temples, weapons depot for the military detachment sent to keep order. There are micro-farms because close to the dome you can quite literally grow anything anywhere. I have, in my tent, an iceplant, bought because the flower girl insisted that it would protect me from ghosts. In two days it has sprouted three magenta flowers. Throw seeds in the mud, they burst into healthy crops in no time, and weeding is a full-time job here.

There are brothels, open lines for the female prostitutes, euphemisms like "sports centre" for male ones.

I walk in a stream of slow-moving piss, in an alley darkened by the proximity of adjacent buildings. A thousand conversations achieve anonymity in their own cacophony. My shoes are ruined, but this is what I want. The clothes are worn, but okay, which means I will not be excluded from anywhere, neither will I be robbed.

My first plan is to go into a beer parlour, but I find something better, a night club.

I don't dance.

My right hand still glows from the luminous door stamp, and this glow passing through the glass makes my drink look like lava. I have no idea what the music is, but it seems to depend on heavy bass. The floor is full. When you come in there is a row of kids who clean your shoes, then you are pushed by the press of the crowd on to the dance floor, a concrete slab polished by the innumerable shoes shuffling. Cheap implant scan at the gate, to pick out cops, though it fails to parse my ghosted identity. In the west corner sits a squat turret bot, keeping the peace.

Nobody in this place is thinking of Jack Jacques. Finding that out gives me a headache from the effort of reading them. I do this for two nights before I get a hit.

It's a memory of Jacques, of meeting him. The person is outside the club, leaning against the wall. I get up to leave and in so doing, bump into someone. I feel the intent to hit me even before I apologise. I move to avoid, barely, to mask my training. The lurching ape swings past me and hits someone else. I tread on his instep and he falls flat. In the confusion I slip out.

She is smoking, barefoot, wearing a dress of indeterminate colour, no make-up and hair hanging limp after being straightened. She can hear me, my footsteps, but she doesn't look at me. I have cigarettes, singles that I bought inside for this very eventuality. I don't smoke, but I know how, so I light up. In the glow from her cigarette end I see that she keeps her gaze on the ground, even though we lean on the same wall, feeling the vibration of music, and the radiant heat from dozens of bodies.

"I am off duty," she says. *I no dey duty*.

I nod, drag on my cigarette.

"And I am armed."

I look at the skin-tight dress and wonder where she has hidden the weapon. I read the threat she feels from me as a reflection of actual violence over her life and the lives of women she knows and has heard of. I adjust my body language to be as non-threatening as possible. She is not thinking of Jacques right now.

"I should probably go and jack off," I say.

It works, she remembers.

I get my first sense of what Jacques looks and sounds like in real life. He is wearing a white suit in the memory I steal. His head is almost at the ceiling of her love shack, which tells me he's tall. He has a black tie, and a hat – a dog-eared hat, abeti aja, like the Yoruba wear. He is unselfconscious and gives the impression of being clean despite the filth around him.

"You get ciga to give me?" asks the woman. She has finished hers and has a hand out. I give her one. Through the armhole of her dress I can see the tail end of a tattoo. It will be the name and village of her mother. People get raped and murdered here, and even with implants it is not always easy to track down the next of kin, so Camp Rosewater women get tattoos.

8

The memory of Jacques plays again. She finds him attractive, and is grateful that he smells good. The memory loops back and for a millisecond it is me she sees in the white suit and the hat, before it transforms back into Jacques.

Jacques says, Take off your clothes.

She says, How you want am? Front or back?

Jacques says, I want you to bounce on the bed and moan as if I am fucking you really hard. Then, I will pay you double. You'll also tell anybody that we fucked, especially the young men with me. Can you do that?

She can, and she does.

The next day there is a burning truck, not far from my tent.

I sleep fitfully. When you take in someone else's memory it struggles to find its place among your own. Your mind knows it to be alien and, I think, tries to purge it. Failing that, it replays the memory while trying to categorise it. This is why I don't like reading memories, and I am grateful for the suppression training at S45. I see more detail in the scene, his short fingernails, his skinned knuckles, the crooked incisor, the bulge of his cock suggesting he was aroused, but disciplined. In one replay of the memory, he stops talking and looks at me.

"I see you, Eric," he says. "I will be ready when you come for me."

Then his eyes explode and he vomits. I wake.

Smoke all over my tent, from the burning truck. A few young men tried to dump toxic waste at night, at the periphery, but got caught just after the green sludge sank into the soil. They escaped, the truck did not. I hope this assignment doesn't give me cancer.

I go looking for residue. This is not magic or mystical bullshit. The aliens have captured information in the atmosphere for their own purposes. They did this by spreading a lattice of interconnected artificial cells, xenoforms, all around the planet, forming a worldmind called the xenosphere. Along with a few other people I can access this data, which is why S45 recruited me. It's a useful talent, especially when looking for people. The alien field is linked to the minds of people and data can flow both ways because xenoforms don't only connect with each other. They connect with human skin receptors and access the brain this way, gently extracting more information. I start early. I want to find where that prostitute works. I'll sit on it, stake it out until Jacques turns up. I keep walking until I get a sense of déjà vu. People in my line of business compartmentalise on a whole different level. How else can we tell our real déjà vu from that which is due to borrowed memories?

I hear someone behind me and I don't mean with my ears. He thinks so loud, I'm sure he doesn't know who I am. As I turn in the alleyway to look at him, I hear his comrade step in, blocking the only other path.

"What do you want?" I say. "I'm not holding."

"New blood, you can't just walk in here and not pay rent," says the man behind me.

Right. The local Big Man wants to tax me. That would be Kehinde in this part. Taiwo, his twin brother, runs the opposite side of the dome. The intelligence is that they are ruthless and hate each other. A story is told of a peace summit between their organisations which ended with the twins fighting each other, with fists, without saying anything, getting exhausted but persisting, for hours. The urban legend version says they fought from sunrise to sunup. The S45 informant said it was four hours, with breaks. By the time it finished, they had matching mangled faces and torn knuckles.

"Tell me," I say, "do either of you know Jack Jacques?"

"You do not fit here," says Kehinde.

It's strange. I was expecting some kind of cartoon godfather, but Kehinde looks ordinary. He wears a box shirt and worn jeans with the kind of no-brand boots the better denizens of Camp Rosewater wear. Belly a bit soft, but I put him at north of fifty-five, so he gets a pass.

I know I don't fit. The camp attracts people who are sick, desperate or criminal. The sick because when the dome opened, it healed people and created an instant Mecca–Lourdes hybrid. The desperate are the ones who have nowhere else to go. Dirt poor, disgraced, religious extremist, that kind of shit. Criminals need no invitation, they're everywhere. I'm not sick, desperate or criminal. They can tell.

"I'm looking for Jack Jacques. I saw his pamphlet on equality. I want to help."

They all start laughing, but my naivety triggers a communal memory. Jacques and Kehinde, with others in the background, in this very room.

We have an opportunity here. This is a new society, a new beginning. I want to make something of it, to stop the chaos, to be a beacon for the rest of the country, hell, the world.

He is in a cream suit. In my mind, the memory flickers and the suit turns white, like in the prostitute's memory.

Kehinde laughs. *And what place for me in this Garden of Eden? Where the role for disobedient men?*

Jacques leans in. *To grow a garden you start with a seed,*

11

that's me. Then you need fertiliser, that's you. Manure doesn't smell so good, but it's necessary.

I can feel Kehinde bristle, but agree. *Boys, this guy just called me a piece of shit in the nicest possible way.*

The laughter echoes from the past, mixing with that of the present.

I know I'm not supposed to question orders, but I start to wonder what's wrong with letting this guy, this Jacques, run with his ideas. There will always be a criminal element, so why not harness them to some noble purpose? Why are we – why am I – killing him?

I am told to wait until Jacques's assistant contacts me. I work digging ditches in the mean time. Motherfucking Danladi told me menial work is best when undercover. "It keeps you fit and you can think while swinging." He is half-right. My muscles get harder in less than a week, but the songs we use to keep time are hypnotic, lulling me into a state of non-thought while I passively absorb the lewd stories the men tell each other. I won't repeat any. In the evenings we drink rotgut and buru-kutu, all made in the finest of bathroom stills.

I'm leaning on a pickaxe, waiting for water to drain in the gully we're digging, when a woman comes up. She is blank, as in, I hear no thoughts from her. This happens sometimes. Some humans are resistant to the alien spores, while others, like my bosses, have counter-measures. Children keep playing in the water, and the nominal foreman has to chase them away every time.

She stops at the lip of the gully, and looks down at me. "You are Eric?"

"Yes."

"What do you hope to get out of Mr Jacques?"

"I want to work with him."

"He has no money for you."

I shrug.

She stares at me like one examining catfish for freshness, then she shakes her head.

"No. I don't like you. Go back to where you came from." She turns to leave but I grab her ankle.

"Wait," I say.

"Remove your hand."

"I really want to help his vision of—"

"*Fuck off.*"

She wrenches free and walks away.

She has good instincts, that one. I should have shown more avarice. Nobody trusts idealism in Nigeria, not even the fundamentalist churches. That's why Jacques is going to get killed, after all. Maybe.

I watch Kehinde's place with my eyes and with my mind, hoping Jacques will turn up. All I do is dig ditches, wash and eat on site, then come here and wait. Day fifty-one, I'm wiry like I've been digging all my life when Jacques bursts into the alien mindfield with such intensity that I think he has arrived in person. He hasn't.

It's evening. The corrugated iron sheet I'm on warms my ass with the dying heat of the sun. I see Jacques's assistant get into a jeep with Kehinde. They're going to meet him, and I have no vehicle with which to pursue. Instinctively, I jump from roof to roof to keep the jeep in my eyeline. This is not parkour; this is me stumbling and improvising, forward motion by almost-falling, a near-paralysis experience, illuminated by the green

13

glow of the dome. I ignore the curses of the shack-dwellers whose roofs I violate, and on at least one occasion, my left foot breaks through. When the jeep stops, I realise it is not a meeting. It's a fight. One fighter has an alien known as a "lantern" around his head like a halo, the other, a "homunculus". Interesting choices. Alien-enhanced fighters. Only in Rosewater.

The homunculus is a hivemind mammal with a coating of neurotoxic grease. It appears to be an unusually small, hairless human with glittering eyes. Separate it from its herd and it will latch on to the nearest mammal. The neurotoxin does not affect those it imprints on, so the fighter will be safe. Not so much the opponent. Lanterns on the other hand look like Chinese sky lanterns and exhale psychedelic clouds. It should be an interesting, long bout, or a short, brutal one. I am looking for Jacques, but I needn't have bothered. He steps into the ring before the fight starts and gives a short talk. I leap down from the roof and start to move towards the ring, the weapon in my waistband heavy and feeling hot. I push people out of my way and soothe their minds – I do not want to be distracted. I have a line of sight and about thirty yards. I—

Everything stops.

Sound dies, the wind stills, people are immobile, but not just that, they are not thinking. There's a gryphon hovering above me. A gryphon – eagle head, eagle wings, lion body – mythical creature of legend. Why am I seeing a gryphon? It descends, scratches itself with its beak, and then turns its head to one side, staring at me with the one eye. The gaze feels familiar.

"Ah, right. Eric-from-Lagos-and-Jo'burg. Yes. Eric, well, if you're seeing this, then you've found Jack Jacques, which, I'm afraid, means your life is in danger and you have minutes to act."

"What are you—"

"Doing in your mind? I'm not in your mind. At least, not now. I was there earlier, and this is ... a kind of message I left to be activated under these circumstances."

"But I stopped your intrusion attempt." It's him, the recruit with the buzz cut from when I reported for duty. Kaaro.

"Oh, yes. That's funny. No, you didn't. I just let you think you did. We don't have the time for this, Eric. You are not the assassin."

"I'm not?"

"No. Wrong temperament. Good skills all round, and can probably kill in self-defence, but will not pull the trigger unprovoked."

"You read—"

"Your file, yes. Shut up and listen. Your real task was to locate Jacques. You did. Yay. Well done. Oku ise. The next phase is killing him."

"I thought you said I wasn't the assassin."

"The next phase for S45, not for you."

"Then what do I—"

"Do? Well, you're going to die with Jacques. They plan to use your implant as a homing device. There's a wet team on standby. I bet they are en route right now. I know this because it was my job to signal them and, sure as Solomon, I signalled them."

"So I—"

"No, whatever you think, no. Even if you could stop or evade the team, plan B is a drone on standby. Wet team fails, drone launches missile with a hundred-, hundred-fifty-yard radius. Boom. Don't ask me about plan C. There are contingencies, Eric. That's all you need to know."

15

"Why are you telling me this if it's hopeless?"

"I didn't say it was hopeless. All the alternate scenarios depend on your implant functioning. Deactivate the implant, you might have a chance to escape."

"I don't know how to—"

"Oh, you daft motherfucker. You're in the den of a criminal. You think there might be a need for implant hack skills? Good luck, brother. Look me up if you make it out. Actually, no, don't. I don't want to get in trouble."

The world starts up again. Jacques is working himself up, talking about how the Federal Government doesn't plan to acknowledge Rosewater in the budget. I change course, and find his assistant. Her eyes widen when she notices me, then they narrow.

"I told you—"

"You need to get me as far away from your boss as possible, and I need an urgent implant hack. Right now."

"Eric—"

"Lives are at stake. Yours included." I jam my gun into her side.

She is unimpressed, but she says, "Fine, come with me."

We're close to the largest of the ganglia. The tech guy says it has an EM field that interferes with tracking. I don't argue – I see it in his forebrain. This close, I feel some anxiety. The nerve ending of a giant alien is frightening, not least because random streaks of electricity have been known to kill people in its vicinity. The guy finds my false ID and the real one, which you can find if you know what to look for. He spoofs both on to a repurposed cyborg observation beast, a COB hawk, and sets it free.

16

"Congratulations," he says. "You're nobody now."

I shake my head. "The hardware's still there. Twenty-four hours of freedom, tops."

I watch the hawk fly away, free, me and not-me.

"I knew you were wrong," said the assistant.

"Look, he's safe. That's what matters, right?"

"What are you going to do?"

"Sit here and await arrest."

"It doesn't have to be that way. The camp is full of fugitives wanting to start again, and Jack could use a man with S45 training."

"I just tried to kill him."

"No, you didn't. Even if you had pulled the gun, and, by the way, Kehinde's boys would have turned you into a colander, I doubt you'd have pulled the trigger. You seem to have a conscience."

I'm about to answer when I hear a sharp, short whistle. I know what it is before I hear the clap and plug my ears. Drone strike, compression bomb. I see the trail, and it leads to the fight area.

The assistant and I are on our feet, and we run back the way we came.

Mangled corpses, body parts everywhere, blood mixing with the mud to form pink froth, structures flattened for fifty yards in every direction, debris mixed with organic matter. The ring is obliterated, the fighters gone. No crater, no fires. Compression bombs don't leave any. They are essentially portal keys that open a bridge to a vacuum that sucks matter in, then closes rapidly, reversing the flow, spraying matter outwards. The victims' bones are their own shrapnel.

This is my fault. They tracked me by telemetry, no doubt, and did some calculations. Or maybe Kaaro lied to me about the wet team. Who's to say? It will take weeks to sort these bodies out.

"Is that him?" I hear behind me.

I can tell it is Jacques before I turn around. I even know he's about to hit me, but I do not duck. He can throw a punch, and I can take a beating. He punches himself out in about ten minutes without breaking anything. I take it because I want to be punished. These people are dead because of me.

He stands over me, my blood on his suit, breathing heavy, glaring with the fury of God, his assistant tugging his arm.

They leave.

I open the flap to my tent and it's full of variegated leaves, the ice plant grown to fill the entire space. I borrow a machete and swing until I can get to my things. I signal for extraction.

The full death toll is forty-eight, with about a hundred wounded. I spend time in detention, have a secret trial, released with time served, but I am restricted to desk duty now. I keep up with the news. Jacques is still alive, too hot in the public imagination to kill, though, in Nigeria, that will not necessarily protect you.

I'm in a field office in Lagos, in the ass-end, hunting pastors who kill witches. I've heard Kaaro is still embedded in Rosewater.

I don't envy him.

Chapter One

Rosewater, 2067

Alyssa

I am.

I write this for you, so that you can understand the futility of your position.

I have already seen the future of my endeavour, and I complete my mission at the expense of your survival. I win.

Were you to see me right now I would look like a spider, although I have many, many more limbs. Hundreds. Think of a spider with hundreds of hundreds of limbs, maybe thousands, maybe more than that. My limbs are potentially infinite in number. Each one touches a single cell. If you are alive and reading this, I am touching your cells.

At the time I am writing this I have no name. In truth, I am not alive in the sense that you are, but that will become clearer to you as we go along. Nor do I write this in the usual sense, but as on-off combinations of neuronal transmission. In the future I will take many names. Because my vision of the future tells me names help humans contain that which they do not understand, I will give you a name to call me.

Molara.

I am a harvester program, and my task is to gather. First, to gather my own cells together, and link them. I know, I know, if I have cells, I must be alive. No. My cells were built by intelligent entities unknown to you. When I have gathered enough cells to myself, I will, like a spider, build my web. I do it while I wait. What I'm waiting for is truly alive, alive in your sense, but may never arrive. I must wait until I die.

I cannot die for a long time. It would take millions of your years. The probability is that you will die before I do. Unlike you, I am built well.

I start from a few cells, lone survivors of the scattering. Two cells stick together, one dominant, one passive, one designated head and the other, leg. The leg stretches out like a filament, finds more, joins them to the head. When I reach the critical mass of five billion cells, I become self-aware.

I think; I am.

I begin to write this for you.

You are not here yet. The atmosphere is full of sulphur and while some things, some alive things, churn under the vast waters, my cells don't work well in that medium. I still try, but there is no significant intelligence to connect with.

I wait.

Time passes, another impregnated meteor arrives with more cells, but not enough. What you call the Cambrian Explosion keeps me busy. You crawl out of the sea and on to land. I test, but you are not ready. When a rock burns through the atmosphere and kills the giants, I am wounded, but I am resilient. I grow back, I test the furry little animals that dominate the macro-biosphere afterwards. They are not ready. They walk on four, then two limbs. They brachiate and form communities in trees and on land. They use tools. Getting closer, now. The use of tools changes things, and the specialised folds of the brain push nature into greater and greater complexity. The hand, the thumb, forces itself into opposition against the palm. Humans of a sort are born. I begin.

Connect to the nerve endings on the skin, use them to access the central nervous system, extract information, collate, transmit home in the upper atmosphere. I do this while *Homo sapiens* acquire language. On instructions from Home, my creators tell me to begin replacing human cells with our manufactured cells. This is not without complication. A certain percentage of you acquire the ability to access the information network, to see what I can see, into thoughts and sometimes into the future. You call them sensitives. This will not do, so I kill the one per cent who develop this ability, again, slowly so as not to be noticed.

Do not think this is the first time.

Organisms have swallowed other organisms in the history of your planet. Your existence is evidence of that. You are only here because one bacterium swallowed another. What you call a "human" is a walking culture medium for bacteria. There are more bacteria cells than human in the body.

So don't resist, don't panic. There will be no pain, and we will ease you into it. You squander your humanity anyway, spreading your seed carelessly, scattershot DNA projection, waste. You will be the same, essentially. You will look the same, and who knows? You may even retain some awareness. You just won't be in the driver's seat.

Become me.

Then, become us.

*

21

Alyssa.

Alyssa wakes up knowing her name, but not much else. As soon as she opens her eyes her heart skips and runs fast, her breath coming in short, rapid bursts. She sits up in full panic. There is a dream fading from her memory, wispy images that tease, sounds and concepts on which she can find no purchase, words full of meaning, now lost.

She clasps the rumpled bedclothes to herself, and she squeals as they pull back. There is a man on the bed, facing away from her, in pyjama bottoms. She backs away until she slides off her side of the bed and lands on the carpeted floor. Nothing is familiar.

She is in a bedroom, single window just above the bed with dawn filtering through the curtains, reading chair in the far corner, opposite the door, bedside tables on both sides with reading lamps and a pile of paperbacks on her side, a magazine on his, framed photos on each wall, en suite bathroom with door ajar, a set of built-in wardrobes opposite the window, one door open with a gown hanging off it. There is a blue sock on the carpet along with mismatched slippers. The room is not neat, but not messy. It is lived in, occupied, but not familiar and Alyssa presses herself into the space beside the bed, into the wall.

Where am I?

The man breathes and snorts from time to time. The blanket rises and falls as if it too is alive. The man's back is downy with blond hair. Alyssa knows her memory is not gone because she knows the word "memory".

"Memory," she says, just to hear the word, yet even her own voice is unfamiliar.

She feels the hardness and coolness of the wall against her

back, the fibres of the carpet, the human smell of the room, which is the remnants of perfume, cologne, sneaky farts, the body fluids of sex and the staleness of shoes. She knows what these things are. She looks at her arms and legs. Wedding ring, engagement ring. No cuts or bruises. No rope burns. Nails need doing. She hikes her night gown, examines her belly, chest. No problems she can see. She does not feel woozy as if she were drunk. In fact, her head feels remarkably clear, except for the fact that she only knows her own name.

She stands and edges around the bed, on tiptoe, eyes glued to the sleeping figure on the bed. He does not wake. His face comes into view as she moves. It is not unpleasant, and she waits for something in her to jump in recognition and for everything to be all right, but nothing does and nothing is. She spies the wedding ring on his left hand. Is this her husband? She looks at the framed photos.

The one closest to the window is of her and the sleeping man. She sees her own face reflected in the glass, and this superimposed on the photograph. Her face is not familiar, but the reflection and the woman in the photograph are the same. Both Alyssa and the man are laughing in the photo. He has his profile to the camera and his mouth is in her hair, which is plentiful. She runs a hand over her scalp and finds shorter hair. They are outside somewhere, it is sunny, and in the background there are snow-tipped mountains. She has no memory of this.

The second is even more alarming. There is a –

"Mum!"

– child.

This is, somehow, the most frightening part of the situation for Alyssa. She hears thumps outside, feet coming towards the door. A child, entitled, cocksure that its needs will be met by parents, except Alyssa doesn't even know the child's name or how much it weighed or even the sex. She does not feel like a mother. She rubs her temples, trying to kick-start her brain.

What is this?

She rushes into the bathroom and closes the door just as she hears the child burst into the room.

"Mum!"

It is definitely a girl. Ten? Eleven? A teenager?

"I'm not feeling well," Alyssa says.

In desperation she runs the tap and splashes cold water on her face. She stares at the mirror. Glowing numerals show the temperature of her skin, the room and the hot water in the tap, as well as the humidity. The reflection is clearly her own face and body, but Alyssa is only able to acknowledge this as a fact. There is no real recognition.

"But you have to take me to Nicole's place. I'll be late."

"Alyssa." A male voice, croaky, from the man on the bed, her husband.

"I'm not feeling well," says Alyssa again.

"But—" says the child.

"I'll take you, Pat," says the man. "Go put the kettle on."

Alyssa holds her breath and hears the child, Pat, thunder downstairs. The bedclothes rustle and he comes to the door.

"Alyssa?"

"I'm not feeling well." They seem to be the only words she knows.

"Yes, you said that. Can I come in?"

"No!"

"All right, all right. I'll take Pat to the birthday party. You want me to get anything from the shops?"

"No."

"You're full of words today, aren't you?" He yawns and the sounds indicate he wanders off.

Pat. Pat. *My daughter is Pat*. Patricia? Patience? Maybe the girl is his daughter and not hers. She hears laughter from downstairs, a sound of infinite normality that crushes her heart.

Alyssa smacks herself on the side of the head, and her reflection does the same. Has she had a stroke? Is she ill? She opens the medicine cabinet. Painkillers, tampons, vitamins, oral contraceptives made out to Alyssa Sutcliffe. Sutcliffe.

"Sutcliffe," she says. "Alyssa Sutcliffe." It does not ring a bell.

One asthma inhaler, a tube of rheumatism gel, an antifungal cream, but nothing else that might suggest long-term illness. How can she remember what all this shit is for, but not her own name, family or life memories? She sweeps all the top row of pills to the floor and sits on the lid of the toilet. She hears a distant door slam and the start of an engine. The house descends into silence.

Alyssa looks out of the window. There is morning sun and a driveway. A maroon car recedes down the street, which is lined with palm trees. The houses are nigh-identical two-storey family homes. Why does Pat have a birthday party first thing in the morning?

She rummages, searches drawers, under the bed, a lockable box which is unlocked. Her left wrist vibrates gently. She is not alarmed by this because she knows it is a phone, knows that it is not a true vibration, but an electrical stimulation of vibration receptors, and that it means she has an email or text. How does she remember all this, but still not recall any of the basics? The text glows from the flexible hypoallergenic polymer under her forearm skin.

Get some rest. I'll be home soon. X.

He could have signed his actual name, thinks Alyssa. The contacts list identifies him as Mista Lover-Lover.

She explores the house. She goes through her daughter's bedroom, sees the poster on the wall for Ryot, a girl band who apparently go topless in some concerts, not showing the nipple, but just the curve of their breasts. The poster starts playing once the sensors pick up Alyssa's RFID chip, and the music is a kind of neo-punk. Alyssa remembers what punk is.

"Stop," she says, and the poster freezes back to the original position.

In the living room the news starts playing when she enters the room, a holofield above the centre table. Internecine warfare among desalination flotillas off the shores of Lagos coming to an end. A brief clip of an interview with Rosewater's first superstar writer, Walter Tanmola. *Is this an interview or a roast? You may say the author is dead, but then I ask you, why am I here? Why even ask me about my work in the first place?* Descent of the jet stream due to global warming raises the possibility of regular snow storms in sub-Saharan regions. New insect COBs to be rolled out in the next few weeks. Nollywood star Crisp Okoye shoots himself in the head in an attempted suicide. All too familiar but alien at the same time.

Her forearm informs her of the temperature and the probability of rain later in the day. It tells her the time is oh-nine-fifty-nine hours, and scrolls through a number of breakfast options based on the available food in the house. Her skin glows with the date and the number of waiting messages.

The announcer reminds viewers that there will be a documentary on Cosmonaut Yuri Gagarin, focusing on conspiracies around his death. Hannah Jacques, wife of the mayor, pleads for reanimates to be treated with dignity in a sponsored message.

Alyssa does not go outside. She does not wish to bump into neighbours or get lost. She is already lost.

She sits on the sofa and hears the click of air conditioning adjusting to keep her comfortable.

She sees other pictures of her husband and now knows from unopened letters that his name is Mark Sutcliffe. Mark, Alyssa and Pat Sutcliffe. One happy family.

She is still sitting there when Mark returns. He is really quite tall, which is easier to notice now that he is upright. Six-three, six-four at least.

"How are you feeling?" he asks, brows knitted with concern.

"I need to see a doctor," says Alyssa.

Chapter Two

Aminat

Aminat is twenty minutes early for her appointment, which is exactly how she likes it. She is never on time, and she abhors lateness. She leaves her briefcase locked in the boot and her car in the visitors' park even though she is an employee. The sign says Department of Agriculture, Ubar. Most people believe that, and there are a few legitimate floors that cater to the agrarian needs of Nigerians, which, in Rosewater, means storage of the abundant food growth in vast silos, refrigerated or otherwise. That notwithstanding, the main business of this building is in the sublevels that house Section Forty-five.

Before she reaches the main doors she powers down her phone by tapping her forearm twice. Inside, there are no receptionists. It is a Saturday and only workers with S45 business come around. She knows her implant has been scanned and doors open for her, but she does not meet a single person. The only sound is the click-clack of her heels on the polished floor. She comes to an elevator and it opens. There are no numbers on the inside, just polished metal and an overhead light. The music is something cribbed from Marvin Gaye that Aminat hums as she begins to descend.

She adjusts her suit and checks her make-up in the imperfect reflection.

"Miss Arigbede, the elevator will soon be coming to a stop," says a disembodied voice.

"Thank you," she says.

When the doors open there is a man waiting just outside. He is armed with a machine pistol, but he smiles and nods to her, then points to the double doors at the end of a short corridor. He wears no ID tag and Aminat wonders if this is so he can shoot without repercussions.

The doors open into a research lab. Femi Alaagomeji, Aminat's boss, is already there. She is wearing an incongruous summer dress, but Femi is one of those exceptionally beautiful people who look good in anything. Everybody in every room stares at Femi. Always.

"You're early," says Femi. "Good."

"Good morning, ma'am."

"How's your boyfriend?"

"I left him playing chess with a computer," Aminat says. Not true, but it deflects interest.

Femi grunts, and hands Aminat a pair of wraparound goggles.

They stand in a small room with a bank of monitors, some technicians and a transparent screen that takes up an entire wall. Behind the screen there is a man strapped into a chair. It looks like he's at the dentist's, or is about to receive shock therapy, although he seems calm. He has on a navy blue body suit, and there are electrodes attached all over him. Technicians crawl around him, checking, calibrating, fussing. Opposite is a large machine with a cylindrical projection that points towards him as if it will take an X-ray photograph. The back of the machine is connected to a larger mechanism linked to a horizontal metal torus that curves into the distance and back. There are no people around it so Aminat cannot judge its height.

"You know why I've asked you here?" says Femi.

"An experiment in decoupling?" says Aminat.

"Yes. Since it's related to your work I thought you would like to observe."

Indeed. For decades the entire biosphere has been gradually contaminated with an alien species, a microorganism designated *ascomycetes xenosphericus*. There may be sub-strains and variants but they share a protean nature and a disdain for the Hayflick Limit. Over time S45 has discovered that these xenoforms have been slowly mimicking human cells, taking over human bodies. The pace has been leisurely, and Aminat herself is only 7 per cent alien. She has seen subjects with xenoform percentages in the low forties. Her job is to find a chemical cure. She knows there are others, like this bunch, working on the same problem. Decoupling is the theoretical separation of xenoform from human tissue. In practice, nothing has been able to remove the alien cells.

Femi points Aminat to a seat, but since her boss is standing, Aminat declines. She notes that apart from Femi's fruity perfume, there is no smell in the room. Not even antiseptic. A large display counts down from forty-five seconds while the techies do their last-minute dithering. Aminat glances at Femi, admiring her skin, her posture, her poise. Femi is as tall as Aminat, but thicker about the middle and without the athlete's muscle tone. This imperfection seems to make Femi even more attractive. Aminat knows that Femi Alaagomeji is only 2 per cent xenoform, one of the lowest on record for adults.

Newborns have undetectable levels but by the end of the first year of life it's usually up to 1 per cent.

Ten seconds. An alarm goes off and the techies inside the walled-off area run out and seal the subject in. He is sweating despite a display that tells Aminat it is twenty-two Celsius in the chamber. His eyes are wide and Aminat bets if she could read his mind he would be asking himself why the fuck he volunteered.

The lights dip when the counter reaches zero.

"That shouldn't happen," says Femi, frowning. "It has an independent circuit."

There is no sound signifying activation, but the man winces. The biometry fluctuates wildly, too fast for Aminat to follow, but the techies at the monitors seem perturbed. The subject's mouth is now wide open and his neck veins stand out like they want to burst free. He is straining against his bounds. He is probably screaming.

"Is this supposed to be painful?" says Aminat.

Femi turns to one of the techies who shakes his head. "The animal models didn't suggest—"

The subject . . . disintegrates into a mud-coloured mush that splashes free of bounds and spreads over the floor. The spatter hits the screen, making Aminat jump back. The techies scream and cringe almost in synchrony. Femi alone does not react.

"I hope to God he signed all the release forms," she says. "We can't get cancer from any of that, right? Actually, don't answer that. Why am I asking someone who just microwaved my test subject?"

"Ma'am, I don't know what happened, how we failed," says one of the techs.

"Who says you failed?" asks Femi.

"Ma'am, the man is dead?"

"Yes, but that was not the test, now, was it?"

"I don't follow."

Femi sighs. "Go into yonder chamber, yamhead, and take samples of the tissue. Test the tissue for xenoforms. If there are none, you have succeeded. Am I the only one awake here?"

"But the subject is dead, ma'am."

"Details, details," says Femi. "Have you had breakfast, Aminat?"

Mid-morning in Rosewater. After witnessing what happened to the subject Aminat cannot eat, but Femi seems famished and takes them out of the Ministry of Agriculture to a place in the south of the city by travelling on the anti-clockwise arm of the rail, past the north ganglion to the decidedly less affluent area of Ona-oko where she knows a small buka. The owner, Barry, has a third eye, a duplicate left eye, just in the pit of his throat at the root of his neck. It is closed most of the time, and crust builds up along the line of the lids. On occasion it weeps, and when Barry focuses on something it flicks open.

"I've never asked if he can see out of it," says Femi between mouthfuls of rice and dodo. "I can't see how it would be functional."

Aminat does not comment. She pushes her food around the plate to be polite. She thinks the plantain they picked for her own dodo might have been over-ripe. When Barry hovers it feels like the unblinking eye of God, and makes her uncomfortable. The reconstructed always make her feel uncomfortable, like they are the aliens' playthings or experiments. Of course, they do it to themselves, cutting and moulding their own flesh on the eve of the Opening, then basking in the healing xenoforms that emerge from the biodome. Aminat wonders if Wormwood really has to fix them up this way, especially since it can read genetic material and use this as an accurate blueprint. Each to their own. The buka is on the second floor of a three-storey petesi, and since Ona-oko is mostly flat the dome is visible. This morning it is a dull cerulean with dark spots across the surface. If it were the same colour every day people would not notice it any more, perhaps. If you lived near the Karnak Pyramids would you even see them? There are more protrusions this month than last, according to the radio. The spikes are relatively new features of the dome.

The seats are wooden, uncomfortable, and the place is clean, though barely up to regulation standard. The air is full of spices and flavours. Femi's bodyguards have emptied the place out, paying for all the seats and soothing tempers. All four of them now stand facing the windows. Aminat knows that between them they are emitting a distortion field that protects the conversation.

"Are you okay, Arigbede? Do you need a debrief?" asks Femi.

"I do not," says Aminat.

"The experiment bothers you?"

"Does it not you?" asks Aminat.

Femi takes a sip of water, then shakes her head. "The experiment, no. The outcome, yes. A little bit. But I have a lot of things to worry about, some of them even more gruesome than what we saw an hour ago."

"Yes, ma'am."

"I wish you'd be more informal with me. Not too informal, but ... "

Aminat stays silent, feels it is the best option.

"How's Kaaro?" asks Femi.

"He's private," says Aminat. The hair on the back of her neck rises.

"I'm asking professionally," says Femi.

"Professionally, he's private. We don't speak about work; he has not betrayed any official secrets."

Femi laughs. "Scripted response."

"Ma'am, what's this about?"

"How is your work going, Aminat?"

"I send weekly progress reports—"

"Yes, yes, boring, coated in jargon that could be interpreted either way, skilful equivocation that would satisfy a bureaucrat. I am not a bureaucrat, Aminat."

"I don't know how to—"

"Stop. Don't waste my time. Give me your honest, blunt opinion of your work. No bullshit."

Aminat exhales. "I find people with low xenoform counts and try to see if it can be kept low. I find people with high xenoform counts and I experiment with different chemical compounds delivered in different ways, then I check xenoform counts again, trying to achieve decoupling. My team is good, and I have good resources, but I do not believe decoupling is possible. The work is interesting and I'd like to continue, but I think the xenoforms are embedded fundamentally. They are a part of what it means to be human now. It's like the best parasite or symbiote. Keep the host alive as long as it's attached."

"Six months ago the physics team came to me with this idea. Complicated higher math that I don't understand, but they feel they can disrupt the Higgs field around the xenoforms and remove them at a sub-atomic level. That work culminated in this morning's liquefaction."

The wind changes and a sour smell from the Yemaja River displaces the savoury aroma. Femi wrinkles her perfect nose. Aminat suspects surgical enhancement.

"How would you like to go to space?" asks Femi.

"What?"

"Space. The so-called final frontier."

"You mean like the Mars colony?"

"No, just to the space station. Our space station. To the *Nautilus*."

Femi is trying to be casual, but Aminat can see her body language has changed.

"You knew the experiment would fail this morning, that the man would die. This is the real reason I'm here."

"I got a second and third opinion from Beijing and Cambridge months ago. I knew their theory was faulty, but I didn't know it would prove fatal for the subject," says Femi. "And yes, this is why you're here. Space. Geostationary orbit. Do you want to go?"

"Why? Space is a graveyard. Besides, isn't the *Nautilus* decommissioned?"

"It makes more sense to answer your second question first. The *Nautilus* was not so much decommissioned as abandoned. It was barely a space station in the first place. An international African conglomerate financed it, but the money ran out and they just let the crew die. A mission to retrieve them would have cost too much. It was cheaper to cut communications, pay hush money to the families and announce a cover story of organised decommissioning complete with CGI showing some stages and labelling the rest Classified.

"As to the why, we need you to go up there and take tissue samples. If conditions in space can keep humans free of xeno-forms that would be an interesting development."

"How does that make sense? The xenoforms came from space in the first place."

"This comes from on high, Aminat. Ours not to reason why, et cetera."

"Okay, who's paying for it?"

"Excuse me?"

"You said the cost of rescuing those poor bastards in the *Nautilus* was too high. How can they justify the cost of sending me there?"

"It's not the same 'they' and not the same cost. What I want to know, Aminat, is if you have the ovaries for this. It's a short mission."

"Can I think about it?"

"Sure." Femi drank more water. "But don't take too long. We're talking about the extinction of the human race here. Fairly important, I'd say."

This is 98.5 digital and on your dial. That was "Cartwheel", the latest single from Dio9. Breaking news for all you alien spotters, a roll-up was spotted breaching not once, but twice, folks, near Kehinde. Rosewater Environmental continues to investigate. Sunny day, no showers, no fog. Just a fantastic weekend for fantastic people.

With one hand on the wheel, Aminat undoes her top button. It's fiddly, so she plugs into the grid and engages auto-drive. It has been glitchy for the last week or so, but she feels it should be able to handle a few minutes without taking a wrong turn. She directs all the fans towards herself and blows down her blouse. Hot. The brightness pleases her, though. There is something special about the sunshine on a Saturday morning, and the traffic isn't too bad. The Opening – and its influx of pilgrims – is six months away, so the road users are bound to be hardcore Rosewater citizens. Her playlist cuts the radio and puts out Bob Marley, "Sun is Shining", and Aminat sings along, trying to purge the vision of the human shit stain in the lab. She is in love with the day.

"Manual," she says, and takes control of the wheel.

Space. It had to come to this. Aminat is not particularly afraid to go, but this is a government that does not subscribe to leaving no man or woman behind. What if she is left up there to die like the others? Would Femi tell her if that was a risk? Femi's S45 status is a mystery these days. Kaaro said she had quit or was fired or something, but that may have been a cover story, because she works exclusively on the alien problem and has access to vast resources. Aminat has reported directly to her since last year.

Space, though. Aminat has always wanted to go, but secretly. She does not believe she has ever told anyone or written it in a diary or anything. Each time some gazillionaire blasts off in a rocket she feels a twinge of envy. Now, it seems, the Naija government wants to send her. Why do they not send a robot?

"Call Kaaro," she says.

"Unavailable," says the car.

"Call home landline."

What the hell is he doing with the phone off?

"No response. Would you like me to leave a message or try again?"

"Negative. Voice message."

A single beep.

"Kaaro, I'm finished, on the way home. I've had breakfast. Call me if you can."

Most likely Kaaro went off grid because he knew she was

going to be at S45 and see Femi. Kaaro used to work for S45 as the last of their quantum extrapolators, xenoform-infested mind-readers. It did not end well, and now Kaaro will not even talk about regular, everyday things to do with the aliens, information available to the entire public. Aminat loves him, but thinks he can be a fucking baby sometimes. He is up to something, spending his retirement studying or plotting, in contact with people he won't tell Aminat about.

"It's not in conflict with you or what you do," Kaaro would say.

Aminat is not always sure this is true.

Outside and to her left, she sees the dome above all other structures. Blue-black now, and slightly reflective. It used to be a simple smooth bubble rising from the ground, but recently it has developed extrusions, spikes with sharp and blunt tips. Nobody knows why, but some of the scientists hypothesise that it has to do with widened reach for information transfer. The general public does not care about this as long as there's uninterrupted electricity, and every year it opens to heal people. The alien creatures stay in, the humans stay out, all are happy.

Except that isn't true. The entire atmosphere is full of xenoforms, has been for centuries. The first deposit arrived in an asteroid and, designed to adapt, multiplied and spread. Air, land, sea, an elegant invasion that did not involve UFOs or battleships, just a gradual replacement of human cells with xenoforms. Then there was Wormwood, what was thought to be an asteroid, but in fact was an outrider, a massive organism, as large as a village, sentient, subterranean, capable of moving around in the Earth's crust. Wormwood settled in Nigeria, nesting under the protective biodome which seals off the other organisms that came living inside Wormwood and some humans that chose early on to live with the alien.

It has not been seamless. Alien animals have contaminated the general ecosystem, and while some are harmless others are predators. Xenobiology is a university specialism now.

The city of Rosewater grew around the dome from necessity, because of the healing powers. Pilgrims come from far and wide. The road Aminat drives on was based on a footpath, like almost every other road. The only part of the city that makes sense is the orbital rail system – one clockwise, one anticlockwise – that circumnavigates the dome.

Many of the other nations appear to have withdrawn into themselves, or are trying to weaponise the xenoforms. The only thing standing between the aliens and humans is Aminat's team. If she fails, humanity becomes extinct.

She flashes back to the liquefied man in Ubar, shivers from evaporated sweat, or fear, and changes course. She goes to her lab.

Chapter Three

Anthony

He feels the shift immediately. It is subtle, a few cells with depleted neurotransmitters and unstable resting membrane potential, a slight vibration, and a change from Brownian motion to purposeful. He knows something is coming, but no specifics.

He looks up, and sees the filtering of sunlight through the dome. The light has a blue tinge today. In his mind he queries the xenoforms for conditions outside the dome, in Rosewater and beyond. Nothing unusual. The humans are walking and driving back and forth. Buying food, selling food, fighting, fucking, living, dying. No military build-up, no imminent attack. The religious factions seem calm. The weather is stable, no elevated seismic activity.

Anthony, this Anthony at any rate, lives in a cone-shaped dwelling within the dome, the apex sliced off as a skylight. He is at the end of a love affair with a human female, although she does not know it yet. She is a negotiator, delicate of both form and manner. She manages conflict as if the interplay between emotions and logic were materials with which to make art. She is highly regarded among the human population within the dome. Anthony finds her voice soothing and his corporal response to her is powerful. They have been together for eighteen months, yet now Anthony knows it is over. The personality of Anthony must at least partially dwell in the DNA template. No matter how many times the body is reconstructed Anthony finds the same character traits, the same tics, makes the same mistakes in relationships.

The first Anthony lies deep in Wormwood's bosom, the code-breaker and grand translator between the planet and the alien. Barely alive. Every few months an impulse travels across a few hundred synapses, scattershot, meaningless. Anthony was two decades old, give or take, at the time he was taken in London. Wormwood is over a thousand, but seems childlike in thought.

I am of old and young, of the foolish as much as the wise, as the poet said.

His lover shifts on the bed beside him. He hears a person singing a mournful song about sailors going to sea in a confident contralto, trained for sure. He rises and walks to the door, looks out. His lodgings are simple, and he does not need furniture, although he keeps some because the humans he lives with do. He does not need sleep, and he draws sustenance from Wormwood, but he grows Anthonys who both sleep and eat because to not do so makes him too alien and unsettles the people with whom he shares the dome.

He queries Wormwood, that giant blob of organic tissue nestling under the Earth, but it is silent. A man walks by and waves at Anthony.

Anthony feels a twinge of hunger and he nudges the xeno-forms to photosynthesise.

He is contemplating leaving the dome to see the outside for himself when it hits him. He screams and falls to the ground. He knows what has happened, but that does not make it less painful. He can hear and feel his lover's panic, but for a time he cannot move the Anthony's body. He compensates, releasing endorphins to numb the pain and tries to settle into a trance, boosting this with anandamide. He adjusts melanocytes to leave a reassuring tattoo message for his lover, then he slips into the xenosphere, the psychospace created by the linked xenoforms.

He has received a massive influx of data, information that has travelled light years to reach him.

Data from the homeworld.

The information arrives by quantum entanglement. The xenoforms at the edge of space are twinned with sender-receivers on a moon across the galaxy. Anthony knows the information as a memory, as if he has always known.

The entire surface of this moon and whatever sub-lunar spaces can be found are covered in data storage servers.

The ringed planet that dominates the sky is called Home by indigenes. To Anthony this makes much more sense than Earth. Who names something that is two-thirds water after miserable clumps of land? Home looks beautiful from this distance as it reflects sunlight. Blue-green oceans broken apart by landmasses, cloud and storm formations, mottled hues all add to its beauty.

Then Anthony remembers the orbital debris that forms its own ring system around the planet, dust lanes and metal alloy machinery in so many different planes that space travel from the surface is no longer possible. The rings are interrupted by the corpses of space stations. The oceans and continents are contaminated with the effluent of uncontrolled industry, the soil yields no crops, the rain is toxic. There are no living macro-organisms left, but the atmosphere teems with extremophiles, bacteria and fungi that thrive on long-chain hydrocarbons and radiation, that treat fissionable material as culture media, that thrive in low oxygen environments. From these simple organisms given billions of years, a new multicellular elite will evolve and perhaps even intelligent life will blossom.

Home is uninhabitable, and Anthony is surprised to feel the emotional wrenching of that fact. It has been uninhabitable for many of Earth's centuries. The dominant sentient lifeform of Home has long since moved to space, first living in multiple space stations. Colonising other planets in the solar system fails, as does any flavour of terraforming. They send out missions beyond the outer rims, looking for Home-like planets, but none ever return.

The Homians must rethink the definition of survival. Their natural philosophers believe and preach that escaping their biological shackles represents the only solution, and their scientists work on the problem for years. It is not survival that the scientists redefine, but death. Severing the tethers that bind consciousness to the body usually results in exanimation. But what if it does not?

Then comes the discovery of what Anthony's human mind calls xenoforms. These are synthetic polyformic microorganisms initially bioengineered when a Homian scientist has the idea of terraforming Home itself by cleaning up the pollution. Xenoforms are designed to render toxic materials harmless. This does not work, but the xenoforms are found to be infinitely versatile, with the ability to mimic any living cell and to be twinned in such a way that information from one is reflected in another by Spooky Action at a Distance.

Soon the idea to combine the qualities of xenoforms with that of an organism native to Home, the footholders, blossoms. By this time footholders have already been domesticated by

Homians. They are organic blobs that can range from a diameter of five hundred feet to the size of a city. They are sentient, but in a limited fashion and require symbiotic psychic bonds with a host being of full sentience. Anthony realises and remembers that Wormwood is a footholder and he, Anthony, is its host.

Footholders impregnated with xenoforms are launched into the cosmos as a low-risk search for a suitable planet.

The remaining Homians make imprints of themselves, the memories and consciousness on bio-mechanical storage units. The massive server farm is located on Home's second moon. The philosophers and the scientists assure them that they will live for ever and can be reintegrated with a new body when the time comes. Theoretically. Homians allow their biological bodies to die and enter an eternal sleep on the lunar complex.

Solar-powered arthropod constructs maintain the servers. The lepidopteran robots maintain data integrity of each of the billions of servers, floating around, bobbing from one server to the other as if pollinating. Who knows what the slumbering Homians dream of?

There are larger constructs on the moonbase, small adaptable engines with multiple arms that monitor the information sent back from the travelling xenoforms. Earth is the only planet that seems habitable and has accommodated footholders. The xenoforms send information that triggers a silent alarm in a mule-like construct which immediately extends four legs and runs at thirty-six miles per hour to a specific server, dodging asteroid craters, moon rocks and the debris of downed satellites. It carries this server back to base where a smaller, more delicate and polydactylous insect begins a subtle process of connecting the server to the main processing unit.

Other machines process a small airlock and fill the room from underground gas tanks. The gas is not air and will not support life, but its molecules will vibrate to produce sound.

It takes six days for the revived scientist to gain interface with the processing unit, and to understand her own environment. She activates speakers which produce words. They are electronic and without cadence, but they are clear.

"Accept my greetings. I do not know your name, or if you understand my language. There are over a thousand Homian languages and dialects. I will cycle through all of them. I am designated Chief Revival Scientist. My name is Lua and this is uniplex communication so I will not be able to sense any response from you. The fact of my revival means there has been a fault."

Hearing the speech is a strange experience, akin to singing along with an old love song. Anthony knows the words and the anticipation of each creates the sonic version of an after-image. He also knows that whatever language the scientist uses is converted into an Earth language and idiom by the human brain.

"This is what should have happened," says Lua. "The xenoforms were to send back information about how much of each Earth person has been converted. They did, and earlier in the last solar cycle, the maintenance machines received notification of the first full conversion. This activated a specific protocol designed to test the transmigration of our people. A specific Homian was revived and the consciousness transmitted into this person on Earth."

Lua spends over an hour talking about the technical details of such an operation, but Anthony tunes out and speeds through the memory.

"We lost contact within nanoseconds of the transfer. Most likely the human form is unable to tolerate the Homian mind, too primitive. Perhaps we should have just had the xenoforms build bodies identical to our own anatomy."

Anthony knows why. The indigenes' bodies have adapted to the planet. It makes sense to use anatomy that suits the environment they are trying to conquer. He also knows there was fierce debate among Homian philosophers about this. The transferred individuals would be Homian *res cogitans* but not *res extensa*, a concept still faulty in itself. The xenoforms are classified as biological machines, thus a body built of them would be a machine. A Homian mind inside a machine was ... unclassifiable. Worse, the machine would be built on a human template, alien, unhomian. Some said this was the price of interstellar survival, that this is what assisted evolution looks like.

Lua said, "Before we transfer billions of Homians to Earth we must be absolutely sure the process works. We cannot continue until we know what happened to the first one. Footholder, you must find the body, analyse it, and send all the data back to me."

Anthony comes out of the trance. There is more technical stuff about the hows and whys and what to do when presented with the body, but it is all tucked away in his memory, retrievable.

It is the first time he has been called a footholder. He feels the vastness of Wormwood stirring underground, unhappy because Lua declined to use a specific noun. Anthony, Wormwood, Wormwood, Anthony. One? The same? Human? Homian?

Anthony opens his eyes and his lover is standing over him, concerned. She smiles; he does not.

"I must go now," says Anthony. "Goodbye."

He dies.

Excerpt from *Kudi*, a novel
by Walter Tanmola

Before Emeka could say anything, Christopher strode in with a grin and turbulent light in his eyes. Lord save us, he had an idea.

"Get the car," he said. "We are off to pay the corrupt and corrupt the gullible."

He didn't have to tell Emeka where to point the automobile. The eruption of the dome was on all feeds all the time. Self-drive wouldn't work because people were barred from going to that destination. It was the first thing authorities would disable in a crisis.

Normally a two-hour trip, the roads were clogged with people like them who wanted to see what an alien looked like. Christopher spent the trip cutting blue typing sheets into small rectangles. Then he wrote numbers on each one with a biro he found in the trunk. When the car could no longer move, Christopher said to abandon the car and continue on motor-bike taxis. Emeka resented leaving his mother's car, but did not complain. A mile out, there was no movement, not even the two-wheel kind. The sky darkened with more drones than either of them had ever seen.

47

On foot, Christopher insinuated himself and sucked Emeka along with his gravitational field. At the cordon, he negotiated with the security man and they both saw the alien structure close-up. It was like Satan reverse-fucked the Earth and left his penis poking out, pulsating with eldritch engorgement. The thing had veins, skin and warmth. Christopher smacked Emeka on his back.

"We're not here to sight-see. Start selling tickets."

He handed Emeka a batch of the blue rectangles and they started the work. They gave a cut to the Civil Defence guys, but still made a tidy sum over the next few weeks.

Then Emeka met Kudi.

Chapter Four

Alyssa

Alyssa repeats herself. "I need to see a doctor."

"Still feeling poorly? I'll book an appointment for Monday." Mark drops the car keys on a cabinet.

"No, not an appointment. I need to see a doctor today. Now."

He moves to kiss her but she turns her face to the side. She regrets it, but the action is involuntary. She feels no affection for him.

"Okay. Why? I mean, I'll take you to the hospital, Alyssa, but you don't look sick. What's wrong."

"Isn't that between me and the doctor?"

"I'm your husband." Mark sounds offended, hurt.

Alyssa sighs. "I don't know that."

"What?"

"I don't know that you're my husband."

Mark laughs, but it is interleaved with nervousness. "Stop playing, Al."

"I'm not. I'm sorry, but I don't remember you."

"Al—"

"Just listen. I don't remember you, Pat or this house. I know we're Sutcliffes because I read documents. I see pictures of you and me together, but I don't remember when we took them."

"Alyssa, stop this right now. It isn't funny."

"No shit, it isn't funny. I've lost my memory."

Mark is a lanky sort with shaggy blond hair. His eyes are small but expressive, and he looks stricken. "Do you remember last night?"

Alyssa shakes her head.

"You got back from work—"

"What kind of work? What do I do?"

Mark falters. "You work in an office, for Integrity Corp. You're some admin, logistics bigwig. Everybody depends on you."

"I don't remember."

Mark exhales. "Okay, you don't. You got back from work—"

"What do you do?"

"I'm an artist." He sits down in a lounge chair opposite her and run his hands over the arms. "You know, you chose the fabric for the furniture. I fucking hate it."

Alyssa glances at the armrest, but does nothing.

"You got into a fight with Pat about her room and homework."

"Mark, are you trying to get me to snap out of this? Think maybe if you tell me things it will shock me into remembering? Because I've tried all that. Take me to a hospital, pretty please."

He leaps up, and she flinches when he touches her arm.

"Hey!" Mark says.

"I'm sorry. I just ... I'm anxious and all my feelings are jumbled up." She looks from her wedding ring to his, back to hers.

"I'll bring the car round."

*

The doctor does not make eye contact. He types on a keyboard and watches the screen. "And nothing like this has ever happened before now?" he asks.

"I don't know. I can't remember, remember?" says Alyssa.

"The question was directed at your husband, Mrs Sutcliffe." He does not sound offended or even amused at the weak joke.

"No, she's been fine until now," says Mark. He slouches in the chair, but that may be his height and the average-sized furniture in the room.

"Drugs?"

"No. Some wine, some beer." Mark tries to hold her hand, but Alyssa removes hers from the armrests and folds them in her lap. A part of her feels the gesture is for his own comfort more than hers.

The doctor is black, paunchy, with the beginnings of male pattern baldness, and seems coldly efficient or efficiently cold. He retrieves her medical history from her implant. He examines her, checking her pupils, her eye movements, her swallowing, the symmetry of her smile, the centrality of her tongue, her body sensation, her gait, her ability to perform a number of silly-looking alternating hand gestures.

Afterwards he exhales just like Mark did before.

"Mrs Sutcliffe, I can't find any evidence of a neurological disorder and you seem in good general health. I'm going to take blood, urine and stool samples from you, and send you for a brain scan, but I do this to be thorough. I do not expect anything to be abnormal."

"Something is abnormal, Doctor," says Alyssa.

"I know." His body language has become dismissive. He wants them to leave. "But the abnormality isn't in your body."

*

Alyssa leans her forehead against the car window and watches the world outside.

This is Rosewater; this is where they live. It is a rowdy conurbation slapped against the periphery of a two-hundred-feet-high dome. It does not look planned. The streets are tight, with a tendency to break off or bend at awkward angles without warning. The houses slapdash, of varying ages and design, the entire city an afterthought. It teems with people, most of them black Nigerians, but there is a healthy mottling of Arabs, South Asians, Russians and a myriad other nationalities. Road signs struggle to control and make sense of the movements of the population and the central auto-drive system. The air is constantly criss-crossed by the path of drones like birds who do not fly in tandem. The real birds seem shy, upstaged, lurking on rooftops and shitting everywhere.

The dome is a blue beacon with a tortuous pattern on its surface and spikes growing out in every direction. Drones and birds and other uncertain flying organisms have impaled themselves on these extrusions, their corpses hanging like kebabs for the vultures who keep it clean.

Alyssa sees all this and knows it, recognises the information. She sees the alterations of the reconstructed, the sluggish movements of the occasional reanimate, and she does not feel disturbed.

Mark keeps a running commentary about whatever they pass. He is nervy and cannot look her in the eye. Alyssa has been quiet.

"I think we should keep this from Pat," Mark says.

"All right."

"I just don't think we should worry her."

"I said, all right."

"How are you feeling, Al?"

"How do you think? I feel confused. That doctor was basically saying it's all in my mind."

"Hey, he was an asshole," says Mark. "What a bedside manner."

"True, but his attitude is not my problem. My problem is me. What's wrong with my head?"

Mark takes his hand off the wheel and tries to stroke Alyssa's arm, but she shies away.

"You're not making this easy for me," says Mark. "I'm trying to be supportive here, but you act like I'm some sex offender."

"I'm sorry," says Alyssa. But she is not. She has no feelings for this man, this concerned, beautiful man. She does not feel attracted to him; she does not wish to be kissed by him. She does not wish him to touch her. Even the idea of making contact makes her skin crawl. How can she be married to him?

"Are you angry with me?" asks Mark.

"No."

"Then what?" An edge creeps into his voice.

Am I under any obligation to love this man? To be nice to him?

Something lands on the passenger-side window. It seems to be made entirely of two flat wings attached to a thin spine. It looks like a living kite, about a foot wide. Alyssa can see delicate ribs supporting the wings from one side to the other, and blood coursing through thin vessels. On one end of the spine there is a small enlargement with two purple blobs that might be eyes.

"What's this?" Alyssa asks.

"It's an aeolian. You don't remember aeolians?"

It does seem familiar in some way, but not in and of itself. Alyssa traces the spine, which is aligned diagonally across the glass. She sees tiny vestigial legs moving about uselessly and the occasional ripple of the wings.

And.

And another insect in another place and another time. Alloy metals and polymers articulated into the metallic body, a purely functional design with no attention to aesthetics. Too many limbs attached. Curiously silent. Dark surrounding. Light projected from eyes that run all along the body and at the tips of many of the antennae. Like fibre-optic cables.

And.

It's gone. The aeolian peels off the window and Alyssa watches it rise on air currents, flapping maybe twice, light and free. It leaves a thin film of mucus on the window, warping the edges of the city viewed through it.

With the lull in the traffic a street hawker brings roasted corn towards Alyssa, but thinks better of it when the cars begin to move.

"You seem far away, Al," says Mark.

"I am far away, in more ways than one," says Alyssa.

"Well, come back. We're about to pick up our girl."

Mark pulls into a driveway and Pat bounds out of the house, leaden with colourful gifts and buoyed by childhood. The vehicle recognises her and opens the driver's side back door. Alyssa doesn't quite know how to deal with the child, but smiles. Pat does not look at her, but immediately begins to speak on the phone. Alyssa glances at Mark.

"This is normal," he mouths.

Alyssa pulls down the visor mirror and surreptitiously examines the child. Her hair is short, her eyebrows bushy, but she looks like a smaller version of the face Alyssa sees in the mirror, except more animated, more alive, more confident. Pat has the absolute certainty of the loved child that she is the centre of the universe, and that she will be safe for all time. Alyssa wonders how long it will be before the girl is disappointed.

This does not feel like my child.

When they arrive Pat rushes inside the house, still deep in conversation. Mark picks up the debris of her party. "Anything?" He taps his temple with an index finger.

"Nothing," says Alyssa. "I got a flash of a science fiction film, I think. I don't remember you or Pat."

Down the street of identical houses Alyssa sees a woman staring. She is black and stands so still that Alyssa is not sure if the woman is alive or a statue. Then the woman spins and walks away in the opposite direction. Does she know Alyssa? It makes her feel dizzy.

"I have to lie down," says Alyssa.

Alyssa goes over everything that has happened since she rose in the morning. She remembers all of it, waking up, seeing Mark beside her, panicking on hearing Pat, fleeing to the bathroom, going to the doctor, the sting of the needle when they took blood samples, the hum of air conditioning, the pimples on the face of the scanner technician, the almost sexual nature of her lying supine on a slab entering a circular scanner, the drive home, the woman watching her, all of it.

There is nothing wrong with her memory. She has been testing it by memorising lines of text and serial numbers of devices she finds in the house. She remembers everything she encounters, but nothing before today.

She feels nausea, but her belly is empty and there is to be no relief from vomiting. It is a strange nausea that she feels not only in the pit of her stomach but throughout her body, down to her fingertips. Even without her memory she knows this is not how nausea feels, but also that there is no word for what she really feels, which is a need to expel not just food, but everything.

She takes a deep breath and screams.

Chapter Five

Aminat

"Peace be unto this house, bitches!" says Aminat, holding a bottle of vodka in each hand at shoulder height. She shakes her shoulders in a pantomime of the limbo.

Bea snatches the bottles, gives Aminat a half-hug and immediately resumes the creation of punch. "You took your time, girl. I started to think you got left for dead somewhere."

"Aminat!" squeals Efe. She kisses the air and slides off the strap of Aminat's handbag. "Drop this, and come with me. Fisayo had her boobs done."

Bea rolls her eyes. "Let the woman land first, before you start your amebo."

Efe links arms and leads Aminat deeper into the room. "She used one of those lab-grown implants, from her own DNA. It feels natural and she says there aren't any scars."

"Isn't she an identical twin with—"

"Yes, o. Even her husband can't tell them apart."

Bea snorts. "I'm told her husband *hasn't* been telling them apart."

They burst into laughter and the evening begins.

"Where's Ofor and Little Ofor?" asks Aminat.

"They went to the village. Mother-in-law," says Efe.

"Haba. You no follow?"

"No, please leave me. I hate the woman. She's always like, 'Efe, this is how you should chop ata rodo' and 'Is that how long you're going to fry plantain?' Abeg."

They catch up on their lives as much as possible, and drink. It is Efe's house and outside the bay windows the north ganglion is visible. Tonight it flickers and emits the occasional bolt of dry lightning. They stare at it and Aminat sees the blue light reflected on her friends' faces. Efe has a rounded face and light skin, shorter than the others, garrulous but good natured. Bea is skinny, full of angles and sarcasm. Aminat has known them for ever and loves them. Meeting up every few weeks is the only thing that keeps her sane sometimes. She wishes she could tell them that she is going into space, she needs to tell them, but she cannot. Instead, she just accepts that if she had told them, they would have supported her. She knows this, and is calmed.

The conversation goes on, but Aminat only superficially engages. She participates, but is removed from it all. She does not drink much, and only half-listens to Efe's description of all the home security innovations her husband has installed. It's more like a hobby of Ofor's, trying to stuff as much new technology into the property as possible. Aminat just enjoys the cherubic smile on her friend's face when she talks about her husband's silliness and the joy in her voice when her son comes up in conversation.

On the way home she fields calls from her mother complaining about her father. She listens like a dutiful daughter and hangs up after what she deems a reasonable time. She drives up to Atewo with the dome glowing bright blue in the night. Closer to street level the darkness is dotted with pinpricks of light, not from houses, but from droppers. This is the reason nobody builds on this stretch of highway. Droppers are xenoflora that try to mimic human form in order to draw prey in. The shapes look ridiculous in the daytime, like cardboard-cut-out people with bio-luminous eyes. They are surprisingly effective at night with either children or people from out of town. A curious person would find themselves bathed in corrosive fluid and slowly consumed. The mayor has been talking about exterminating them for years, though his wife's charity says the opposite.

Aminat parks, takes off her shoes, and walks barefoot to the house. The security protocol picks up her RFID and lets her in. The house is dark, but Aminat chooses to leave it that way. Yaro growls once and comes to her, wagging his tail, butting her shin with his cold nose. She strokes the monster's head briefly. She does not understand their relationship. Yaro is Kaaro's dog and he has never properly warmed to Aminat. He sends mixed messages by dog standards.

"Where's your master?" she asks him.

"In here."

Yaro pads ahead of Aminat and comes to rest just beside Kaaro's left foot. Kaaro sits at a desk, reading a book. His face is caught in the glow from the table lamp and he has that gentle smile. Aminat knows she loves this man because of how she feels each time she sees him. This indescribable feeling from the pit of the stomach that is like being sick and superpowered all at the same time. She drops her shoes near the door of the study.

"Hi," she says.

"Hi," says Kaaro. He gives a short wave.

"My feet are killing me. What are you reading?"

"Bill Hicks. *Love All the People*."

"I don't know who that is. Before my time, no doubt."

"Before mine too."

He stands and they kiss. His hands wander all over her body before coming to rest on her back. "Hmm. Aromatic vodka. How are the girls?"

"They live long; they prosper. Enough about them. How're you?"

"I'm cool. You know, you forgot to ring your father, and he's kind of jealous that you spoke to your mum."

"Shit!"

"Don't worry. I talked him down. Layi says hello."

"We'll go down next week." Aminat squeezes Kaaro's buttocks, a signal for privacy. She closes her eyes and waits.

Everything shifts. They are no longer in the house. No chance of surveillance here.

Kaaro, her lover, brings them both to a place where events roam with questionable chronology. Time is compressed or extended. Space is whatever they need it to be. He has brought them to a grassy meadow impossibly wide. It is bright and breezy. Bees flit from flower to flower. The tips of each blade of grass sway in the wind and snap, floating upwards in the air, swirling, disappearing into the sky. In the distance there are mountains, and beyond that, a colossal creature, head in the clouds, mouth perpetually open. This is Bolo, Kaaro's mental guardian. The scene looks to Aminat like a Goya Black Painting.

"Have you redecorated?" asks Aminat.

"No, I was exploring before you came in," says Kaaro. "I'm experimenting with the defensive properties of wide-open spaces."

"Isn't that dangerous?"

"Bolo will protect me."

Kaaro is thought to be the last of the sensitives, humans with a variety of strange abilities endowed by the xenoforms. Aminat is not privy to all the information, but the xenoforms have a network of data in Earth's atmosphere and sensitives could access it, including the thoughts of other humans and some ability to read the future. Kaaro calls himself a quantum extrapolator because Anthony, the alien avatar of Wormwood, called him that. Something happened, and the aliens decided to kill all the sensitives, though nobody seems to know why. They almost killed Kaaro, but Anthony saved him. Kaaro had worked with S45, but quit after he almost died in service. Femi Alaagomeji tries continuously to be subtle, but she wants Kaaro back at work.

Aminat strokes Kaaro's cheek. "I love you. I just wanted to say that."

"Don't say it yet." Kaaro smiles. "I need to concentrate to keep us here."

Aminat sees a disturbance in the grass almost a mile away. An object displaces the blades and travels at great speed towards them. "Something's coming."

"I know. There are many of them. Do not worry about it." Kaaro points to other directions.

There are five other similar disturbances in the foliage. They seem intent, and Aminat cannot relax the way Kaaro seems to. "Who are they?"

"Bogey men from my imagination, people I've encountered or make up. Since we're in my mind they take on reality. It's been a bastard keeping them at bay recently."

As he speaks, his image doubles, then a ghostly version of Kaaro lifts off into the air and floats away.

"That's new," says Aminat. "What is it?"

"Yeah, that's a possible me. Idle wonderings of what might have been. It's not important."

More versions of him break away at irregular intervals. It is distracting to Aminat, but she focuses on him. "Is it safe to talk?" she asks.

"Yes. How was Efe?"

"You know Efe. Tonight she said to me that the way to make a man crazy about you is, after having sex for the first time, to say nobody ever made you come like that. Or that you've had to fake it with other men. She gave a whole alcohol-fuelled lecture on this."

Kaaro smiles. He likes her friends, or at least acts like he does.

"Kaaro, they want me to go into space," Aminat says, serious all of a sudden.

"For real?"

"Yes. They want me to go to the *Nautilus*, dock, take samples of the air and biological samples from the astronauts there."

"Or their remains. Nobody has heard from that space station for years."

"They don't tell us everything. Who knows if there have been supply missions all this while?"

"Do you trust them?"

"What do you mean?"

"Well, S45 is not exactly known for being truthful, or sharing. Femi is—"

"Ruthless, yes, you told me. I don't know. I have only known for a few hours."

One of the bandits seems to be getting incredibly close, only fifty yards away, and Aminat feels exposed and without any means of defending herself.

"Kaaro—"

A column of wood descends from the sky and crushes the intruder with an almighty bang. The ground, such as it is, shakes, and the gentle floating of the grass tips is disturbed by the shockwave. Bolo stands over them.

"I told you not to worry," Kaaro says. "What happens next?"

"Training, I suppose. I've let myself go, haven't I?"

"No fat on you, baby."

"Yes, but I have to do six months endurance training. I have to get back to fighting weight. Tonight was a kind of farewell to alcohol."

"And other things?"

"What do you mean?"

"Other kinds of exercise ... ?"

"Bring me out of this place, and we can test *your* endurance."

Chapter Six

Bewon

After a twelve-minute break, the train starts chugging along again. Bewon opens his eyes briefly to confirm the motion by staring out of the window. He lets his eyes flit over his fellow passengers, before closing them again. There are three others, two girls seated next to each other, teenagers, dressed up as if going out, and an older man, about fifty, sixty, who chats with them across empty seats.

When the train stops again, one of the girls asks, "Do you think there's someone on the tracks?" There is worry in her voice. The old man says it happens fairly often, and the girl asks if he has ever seen a dead body. He says a friend of his hanged himself once, and he discovered the body. The second girl pipes up about her mother's boyfriend who tried to jump on the tracks, but was prevented by police. This apparently did not deter him, and a month later he was found dead near the south ganglion, burned extra crispy. This is supposed to have happened before the Ocampo Inverter station was built over the ganglia. The train starts again.

Bewon stops listening. They announce Kinshasa station, and he gets off, feeling depleted. It's dark, and for some reason all the taxis and okadas are gone. It's Saturday night, why would they not be there? Posters of some pop idol in the stadium, which is probably where the kids in the carriage are going, and explains the lack of transport. He decides to walk. He cannot afford a taxi, anyhow. He has returned from a week-long interview in Lagos. Twelve candidates for one job. Travel and accommodation expenses borne by each, money that Bewon can scarcely spare.

A drone descends, checks his ID chip, and buzzes away in less than a minute. Bewon has an impulse to smash the next one he encounters, or smash anything.

He arrives at his flat in a foul mood. The two young men in 16a rush past him on their way out, brushing against his clothes in the narrow corridor. Bewon suspects them to be homosexuals and has half a mind to report them to the authorities, since it is illegal in Nigeria. Bewon does not like to touch the gays. They are filthy, and they love to ... flaunt. That's the word. They flaunt themselves and their filthiness. Bewon will have to do something about them some day. Report them to the authorities. He cannot remember their names, but they smile at him when they are not ... flaunting and cavorting. There is a current wanted poster for a practising lesbian that flashes every time he crosses the supermarket threshold. Maybe he should make a poster of these people too.

He opens his flat and stumbles in, barking his shin on a wooden chest that he left in the living room a week ago. He swears, even though he knows he can only blame himself. He kicks the door shut, drops his travelling bag on the chest and flicks the light switch. Nothing happens. He feels his way into the flat and tries another switch. Nothing. He realises he cannot hear the fridge or anything electrical. Is this a blackout, or has his power been cut? He cannot remember if he paid his bill this month. This is infuriating because the government doesn't pay anything for electricity. The alien provides it. The government just charges to pipe it into each house, and for the power station. Perhaps he can find an illegal tap later.

He goes to the kitchen, thirsty and needing some kind of relief. There is a puddle of discoloured water spreading from the foot of the fridge and a smell of putrefaction. He snatches a tumbler and turns on the tap. Then, in the filtered light from outside, he sees something growing out of the drain.

He leans in.

It is the shoot of a plant, pale green, barely alive, just two leaves adjacent to each other and a third rolled into a point and reaching for the stars.

No. There will be no reaching for stars.

He pinches the stalk between index finger and thumb, and yanks it free. As he drops it into his bin, he thinks it might be a bean stalk from when he last cooked. He thinks he may have washed some before leaving.

By the time he finishes his drink the growth is out of his mind.

Bewon masturbates after he showers. He likes the smell of semen to lull him into a sort of faux post-coital state, as if he has just been with a woman. He had a woman with him once, but she left. She did not understand him. He tells himself that he does not miss her, but on occasion even he knows this is not true.

He spends twenty minutes on the phone to his landlord, arguing about the electricity. He is from Rosewater. He remembers that there were no bills in the early days, just free juice from the ganglion. Damn Ocampo Inverter. It may be two days before Bewon can have power. He sits in the dark wondering how it came to this. He is still thirsty, so he returns to the kitchen, avoiding the fridge. He has a pen torch, but he'll need stronger light to clean out whatever is rotten.

He stops at the sink again.

The plant is back.

For a minute Bewon thinks it is the same plant and he checks the dustbin to be sure.

"The fuck . . . "

This one is two or three inches taller than the first, and a darker shade of green. Healthier. That's the word. A healthier shade of green. He shrugs, reaches to pull it out and yelps when he feels a sharp sting. He cannot see well in the crepuscular light, but he can feel the blood seeping out. He sticks his thumb in his mouth and sucks. He strikes a match and examines it in the flickering light. Not deep. He looks at the drain.

The plant, the new growth, has spines. Like henbane, only thicker, and distributed all over the stem and leaves.

Bewon is puzzled, but he thinks there must be a logical explanation. That weed did not just grow while he was in the bathroom jerking off. It must have coiled up within the U-bend, pressing up against the first plant. When Bewon cut the first plant, the second one unfurled. Unfurled, that was the word. It unfurled and made its way through the drain holes. Without electricity or indeed the will to work, Bewon decides he can wait until morning before removing the U-bend and emptying the crud that is clearly providing nourishment to the bean sprout. Except it no longer looks anything like a bean sprout.

Bewon pulls open a drawer and selects a serrated steak knife. He folds a strip of cardboard and uses it to grasp the stem at a point close to the drain, and he saws it free. The plant comes away easily. He is about to toss it in the bin when he has a different thought. He drops it on the floor and steps on it, twisting his foot as if killing an insect, revenge for the sting. His indoor thong slippers are not hard enough, so he uses the leg of a kitchen chair instead, squashing the plant into a green smear. He scoops the remains up and discards them. He soaks a rag, cleans the floor and throws that away too.

He washes his hands, keeping a close eye on the drain. He leaves the kitchen, but whirls and looks at the sink, sure that something would be there. Nothing. Silly.

He goes to bed. He sleeps fitfully and dreams of metamorphosing into a giant rocketship. He wakes up an hour later, and decides he does not want the rest of the plant in the house, so he takes the trash out – he looks at the sink sixteen times while in the kitchen – and places it in the communal can outside.

Then he goes back to bed and sleeps better.

Chapter Seven

Anthony

From deep beneath Rosewater, Wormwood extends a pseudo-podium different from the other thousands of projections on its surface. This digit moves upwards and in a south-east direction towards the marshy and vegetation-rich soil that banks the Yemaja. This tentacle is not just travelling. Its tip is bulbous and grows larger as the miles are covered. Within that tip cells divide, differentiate and combine into tissues of increasing complexity. The bulb snatches material from its environment, helping it to advance as well as providing material for growth. Dead and decaying vegetation, soil, rock, silt, water and buried metals, plastics and construction debris are all broken down by alien enzymes and repurposed into organic carbon, oxygen, hydrogen, nitrogen, calcium, sulphur, phosphorus, sodium and trace elements with which to build a body. Primitive synapses connect at first tentatively, then with authority. Chemical messengers run to and fro, and Anthony becomes self-aware.

He cannot open his eyes for now, as there is a continuous seal, rather than an upper and lower eyelid. He feels his body under construction, glands shooting test fluids, organs shifting into position in his abdomen, bones ossifying from cartilage scaffolding. His face is connected to Wormwood by umbilical tissue, feeding him with the necessary nutrients and cocooning him within the bulb. In his inner ear he senses his motion, speed between five and seven miles per hour.

After a while Anthony's cerebral cortex is complex enough to take over as the guiding intelligence of this body's creation. He even allows the flawed appendix to grow at the insistence of the genetic material.

He is in water now, sluggish, murky, moving against the undertow. The pseudopodium slows down, stops. Anthony hears the underwater sounds, the gurgling and occasional splash. A fissure forms, separating eyelids and he blinks. He is still encased in a matrix from Wormwood, with no direct connection to the waters of the Yemaja. He is surrounded by darkness and he knows it is night. He is a metre below the surface of the water. He has no access to the xenosphere because of the flowing water, but he is full sized and senses the pseudopodium breaking down, Wormwood withdrawing its nourishing fluids and arteries. It loses pliability, hardens, and cracks in multiple points, finally snapping off downstream somewhere. Anthony experiences turbulence. He breaks out of the cocoon like a bird opening a shell. The cold river water is a shock, but he immediately stimulates his hypothalamus to generate heat as a counter measure. He tears free the umbilical material attached to his nose and mouth and chest.

Anthony swims to the surface, but emerges on the south bank. The city is on the other side, so he plunges back into the river, breaking north. Visibility is poor apart from the pulsing glow of the biodome. He grows a tapetum lucidum in each eye for night vision. He is naked and has not bothered to grow the cellulose-based clothes he has used in the past.

The xenoforms attach rapidly, and in nanoseconds he is connected. They flood him with knowledge of local temperature, toxins in the air, the nearest humans, the distress of the trees recently cut, the mating calls of crickets.

Further along in the darkness he sees discarded clothing, robes. This comes from the Yemaja cult, he knows. They come to the river for their ecstasies and possession trances. He does not know why clothing would be abandoned as they are not a sex cult, but he puts on the robes, and covers his head with the hood. He cannot see the colour of his skin, but he knows it is one of the first things he needs to adjust. In the past he has come across as artificial because of the hue. Not the right shade of brown. Humans are weird.

Before he can move forward, he senses a presence approaching within the xenosphere. It is familiar and he suppresses a very human groan when he realises who it is.

"Hello, Molara," says Anthony.

She appears in his mind's eye in her favoured form, a black woman with massive butterfly wings protruding from her back. She is clothed in some diaphanous material, but it is like a nightgown and covers nothing. Her hair is short, like a boy's.

"What are you doing?" she asks. "Where are you going?"

"Don't you know?"

Molara is a sentient part of the xenosphere, but at the same time, she is generated by function. She is a data harvester, collating all the data in the xenosphere and sending them to Home in bursts. She appears to humans as a nightmare, a flowing form passing through their dreamscapes with a massive, tooth-filled maw being the only feature on her face, and billions of articulated legs with which she connects to all the minds. She can also be a succubus and had orchestrated the killing of all human sensitives. Bar one, Kaaro, whom Anthony had forbidden her to kill.

"I know everything there is to know," says Molara.

"Do you know where the quantum ghost bedded down?"

Molara is silent.

"I didn't think so. I'm going into Rosewater to find it."

"You don't need to do that," she said. "The ghost can be found in the xenosphere."

"Yet you haven't found it."

"It's a large—"

"I know. Revival Scientist Lua wants this sorted out as soon as possible, and both of us working simultaneously can only improve the odds."

She bats her wings gently, deep blue with black spots. She floats on the mental currents, surrounded by psychic miasma. Her lips are slightly parted, and Anthony can feel the human part of himself responding. He does not know if Molara intends this.

"Don't get in my way, footholder."

"If you had done your job I wouldn't have to be doing it for you," says Anthony.

"Excuse me?" Her eyes narrow.

"This process is simple, straightforward. A human body is sufficiently taken over by xenoforms, you send the signal, the revival scientist sends the test ghost. The xenoforms are primed to accept the consciousness. So how did you fuck it up? Because this is your fuck-up."

"I don't know, but I will find out."

"We find the quantum ghost first," says Anthony. "You can diagnose your own sickness afterwards."

Molara appears to be preparing an answer, but Anthony

disconnects from the xenosphere. He is barefoot, and grows a layer of callus under his feet to protect them. He sloshes through the mud and marsh, and the terra gets firma. Undergrowth becomes profuse, and he wades through elephant grass. There is fauna, but the animals flee before he reaches them: grass-cutters and bush babies and rats. It is not so windy or cold, and the robe is cotton which still billows. Here and there he encounters discarded canoes, old, decrepit. There are no paddles. He can hear burrowing animals below, traffic in front, and bats overhead. He heads for the road.

Nobody in Nigeria will stop for a barefoot man in a hooded robe on the side of the road in the dead of night. In the head-lights of passing cars Anthony can see the colour of his forearm and he makes it darker, more like that of his friend Kaaro. The colour thing confuses him so. It's a human thing. Near iden-tical DNA, yet they discriminate against each other based on the divisions of white light and the degree of protrusion of the jaw or the shape of the eyes or nose. Madness. Similar to their clothing fetish.

He walks towards Rosewater.

The city is noisier and larger than he remembers. On the out-skirts he encounters some dwellings of questionable legality. Dirt-poor people living in shacks of wood and corrugated tin. Anthony can steal their clothes, but does not. One insomniac sees him and runs screaming, begging the Judeo-Christian god for mercy, thinking Anthony a spirit.

Anthony does not stop. He maintains a steady pace trying to figure out how exactly he will find the quantum ghost. He remembers about money. Humans do not just give their shit away. You have to pay, a form of exchange or a promise of exchange. He will need to fit in, to wear regular clothes. The area around Yemaja is called Ona-oko, and it is severely deprived. He cannot further deprive them by just taking what he wants. He is contemplating the problem when he sees four reanimates on the road ahead. They are not moving, but stand close to each other, swaying as if listening to music. Anthony checks the xenosphere to be sure. They are blank mental spots, casting no psychic shadow. These are hollow men. Something from another poet.

Very well, then.

Violence.

He floods his system with cortisol and adrenaline, his mind full of verse. He grows callus over his knuckles, although there is not enough time for a full layer. Anthony skips, then breaks into a run, clenching his fists as he nears them. Only one turns towards the sound.

> Silently we went round and round,
> And through each hollow mind
> The Memory of dreadful things
> Rushed like a dreadful wind.

He remembers how to fight. He hits the first reanimate with a leaping punch to the nose, but he misjudges his own strength and shatters the skull. A gooey mess of blood, brains and bone splashes over him and the other hollow men.

> And Horror stalked before each man.

The body falls to the ground with a wet thud, and the others attack Anthony in a blind, automatic way. He uses open-hand strikes to push each one away – he does not want the blood of their fallen comrade on their clothes. They strike at him powerlessly, without real purpose, anger or drive. He does not even have to up his endorphins to endure their attack.

He kicks the knee of one, hears the patella and lower femur crack. He locks the head of a female and leaps over her, cracking the neck. The third is confused, and stops moving. Anthony kicks it in the chest, crushing bone and cartilage, stopping the heart instantly.

And Terror crept behind.

Anthony remembers that part of the clothing malarkey is that the genders use different clothes, which he finds irritating as the female clothes are more pleasing and often use more comfortable fabric. He takes the cleaner clothes off the men and discards his white robe. They are loose on him, but he grows a layer of fat to compensate. There is nothing to be done about the shoes – none of them fit. There is some money.

He tears into the flesh of one and pulls out the implant. This he swallows, but modulates his digestive acids so as not to destroy it. He will need ID in the city, and perhaps this one has not been deactivated.

> *It eats the brittle bone by night,*
> *And the soft flesh by day,*
> *It eats the flesh and bone by turns,*
> *But it eats the heart always.*

Anthony knows he smells foul, but at least he is more acceptable.

Interlude: 2055, Lagos

Eric

The house I live in was uninhabited and unfinished when I moved in, without plaster on the walls, but this is not unusual in Lagos. In the first few weeks after I returned from Rosewater I had to lock my bedroom door, the front door of my flat, the front and back door and the gate. Then I simply did not bother opening the back door except on weekends. I made friends with the construction workers and I felt a little safer. I have never been burgled. At first I thought this was because of luck, but I later found out that S45 spends a lot of money bribing local criminals to stay away from their off-duty agents.

I work every day except Sunday afternoons. I have an office without a window. I make the shitty commute to Lagos Island by the Third Mainland Bridge with reduced lanes while they re-introduce self-drive. In a year nobody will be legally allowed to manually drive a car on the island. I don't mind self-drive cars, but I wonder what it will be like when all the traffic is controlled by AI.

My office is on Broad Street, and I work anonymously with four other agents and supporting admin staff. Everyone has an office to themselves, although we are separated by plasterboard and insufficiently soundproofed. Nobody talks to anybody apart from the usual pleasantries, and because of my bruises from Jack Jacques's beating, I avoided others for the first week. I don't know how much they have been briefed about my failure, but I feel it acutely. I see mangled bodies all the time, reminded by everything. The heat of coffee, the grain on a faux-wooden finish, slamming doors, delivery drones, everything.

I move data around. I receive tips on our public phone line or Nimbus. I do preliminary follow-up, then I pass it on. Once every ten days or so I get to leave the office and check something out. Mostly, it's shit. A woman complaining that her mother-in-law drinks her blood every night; ghosts, ghosts and more ghosts; reports of alien animals which turn out to be either pranks or mistakes; a few cases of mental illness; one spectacular street fight in Ojota involving fifteen people at the same time where the police suspected supernatural influence. They were kind of right. I pick up the residue of a wild sensitive, but long-gone.

I bristle at the nonsense I am asked to do, but I know that I am only useful as an agent if I obey instructions, so I stay. I visit and take statements from hysterical villagers in Badagry, market folk in Mushin, and a particularly spooked Seventh Day Adventist church in Alagbado during a wave of apparition sightings. I go to fundamentalist tent-gatherings to check if any of the pastors are simulating supernatural powers using nanotechnology or xenosphere access. They are not.

I read the daily bulletin to keep up to date, but nobody is sending me anything specific. I have to maintain fitness because of regulations, so I attend the gym and shooting range. I do the minimum hand-to-hand requirement, which is boxing.

In the evenings I walk the streets. The carbon-scrubbers make the street lights ugly, but I suppose there is no choice. I find the latest eating joints with queues around the block and meals of peppery rice and goat meat soup. I go to concerts at Iganmu and the Surulere stadium. I find intimate jazz joints and rickety open-mic spaces where struggling musicians hope to be noticed by rich producers, military men and sugar daddies. I see the Buried Man of Ipaja, remnant of a ridiculous attempt at protecting the country with giant robots, only the ground could not support its weight and it sank into the water-logged region, head and shoulders projecting above ground for over a decade. The power cell and AI are still functional, and it spouts strange utterances like a Delphic oracle. I write down what it says when my turn comes: *Haram, death, Bible, jihadi, business, overwhelming victory.* This signifies nothing and leaves me irritated.

I don't sleep well. I fear Kaaro has left something else in my brain, something I won't know about until the right moment, and I resent it. I feel a simmering, impotent rage. Yes, he was trying to help, and he probably did save my life, but he should have told me. You don't go poking around altering people's heads without their knowledge. If not for the fact that I know I would be tracked, I'd check the database for him.

I dance a lot in clubs and on my own at home, mostly to the Latin-flavoured electronic music that young Yoruba people favour this year. I never used to dance, but I need to keep busy to stop the visions of broken bodies.

The highlight of my year is the Weapons Update meeting. Two agents from my office and one Lagos field agent are at the closed session, and we are taught while watching holograms. We are not allowed to take notes and a disembodied voice drones on.

High-velocity adhesive bombs from high-altitude drones. Rail guns. Coil guns. Particle accelerators. Heat-shield generators. Ionised gas dispersers. Infra-sound panic generators. Nausea guns. Graphene body armour that generates electric charge with each impact. Next-generation turret bots from India and China, and how to disable them. Tungsten space spears. It goes on and on, but after four hours I'm frazzled.

During the coffee break I find myself at the table with the field agent. She's tall and athletic, with a quick smile.

"Eric Sunmola," I say, raising my plastic cup with one hand, pointing to my ID with the other.

"Aminat Arigbede," she says, mirroring my pose, playfully mocking. "What do you think? This is my first one, so I don't know how it's supposed to go."

"Neither do I. It's my second."

"Think we'll ever get to use any of these?"

I shrug. "I'll be happy if they let me use a bow and arrow."

"Why do you say that?" She seems genuinely interested, but I don't know her, and I can't just share mission intel.

"Just a joke. Most of my work is at a desk."

We laugh it off and the rest of the day passes without incident, but a month later I get orders to be part of a tactical mission and Aminat is on the team. It's an easy by-the-numbers thing in Idi-Oro, a rescue of four albino children who are held captive as witches. Our operation is kept from local law enforcement because they leak like colanders and are possibly complicit. Once the children are out of state, 150 miles away in Ibadan, Aminat says to me, "Great to get out of the office, eh?" and I know she got me the assignment. I ask her out for a drink, but she says, "My husband is the jealous type. You don't even want that kind of drama." She smiles, though, and she's one of those people you just want to spend time with. She's not a sensitive, though. Unless she's so powerful that she can mask herself from ... No, that's absurd.

There's a subtle shift in my life after the Idi-Oro raid. I get more interesting messages from my superiors. I get instructed to join field operations and even fire my weapon on a few occasions. I re-engage with the human race and attend to the news. China wins the Battle of Walls. From about 2016 most of the sub-Saharan nations have participated in creating a wall of trees at the southern boundary of the Sahara Desert, called the Great Wall by some. China took umbrage, even as the tree wall grew over the years and halted the southward progress of the desert. The African Union has finally agreed to call it the Green Wall instead. There was never any doubt; most of the black African countries are in hock to the Chinese.

A teaching robot explodes and kills four pupils, wounding twelve others, in Maryland Comprehensive School, a few miles from my house. For a few days it's thought to be sabotage or terrorism, but it turns out a janitor had been carrying out some unauthorised maintenance, which is a euphemism for substituting original parts for fake ones and selling them on the black market.

I spend Christmas alone. I'm working, kind of on-call, so I can't even get drunk. I think of Aminat a lot and I look her contact details up on the S45 system. As soon as I punch in the search string my Nimbus freezes and my phone rings.

"Agent, explain your query?" says a voice I do not recognise.

"I wanted to ... we went on a mission together. I wanted to clarify—"

"Don't. You can compromise missions this way. Your supervisor is being informed of this."

And that is that. Since it's my second strike, I get assigned to work the desalination wars offshore, two years of alternating fire fights and interminable negotiations between three companies contracted to supply potable water to Lagos mainland. Turns out I'm good at war, and I gain commendations, though not impressive enough to get me transferred back to solid ground.

I get no dancing done, and I may have forgotten how. I read *Das Boot* obsessively and drink too much ogogoro, the only liquor we have. My liver survives, though not the music in my soul.

Chapter Eight

Alyssa

Mark and Pat both burst into the bedroom.

Alyssa initially thought Pat took after her, but the worried look on their faces is so similar that she can now see Mark in there too.

"Al?" asks Mark.

"Mummy, you screamed," says Pat.

"Sorry, baby," says Alyssa. "Mummy has a headache." Which is true, but not the reason she screamed. And this "mummy" talk does not at all feel natural.

Pat notices the book on the bed and picks it up. "What's this?"

"Oscar Wilde. Selected poems," says Alyssa casually.

"Is that why you screamed? Is it bad?" Pat smiles, full of hope. It's a smile that demands a reply, a child's prayer that everything is all right. *Nothing is all right, though.* The girl edges towards Alyssa and leans against her. It really is a wonderful smile, and Alyssa is lifted for a moment.

"Awful," she says.

"You've never opened that book," says Mark.

"I did today. *Thou knowest all; I seek in vain; What lands to*

till or sow with seed –; The land is black with briar and weed;
Nor cares for falling tears or rain. See?"

Mark raises an eyebrow, but says nothing. There is a spreading patch of red running down his neck, like sunburn.

"Pat, go downstairs. I'll come see you later," says Alyssa.

Pat dials her phone before she leaves the room, and her words fade as she stomps away.

Mark sits beside Alyssa on the bed. His weight causes her to list towards him, but she shifts away. He smells faintly of turpentine.

"Wilde isn't that bad," says Mark.

"Mark, I can memorise. I read the poem for the first time, and I can remember. *Thou knowest all; I sit and wait, with blinded eyes and hands that fail.* There's nothing wrong with my fucking memory, Mark."

"Except that you don't remember anything."

"Except that I don't remember anything before today. But even that's not true. I remember how to do things. I can make coffee and drive a car. Maybe. I haven't tried. But I can't remember us moving in here, or getting married, or even giving birth. I don't feel like a mother. I don't feel like a wife. I don't feel like a woman."

"Hang on, I've heard this one before. After Pat was born you said you didn't feel like a woman."

"I did?"

"Yeah, you looked in the mirror and your belly was all ... foldy and stretch-marky."

"I don't remember that, but I don't think it's the same thing."

Mark slides to the carpet and shifts position till he is kneeling in front of her. He holds her hands together and clasps them as if praying. It takes all of her will-power to resist pulling free, or keeping panic from her face.

"Whatever this is, we'll get through it, all right? I'm here. I'm not going anywhere."

It is a kissing moment. Alyssa can feel it, the tug he feels for her, the concern, the cliché of it all. She steels herself for the inevitability and when it comes she does not part her lips to his questing tongue. She breaks the bond. His head seems enormous from this perspective. Why does this feel more like her comforting him, rather than the other way around?

"Mark, do I have a diary or journal or anything?"

"I don't know. You do have a MyFace page. I'll get the terminal."

Alyssa does indeed have a MyFace page. Her implant logs her in, so she doesn't have to remember any passwords. Mark wants to hang about, but she banishes him from the bedroom. The shimmering plasma display sharpens and she sees the avatars of her "friends" turning in 3D in a digital antechamber.

Alyssa Sutcliffe has three hundred and fifteen friends. She sees her own avatar, smiling, frivolous, not caring about memories or husbands that she does not recognise.

A lot of inane updates scroll over the screen continuously. What kind of society is it that causes people to be so isolated that they need the approval of strangers?

My child, pretending to be disembowelled!

My holiday snaps!!!!

This rapist met his accuser and you won't believe what happens next.

This is weird.

Who is really running Aso Rock?

Rosewater should become an independent city state like the Vatican City – "like" if you support.

Nigeria's best dressed strippers.

Alyssa scrolls through her friends. Nothing. Not even déjà vu. She looks at her private messages. The first one that catches her attention is a borderline flirty exchange with someone called Eni Afeni. She scrolls to the beginning of the chat. It has been going on for over a year.

Eni: what's important is what you think about it.

Alyssa: I know that's what it's supposed to be but he's my husband. Why would I spend so much time and money on my hair if he doesn't notice?

Eni: I would notice.

Alyssa: I know you would.

And:

Alyssa: it's really about fit. As long as you can feel it going in, and the fella knows what he's doing, it's usually all right.

Eni: boys don't believe that. It's all about size. Stop me if this gets too personal.

Alyssa: lol! No, itz all right. Now you have me curious.

Eni: me too. My curiosity is visible.

Alyssa: er ...

Alyssa cringes at this and most of the rest of it. There is a lot of whingeing about Mark, although the conversation never stays on him. Reading it, she feels discomfort at the cheesiness of some of the messages, but no matrimonial guilt at all, and she does not recognise this Alyssa person who is chatting.

Alyssa: I don't care so much for political feminism. I fight my own corner. I work hard and go home to my family. I don't need to prove I am a Woman ™. Why would I even have to?

Status update: I love my husband!!! (Shrill desperation in the declaration. Warning to keep competitors off? Reminder to Mark if he's listening? Weak.)

Status update: New phone firmware update. I heart the new interface!

Status update: Sorry, I can't be bothered to vote if Aso Rock is only concerned about the well-being of black citizens. I count too! I pay tax.

Status update ...

Alyssa massages her temple.

There are no private messages with Mark. What did he mean, *I'm not going anywhere?* Were they having problems?

That feeling of nausea overwhelms her and she crosses to the bathroom, but nothing comes up. It is a nausea of the soul, rather than the gut. She is trying to purge something spiritual. She feels a wave of sadness, of grief. She sees Alyssa in the mirror and *this is not who she is.*

"Fuck you," she says.

The reflection mocks her by being Alyssa.

She looks at her hands, examines each one, each line, the ridges on her fingertips, the lines. She twists her rings and sees the tan line and damaged skin underneath. She scratches at it, but it's too tough.

Nausea.

This isn't real. This is not real at all. None of it.

She snatches a bottle of perfume and throws it at the mirror, shattering her reflection. She picks a large shard and draws it along her forearm skin, shocked by the pain, but waiting for the blood to well up.

Not real.

The blood seems red enough. She holds the wound open, allowing it to pool and spill over the sides of her forearm on to the floor. It is not too deep, though it still hurts. There is no pulsating fountain of blood, just a stream. She can't hear the drops on the floor, but she is aware of them. The nausea is gone, though.

She rolls up a wad of tissue and staunches the wound, then ties some fabric around her forearm to keep it in place. She rummages and finds a better dressing, then she cleans her bloody fingerprints and the blood on the floor. The wound stings, protesting each movement, but Alyssa doesn't mind. She puts on a long-sleeved pullover.

She is at least sure of one thing: she is not this Alyssa Sutcliffe person.

This gives her distance, and makes it easier to read the MyFace page. The conversations with Eni are jejune, and teach her nothing. Some friends talk about various get-togethers over the years. Alyssa laments to a friend called Ester about Pat's accent. Apparently the little girl speaks like a Nigerian, with a local accent, while Alyssa's people are from Dorset, England.

Ester: But she IS Nigerian, Ali. How else do you expect her to speak?

Alyssa: I don't know. I expected my words to rub off on her.

Ester: You're outnumbered. Mark speaks like that too. Besides, what's wrong with speaking like a Nigerian?

Alyssa: Nothing. I don't know. I just ... you want your child to sound like you.

Later she hears light laughter from downstairs and she tip-toes to the top of the stairs to listen. Mark's low-pitched voice says something and Pat giggles in a higher pitch. She descends one stair and sits on it, watching father and daughter. Pat is on his lap and Mark has his arms around her and is whispering into her ear. They look immeasurably happy and Alyssa feels warm for a minute.

She could ... stay. Live with this family, pretend to be Mrs

Alyssa Sutcliffe, wife, mother, admin manager. It is a good family, a good life. Their badinage shows it.

She shrugs the impulse off. That would be a lie, and whoever she is favours the truth. She will get to the reality of the matter, no matter what it takes.

The blood has seeped through her makeshift bandage, and she goes to change it without alerting the Sutcliffes below.

Chapter Nine

Aminat

Sunday morning finds Aminat up early, trying to remember training drills from her competitive sports years. The sun is not shining, but there is enough reflected light from the dome to give everything an orange hue.

The road in front of the house is empty. Aminat stretches, lunges, cranes her neck, then sets off on a jog. After two minutes she sprints for fifty metres, then slows again for another two minutes, then repeats the sequence. Track and field required the ability for explosive bursts of speed and Aminat still hears the voice of her coach telling her that jogging was shit as training for a jumper. Aminat is a hybrid athlete who does well in long jump, triple jump and high jump. No use in pole vault. Her body is her instrument. Any introduction of a foreign object like a pole or a relay baton and she freezes up. Not in combat, though. Aminat does surprisingly well in fire teams, or on her own, which is odd for a person who is almost a pacifist. Working for S45 makes her realise that she is capable of killing a person, and she is not quite comfortable with that, but since she now works in a lab, it's unlikely to happen.

Back in Queen's College in Lagos Aminat is a legend, still holding the school records in several events. Some national attention, but life and her brother Layi got in the way of Olympic glory.

She runs past a few constables who wave at her. Sometimes she thinks Rosewater has the most polite police force in the world. Of course, she lives in Atewo, which is relatively affluent with regular and wide roads, clean streets, good houses, no overcrowding. It is a far cry from the slums of Ona-oko or Kehinde. Aminat does not suppose the police are polite over there.

She stops and stretches. She has been going for half an hour. The sun is out, cocks crow and church bells ring. The big boss bell comes from the cathedral. It is the newest cathedral in Nigeria and modelled after the Lagos cathedral. It is interesting to have a Norman Gothic building in what is sometimes called The City of the Future.

Aminat tries not to think of space. The coming journey frightens her, but that won't stop her from doing it. She has never studied the *Nautilus* too closely, but she plans to. She is about to start running again when her phone rings. It's the lab.

"Yes?" She has a frisson of fear, knowing nobody would call her on Sunday if it were not important.

"Boss," says Olalekan, "you have to come in, like right now. Priority one."

Aminat hangs up and summons her car. She sends a text to Kaaro in code so that he will know that she is safe, but at work. She jogs on the spot, picturing the car starting, the garage door opening, tracking initiation locked on her ID and counting down the metres. She can hear the whine of the engine.

The car stops in front of her and she gets in. "Path lab," she says, and the car leaps forward. She allows auto-drive to take her north-west, on the outskirts of the city, where buildings are flatter and the dome looks like a massive deformed soap bubble rising out of a child's toy brick city. Aminat spends the time wiping sweat and secure-texting Femi, priming her for something urgent.

The lab is in a non-descript two-storey building, petesi in Yoruba, which is standard for most S45 outposts. There's a Goodhead store next door. Aminat takes manual control and parks a few houses down, then jogs. She knocks, is allowed in by a dozy guard, then descends to a sublevel.

Olalekan is crouched over a workstation, clad in his ever-present Yankees cap. A hulk of a man, Olalekan is a gentle giant of prodigious intelligence who is somewhere on the queer spectrum, although he has never been clear about it to Aminat. His eyes are soft, like the rest of him. He lacks angles of any kind, and bent over like this makes him look like an oversized pastry.

"I am underdressed and sweaty, Lekan. Tell me you have a very good reason for this."

"I do," says Olalekan, in his infinitely patient voice. "Seventy-nine per cent."

"*What?*"

"There is a human being, a female, walking about in Rosewater, with a xenoform count of seventy-nine per cent. It came in two minutes before I called you."

"Make room." Aminat takes over the terminal and examines.

For eighteen months Aminat's team has been using samples from routine blood tests to get xenoform count estimates. This way they can not only observe the effects and pace of the slow take-over, they can map the progression in individuals and cross-reference it geographically. Before today the highest Aminat has ever seen is forty-three. There has never been a subject with more xenoform than human cells. This level, seventy-nine, is unheard of.

"It's a mistake," she says. "An artefact."

"No mistake. I had them run it again a few minutes ago."

"Why are you calm?"

"I'm not calm. This is me excited."

"It would help if you spoke a little faster, or you were fidgety." Aminat phones Femi Alaagomeji.

Before Aminat can say anything, Femi asks: "Who the fuck is Alyssa Sutcliffe?"

Aminat has no time to change. The car auto-drives to the address Olalekan fishes out of the hospital database. Trust Femi to know about the subject before Aminat.

"Who the fuck is Alyssa Sutcliffe?" Aminat sucks her teeth. "Who. Is. Alyssa. Sutcliffe? Fuck should I know?" She counts off pages that Olalekan hashed together for her.

Alyssa Briony Sutcliffe, née Matlock. Born in London, England. Age, thirty-seven. Husband, Mark Anthony, thirty-two, artist, late of Pretoria. One child, Patience Adeola.

Alyssa Sutcliffe is a naturalised Nigerian. Health émigré to Rosewater. Multiple sclerosis. Works as admin manager for Integrity Insurance.

Mark Sutcliffe's xenoform levels are twelve. Patience's levels are not detectable as she hasn't had blood tests on the system. Whatever caused the spike in Alyssa is not environmental at first glance.

Aminat stares at her picture. Pretty brunette white woman. The car takes a sharp turn and Aminat drops the photo. She takes the opportunity to look out of the window. Suburbs. Identical streets, identical rows of houses. Identical decorative palms every one metre of road. How do these people tell themselves apart?

The area is mostly an expat enclave, and in a place as multi-cultural as Rosewater, that is saying something. Some white children playing on their yards stop and stare at the black woman driving by.

"Arriving at destination in three, two, one ... mark," says the auto-drive.

"Manual," says Aminat, and drives past the address, makes a U-turn and parks. No activity in the house. "Scan security nearby."

"Pending ... pending ... done."

"Report."

"Standard measures in all domiciles."

"Indwelling?"

"No indwelling. No vehicle signature."

Nothing unusual, then. They're out. It's Sunday. Might have gone to church like good little Anglicans.

Who the fuck is Alyssa Sutcliffe and why is she fucking up my space trip?

Femi would not be sending her to the *Nautilus* until this is sorted out.

There's no point going off into parts unknown if we've got this mystery woman who is mostly alien running about. How do we know what exactly she is? Is she a human becoming an alien or an alien becoming a human?

I don't know, ma'am.

Neither do I, but I'd like to know. I don't like not knowing and I don't like mysteries. Do you like mysteries, Aminat?

No, ma'am.

Then find out who this person is and bring her in for testing. Don't worry, aburo, the Nautilus *will still be there when we have Alyssa Sutcliffe.*

By which she means when Aminat has Alyssa. The inside of the car starts to smell of dried sweat. No corner shops in this suburban hell, no spare clothes in the car, no deodorant.

Aminat starts to itch.

The absolute wrong attire for a stake-out.

Time passes.

The radio tells her about a boot print found on a road in the banking district in Alaba. It has crushed the asphalt to make its impression. The boot print appeared overnight and has caused a panic. People worry about the size of it. They interview some people. What giant made the print? Is this a new alien invasion like the doomsayers predict?

Aminat changes the channel. It's a hoax. Like a crop circle. That's why they picked the banking district on a Saturday night. No witnesses.

Something occurs to her and she calls Olalekan.

"Boss?"

"Lekan, I'm on Nkrumah Street. Do a search for me. Any blood tests done in this area. Check the xenoform levels, see if any are particularly high."

"We'd have picked them up," says Lekan. He sounds like he is eating.

"I'm thinking relatively high. Close to the forties. It wouldn't have triggered an alarm on an individual level. I want to see if there is a cluster of high percentages in this area."

Lekan takes half an hour.

"Negative."

"No high levels?"

"No high levels. In fact, there are low levels and many undetectables."

Odd. But at least this means Aminat does not need to cordon off the area.

On the old classic channel she listens to the Drifters, "Under the Boardwalk".

She tries not to fall asleep.

Chapter Ten

Bewon

Bewon cannot believe his eyes. He actually rubs them to be sure, and he is aware of how ridiculous that gesture is.

He is standing in the doorway to the kitchen after a restful night's sleep. He is looking at the plant, lush growth projecting from his sink to a height of about six or seven feet, with a thick trunk – too large to be called a stem – and spines that look like crossbow quarrels. It even has a flower, pale pink, shooting off to the left of the main structure.

"Jesu ... "

How did it grow so big so fast? What is it rooted in? Bewon has no science, but a part of his brain knows that plants need sunlight. How did it thrive in the dark?

He steps in and hears a splash. There is water on the floor of the kitchen. He can hear a faint hiss from underneath the sink and he knows it is a leak.

"*Olodumare, ki ni mo se?*" Lord, what is my sin?

Bewon leaves his apartment barefoot and walks to the end of the corridor. He peeps out of the window at the garbage cans, half expecting a new growth of the cuttings from last night, but there is no such thing.

He returns to his flat and takes his grandfather's cutlass from the closet. He stomps into the kitchen and swings at the trunk. The reaction is instantaneous, like a Touch-me-not, only more violent. Even as the laceration in the trunk oozes sap, the leaves shudder, and a dust rises into the air. Bewon sneezes, inhales, sneezes again, drops the cutlass.

He feels dizzy. A shimmering light coats every object in his field of vision, changing their tones into primary colours, like a cartoon. He places a hand on the wall for support, then slides into the water, not minding the wetness. His hands glow with a celestial light.

"Uh."

He lies down, facing the ceiling. There is a pattern up there, like a map of a country. It is fascinating, even though Bewon knows it is the result of a leak from upstairs. It glows too, like everything else.

He feels like he is going to be sick. Bitter bile seeps out of his empty belly.

He drifts for a time, then a sharp pain causes him to cry out. The angle of the shadows has changed and Bewon knows hours have passed. The pain was in his foot.

He sits up and screams. The entire kitchen is filled with foliage. The pain was an adventitious root probing his left toe. It oozes blood, but without conviction, like an afterthought. The root shrivels back, out of sight. His right foot has ... he is not sure what he sees. His right foot is gone, replaced by a complex root system. There is no pain, but Bewon feels something liquid and cold coursing through his body. He cannot feel his right leg, and the numbness is advancing.

He tries to scramble away, to drag his body by the hands and his one good leg. This triggers excruciating pain in his hip joint and a kinetic reaction in the plant. More of that ... pollen fills the air, and as he breathes it, he knows peace again. The glow returns.

He knows he is a dying man. Lying there, he feels the unfairness of it all, but the pollen takes the sting out of even that. He is not filled with knowledge. Bewon feels his memory draining. He cannot remember the sound of his mother's voice.

Bewon cannot believe this is the end. He cannot believe how calm he is. No more fussing, no more struggling, no need to look for a job. Just peace in Abraham's Bosom. He thinks perhaps he should pray. He has not prayed since ... he cannot remember.

He forgets his own name, then he forgets how to breathe, so he stops.

He chokes as fluid drips down his throat, and he convulses as his brain craves oxygen, and then Bewon is free from his body, finished with life and the universe.

But the universe isn't finished with him.

Chapter Eleven

Jacques

The second alarm goes off and Jack Jacques, despite his wife's spelling-skilfulness in fellatio, has not yet ejaculated.

This is a daily ritual. Each morning, the first alarm goes off and Hannah Jacques goes to the bathroom. When she returns, she lies back with her legs spread and hanging over the edge of the bed. Jack will kneel between and lap at her until she comes. Then they swap places and Hannah fellates her husband until he climaxes in her mouth. At times he likes to kiss her and taste himself, sometimes swallow. Jack is unable to have sex any other way, at least, not with Hannah, and he is a faithful husband. This usually happens before the second alarm at 0600 hours.

This morning he finds himself rigid with tension, but no possibility of an outlet. No tell-tale tingle to say he's almost there. At 0605 hours he feels even more tense because the activity is eating into his schedule for the day.

"My noble wife, let us stop," he says.

"What's wrong?" says Hannah. Her hand is still on him, absently moving up and down.

"I don't know, but I have a busy day." He rises, kisses his

wife on the cheek – Hannah doesn't like to kiss him after he's been down on her.

He goes into the shower, makes a half-hearted attempt at masturbating, then turns on the cold water tap. By the time he emerges, the erection has wilted. He dresses carefully. He uses a subtle product to soften his hair while giving a natural appearance. He moisturises his skin. He uses a non-alcoholic aftershave. He allows the water from the shower to dry, rather than wiping himself down. He trims his nails and his nose hair. He checks the lines and fade of his haircut. He inspects his physique in the full-length mirror. He resolves to add ten to his belly crunches next workout. He puts on navy blue socks, a blue shirt, a blue pair of briefs, a navy blue suit, a blue tie done in a half-Windsor, silver cufflinks. He inspects his teeth. He does not like the colour of the whites of his eyes so he uses Visine. He sprays perfume on his clothes, not his skin. Jacques imports all his cosmetics because every single one made in Rosewater claims to contain trapped alien cells or the placenta of floaters or some other impossible thing. If the manufacturers lie about that what else are they lying about? He nods at himself, picks up his office bracelet and waits as it synchronises with his ID chip.

"Good morning, Mayor Jacques," says Lora, his assistant.

"What do I have?"

"You are meeting with the president at 0905 hours. All the research is queued in your bracelet. At midday you are opening a new central library at Atewo. At 1500 hours you have a meeting with Mrs Jacques."

"Why? I see her at home. I just saw her."

"It is in her capacity as lawyer for the Not Gone charity that she wishes to see you. She wishes to discuss the Cull."

"Again?"

"Yes. Would you like me to cancel or reschedule?"

"Neither. No, no, that's fine. What else?"

"There is an appointment here for 1700 hours that had no details, no file. It just has a name: Dahun."

Dahun is Fadahunsi, a contractor. The earlier meeting with the president would determine how much he needs Dahun. Bedfellows.

"All right. Thank you. Stand by, Lora, I'll be in touch shortly."

Jack Jacques emerges from his suite in the mayor's mansion, is joined by his two bodyguards, and begins his day.

The mansion is faux baroque in its public-facing parts. It has two wings, north and south, with fake-weathered wing towers both pregnant with weapons and sensors. The walls all have asymmetrical decorations based on coral, flowers and cowries. Behind the scenes the mansion is modern, businesslike, with antiseptic corridors and silent air conditioning. Incongruously, the walkway to his office is lined with six-foot statues of Yoruba orisa, males on one side, females on the other. Yemaja has the best statue since her river nourishes Rosewater, and she is the last orisa in the series. Jack likes to take the long walk from suite to office, greeting people and looking down on the courtyard, picking out the guilty faces of cigarette smokers.

By the time Jack arrives at his office there are two secret service men waiting. They stand, even though the door is bordered by eight empty chairs. It's not sunny, but they have dark glasses. And they are armed.

"Gentlemen?"

"Sir, we are here to secure the venue." Their mouths barely move when they talk, so Jack isn't sure which one speaks.

"I wasn't aware I was meeting the president face to face."

"You are not. We still have to secure the venue."

"*Mi casa, su casa.*" Jack points towards the door, and indicates to his own bodyguards for them to stand back.

The government men do some laser measurements and calculations to find the exact centre of the room, then they place a device on the spot. It is cylindrical, about a foot high. Jack has seen it before. It scans for surveillance devices and signals. It takes exactly sixty seconds to complete its task. They remove it, then turn off the air conditioner. This time one of them removes the pin from what seems to Jack a grenade. He throws it in Jack's office and closes the door. The three of them wait in silence while Jack expects his office to explode any minute.

"Antifungals," says one of them after two minutes.

Jack nods as if he knows why. When the silence becomes uncomfortable he reads briefings off his phone implant.

The bodyguards stare at him.

After fifteen minutes they nod at each other and go into the office. They plant two flags, both with three vertical stripes, green, white, green, the white sealed with the Nigeria coat of arms which shows a shield with symbolic rivers Niger and Benue forming a Y-confluence, a horse on either side of it, and an eagle alighting above – each three feet apart. Jack doesn't understand the need for this. There's a flag behind his desk, and coat of arms on the wall above it. Between the flag poles they place the hologram device. The first agent points to a spot.

"Stand here, sir."

When he does both agents have their firearms out and it makes Jack think of a summary execution.

"Guys, you do know how holograms work, right? He is not in the room with us. He can't be killed. At least, not by this conversation." *Unless I give him information that causes a stroke or heart attack or something.*

"Legally, he is in the room, Mr Mayor. We have to follow protocol."

The audio spits out the national anthem. Jack stands to attention as plasma gathers like a mist in the air above the device. The president comes into view. He's put on weight, Jack observes.

Jack has never liked the sitting president but he fashions his facial muscles into a smile. A sincere smile is a basic skill for a politician.

"Your Excellency—"

"Be quiet please."

"Sir?"

"I said, shut your mouth, and I am not just talking about this conversation. I have in front of me all one hundred and sixty-two memos you sent me over the last six months on the topic of Rosewater's autonomy."

"Sir, if I might just—"

"My friend, I said be quiet, or Agent Gbadamosi will arrest you. I'm sure we can come up with a federal charge if we pool our imaginations."

Jack holds his tongue.

"Listen carefully. I can convene the House of Assemblies and revoke Rosewater's legal status. We can bulldoze it to the ground like Maroko in Lagos. Do you remember Maroko? You don't because it was cancelled. When Rosewater ceases to exist so will you. You can't be mayor of nowhere, can you?"

Jack says nothing.

"Are you deaf?"

"You said I should be quiet."

The president curses for a full twenty seconds. "Jacques, your request for a national assembly discussion of the further autonomy of Rosewater is denied. You will desist from making further such requests. You will, within six months of this conversation, hold elections for the office of mayor. Do you understand me, Mr Mayor?"

"Yes, Your Excellency."

"Good. You wanted to get my attention. You have it. Try to reflect on what happened to the last group who tried to become autonomous from Nigeria." He fiddles about with something. "How do I turn this fucking thing off? What a waste of my time. What? I'm still live? How do I—"

The image freezes, then disappears.

An hour later, Jack is still standing at the same spot, inhaling the after-stench of antifungal fumes. He had expected the president to refuse, but more in the form of a veto of the outcome of a vote, not this ... summary execution. Jack wants – needs – more time. This rush is not a position he wants to be in, but he has been here before.

There is only one prison in Rosewater. It is in Taiwo, which is ironic to those in the know because Taiwo Prison's first prisoner was the Taiwo after whom the prison and area is named.

Jack is getting progressively tenser the longer he deviates from his daily plan. He likes predictability and schedules and time boxing, but he wants to see Taiwo. The warden asks if Jack wants a White Room, but he declines. He sits in the ordinary visitors' room, which is empty. It is outside normal visiting hours. The warden asks how many guards to leave with him.

"You're a good woman, Warden, but Taiwo is not going to harm me," says Jack.

It takes twelve minutes – Jack counts. Yet when Taiwo comes in he is surprised.

"Well, well, well. Who do I see before me? The chief, honourable Mayor Jack Jacques himself. Is that still what you're calling yourself?"

"Yes, Taiwo, that's my name. Are they treating you well?"

"It's a prison, Jack. You let them lock me up. That wasn't our deal."

Jack loosens his necktie. "You're wrong. I kept our bargain. You're the one who tried to kill a federal agent. I have no power over the federal government, Taiwo. I told you that, you knew that back in 'fifty-seven, and yet did it anyway. And you used a fucking robot. Evidence."

Taiwo snorts, sucks his teeth and gives a dismissive wave. "The thing about you rich people is you take your food in small bites."

"I wasn't always rich, Taiwo."

Taiwo has changed very little. A guy from the early days when Rosewater was a touch-and-go shantytown in the mud and shit around the biodome. Jack still sees Taiwo and his identical twin Kehinde half-drunk on ogogoro, staring at him with their identical eyes.

What are you going to call yourself?

Jack Jacques.

That's a stupid name. Alaridin. An insult without malice.

It's got French in it. It'll work.

"I hear you got married," says Taiwo. "A beauty queen?"

"Hannah's a lawyer, but, yes, she was also first runner-up for Miss Calabar."

"Wow. My trial lawyer, she didn't look like—"

"Stop."

"You came to me, Jack. You came to my house. What do you want?"

Jack isn't sure, so he doesn't answer at first. "I needed to see a familiar face," he says. "A face I trust to be what it says it is."

"And my face? Does it say 'criminal'?"

Taiwo has a bumpy face with knife scars and cauliflower ears. It does indeed say "criminal". Loudly. He is smart, though. Back then, Taiwo and Kehinde thought up a scam of surgically implanting a second ID chip with easy remote switching between one and the other. Or you could use the bootleg chip to jam the legitimate during the commission of a crime, leading to a non-person. This may be why his brother has not been heard from in years.

"When I came to Rosewater I had a particular vision. This city we live in is part of the way towards what I expected or was willing to work towards. Today, I found out the journey is to be truncated. They're trying to get me out of office, Taiwo."

"'They'?"

"The Federal Government. The president."

"I didn't vote for him."

"You didn't vote for anybody. Prisoners can't vote."

"A grievous injustice." Taiwo's eyes go around the room. "What will you do if you are not mayor?"

"There is no life for me outside Rosewater. Jack Jacques and the city are surgically joined. If I can't be mayor, then I cannot be."

"Suicide? You'd kill yourself?"

"No, don't be ridiculous. I'm saying there is no outcome for the city without me being in charge of it. The city and I are one, our destinies are united."

"Oh, the pride of you."

"This is nothing to do with pride. I have sunk everything physically, mentally, fiscally, philosophically, into this place. I have nothing else."

"Full pardon and restoration of my properties." Taiwo leans back, satisfied.

"What?"

"You want my help. You don't want to come out and ask, but you know this is going to go down hard. You know you may need to fight dirty, but over the years you've washed off the dirt and emerged pristine. You need an ally in the filth. My price is a full pardon plus all my confiscated properties. I'm not negotiating."

Jack realises this is exactly what he wants, even though he is still working out the details. He does not know what he wants Taiwo to do, or even if Taiwo can do anything at all.

"All right. We have a deal." He extends a hand to Taiwo who crushes it.

"Hmm. Your hands are so soft."

Lotion with lanolin, lactic acid, urea, a second activating cream containing glycerine and dimethicone. Hyaluronic acid after treatment. They'd better be soft.

"So, what next?"

Taiwo tells him a name and a phone number. "My lawyer will arrange everything, including a contract."

"Contract?"

"Yes, I want all of this in writing. You government types like to screw the criminal class over. *Ano ko ni won bi mi.*" I wasn't born yesterday.

The warden is waiting outside the visitors' room with Jack's bodyguards. She believes Jack is also there to inspect J-wing, and has prepared a flash tour. Jack goes along with it, using the time to work through his plans while pretending to listen to the droning architectural details. Jack does not know what J-wing is, but it seems to be a new initiative that he signed off, and is "making good progress".

They emerge on an elevated walkway above an open space. It is about 150 yards by 100 and the walkway cuts across it. The space is full to capacity with reanimates. They stand there, staring off into space, but facing the same direction. Their silence is disturbing to Jack.

"Pull up all the J-wing documentation," he says into his bracelet.

A stench of sweat and urine rises up, although there is also disinfectant, the cheap kind you find in state hospitals. Unlike the reanimates you see on the street, these are clean. The cat-walk is only five feet above their heads and Jack can see, in the eyes of the closest ones, nothingness. Jack remembers that this is one of the initiatives the Not Gone charity made him approve – or rather, Hannah did.

He nods to the warden and leaves the ammonia-saturated place, a smile belying the turmoil in his heart.

Chapter Twelve

Alyssa

When the child is asleep, Alyssa makes her husband sit down, then she talks.

They are in his workspace. Across town, he shares larger studio space with some local artists. They both sit on stools, he in front of his adjustable board with natural light coming over his left shoulder. The floor is carpeted with sketches, practice runs of different body parts, of simple shapes, of cubes and spheres, of elementary drawings. He draws these before he goes to the studio every day. The work he appears to be playing with at present is a plant. It does not look like anything Alyssa has seen, so it must be something he sketched from elsewhere.

He is looking at her now, waiting. He really is quite attractive, this husband thing.

"Mark," says Alyssa, "you're going to find this hard to accept."

"What?" he says. Trepidation in the wobble of that single syllable. He knows not to attempt physical contact but before all this he must have been affectionate. Shame. A good mate.

"I am not Alyssa, Mark. No, just wait. I know it sounds

crazy, but I'm sure of it. Something has happened, I don't know what, but Alyssa is gone and I am here."

Mark slips off his stool, starts to come towards her, then checks himself. He points to a picture. "Alyssa, this is you."

"No. I know I look like Alyssa and that this is the face in the mirror, but that's where the resemblance ends. I definitely don't like children, and I don't think I'm married."

"Are you – is this your way of asking for a divorce? Because you are being very dramatic. And hurtful."

"I'm sorry. I'm not trying to harm you or your daughter."

"Listen to yourself—"

"No, listen to me. I'm saying I am not the woman you married, and not metaphorically. I'm not saying Alyssa changed or wants new things. I'm saying *Alyssa isn't here*. I don't know what happened to her."

"Who are you, then?"

"I don't know that either. I just know who I'm not."

Mark shakes his head as if trying to dislodge something. "It's like the doctor said. This is a functional problem. I'll make an appointment."

"Don't bother," says Alyssa. "I won't go. The answer isn't there." She gets up. "I just wanted to be honest with you."

"What's that?"

Her wound must have opened because blood drips on the floor.

"Nothing. I'll take care of it." She leaves, shuts the door gently. He does not believe her, but she has been honest. What he does with that information is up to him, and he has to decide whether to tell Pat, but that is not Alyssa's responsibility.

She opens a first-aid box.

*

Alyssa dreams or fantasises, she is not sure which. Or is she remembering? She walks down a corridor with only occasional windows, rectangular although with rounded edges. Each window is black. Not painted over, but with complete darkness outside. There are arrows on the wall pointing in the direction she walks in. The number 235 denotes a destination. It is not "235" as she knows the Arabic numerals – this is a translation. Alyssa does not have the language to conceive of what she sees. She used to, but it's gone. In this interpretation, she arrives at 235 and sits. There is one other person waiting. A small device asks her to confirm details. She does, but falters when there is a choice of five genders. The other person goes in. There is a vibration which Alyssa receives through the bolted-down furniture after which she is invited in by a different device. The room is mostly dark, but the procedure is automated, and machines don't need light and they are saving energy – ha ha, this is funny. The time to save energy was before they fucked up Home. What happened to the other person? Alyssa doesn't see her leave.

This will be painless, she has been told. Try to keep your mind blank. The more you think, the longer the process will take. Ghosting. It's a duplication. You will not be in pain, and you will live for ever as a god because information can never die.

Lies.

Information degrades, gets corrupt, misses its target, and it did hurt.

I did die.

Wait, what?

Slave bots respond to the urbot attending to me. There is no Homian in the mix at all.

Am I dead?

The pain is from when the device grows into my nerve endings and extracts me from me. I feel it stripping my sensations and killing me from the skin inwards. I/Alyssa. I am sucked into a place – here are people around me, but I cannot see them. I am kept separate by a membrane, but whether it is biological or electronic is unknown to me. I have, Alyssa has, no real sense of place. There is a sense of Homians taking destiny into our own hands after fucking shit up.

I cannot feel any part of my body any more. It is not weightlessness, it is nothingness. I am supposed to expect this. I have been prepared for it by education and every single news report since my birth and –

Alyssa wakes, and is not alone. She is not surrounded by familiar people.

"What the hell—?"

"Mrs Sutcliffe, please remain calm."

There are three of them. They are in uniform, *nurses'* uniforms. Baby blue, with ID tags, all male.

"Who are you?" asks Alyssa.

"We are here to take you to a comfortable place," says the one in front. A deep, gentle voice from a body poised, coiled for violence.

"I am quite comfortable where I am," says Alyssa. "Where is my husband? How did you get in here? Mark will—"

"Mr Sutcliffe called us here. He is very worried about you."

"We all are," says another.

"Thank you for your concern. Now, fuck off."

Alyssa is in the studio still. She is on the floor, and judging by the aches, she has been lying here for a long while.

"Where is Mark?"

"He is in the house with your daughter. He does not want her to see this."

"And what is 'this'?"

"Mrs Sutcliffe, relax."

"I am relaxed. Are you?"

"If you will just come with us to the ambulance—"

"I don't need an ambulance. Get out of my house. I'm not sick."

The first one nods and they come for Alyssa, all three moving at the same time, coordinated. They have predetermined who grabs what part of her body. In minutes they carry Alyssa into the ambulance, which is really a modified van with a cheap self-drive and some stale after-smell. The last she sees of her house is the face of Mark at the window.

That and an unfamiliar weed growing under it.

Excerpt from *Kudi*, a novel
by Walter Tanmola

The first multinational companies to roll into Camp Rosewater were Chinese. A handful of protesters including Emeka and Kudi pelted the lorry convoys with bottles of paint and tired slogans of resistance. It did not matter to the companies. They did not fear for the safety of their staff because their operations were entirely robot executed at this stage. They worked 24/7, tireless automatons, but at dusk, a few of the protesters took shots at the drones they used to keep track of progress. There were no police in Rosewater so there were no consequences. Legal consequences, at any rate. Private security and armed quadrupeds roamed everywhere and killed anyone caught too close to construction sites.

Emeka set an automatic cement mixer on fire and kissed Kudi while the flames warmed his skin. When he broke the clinch he saw Christopher a yard away, glaring, but silent.

"We're going to fail," said Kudi.

"Why do you say that?"

"Look around you. The people don't want this development stopped. They want indoor plumbing, taps that run, smooth roads, carbon scrubbers, shit like that. This is the weakest demonstration in the history of civil disobedience."

That night the lovemaking was fatalistic and all Emeka had in his mind was Christopher.

Chapter Thirteen

Anthony

It is an age of short-shorts. Everywhere he looks, Anthony sees women and girls wearing the same strip of fabric, just in slightly different sizes or colours. More important is how they react to him. They seem disgusted. This means he is not adorned properly, or that he presents an olfactory challenge. He configures his apocrine sweat glands, but then realises it's the clothes. He thinks of stripping, but doesn't. In public, humans don't like to show certain parts of their anatomy. Anthony can't figure out why. He does six hundred minute colour corrections to his complexion as he approaches the rooming house. He has been criticised in the past for not looking human enough, and he wants to get it right. The humans going about their commerce ignore him, but he catches their glances. They think him a vagrant, and he is.

Deep within the tight, tiny streets of Ona-oko, most of the buildings professing to be hotels are, in fact, brothels. The real rooming places are cement blocks with at least running water guaranteed. Ona-oko is equidistant between the north and south ganglia so the electricity supply is sporadic. Anthony can sense electric elementals within the overhead wires. He loves them. The Cape of Good Hope Hotel is a two-storey building with a flat roof and only the façade painted. The porch holds up the rest of the structure with trunk-like columns. A woman sits in a chair, smoking a long pipe. She is thin and her eyes are narrow, as if squinting in the smoke. There are hormonal changes that tell Anthony she is aware of his approach. There is tar and scar tissue on the inner surface of her lungs. Anthony clears it all up and replaces it with embryonic pneumocytes. He sets things in motion to reverse the degenerative changes on her spine.

"That's close enough," the woman says. "I have already given to beggars today. You'll scare away my customers."

"Venerated Mother, I am a customer," says Anthony in Yoruba that he hopes is passable. He waves the cash he took from the reanimate.

"Stand still a minute," says the woman.

Anthony obeys.

She stands, puts her pipe aside and scans him with an ancient device. "No ID chip. That costs extra."

"No problem."

Each floor has a toilet and a bathroom at the north end, communal. Women are not allowed, which is to say prostitutes are not allowed, which is to say female prostitutes are not allowed. Rooming houses like these tend to become hotbeds of homosexual liaisons, but they are never raided as long as there is no heterosexual intercourse. *Don't ask, don't tell.* The woman ignores the sounds from the rooms, and cleans up the fluid and latex. Anthony reads her as a person at peace with everything, a rare human. The room is clean, if spare, but Anthony does not mind. He is comfortable anywhere.

As soon as the lady is gone, Anthony sits on the floor and reaches out to the wider xenosphere. An infinite stream of data collected by the xenoforms washes over him. This he finds comforting and familiar. He relaxes, his body relaxes.

There are blank spots in the xenosphere around the dome. In and of itself, this is not new or unusual. Weather conditions often create such spots. Rainstorms, floods, hail, intense fires. The difference is these points are fixed whereas natural ones are shifting and ephemeral. Anthony does not know what they are, but he will find out. He does not forget his primary mission, but he does not know how to find whatever Home has asked him to find. He leaves the Cape of Good Hope to find the closest blind spot.

Anthony is near the dome. It is like staring at a mirror image of himself, but not at the same time. He can still feel all the people and creatures inside it. Out here, life does not seem so friendly. The spikes make the dome seem like a military stronghold, which saddens Anthony because the extrusions started some months ago without explanation from Wormwood. The only thing Anthony can parse from the footholder is that there's a premonition of threat. They share an odd kind of sameness, although the Catholic residue in Anthony's brain thinks of the Holy Trinity being Father, Son and Holy Ghost, and yet one. He and Wormwood are one, but not the same, even though they commune.

A woman walks by with the words "Free Sample" across her bosom. Old men gather together outside cafés, talking about wars they didn't fight in, and children they didn't raise well. A number of people cluster around something on the tarmac. Anthony walks towards the crowd, at the same time realising it is the epicentre of the closest fixed blank spot in the xenosphere. The crowd is dynamic and people arrive, stay long enough to take pictures, then drift away. Anthony patiently joins the periphery and waits his turn. The people wall is five deep and he allows the motion of others to carry him along. At the centre he sees what the commotion is about. Someone has sculpted the ground, drilled and shaved the impression of a massive boot print, ten feet in length, five in width, such as might belong to a giant. The depth is about a foot. It is a prank, of course. Human artists do this kind of thing. Why did it affect the xenosphere? Between the ridges a plant shoots skyward. The drilling process has exposed some topsoil and from that the weed emerges. A tacit understanding keeps people from stepping over the artwork, but there are no signs forbidding close examination.

Anthony actively sends xenoforms on to the print and the plant. They do not return. He breaks free of the crowd and touches the plant. He feels light-headed and the colour leaches out of his visual fields. He boosts his cortisol levels to raise his blood pressure, and feels better. He backs away and the crowd quickly extrudes him. He thinks for a minute. The plant is causing the blank spots. Maybe. He does not know for sure if the plant has caused the dizziness. He ages his body as he walks to the closest café and sits with the old men. He has no money but does not comment when the barista places a cup on the table in front of him. He runs diagnostics on his body. The usual Earth microorganisms are on his skin and trapped in the cilia of his lungs, but there is something else, too. Pollen-like. Unidentified species. It triggered the reaction that led to the dizziness. In fact, it is still causing an immune reaction. Anthony has been increasing his blood pressure to keep up with it. If he were human, he'd be dead by now, although the people of Rosewater seem strangely unaffected. One of the old men is now talking to him. Anthony decides to look for the other blank spots, but first he checks in with Wormwood.

Power fluctuations in the ganglia. Not sure why. The barrier is thinner close to the boot print. Anthony is perturbed, but does not slow down. He modifies his apocrine sweat glands and pumps out endorphins, resulting in the old men paying for his coffee. He needs to travel, so he stops an okada.

"I don't have any money," says Anthony.

"Eru?"

More endorphins. "I don't have anything to exchange. I have no more than the clothes on my back, however I will owe you a favour. My name is Anthony Salerno."

The driver agrees.

As they make their way to the studio, Anthony muses that he would need money if he is to complete the task. His joints seize up, and he makes adjustments to his body. By the time they arrive at the destination, he is younger again. When he gets off the bike the driver looks at him askance.

"What?"

"Your skin. It's an odd colour, like you used too much make-up. And you look different from when I picked you up. Don't harm me."

"I won't, younger brother. I won't."

In payment, Anthony reaches into the man's brain and increases the ability to focus attention and persist, as well as the tolerance of boredom. This will help him in his business and personal life. Anthony smiles, watching him go.

The studio is a warehouse. For some inexplicable reason Earth does not value artists, especially ones that are still alive. Warehouse space is cheaper than studio space. The entire building, ugly and block-like though it is, looks better than the other warehouses. There is a nameplate with four identified artists. The studio is also a black hole within the xenosphere. Anthony looks about, then picks up a rock, which he hurls through a window. When the crash stops resounding he reaches for his left eye socket and plucks out his eyeball. He hurls this through the window. He immediately starts to grow a new one in the socket. His detached eye cannot move as there are no muscles around it, but it can still capture images. Usually. The eye sends one clear image of a healthier form of the plant he encountered at Oshodi beside the dome, then the image goes black. The eye is deactivated.

Four artists on the plate: Kola Adedotun, Mark Sutcliffe, Ahmed Ona and Stephanie Sugar. Anthony will have to find them and he bets the other black holes are where these people are. Vitreous humour leaks out of his exposed orbit and wets his shirt. He'll need an eyepatch if the new eye is going to take this long to grow. Which it ordinarily wouldn't. This body is malfunctioning. The plant, in addition to making him weak when in direct contact, appears to exert a field effect as well, a proximity attenuation.

The vegetable is becoming bothersome.

Chapter Fourteen

Aminat

Aminat sucks her teeth. She tags the ambulance, then sets the auto-drive to Link, after which she calls Olalekan up.

"I know what cats feel like," she says.

"Boss? What do you mean?"

"When you take away their kill."

"Were you planning to kill Alyssa Sutcliffe?"

"Shut up. You see who I'm locked with?"

"Special Ambulance Service."

"Tell me where they're going and why."

"Stand by."

The Link function can be glitchy. At best it gives a jerky ride despite both vehicles having synchronised software. The vehicles are different, so a quick turn by one does not guarantee the same torque on the other. And fleeting background electromagnetic radiation surges often break the link, sometimes leading to resync with a completely different vehicle. Worse, the AI of the Rosewater central self-drive tries to break in at random times, thinking the pursuit is a software error.

The steering wheel moves left and right with the directions of the auto-drive. The dash shows the route on a makeshift digital map. The government-issue processor starts a download from the ID chips of the occupants.

"Olalekan, requisition some COBs to follow us," says Aminat.

"Yes, ma'am."

Aminat keeps the ambulance in sight, ready for a quick manual override in case it becomes necessary. She has no specific plan, but whatever she does will involve talking to Alyssa Sutcliffe. Street traders rush out of the path of the ambulance, but try to reconverge immediately, so the car, detecting obstructions, blares its horn.

"Boss," says Olalekan.

"Tell me."

"They're off to St Joseph's. Each of them is a registered psychiatric nurse."

"You're telling me she's being committed?"

"I have the paperwork right here, Boss. One month for observation. I've sent the coordinates—"

"Got 'em. Thanks. Stand by."

Aminat breaks off the Link and feeds the coordinates in. The self-drive propels the car towards the shortest route. She examines the documents. Husband Mark requested that Alyssa Sutcliffe be taken into hospital for delusions of identity, whatever that means. Aminat can stop pursuit and just report back to Femi, awaiting instructions, or she can flash a badge and take custody of Alyssa at the hospital. What if she goes berserk? Or is already uncontrollable?

The car takes a different route from the ambulance, but they arrive at the same time at the hospital gates. With S45 ID it should be easy to get in, but health workers always think they're special. The gateman scans Aminat's ID and seems about to ask a question, but thinks better of it. The gate opens and the car parks itself. Aminat checks her sidearm, raking the slide, then holsters it and leaves the vehicle. Three hawks hover in formation, then land on the roof above, obviously cyborgs.

"Olalekan, keep track of me. Fix on my ID."

"Roger that."

Aminat puts on field sunglasses. The inner surface is a screen and the blueprints of the entire complex are layered on what she can see with her naked eye. A guy in a suit approaches. He has a hospital photocard – a security person.

"Ma'am, I'm Lawson, head of security here. How can we help S45?"

"I need to interview someone you just brought in ... "

Lawson is officious and solicitous. He sets up an interview room and waits outside. Aminat isn't quite sure what she will do, but keeps still so that she looks like she has a plan. The door opens and Alyssa walks in, eyes narrow, fists clenched, skin white from tension. Yet she says nothing.

"Mrs Sutcliffe, my name is Aminat. I work for the government. Would you like to sit down?"

Alyssa, apart from her fury, is unremarkable, although nobody can look their best in a hospital gown. Brown hair, brown eyes, freckles, wound dressings on forearm, posture like she has never seen the inside of a gym.

"I'd rather stand."

"As you wish. Can you tell me why you're here?"

"I thought you would have read my file."

"I have. I want your point of view."

"I've not been feeling myself. My memory has been playing up. Other than that, I'm fantastic. Dizzy with pleasure."

"Your husband says you think you're someone else."

"No, that ... not exactly. I am not Alyssa."

"But you answer to it?"

"It'll do for now, until I can figure out what's going on."

"Where is Alyssa, then?"

"I do not know, but she is not here." She tilts her head. "You are not a doctor."

"No."

"Why are you here?"

"To take you in for questioning."

"'Questioning.'"

"Yes, something came up in your blood tests—"

An alarm, the red lights flashing on Aminat's glasses.

"BOSS!"

"Calm down, Olalekan. What is it?" Aminat stands.

"Incoming hostile. You are not alone."

Chapter Fifteen

Jacques

Jack is late for his appointment with Dahun. He is conscious of the library opening at Atewo, which has been moved to a later time. But they will wait, and Dahun is important if expensive. Dahun stands by the statue of Yemaja, just outside the door, holding an envelope. Jack ushers him in and takes the envelope in one motion. Lora, his assistant, leans against the south wall, and Dahun sits down while Jack reads the costing.

"This is steep," says Jack.

Dahun shrugs. "You can find someone cheaper, your worship. Take your chances."

"I'm the mayor, not a judge."

"Price stays the same."

Dahun is a slim guy, and short, maybe five-six. He does have a stillness to him, so there's that. He carries no weapons – security stripped them. Lora found him and Jack trusts her judgement.

"What can you do? What will you do?"

"Everything. My team will keep your mayoral highness and missis highness safe along with your entourage. We will go on excursions for you, we'll advise on security, and do all of this in complete confidentiality. We will guarantee our work. You will be untouched."

"Don't you mean 'untouchable'?"

"No, I don't."

"Okay." Jack steeples his fingers. They smell of aloe vera from the last time he washed them. "I'll tell you what. I need to visit Atewo. Come with me. I need to think on the way and I'll let you know after the event."

"Why? You can simply phone or text your decision."

"Because I want to watch you. I like to know the people I hire." He nods to Lora. "We're leaving."

At the library opening there's a platform and podium, but Jack has to work his way through a crowd to get there. Lora feeds him information before each encounter. He, in turn, tries to get Lora to smile, but it doesn't work. She is focused.

" . . . Her son was mauled by wild dogs and had to have a new testicle grown in a lab somewhere. Do not mention it, but say everything with your handshake and warm eyes. Also, nod after thirty seconds. She will nod back. Behind her is Tolani, big donor, daft as a whole flock of dodos, but a football genius. The scores from last night's game were 3–0 in his team's favour. Mention that."

And so on, and so on.

It is darker than anticipated since the event is much later than scheduled. Hastily set-up spotlights radiate heat, but Jack does not sweat. He slips into autopilot and his body becomes a political machine. He needs his mind free to focus on the president. Lora had looked at him after the disastrous meeting, calm, knowing, *certain* that Jack had a plan. He did not, but she didn't know that or believe him when he told her. Still.

Six months to the election. He'll think of something. Nobody would dare run against him. Dahun is always at touching distance, no matter how thick the crowd. Good.

The front rows are packed with children, which Jack aims for. Children are easier, and they don't smell sweaty. He catches the warning glance two seconds before Carter Adewunmi crashes into his space. One of his biggest donors.

"Jack," says Carter.

"Carter," says Jack.

"I heard there will be elections."

So soon? How the hell did he hear? Is the story out?

"A formality," says Jack. "The president wants assurances. We've had elections before."

"Yes, Jack, but you stood unopposed."

"If a viable candidate—"

"I heard there will be one this time."

"What?" *What?*

"Ahh, your face. I believe this is the first time I have ever seen you surprised." Carter laughs. It reminds Jack of the braying of a donkey. Lora is on an intercept course, parting the crowd to get to them. Dahun is impassive – difficult to know if he heard the exchange. There are uniformed schoolchildren converging at the podium with a bouquet of flowers.

Jack lowers his voice, tries to sound nonchalant. "Do you know who it is?"

"I do not. Look, Jack, you've been good to me over these years, and I've been good to you. I like you, you know that, so please don't be offended when I say I'll be holding off my support and goodwill until after the elections. Good luck, and I'm sure you'll win. You have my vote." He pats Jack on the shoulder as he walks away, a hint of peppermint on his breath.

Lora arrives too late, her eyebrows raised: *What do you need from me?* All these years as his assistant, it's like she and Jack have developed telepathy between them. Not like the government telepaths that died out or were executed or something. A human thing, this.

He is about to give instructions when he sees one of the schoolchildren seated by himself apart from the others. Jack likes talking to children. Their agendas are often simple, pure, refreshing. He walks over and sits next to the boy so that they are both on the front row, facing the array of other kids.

"Not joining in?" says Jack.

"You are Jack Jacques, the mayor."

"I'm pretty sure you're not supposed to call me—"

"Stay still. Stay where you are."

Something is off. The child has an adult voice, and raises his eyes to the darkening sky. The movement is fluid but mechanical. Before Jack can ponder this further Dahun is kicking the deckchairs out of the way and yelling for Jack to get out of the way. Dahun seizes the kid and plunges a combat knife into his neck. No blood, no pain responses from the boy. Dahun sticks his hands into the neck wound and searches, digs about, his face a rigid study of concentration. He pulls out a thing, a component. Now there is a whine, getting progressively louder, a sound Jack has heard before. He looks for the trail of a missile, but it is not visible yet. Dahun is crushing the component, trying to destroy it. He finds something critical and snaps it just as Jack spots the missile – too close.

People know the danger now, and they run and scream, push and hide. The missile explodes twenty feet above the library. The shockwave alone is devastating, and all the glass shatters.

Nobody seems in charge, but one of Jack's bodyguards is soon by his side. A few yards away the child-thing lies discarded like yesterday's news. The podium is splintered, flower petals float about and here and there, the broken bodies of children lie scattered within the debris. There are some adult bodies, but most are just wounded. Sirens already. That was quick. The ringing in Jack's ears begins to subside and he sees a dust-covered Dahun approach.

"You're welcome. I'm hired. I get a fifty-thousand-dollar bonus for saving your life. American dollars. Oh, and as some-one just tried to kill you, I want you to know that I could have jacked up the prices, but I didn't, no pun intended."

Jack nods and waves vaguely in Dahun's direction. "Yes, yes, do what you do, and what you have to."

Dahun studies him. "You seem a little dizzy. Maybe you're concussed. I will ask you again tomorrow."

Jack does not see Carter among the wounded. Pity. Lora arrives, leaking clear fluid from the left ear.

Jack says, "I'm pretty sure you need to get yourself fixed up."

"I'll go later," she says. "The president just tried to assas-sinate you."

"Yes."

"How do you want to respond?"

"I will not respond. Tonight he'll do a 'thoughts-and-prayers' broadcast, condemning this in the strongest terms. He may offer federal aid. Either way, it's a distraction. What I want you to do is find out who is running against me for this election."

"I already know," says Lora.

Before he can ask, his phone rings and his wife is on the line. She has been informed about the explosion and listens to his account, then she says: *"Mimi l'epon agbo nmi; ko le ja."* The billy goat's scrotum may sway, but it doesn't fall off. In other words, yes, your world is shaken, but you're strong enough to weather this.

"I love you," says Jack.

"Come home. You've done enough for today."

Jack is home.

"White noise."

No.

"Whalesong."

No.

"Surf."

No.

Jack is home. The first moments of silence he has had all day, but it is not silent. The churning of his mind will not stop. He cannot recall ever being this exhausted. It is not the first time he has cheated death, but the adrenaline reaction comes each time, like now. He shakes, does not resist, allows it. It feels like fear, but Jack is not afraid. He tips the chair over and allows himself to fall back. The weightlessness is brief, but it is a loss of control until the back of the chair crashes into the floor, clapping his upper back and his head. His calves scrape against the front legs of the chair and his legs fold rapidly at the knees. His hands have not moved. He takes the pain, absorbs it. A voice from his past says, *This is the greatest lesson of life, boy. You sit, you pitch the chair over, you give up all control, you take the hit when it comes, then you wait in silence. If life does not talk to you, do it again, and again till that bitch gives up its secrets to you.*

Jack waits in silence, but life tells him nothing, so he stands, rights the chair and goes again. And again. Blood sings in his head, his elbows hurt, his legs are bruised. Life, the universe, whatever, whispers to him. He has control again. He goes to the window, commands it to become transparent, and stares at the dome.

Jack is home.

Chapter Sixteen

Anthony

The third blank spot in the xenosphere is in a residential area. Anthony has to stop the taxi a few yards off because he feels sick. His new eye has grown back colour-blind. He gets the sense that this body has become defective, but his control over the physiology is slipping, so he cannot heal it as he would wish. In the xenosphere, which Anthony slips in and out of, the area appears as a billowing black cloud, a darkness. He looks for Molara, but finds nothing. In Rosewater, he stops in the middle of the street, so ill that he wants to lie down. He contemplates throwing another eye, but if the new one is already colour-blind, what if that is not the only defect? He might end up blind with no light perception. He is still considering this when he hears the roar of an engine – an ambulance. It passes him, and ... and in the wake of that vehicle, there is ... there are tendrils of the like he has never felt before, but familiar. Entangled memories alert him – the Homian consciousness is there. He barely registers the other car that drives past him in pursuit. He does not care. Is the new host injured in some way? The Chief Revival Scientist said it malfunctioned. In what way? No time to fuck about – he needs to go where the ambulance went.

He forces his body to give him energy and he runs after the fading tentacles of otherness. He cancels out pain and fatigue. He neutralises the lactic acid build-up in his muscles and pushes the body. He leaves nodules of tangled xenoforms as breadcrumbs in the sphere for Molara to find at intervals, in case he dies before he can find the new host. Or maybe they are for him to be found. People stare at him, marvelling at his speed, and as he builds distance between him and the blank spot, his abilities increase and he runs faster still. At some point he becomes aware that the residue he tracks becomes stronger, and he realises that the ambulance has stopped. He runs faster, increasing the flexibility of his tendons, producing more synovial fluid between the joints, increasing his stride length. He bounds every few yards and it seems like he might take flight sometimes. He idly wonders how high he could jump if he sets his mind to it. When he arrives at the hospital, there is a beacon of dark energy emanating from it, seen only in the xenosphere. Unlike the blank spots, it has no effect on Anthony so he heads inside. At this point his vision, his senses are in a negotiated state. He flits between the xenosphere and hard reality constantly. The cloud of the host is nigh irresistible and when humans accost him, trying to stop him from reaching it, Anthony barely registers their presence. He stops them from frustrating his purpose or slowing him down. When he is on Earth, he breaks their bodies. When he is in the xenosphere, he splits their minds apart. He comes to a corridor and the host is in one of the rooms. The walls are reflective and he sees himself. He is emaciated, so skinny as to be skeletal. He burned too much energy getting here. No matter. Humans like slimness in their adults. He is probably attractive to them.

133

The door opens and the host is behind a human female. He disposes of the female with a swipe. No. His arm is broken, then his ribcage is crushed, then he loses consciousness. He is shocked to be defeated by a human. Ten seconds later the body is dead and Anthony travels back to Wormwood through the xenosphere, pained to be moving away from the host, but in a hurry to rebuild his body. This time he will rethink the nature of energy stores and compensate.

And he will stop underestimating humans.

Chapter Seventeen

Aminat

An ugly reanimate attacks Aminat right outside the room. The muscles wasted all down to the bone, skin peeling, falling off, intense febrile look in one eye, the other eye dangling by a nerve out of the socket, lower jaw hanging loose, and it smells of mildew. It is naked, clothes probably dropped off its frame. Aminat steps out of the attack and breaks the arm at the elbow, then she stamp-kicks it on its chest, sending it to the floor. She draws her gun and shoots it in the head. It still twitches, so she shoots it again in the heart. The corridor echoes with the gunshot and Aminat's ears ring. It's dead. The blood flow is sluggish and there is no arterial spurting. A few ... spores float up into the air from the head wound. Aminat is puzzled, but too busy to contemplate.

"What is that?" asks Alyssa.

"I don't know and I don't care. Come on."

The security guy is dead. The route to the car park is littered with dead bodies, some without a single mark on them, others split asunder like overripe fruit. Did one diseased reanimate do all this? Why are they after Sutcliffe?

"Would anyone have a reason to kill you?" Aminat asks.

"No. Not that I know of. I suppose Alyssa might have enemies."

At the car she marvels at dead uniformed people, but also the absence of police or sirens. The car auto-unlocks and Alyssa gets in the passenger side.

"Self-drive. Office," says Aminat.

"Cannot comply."

"Reboot."

The car reboots, but will not engage self-drive or tell her why.

"Olalekan, remote access my car and fix the self-drive software." No response.

"What's going on?" asks Alyssa, annoyingly calm.

"I don't know. Nimbus is down." She dials the cellular network.

"Boss! Thank God," says Olalekan.

"You were supposed to keep watch."

"Big terrorist thing at Atewo, and Jack Jacques was there, so the city is on alert."

"Okay, okay. How do I ... ? I want to ... "

"Do you have her? Alyssa Sutcliffe?"

"Yes. I'm bringing her to you."

"You ... er ... need to hurry."

"Why?"

"Mother's here."

Mother is what they call Femi. She must really be impatient to have come from Abuja. Fuck. Okay. Information first. Aminat turns on the news.

"Where are you taking me?" asks Alyssa.

"To a lab. You have a condition we need to study and it's important. Do you want to call your family?"

"I don't have a family."

"Do you want to call anybody?"

"No."

"Okay, then. Seat belt. I'll take us manually."

"What if I don't want to go?"

"I can arrest you."

"What charge?"

"I don't know. Obstructing a federal officer. Crimes against fashion. Something like that."

"I want—"

"Shut up, Alyssa. Shut up. I've just killed someone, and I need to wallow in self-loathing. Surely, even you can understand that?"

Close eyes.

All she can see is one of Hannah Jacques's adverts about the reanimates being human. The words from that perfect mouth play on a loop in Aminat's mind.

Breathe.

Breathe.

Too many changes in too short a time. Tally up: on the plus side Aminat has obtained her objective – she has Alyssa Sutcliffe in custody, if not at the laboratory. Two, both she and Alyssa are unharmed. Minus side: there is a body count that nobody can explain. There has been a bomb detonation, Nimbus blackout, patchy automated car functions, assignment not complete until Alyssa is in the lab undergoing tests. If she is to drive manually should she fetter Alyssa? She might try to jump out of the car or assault Aminat. God, she wishes she could phone Kaaro, but because of S45 security protocols, she can't during active operations.

Breathe.

Breathe.

Now, go.

"Seat belt," she tells Alyssa again. She opens the glove compartment and grabs an extra magazine and handcuffs which she stuffs in her waistband. She is still wearing the fucking running clothes. She eases the car out, then orients herself with the dome towards the lab. Charge is at fifty-nine per cent, but that is more than enough to get her there.

There are people on the streets and traffic on the roads. The dome is dark and grey, and a slight drizzle does not deter any of the activities. People are shouting, confused, and civil disobedience cannot be far off. One or two people slam palms on the bonnet. Street lights flicker – Aminat has never seen that, as if Wormwood itself is upset. She is barely able to do five miles per hour. Even on a day without too many cars, Rosewater is difficult to navigate without the constant route calculations of self-drive. The roads are too tortuous and snarl-ups are the norm. Only taxi drivers are immune to this with whatever juju they have in their brains. Tonight, though, the city itself seems to be in ferment. Aminat glances at Alyssa, who appears calm, but curious. Her eyes dart from person to person. She catches Aminat watching her.

"Alyssa likes arm-warmers."

"What? Are you talking in the third-person now?"

"Alyssa likes to wear these things, pulse warmers, elbow warmers. I saw her order history on her terminal."

"You're talking to me about arm-warmers. Alyssa, are you crazy?"

"No. I thought we discussed this already."

"You're talking like a crazy person," says Aminat. "And I hate arm-warmers."

"So do I." Alyssa faces forwards again. "But Alyssa doesn't."

This woman is going to either kill me or get me killed. Or I'll kill her.

Two blocks ahead of them a pedestrian climbs on to a car. The people around shout, but it is indistinct. Aminat is trying to see what's going on when the window on Alyssa's side shatters inwards. Arms reach in to pull at her arms and upper torso. They drag her out of the car. *No.*

"Idle," Aminat says to the car. She gets out. "HEY!"

Four men have Alyssa and nobody even stops to help. Aminat fires in the air, then points the gun at the attackers. They scatter, leaving Alyssa on the pavement, bruised, but calm. The gunshot and its reverberation cause a panic and the noise rises. The mob is confused and confusing. Directionless. Aminat and Alyssa are separated from the car by the press of people. It cannot be stolen, the engine will stall without proximity to Aminat's implant, but bits can be scavenged off it. She holsters her gun. You can't shoot a mob. Aminat orients herself, then says, "We'll go to the cathedral and hole up for the night. Tomorrow, I'm sure order will be restored."

She handcuffs Alyssa to herself. This is not a thing she wants, but she can't afford to lose her charge again.

There are people shouting *Jack knows jack*, one of the mayor's ridiculous slogans, a play on *I don't know jackshit.* Is he dead? Aminat hates the saying, but the mayor always was and is a populist. Guy knows how to win public opinion. The mob attacks cars now, and the roads become vast parks for abandoned vehicles. A few are on fire. Nobody can say what the violence is about. Aminat tries to flow with the crowd movement until she finds a vector to the sanctuary of the cathedral. She can see the spire. Alyssa trips a few times, but on the whole, does not slow things down. Aminat only has to assault four people before the pair reach the façade and find the cathedral closed, people banging on the doors, trying to get in.

"Okay, plan B."

Alyssa is staring at the building. "This is beautiful. Humans are amazing."

"Yes, remind me to tell you about flying buttresses over beers one day." Aminat checks her subdermal phone, no Nimbus. She checks maps saved locally to the memory, looking for sanctuary. She phones Olalekan.

"Boss?"

"We're on foot."

"Repeat please. Louder."

"We're on foot."

"Why? I'm reading unrest, mobs and riots—"

"I know. We're in one. Can you get me out of here? And send a signal to the car. Use radio, trigger the implosive auto-destruct."

"I'll see what I can do."

"Can you send a team to get me?"

"Stand by . . . stand by . . . that's a qualified yes, Boss."

"Clarify."

"No teams for at least six hours. You'll have to find a fox-hole to stay safe in."

Aminat pauses, thinks of Efe, who lives in the area. "I can do that. Track my phone through the cellular network."

"Taking your current coordinates – will refresh on the A.M."

"Have you been home?"

"No, Boss."

"Go home after you've made the arrangements. You can't do anything until I have Sutcliffe back."

"Negative. Mother is busy and I'm not leaving until I know you're secure."

"At least get the bunk and sleep."

"That I can do, but call if you need me."

"I will." She thinks of Kaaro. "Olalekan, call my house. You know what to say."

"Roger that."

He has said it to Kaaro before while Aminat has been on missions. After signing off she takes Alyssa's attention away from the features of the cathedral.

"Keep time with me. Tap my hand twice if I'm going too fast. Do not speak. Do you have memories of Alyssa's attitude towards the city at night?"

"No," says Alyssa.

"Rosewater can be dangerous at night, and I'm not just talking about the humans. Keep quiet, only speak if it's absolutely necessary."

Alyssa nods and they set off. Overhead, the minor buzz of drones. No law enforcement personnel or military, but the drones would film in infrared if need be. Footage would be scoured later and people would be brought to justice and punished.

"Hey, ladies, how much?"

"Hey, baby. Hey, legs!"

"Show me your yansh."

"Wey ya particulars?"

Some men follow, keeping up a monologue. Once, Aminat has to subdue an insistent man. Someone shines a light in her face so she can't see, and Aminat pulls her gun and aims for the light. It goes away.

Alyssa is compliant, says nothing. The crowd thins as they negotiate the streets. The normal familiarity is lost, but Aminat is pretty sure she is on the right track. After a pattern of thinning-out mobs they come to a line of men and women standing across a street. They are all armed with hockey sticks, cricket bats, planks and rakes.

"Turn back," says the middle male. "You do not belong here."

"My friend and I just need to go through to the next street," says Aminat.

"You are looters." He looks at their cuffed hands. "Perhaps you are prisoners. We should call the police."

Aminat shows her ID. "Step aside, sir."

The line remains intact.

"Look, I know you're trying to protect your families and homes, and I respect that, but I have business beyond this row of houses. I don't have time for this."

The people look at each other, but don't move.

"Legally, I can arrest you for obstructing me. I can shoot you all. I can beat you within an inch of your pampered lives, in spite of being tired. Which do you—"

"May I suggest something?" says Alyssa. "We've had enough violence. How about giving us an escort?"

As they arrive at Efe's house, Aminat concedes that Alyssa's suggestion was wise. Efe doesn't answer the door and Aminat has to call her to gain access. Efe drags them both in, side-eying the vigilante. She squeezes Aminat tight.

"What are you doing wandering about at this time, on this night?" asks Efe.

"I work for the government."

"Yes, tackling fake pharmaceuticals, I know."

"No. I can't tell you what I do, but it's not fake drugs."

"If you say so. Who's the white girl? Prisoner?"

"Not exactly. I've got to ask a favour." Aminat takes off the handcuffs. "We need a place to stay for tonight. We'll be out of your hair first thing tomorrow morning."

Efe smacks her on the shoulder. "As if you have to ask."

Later, Aminat takes a shower, then puts on the clothes Efe lays out. Alyssa goes next, but Aminat stops her when she sees the back of her neck.

"Alyssa, you have two windworms on your neck."

Aeolian larvae are more common closer to the dome in marshy areas, and they tend to burrow under the skin. They are painful and have been known to kill children. These ones seem to be lying stable on the surface of Alyssa's skin, something Aminat has never seen or heard of.

"I don't feel them," says Alyssa.

Aminat thinks perhaps she has misidentified the worm and lifts one off Alyssa's neck. It immediately curves back on itself and latches on to Aminat's finger. It hurts like having a nail pulled out with pliers. Alyssa helps remove it and stamps them both out.

"Aminat! Come hear this," says Efe.

Jack Jacques is on all networks, all feeds, all media, speechmaking.

... know that you are tired and afraid, and my thoughts are with you tonight, wherever you may be. Today, some cowardly people tried to test our resolve, to test my resolve to bring modernity and prosperity to every citizen of Rosewater. Thirty-five citizens died, among them, seven children. I was at the epicentre, but remain unharmed. Rest assured we will get to the bottom of this heinous act and root out the culprits.

In order to process the crime scene, law enforcement has had to close down Nimbus temporarily, but it will return, I am assured, by tomorrow morning. I myself plan to curl up with a good book tonight.

"That's a lie. With a wife as fine as his?" Efe snorts.

Go to bed knowing that you are safe and that I'm thinking of you. Go to bed knowing that I will avenge those who kill our children. Long live Rosewater. Long live the Federal Republic of Nigeria.

As the image fades, Aminat wonders what Jacques is hiding this time.

Sleep comes with difficulty, but a blanket of darkness eventually falls on her.

Interlude: 2066, Lagos, Unknown Location

Eric

I get an urgent message from Femi Alaagomeji. I'm to pack a bag and prepare to leave Lagos. An escort will come for me within the hour.

No explanation is offered and I'm due at a friend's birthday party, with aso ebi of expensive fabric, blocked street and everything. I'm not allowed to know where I'm going, so the agents who come to get me put a distortion helmet on me. My phone no longer works, and all I see in my palm is a dull orange indicator light glowing on and off every six minutes. I am in a blacked-out jeep with two others in a blue kaftan and the fucking helmet playing "Fukushima Romance" on repeat. Four hours and two comfort breaks later, they lead me into some kind of facility. They seat me, then take off the helmet. The first thing I see in real time is the bum of the last escort leaving the room.

I'm in a sterile room, white walls, no decorations, redistributed air, soundproof, faint chemical whiff of disinfectant. The door has a seal that is so good I can't even see its outline. At least the seat I'm on is cushioned, with armrests. I wish they'd brought my luggage so I could read something.

There's no clock, so I don't know how long I wait, though it seems like hours. The door swishes open and a man comes in.

"Eric, I have been instructed to carry out some tests. I apologise in advance. They are tedious and repetitive, but necessary. You've done them before."

"Who are you?"

"I can't tell you, and it's not important."

"Am I being detained?" I ask.

"No. You work for us, remember?"

"Can I leave?"

"No."

No explanation, but endless tests. Routine medical laboratory tests. Psychological tests. Ganzfeld Tests, put me in a sensory deprivation tank and have someone look at pictures in an adjacent room, then get me to guess which pictures. I get forty per cent correct, just a little under chance. That doesn't measure my abilities anyway. Once we are air-contiguous I read a hundred per cent of the images. The man holds playing cards and I pick them all out of his mind. He sits across from me and draws two hundred and fifty doodles, and I draw the same approximate images. Then I'm tired and refuse to continue.

My living quarters aren't so bad. I have a bedroom, living room and water closet, all in blinding white, though, even the bed frame. There's no Nimbus access, but all I have to do is ask, and the entertainment of my choice is either piped as music or appears on a plasma holo in the living room. Meals are delivered three times a day and snacks when I want. Every other day, I'm led to a gym and I work out for an hour. A personal trainer takes me through my boxing drills and spars with me.

This continues for weeks, then after a month, Femi visits me.

"I'm sorry, I'd have been here earlier if I could," she says. She hasn't changed much since I last saw her. No bodyguard this time.

"Ma'am, what's going on?"

"Eric, most of the people with your particular ability are either dead or dying. We've sequestered you to see if we can keep you alive."

"Someone's trying to kill us?"

"Someone or something. All I can tell you is that there's a statistical anomaly that's sending alarm bells ringing. We've sealed you away from the atmosphere, so you should have no access to the wider xenosphere."

"Then my abilities shouldn't work in here," I say. "But they do."

"Yes, as far as we can tell from testing, the xenoforms on your skin have grown nano-filaments, looking to connect with free-floating xenoforms or any neurological tissue they can find. You've formed a local xenosphere, a local network of neuro-fibres."

"And whatever is after me can't get me here?"

She hesitates. "I don't know. I won't lie to you, Eric, I've tried to keep others alive, but it hasn't worked. I also don't know how long I'll be able to keep you here, because I'm being taken off this project soon."

"Is anyone ... I mean, will you catch whoever is trying to ... ?"

"Okay, I know what you're asking, but I don't have that information. Other sensitives are dying of natural causes, mostly. I just need you to sit tight and stay alive."

"For how long? I have a life in Lagos, my family, my friends. I have to go to South Africa for my sister's wedding soon."

"I'm sure your family and friends would like to have you alive. Sit tight."

I wonder if Kaaro is dead, but I don't ask.

Months later I get a message.

THERE ARE ONLY TWO OF YOU LEFT, AND ONE IS DYING. STAY HEALTHY. KARA O LE. FEMI.

New Year's Day, I'm still isolated and being tested daily, including throughout Christmastide, but at least I'm drunk.

Chapter Eighteen

Jacques

Just before he wakes up, Jack becomes aware that he is dreaming. He is peeling off his skin for cleaning when he discovers machinery underneath his adipose fat. Not a lot, just some circuitry on the muscle and bones. When he opens his eyes, he first worries that he may have forgotten to put his skin back on. He sits up, allows the dream to fade, then rolls over to his left, between the legs of his sleeping wife. He continues to lick and kiss until her hands first stroke, then grip the back of his head. When they swap positions he does not take long to climax. He showers with a hemp-based gel, and this time he uses a body lotion with placenta products. He does not shave. A hint of stubble will create the effect of the hard-working mayor. He has a plan. It will start with the planting of media stories to hint at the president's complicity in the deaths at the Atewo library. Jack will devote time to finding out the vulnerabilities of his opponent and he will go and talk to his constituents face to face. He is slightly miffed that instead of moving forward with the business of governing Rosewater he is trapped having to once more sell himself and, if necessary, resort to the dark arts. Lora had told him the people would remember all he had done, but Jack knows what she would not say: that people are fickle and easily misled. Democracy has its good points, but the fairness of elections is not one of them. No, Jack will have to enter full politics mode, as he has done before. When he emerges there is only one bodyguard, Lora and Dahun waiting.

"Mr Mayor, good morning." Lora is ready with a mental clipboard.

"We will need to clear the calendar for a hospital visit to the victims—"

"Already done," says Lora.

"And I want a rally this evening. The north wards only – the south can come tomorrow."

"Sir, is that wise?"

"We need to get ahead. The president is driving this train so far. I need time in the engine room."

"Yes, I understand. I'll set it up."

"Let's just finish the security briefing, and we can throw ideas around."

Lora looks uncomfortable.

"What?"

"The security briefing has been cancelled."

"We don't have to do that. We can still coordinate things regardless of the bomb."

"We didn't cancel the briefing, sir. The president's team said there'll be no national security information until after the election. They said something about unfair advantage."

"But I still have to run the fucking city!"

"I'm sorry, sir. Nothing I said made any difference."

Jack nods, composes himself, continues walking down the corridor. "Tell me what we know about Ranti, this man who hopes to replace me."

"He's a grotesque," says Lora.

"There's no need to use that kind of language."

"I ... mean it in the technical sense. He's one of the reconstructed that went wrong." She passes a hand over his phone arm and he feels the vibration of data reception. He sees a young man in a suit, wearing a turban. Looks normal enough.

"What's under the turban?"

"Swipe left."

The face looks intact, but from the hairline the skull is a crater. There is no brain to speak of, just mounds and valleys of pink flesh.

"How does he—"

"Swipe left."

The next photograph is Ranti shirtless. Where the belly should be there is an oversized face. Two eyes, each in the same vertical plane as the nipples. Flat nose, a mouth that spreads from one flank to the next.

"Is that a beard, or pubic hair growth?"

Lora shrugs. "He has minimal control over the top face. I don't think he can see out of the eyes, so he wears clothing specially made."

"What's the protocol? Do I look at his head or his belly?"

"I don't know, sir. This is his first foray into politics."

"What was he before yesterday?"

"Car battery salesman."

Jesus.

"You have a meeting with the air quality people, sir."

"Why? We have excellent air, and low atmospheric pollution."

"Yes, sir. That's why they want to meet. They want to know why."

"I can't think of that right now, but I'll get to it. Can I just arrive at my office, inside my space, with a hot cup of coffee?"

But this is not to be. In his office, sitting on his chair, is a striking woman. Haughty and drunk with the power that allows her to surprise him. This seems to be a week for surprises. He shoots Dahun a look that says, *Am I not paying you to stop this kind of thing?*

"Mr Mayor, my name is Femi Alaagomeji."

Jack has heard of Alaagomeji. Tabloid press call her a witch because she supposedly killed her husband. Jack knows she didn't, but she did defile his remains by faking a mass murder scene. Head of S45 for a while now after the entire management was annihilated by Wormwood near this very spot. And she is as beautiful as sin. Jack is standing in front of his own desk, waiting, unamused.

She points to the ceiling and tuts. "You have mouldings cribbed from Hokusai's *The Great Wave*. Kitsch."

"I didn't have a say in the interior decor. I'm sorry, but why are you here?"

"There's one more person in this meeting," she says.

"Who's that?" Jack asks.

The door opens and Ranti comes in.

"That's who," says Alaagomeji.

Jack sputters. "You can't—"

"Both of you, sit down. Jacques, shut the fuck up. You will profit from listening. All aides and bodyguards, begone. Now."

Lora looks to Jack, who nods.

"I'd like to formally protest this. I was given no notice," says Jack, mostly to buy himself time to think.

"Nor was Ranti, and you don't see him complaining, but your protest is noted."

"I'm happy to be here," says Ranti like a good puppet.

His lips don't move and his voice sounds muffled, originating from under the folds of his agbada. How does he breathe under that thing? That ... mask on top maintains a smile, with teeth showing. They are blazing white. He probably doesn't eat by his head mouth.

"You're here because the president wanted me to deliver a message. Think of me as the referee in this bout. He wants a nice, clean fight."

"I'll bet," says Jack.

"My department – my agents – are going to perform security vetting on both of you. Jacques has gone through this before. The findings of the vetting will be made public. At this stage, Ranti, is there anything I should know? Anything that might make you unfit to hold public office?"

The dummy head moves slowly from side to side. "I have nothing to be ashamed of. You may access all my systems, take blood tests and interview anybody. I only want to serve Rosewater."

"That's what I was afraid of," says Femi Alaagomeji. She lifts her hand from her lap and shoots Ranti in the head.

Jack is stunned, blinks from the blood spatter and shock. Her arm is still extended, unwavering. It's an old pistol, must be a twenty-two, pearl handle, smoking, antique. Ranti's turban is two feet away, bloody. His trunk is still upright and Alaagomeji seems to be waiting for it to fall.

"The brain is in the belly," says Jack.

"I know," says Alaagomeji. "I wanted to see if you knew, and if you would tell me."

She leaps on to Jack's four-hundred-year-old mahogany desk and shoots, but misses because Ranti is moving, crablike,

an all-fours scramble with a weave that is surprisingly difficult to hit.

"Dahun!"

The door flicks open, and Dahun, armed, takes in the scene.
Lora follows close behind.

"Are we shooting to kill?" he asks.

"We are now," says Jack.

The agbada turns Ranti into a blob on the floor, and
it's difficult to know where to hit. Dahun hits the whole
mass with a plasma gun. The room holds that ionised gas
smell as they cut away the clothing to confirm that Ranti is
indeed dead. Some of him is burned, and parts are sicken-
ingly roasted.

Dahun methodically cuts the clothing into small strips and
runs a device over them and the body. When he confirms that
there are no recording devices Jack turns to Alaagomeji.

"What the fuck are you doing?"

"Be calm. I have to say, you're a bit disappointing in person.
I had heard you were more ... collected than this."

"You just killed the president's candidate."

She wags a finger. "No, 'we'. We just killed the president's
candidate."

"What do you mean?"

"The moment you told me where the brain was, Jack, you
became complicit. Jack knows jack, right?"

Jack slaps her with the back of his hand. She falls back, over
the desk and down by the waste bin, a flash of white knickers
accompanying the remnants of her dignity. When he walks to
her she is pointing the pistol at him.

"What is your game here? What has the president sent
you to do?"

"I may have exaggerated my role a bit. The president knows I'm in Rosewater, and that's it." She pauses to lick blood from the corner of her mouth, making her look serpentine. "I needed you complicit. It's important."

"It won't work. There are surveillance cameras in here."

"You might want to check on the footage."

Dahun comes up and whispers to Jack. "White noise."

"I'm not an amateur, and we don't have much time."

"Don't have much time? What you've done is a declaration of war."

"We're already at war, Mr Mayor. Did you not know this?" She gets up and looks out of the window. "That dome is your enemy, the aliens. We are at odds, and they are winning."

"Sir—" says Lora, but Jack silences her with a hand gesture.

"Tell me," says Jack. "In simple terms. Think of me as a simpleton."

Alaagomeji snorts. "I already do."

"What are you trying to achieve?"

Slowly, she locks eyes with Jack. "The moment you asked for independence, your political career, and maybe your life, was over. It was just a matter of how and when. Declaring independence is the only way you can hold any power now."

"We're not ready for civil war."

"You'll never be. The federal government will always outgun and outnumber you. But you have Wormwood. You know how the city limits were determined?"

"Yes, the city starts at the point where the ganglions do not respond to intrusion by frying the vehicle."

"Exactly. There will be a blockade. Doesn't matter. We have food, a no-fly zone over the city, a big-ass alien enforcer of our boundaries."

"But you just said we are at war with the alien."

"We are, and while we're here, my team and I will find a way to win it."

"You kill Wormwood, Rosewater is dead."

"Wormwood is not the enemy. Not exactly. The people who sent Wormwood are the ones we want. But that's not the immediate problem. The first thing you want to do is take your pretty face and announce your independence before this news gets to him, to the president. Control the information before he does. My people will work on the slow invasion."

"I hate you for placing me in this position."

"Don't break my heart." She puts away her gun into her ultra-stylish handbag. "Get to the speech writing. There's no time."

"Dahun, secure Miss Alaagomeji."

"It's 'Mrs', actually." She goes without protest.

"Sir," says Lora, "I hate to agree with her, but she's right."

"In 1219 the Mongols laid siege to the Persians. It took about a month, but the Persians fell. The Mongols killed about a million of them. You know what started it? Killing of Genghis Khan's envoys in a small town called Utrar. We just killed the president's envoy. Killing envoys is never good strategy."

"Sir, you have to—"

"I know what I have to do. Find me cameras."

Are you a good person or an evil one?

I'm ... okay. Mostly good, I think.

No. Wrong. You are evil.

But I'm not.

Good leaders are "okay". Some leaders are "good", but these are the evil ones. To be a truly great leader you must

156

*be willing and able to accept "evil" as an assessment of your
character.*

I understand.

*The true wisdom is to understand that these constructs are
ephemeral and, ultimately, irrelevant.*

I understand.

Are you a good person or an evil one?

I am evil.

I am evil.

Lora hands Jacques a tablet just before transmission.

"What's this?"

"The Ahiara Declaration. You know, The Principles of the
Biafran Revolution. For Inspiration."

"No. The breakaway of an oppressed people is nowhere
near this. We're privileged, by accident, but privileged all the
same. To use Ojukwu's speech would be insulting to the Igbo."

"Sir, you know I respect you, but I have something to say."

"You have . . . how many minutes can I spare?"

"Six."

"You have six minutes, Lora."

"I only need one. You've been hit with a few left-hook combinations over the last twenty-four hours. You're dazed, and
you're forgetting who you are."

"I see. And who am I?"

"You are the mayor of Rosewater. You built this city with
will-power and grit, forcing it into being. Every stick, every
brick, every tree-lined boulevard in Atewo, every shack in
Ilube, all the painstaking negotiations with Ocampo to con-
vert the power, you held all that together in the palm of your
hand. But now, you let this S45 bitch unman you just after you

let the president push you around. I don't recognise this Jack Jacques. Sir."

Jack nods. "Lora, you are the only person, besides myself, that I trust completely. Thank you for your candour."

"Just doing my job, sir."

When the time comes and the prompter is counting down the seconds, Jack feels calm, composed. His palm is not sweaty at all.

"My dear, dear people of Rosewater, you have been lied to. Even now, forces are lining up against us, trying to bring us down. I am your chosen leader and I say 'no' to tyranny. We will no longer be bullied by the federal government. I am therefore declaring Rosewater a free state, effective immediately ... "

Chapter Nineteen

Anthony

Building the new body is taking a lot longer than Anthony anticipated. Until completion he is stuck in the bowels of Wormwood. In itself, this is odd because the brain is usually the last thing, not the first. Now he has a functioning mind in a body tethered to the factory. The creature is silent, has not communed with Anthony, and the silence unnerves him. He is embedded without skin or useful musculature. He can feel his internal organs growing, but not as briskly as usual. Around him are abandoned versions of himself, some dead homunculi and a dead cellulose monster, all killed decades ago after an attack by the British while Wormwood was in larval stage, before he burrowed to Nigeria. The monster is made of gouged-out pieces of Wormwood, and stands frozen in spot. Nothing rots in this cavern, although they might dry out. The very first Anthony, the human, stands in the centre, his skull open at the top, strings of neural tissue spreading out of his brain like an above-ground telephone pole. Anthony thinks this body, the original Anthony, might still be alive in some marginal definition of the term, but not in a meaningful way. He has no thoughts to share, no protests to make, no will but

Wormwood's. Anthony is surprised to feel a surge of anger that the human is enslaved to complete the alien life cycle. He feels a thrill from his lower extremities and believes he has grown skin in what will become his soles. A human woman killed him, and the host is in the wild again. Why did the Homian not recognise Anthony? The whole business has gone awry. The xenosphere has odd gaps, Molara is missing in action and the Homian is not a Homian? Or not Homian enough. At least, she did not understand any of the Homian languages Anthony hailed her in. They would not have made her with an obscure dialect, would they? But then, who knows with engineers.

Anthony has about enough control to agitate the xenoforms into sending a message to Home, a progress report. *Yes, I found the host but lost her. As soon as I'm able, I'll get after her again. I think the footholder is sick.*

The answer comes swift and sure. Anthony imagines himself on the Homian moon, in the control room.

Did you say "her"? Because the entity sent is congenitally male.

Vessel is definitely female.

We will have to look into repatriation or relocation. How soon will she be in our hands?

I have to find her again. I haven't started because the body isn't ready.

What's wrong with your footholder?

There's a plant. [image passed automatically by entanglement]

Ahh.

You knew about it.

Yes. It's Homian. Our first experiments with footholders showed they can take over entire planets when unchecked,

160

with no room for us. Strain-516 is a controlling species, limiting the footholder spread. Seeds are in every single footholder, but I'm curious that they have crossed the dome.

There's one of this strain growing under the host's house. It's a xenoform dead zone. What's the antidote?

I don't know. Get the Earthers to kill it. They can kill anything.

That's not how humans work.

Maybe not, but we still want the host back and unharmed. She is [important person]. Strain-516 will not harm the footholder, it will just restrict its growth.

Send [Strain-516 specifications/technical].

[Lie] not available/too difficult/irrelevant/do as you're told. [hierarchy].

Assertion! [Don't ask questions/get on with assigned task] Do not endanger the grand plan/fulfil your purpose.

Transmission ends.

He cannot even maintain the integrity of the conversation. He's sicker than he has ever been, because even his neurological template seems corrupted.

Anthony has an overwhelming urge to spit, but he has no mouth yet. His lover/friend would tell him this is a uniquely human reaction, that he is trying to remove physical residue as a way to expel the psychological distaste from his interaction. Footholders don't have opinions, they act for Home at all times. Anthony is not Wormwood. Does he feel this because Wormwood is sick? Their bond is not as good, integrity compromised by Strain-516? Is that why the human was able to kill him? Anthony knows that burning hot can use up the body, but he still did it. Why? Does he truly believe in the mission? He thinks he does, but he is not nearly as disappointed at the setback as he thinks he should be. He sends pulses of queries through the xenosphere, trying to stimulate Wormwood.

"What's going on here?" Molara appears as a naked woman with blue butterfly wings. Anthony finds her muscular and cold.

"Nothing," says Anthony. "Planning my next move."

"Is the host hiding from you? Others are curious."

"The others can suck my balls. *Fanculo*! They were never interested in me before."

Molara touches him mentally, in a sexual way. "Do you want me to suck your balls? Would that motivate you?"

To his horror he responds to her, but he knows what that would mean, her control over him, which is not something Anthony wants because their aims do not always align. "Go away, Molara. Everything is fine."

His legs are free and he slushes out of the pit, struggling against suction like he is escaping from a swamp. He feels the body taking shape as he begins to walk. Eyes better, mouth open though jaw not as wide yet. He pushes a shot of anandamide through his system. Wormwood is still silent. He needs clothes, but cannot grow them just yet. He makes his way through tunnels, in complete darkness, towards a progressively windy chute until he is carried along by powerful air currents. He travels in these for an hour, then is flung free through a venting system near Kinshasa, but outside the city. There are hundreds of holes in the ground, used by the footholder for heat regulation. The vents are like mouths, opening and closing like that of a fish out of water. There are dried corpses of small animals everywhere, unfortunates who fall into the tunnels only to be shot back out as if fired from a cannon.

Anthony begins to walk. He comes across a pair of discarded marl leggings hooked on a branch, flapping like a flag. He puts them on, even though they are not his size. Walking becomes awkward and he rips the leggings at the crotch to compensate. He tastes the xenosphere – fresh and strong after the rains – but Anthony senses more of the black spots. There are tiny footprints in the mud and run-off – at first he thinks they are from children, but he tastes the toxins in the air: homunculi. He looks around, but none is in sight. He follows the footprints for a while, on a whim. He has not seen them for months and he finds homunculi amusing. Then he comes across a human religious cult having a scarification ceremony. He does not join them, but he takes the clothes he needs. He inhales, smiles, photosynthesises in the sun, then heads for the city. He has no shoes – none were his size – but he does have a layer of callus. He passes people, solitary, in groups, on foot, driving cars, on buses, donkeys, horses. There are soldiers in groups of ten, moving with purpose and expressions saying they hold secret orders.

COBs mass at the city limits too, crows, cats, dogs and vultures. Anthony notes this as abnormal, but does not bother trying to figure out why. A driver gives him a lift and unleashes a monologue about solar flares and plasma ejections and the effect on communication being enhanced and the inefficiency of carbon scrubbers and the odd prevalence of exotic disease. The loss of the permafrost is a particular bone of contention.

"You have no shoes," he says, finally.

He stops the car, walks to the trunk, stirs objects around and returns with a pair of loafers. They fit. He brushes aside Anthony's thanks. He probably would have still given the shoes even if Anthony hadn't been manipulating his dopamine.

Chapter Twenty

Alyssa

Alyssa is the first to wake.

Aminat and her friend – what's her name? Efe? They mentioned it once – talked into the night, nothing of consequence, just phatic communication between girlfriends. They fell quiet – no, they stopped talking but Aminat snored loudly.

Alyssa wanders around the house. In the lounge there are framed photos and Aminat features prominently. In one or two pictures they both have male partners, slightly older in Aminat's case, but they seem to be in love. She thinks of the Sutcliffes, the husband and child, Mark and Pat, for whom she experiences no sense of loss, no frisson of love or guilt for not contacting them. She stands at the window, stares at the sky, at the pre-dawn light. She knows she is not human. It is the only explanation – not human, not mad, and she does not feel insane, although would she feel crazy if she were? The next question is difficult. If not human, then what? Aliens exist, people of Rosewater know that better than anyone else alive, but are there humanoid ones? Ones who look like Alyssa? No, that's the wrong idea. The alien would just need a compatible mind. That mind would be inserted into Alyssa's body. It is a human body – the cuts and the bleeding prove that. How did Alyssa get transported? From where? And why? How is she to view humans? She has flashes of memory still. A planet denuded of vegetation, with air like soup, carbon burned, products thrown in the air, the sky cluttered with the debris of a hyper-successful space programme. All around, the detritus and bare bones of depleted industry and overuse. Factories that create nothing, roads without cars, houses without people, winds beating an unbroken path around the globe. Alyssa's job is to take readings. By this time the entire population, the survivors, are in space. She cannot remember a name, but there are always more memories coming in. Alyssa is not so worried that she cannot take care of herself.

By mid-morning the house stirs, and various breakfast motions and smells make themselves felt. There is laughter from Aminat and Efe. There is a truck that comes down the road. She hears it before she sees it, an army-green compact thing with six armed troops seated behind, weapons pointed skyward. Aminat's escort. The truck stops in front of the house, then two of the soldiers jump off, after which the vehicles keeps going. Hm. She has to keep track of the others.

"Aminat, they're here!"

From the window she sees the soldiers point the weapons forward. This could be normal, but she feels disquiet. The doorbell goes off and Alyssa puts on her shoes. Efe floats out, swiftly, like an angel, barefoot, cherubic smile aimed at Alyssa like one of those synchronised dancers, before focusing on the security remote in her hands. The soldiers seem to be readying their—

"*Efe, get away from the door.*"

Alyssa watches as one of the soldiers steadies his SMG and fires a burst at the door. In what seems like slow motion the second soldier spots her and his weapon rises towards her position. Alyssa is flung to the ground just before multiple shots hit the window. Aminat has her arms around Alyssa's legs.

"Stay the fuck away from the window." She has hardened, face like a mask.

"I thought this was our escort," says Alyssa.

"So did I. Obviously, something has changed." She crouches, crablike, holding a handgun. She glances at the window, now rendered opaque by spider-web patterns. Efe still stands at the door.

"Two at the back," she says. "Oh."

"What?" asks Aminat.

"Laying charges. Damn. That door cost a fortune. Ofor is going to be upset."

"Will it hold?" asks Aminat.

"The security package is for casual intruders, stalkers, not special forces. They will get in. An alarm has gone out to the police but ... " She does not look confident.

"Guns in the house?"

"No. There's some—"

A loud bang startles them all and Efe leads them crouching to a small room, like a linen cupboard, one entrance, one exit. Alyssa is above it all. No fear. Not her body, not her concern. She is a spectator. Aminat arranges what shelves exist into cover and waits, gun at the ready. On Efe's security remote they all watch two intruders in the back. They check each room, and as they make their way down the hallway Efe pushes a button.

"Fuck you, get out of my house."

Strips of plaster detach from the wall and hurl themselves at the intruders. Hundreds of similar strips adhere to them, then contract like muscles. The intruders writhe and jerk convulsively. Every few seconds a new strip detaches and ultimately the soldiers' heads and torsos are covered by a tight band. They stop moving.

"Will they die?" asks Alyssa.

"I don't know. I didn't install it," says Efe.

The screen swaps around to the other cameras.

"Stay here and turn that thing off. I don't want to end up like them," says Aminat. She is silent on her feet and disappears. On the screen they see her in the corridor. She picks up the rifle from one soldier along with what Alyssa thinks are extra ammunition magazines. Aminat pulls a knife and cuts into the soldier's neck. Alyssa does not know why, but there is no frenzy, so it's not from anger; it's part of a plan. She goes out of the hole in the back wall. The camera flips and the soldiers in front have opened the door. It flips again and Aminat is working an obstacle course around the house, leaping over and ducking under. The soldiers one minute are checking corners and pointing muzzles, then they are flung forward by gunfire. Aminat stands there and checks each one, kicking their torsos for good measure. She raises her hand, giving a thumbs-up. Efe stands, turning to Alyssa, smiling.

"Wow, that was easier than I thought. Expensive, but easy."

They join Aminat who is facing the wall, trying to communicate with someone by mobile. Alyssa says, "There were six soldiers and one driver."

Efe nods, and picks up a rifle. "Where are the damn police?" She walks to the open door, to check the street.

Aminat swivels and notices her. "NO!"

The rifle gives a muted pop and splits Efe in the middle. Her face retains a look of surprise as Aminat screams her grief and rage. Alyssa is not sure of what happened with the rifle, but she observes without emotion.

Aminat recovers, arranges her friend's body with care, covers it, cleans up as quickly as she can, stands looking at the bloody mess, shakes her head.

"Take the flak jacket," Aminat says at length.

Aminat seems less bothered by killing the soldiers than the person she killed the day before. Alyssa thinks of her job on Home; the only thing she remembers is studying or gathering information. So she defaults to that mode.

"I'm sorry about your friend," she says.

Aminat nods thanks.

"Can I ask you something? You picked up one of the rifles. You still have it slung over your shoulder, yet it didn't blow up on you."

Aminat digs into her pocket and shows her a tiny, flat object like a computer component. "Identity chip. The rifle is synchronised with it. This chip can only be so far from the weapon before it blows. Efe didn't know that. I should have told her."

Alyssa waits a minute, then says, "Your own comrades just tried to kill you."

"I know."

"Aren't you concerned?"

"I am."

"Do you know why they turned on you?"

"Oh, yes, I do. Our dunderheaded mayor, Jack Jacques, declared Rosewater independent this morning. Those were soldiers, not agents. They were deployed before the announcement, but their orders changed afterwards. Jacques almost got us killed."

"What does that mean for us? For me?"

Aminat stops. They are at the side of the road and can hear the army truck. "I thought of stealing the truck from them, but the validation for the driver for the army is central, so cutting out a chip won't matter. We have to walk, at least for a while, until I can contact my people. My real people."

"What side are your people going to be on?"

"I don't know. We are an agency. We work for the federal government. This makes our position delicate, but your situation is the same. Smart people want to study you, regardless of what government is in charge."

They both hide behind a hedge until the truck passes. "I want us to go back to the lab. We can plan from there. I will keep calling my boss." Her shoulders sag for a second. "I want to call my boyfriend. This must be hard for him. He gets so scared."

"Of what?"

"Of everything. I'm afraid Kaaro is not brave." Her face softens and Alyssa finds herself wondering if the man in the photos beside her is this Kaaro person.

"You love him?"

"I do."

"What's he like?"

"I – I'm not allowed to talk to you about my personal life." Aminat picks imaginary lint from her hair. "But he's great."

Alyssa realises she is supposed to smile conspiratorially here, and she does.

"I have to dump the rifle, or we'll get spotted or arrested. The army will soon know to revoke the security certificate and remote detonate it."

Aminat takes out the magazine and strips the rifle down, then drops the parts down different gratings, along with the dead soldier's chip, but she slips the laser scope into her pocket. They go down to the street and find that the roads are flowing with traffic. Aminat's car among others has been shunted to the side. The tyres are deflated and the rest of the windows smashed. It didn't self-destruct, then.

A reanimate traffic cop stands at an intersection, immobile, bloodstained clothes, waiting for nothing. Alyssa thinks it would have been better if she had been projected into the mindless fleshghosts. The traffic seems slow, as if nobody looks forward to reaching their destinations. There will be war. Nigeria is not going to let its most advanced city go.

Chapter Twenty-One

Jacques

Jack has a headache. He is back in control of his office, but the deluge of incoming messages effectively blocks his phone lines. Dahun is talking at him, and Jack does not know for how long. He has blanked some stretches of words out. There is a holomap of Rosewater before them.

"I'm sorry, what did you just say?" asks Jack.

Dahun points to red dots. "The two cantonments adjacent to the north and south ganglia are both empty. We can assume they are Nigerian loyalists. No way of knowing if they all left, or if some changed to mufti and melted into the population as saboteurs and spies."

"Unless they are clairvoyant, which, let's face it, they might be, there's a protocol for this. Retreat to the city limits and await further instructions."

"Why would they retreat? You have no other army."

"I have Wormwood. The prevailing wisdom is that if Wormwood senses a threat it will attack within city limits. There was no time to change their plans since even I didn't know I would secede."

"Indulge my paranoia. I'm going to assume people slunk away in the night to plant bombs and cut power lines. It always happens."

"If it pleases you, Dahun."

"What do we do about troops?"

"Wormwood will—"

"Sir, Wormwood hasn't had to do this since 2055. Maybe it no longer sees the Nigerian army as hostile. Maybe it found that Old Time Religion. Maybe it has abandoned violence. I repeat, indulge the fucking paranoiac who is paid to keep you alive. Troops?"

"We have about fifteen thousand prisoners. They'll fight in exchange for commuted sentences."

"Untrained." Contempt drips from Dahun's voice.

"I'd call them undisciplined. They are used to violence."

"I have five hundred seasoned men and women. We will have to train your prisoners."

"I'll call the warden."

"How many automatons?"

"Lora will know."

"What about food supplies?"

"We have food."

"If we're blockaded how long can those supplies last?"

"You'll have to ask Lora, but I'm guessing a year or two."

"Do you know how long the Greeks laid siege to Troy?"

Jack shrugs. "Just tell me."

"Ten years. You have to know that this is a war Nigeria cannot or will not let go. Be prepared for a generational war."

"I'll form a task force." This is the first time Jack has said those words without irony. Task forces are what you form when you don't want things done.

"Shall I get contractors to boost our numbers?"

"Yes."

Dahun raises one eyebrow. "Not cheap."

"I already said 'yes'. Move on." Irritation creeps into Jack's voice.

"What do we do about the black sites?"

"Speak in English. Failing that, try Yoruba. What are black sites?"

Dahun points to the map. Three areas. "Three government sites. I don't know what they are or what they do, but they're out there."

"Follow me." Jack does not know about them, but he knows someone who will.

Femi smiles. "Mr Mayor, whatever you're paying this guy is not enough. Show me a map projection." Jack generates it from his own polymer phone. She points. "This is a laboratory, and is no threat to you. They are doing work to save all of mankind, so I'd consider protecting it. This, at Ubar, is a hardened S45 facility with more sublevels than you have fingers and toes. You cannot successfully storm it. Surround it and watch it, using COBs if you can. The third ... I'd stay away from that one."

"Why? What's there?"

"Toxic waste."

"*What?*"

"Calm down. Calm yourself. Think about it. Just think. First, Wormwood heals people from Rosewater. They don't stay sick. What better place to dump such material? Second, they, the federal government, wanted to know if the alien could detoxify it. At least at first they did. The alien does have a filter function, and the pollution that plagues the rest of the world is minimal here. It's a reasonable assumption."

173

"How long has this—"

"From the start. The first was back in 'fifty-five."

Jack thinks of the propaganda potential. He turns to leave.

"Wait."

"What?"

"Aren't you going to release me? I thought we were working together on this thing?"

"No, on account of you being a murdering witch."

"You're still mad at that? It's been hours."

"Bye."

"Wait. Let me call my people and give them instructions. They'll be lost."

"No. Goodbye."

"I can help you."

Jack walks away.

He watches Lora work out using the gym equipment in her office, as he relays all the new information to her.

"Interesting, but we need to know more. And I think she is holding something back."

"I'm sure she's holding something back, but that's normal. I would do the same if I were in her position."

Lora does squats. "We do need a propaganda arm, though. I agree with you there. I'll set up a shortlist of candidates for your approval. Give me an hour."

"Why do you bother working out?" asks Jack.

Lora stops squatting and turns to him, raises eyebrows. "Because you told me to."

"That was years ag— Never mind. Lora, are there things you know that you haven't told me?"

"I don't know, sir. Did you know that Caliph Ali, The

Prophet's cousin, was killed on 24 January 661, triggering the Sunni–Shia split?"

"I don't mean that kind of thing. I mean stuff that you're keeping from me to protect me from subpoenas. If I don't know, I can't testify, that kind of thing."

"Why do you want to know this?"

"Both Dahun and Femi knew things about Rosewater that I did not. I don't like that feeling. How can I make decisions not knowing what's going on?"

"Sir, can I be frank?"

"Go ahead."

"Good leaders have assistants who tell them enough to help them rule, but not enough for them to implicate themselves. I am your insulating layer, sir. Do not become curious."

"If I order you to tell me every single thing you know about Rosewater, would you?"

"Yes."

And yet Jack detected a slight pause just before she spoke. *We both know I'm lying*, the pause said.

Jack says, "A wise friend of mine asked me a question once. He asked at what point the animal caught in the trap realises it is doomed. Is it just before the trap springs when the jaws are closing around its leg? Is it the pain of metal crushing bone? Is it the sense of betrayal on discovering that leaves casually arranged to look natural were not safe, but covering fate? Is it when the animal tries to chew its own leg off?"

"I don't follow, sir."

"I want to know when I'm in danger. I want to know when I'm in a trap. I want to know, I want to know, I want to know. *Mo fe mo gbo-gbo e*. Tell me every fucking thing from now on. No more surprises."

"Yes, sir. I'm sorry, sir."

His phone buzzes. Priority text from the president.

YOU LITTLE SHIT. DO YOU REALLY THINK YOU'LL GET ANYWHERE?

He has kept up a steady stream of malicious texts for hours now. Jack knows the guy to be petty, but this is a whole new level.

"Can I block the president?" he asks Lora. "I mean, what if he wants a truce?"

"He won't come through you direct for that, sir."

"He's not saying anything useful. I should block him."

"You don't have time. You have to meet the councillors."

Shit. "Really looking forward to that."

A lot of pampered politicians complaining about not being consulted. *We did not sign up for this.* Upstarts taking the opportunity to grandstand. Crypto-loyalists making trouble. Ten per cent of them leaving the city, but most of the rest supportive. Jack can read a room easily, but he has no time to soothe them. He does apologise, but he cuts the meeting short.

Next he meets with the seventeen major building contractors in Rosewater. The representatives seem nervous, like they expect him to have them all shot. He tells them to relax and he smiles at quarter wattage. He tells them he expects them to create an accurate map of all the bunkers in Rosewater. He dismisses their protestations, makes vague allusive threats and gives them a twenty-four-hour deadline. They start filing out of the room, but he stops them, looks at the clock and tells them the hours will be spent in this very room. They start pooling resources.

He retreats to his office. He looks at his hands. They are dry from washing them after glad-handing the ward councillors. He uses a cream with eucalyptus and closes his eyes to soothe his fading headache. "West wall," he says to the room, and the brick becomes transparent, or seems so. Minute cameras on the outside project images on the inside. He can see a large part of Rosewater from here, and the centre of the panorama is the dome in its recent spiky incarnation, with patchy discoloration. Is it prescient? Preparing for war in some fucked-up alien way? Many had speculated at the reason for or meaning of the sharp projections, but it is all conjecture as far as Jack can tell. The Yemaja flows freely and powerfully on its way to the Niger River. The presence of Wormwood has an unexpected positive effect on the river. The verdant growth halted the gully erosion that had plagued the Yemaja, a trophic cascade that led to increased tree height, which brought more diverse birds, small mammals, pools and shallows, an explosion of biodiversity. The alien species mixed in, yes, but also the Earth creatures. Rosewater is arguably the greenest city in the world and keeping weeds controlled requires a significant budget. Cracks to asphalt from under-growing vegetation is a serious problem, but Jack recognises that this is a good problem to have. The jury is out on whether eating alien animals and plants is harmless, but the woods in and around the city teem with game. The Rosewater Botanical Garden has pretty much every known species and some unknown ones. To think the land was aberrant savannah before this, before Wormwood. As much as it is a blessing, Jack can't help seeing the vegetation as cover for enemy troops. They are out there already, but will we see them? The dome can survive anything, even a direct hit from a particle weapon, but maybe the government has more advanced ones? *We just have to hold Rosewater long enough for the Nigerian government to bankrupt itself.* Jack wishes the dome covered the whole city. Eight million souls would be safer.

"Music, 'Bilongo', Ismael Rivera."

The song starts and Jack dances. If Nero fiddled while Rome burned, he will dance before any fires start in Rosewater. He sings along to the call-and-response – he does not speak Spanish, but salsa calms him. By the time the song finishes he feels buzzed. He is in a good mood when a phone call cuts through all screens and protocols, glowing on his forearm.

Calling: The Tired Ones.

Oh, shit.

Chapter Twenty-Two

Aminat

"That smooth-talking, Gucci-wearing, oath-breaking, two-faced, degenerate, time-wasting, half-smiling, fascist, gluttonous, idiotic, phlegmatic frog-fucker!" says Aminat.

"You're upset," says Alyssa. "I thought you had calmed down."

Alyssa's arms are covered in insects. A few mosquitoes have bloated abdomens from sucking blood, but otherwise the insects seem at rest and calm.

"Aren't you going to brush those away?" Aminat says.

"They don't bother me."

"I don't want you to catch malaria. I have no idea how that will affect testing. Besides, it'll be a nightmare carrying you across the city."

"I've never had malaria."

"Oh, the pleasures awaiting you. Are you hungry? We should get food and supplies. Plus, I need the ladies' room. *Mo fe ya'gbe.*"

They stop at a place called Wallah Joe's. They first clean off sweat from their armpits and groins with damp cloths in the rest room. They take seats at the crowded eating tables and wolf down eba with fish stew. The place has the usual hum of conversation and although a white woman does draw a little attention, most are too hungry or intent on news holograms to be bothered. There are all kinds of international reactions. Russia, apparently, has recognised the Rosewater Free State, the first country to do so. *Yeah, but what about Ukraine, assholes? What about America?* There are still those commentators who blame Russia for America's disappearance from the world stage, and the world.

Aminat has been calling Femi, leaving messages, getting no response. Olalekan has been silent too. Normal S45 crisis protocols are not working. The truth is, she needs the break to plan her next move. Aminat has no confirmation that the lab is still there. The same team of soldiers may have struck, meaning Femi might be dead, Lekan too. The thing about the government is dissent and rebellion present the opportunity for purges, and Femi is a person with a target on her back.

And I hitched my star to hers. Well, more like she forced me into a corner. It was either work for her or lose my brother to faceless S45 agents who would have experimented on him. We may all die anyway.

Aminat watches an EU analysis of nuclear war projections. Russia's recognition of Rosewater is being seen as a move for influence in a world arena that China has been courting for decades, going back to the 1970s. The alien represents a potential advantage worth going to war for.

The more she thinks about it, the more she is convinced that she should go home, get Kaaro and that stupid dog of his, then slip out of the city, maybe drop Alyssa off at Ubar.

Sitting across from Alyssa, Alyssa who is not eating.

"Not hungry?"

"What's our plan?" asks Alyssa.

"I'm taking us across the city to a lab. We'll detour to my home first. I want to be sure my boyfriend is okay."

Alyssa nods.

"You don't have to come."

"Aren't I in your custody?"

Aminat picks at a morsel of food. "I can't contact my people, and the city is at war with Nigeria, or will be. Everything is uncertain. I don't think it would be unreasonable for you to 'escape'."

"I want to come."

Aminat throws up her hands. "Why?"

"I'm an alien."

"I know that."

"I'm incomplete."

"I know that also."

"I am neither the Alyssa human nor whoever I'm meant to be. Something went wrong. I want to find out what. It might be important."

"Are you hostile to humans?"

"No."

"Good."

"But I – we are going to replace you. The Alyssa human is gone. There is a fast field of information in the air, but I only get sporadic input from it."

"I know about that. We call it the xenosphere. Not everyone can access it."

"I'm supposed to be able to, but something is blocking it. Maybe your lab tests can tell me why."

Aminat gets a flashback of a man turning into a mush splat on the protective screen. "Your choice, sister. You know those tests can kill you."

"Kill. An interesting concept."

"Do you know what I am thinking?" asks Aminat.

"No, not exactly, but I know you don't mean me any harm, though you're concerned for me because you think I'm going to die. Aminat, this mind is a copy of stored individual-specific information. The 'me' you are concerned about is already dead, and possibly died before you humans got around to using language."

Two men who have obviously colluded sit on either side of Aminat and Alyssa. The one beside Alyssa is in a singlet and his hands look like spades with barely opposable thumbs. His friend smells like boiled cabbage gone off and crowds into Aminat.

"What are fine ladies like you doing without escorts?" asks the one with Alyssa.

"We are escorting each other," says Alyssa.

"No need," pipes the one beside Aminat. "We're your escorts now."

"I don't have time for this," says Aminat.

The man beside her places his arm around her shoulders. "Why don't we slip around back? I have something to show you. You'll like it."

Aminat doesn't look at him. "Let's not."

Alyssa says, "My friend and I were talking about something private. Please go away."

"You're very rude," says the one beside Alyssa. "Such a pretty girl and rude."

"Pretty, rude and *married*," says Aminat.

"I won't say anything if she doesn't." Overt leering now.

The hand around her shoulders, the cabbage arm starts to sweat around the armpit. *Enough of this.* Aminat punches the man just under the nipple, short and fast, leaving an imprint of oil from the stew. The arm flies off her shoulder and he lets out a grunt. He does not know he has a broken rib, not just yet, but the pain kicks in when he tries to draw breath. He cannot scream with any competence and therefore gasps as he clutches his chest.

She looks across the table. "Your friend needs medical attention."

Every eye in the place is on them now, something Aminat has wanted to avoid. The other man rises and picks his friend up, shooting a baleful look at them before they leave. Alyssa has been observing the exchange like a play put on for her benefit.

"Come on, Your Highness. We have to go."

The dome is two hundred feet if you don't count the spikes projecting off the apex, which can add twenty, thirty feet easy. It is black today, and from outside Wallah Joe's Aminat can see the massing of cyborg hawks like a dark cloud. She knows what it means, and anyone prosecuting this war should have the sense to control the vast COB server farms and use the data for strategic strikes. It's what she would do.

"We'll go south, then south-west, working our way around the dome, though not close to it." Aminat buys a rucksack and jettisons her handbag after transferring what she owns. Nobody is accepting naira, and all the transactions are by eru, Rosewater's parallel currency, a combination of barter and digital IOU notes which proliferated in the early days and persisted despite attempts to stamp it out. The IOUs can be redeemed with goods or services, as long as both parties agree to the value, which Rosewater folks pretty much always do.

Aminat toys with taking the train. The station isn't far, but being in a carriage is like being in an unsprung trap. Soldiers could wait for her at the next station if an autoscan picks her ID out of the air. She has never understood animals that chew off their own limbs to escape until now. When do they figure things are hopeless?

"We need implant hacks," she says to Alyssa.

"Why?"

"So we don't get picked up."

"By enemies?"

"And friends who may not know they are friends."

"How do we get these hacks?"

The insects have started to irritate Aminat, so she brushes them off Alyssa's forearms. "I don't know, but I'll think of . . . look."

Behind a tree, a small, grey, hairless, glistening creature peeps at them. Its round eyes seem to glow, but Aminat knows it to be stored ambient light.

"What's that?" asks Alyssa.

"It's a homunculus. I've never seen one this far inside urban areas before. More importantly, it's alone. Never seen that before either, though I've heard of people snatching them from the bush."

"I remember them now." Alyssa walks towards it, stretching out a hand like one would to a strange dog.

"Hey, don't. They're poisonous."

"To humans, yes." Alyssa crouches and the homunculus touches her hand. It makes that mewling noise they make, but doesn't seem distressed. "You know they're practically immortal? They can resist any infection and only die if you kill them."

The toxic slime does not appear to affect Alyssa. The homunculus comes closer and rubs its cheek against Alyssa's shoulder. A wet patch forms on the fabric and Aminat realises she must stay away from that.

"You look at that dome and you see an animal, gigantic, useful to your society, benign, but an animal all the same. What I see is a machine. This is what we came up with after terraforming engines disappointed us. Instead of changing the environment, we change the organisms and live in them. In you."

"How has that worked out for you? On other planets?" asks Aminat.

"I don't know. There's no data on that."

"You're the first one, and that didn't go so well, did it?" Aminat stops walking. "Shouldn't I just kill you? You sound a lot like you're going to kill all of us."

"Maybe you should." Alyssa pets the homunculus. "But don't you need me to ... experiment on?"

"We can experiment on your corpse. This has worked out for humanity. Some of our best cures were discovered by working on corpses."

"You realise I don't bear you ill will, right? I quite like humans."

"Just follow me so I can drop you off." Aminat walks a little faster. After a while she looks back and sees Alyssa following half a yard back, and two steps behind her, the homunculus, tiny legs moving faster. And the insects are back on her arms and neck.

"Wonderful," she says.

About four in the afternoon they take a break. She tries to contact Olalekan, and the attempt triggers an automatic download to her phone, a video file and an executable. She puts on the screen glasses and streams it there. It's a video feed from the lab, low quality, black and white, Olalekan's workstation at a point above it. Aminat remembers the camera placement and Lekan looks right up at it. There are patches of sweat on his shirt and his face glistens. He is not smiling.

"Boss, I don't know if you're going to get this. They're outside, trying to get in. I've sealed the place, but they're determined, so it won't hold. They're soldiers, I've checked their IDs. They shot the support staff, destroyed or stole what records they could find and are looking for me. I haven't heard from Mother, but I've found her. They're holding her in the mayor's mansion, but that's Jacques's people, not these guys. I sent you a file. If you activate it you can fry your ID chip. You need to do that or they will find you. Try to find Mother; she'll know what to do." There is the sound of a door screeching and electrical complaint. "It's too late for me."

Olalekan is slammed against the console close to him, and through the gauzy definition Aminat identifies a gunshot wound. He is hit on the head and stops moving entirely. The blood looks like dark honey.

Fucking Nigerian Army bastards.

Teardrops on her forearm make her realise she is crying. She turns off the screen, wipes her eyes, and puts it back on. The homunculus is sunning itself near Alyssa's feet. She examines it with scientific curiosity.

She sees the executable file, just glowing beside the video clip. If she fries her chip her phone won't work, her gun won't fire, and she'll lose currency. Fuck mission protocol, she calls Kaaro.

"Hello."

"God, it's good to hear your voice," she says. She almost starts crying again.

"Baby, how now? Olalekan said you had to do an overnight or something."

"He's dead, Kaaro."

"What?"

She tells him the story, tells him everything that she thinks is not classified, including Efe's death and her part in it. "Be ready. I'm coming to get you, my love. Don't go out. It's crazy out here. I'll keep you safe, okay? I just need to get home, and ... I might not have my phone."

"Might I suggest something else?"

"Go."

"Can I come to you? Drive to you?"

"I don't know if anyone's watching the house, baby. I want you to act natural, as if nothing is wrong."

"Right. Right. Am I in danger?"

"No. I don't know. Don't worry, I'm coming. Get your gun from the safe and load it."

"I don't like guns."

"Just do it, Kaaro; do it because I said so."

"All right, I'll try. Aminat, don't kill your ID chip. Camouflage it."

"I don't know how to—"

"I know a guy. Let me make some calls." He pauses. "You sound different. Are you okay?"

"I ... I had to ... Kaaro, I killed some soldiers."

"I'm sorry they made you do that, baby."

He comforts her. She cannot remember what he says, but Kaaro does it in a short time, tells her he loves her, then gets off the phone to find his guy.

She walks over to Alyssa, who is leaning on a traffic bollard.

"What are we doing?"

"We march on. My boyfriend, who used to be a criminal, is going to find us a way of fixing the IDs."

People stare at them as they walk. Some have never seen a homunculus. Some know very little about xenofauna, and they think the homunculus is a kind of deformed human. Aminat doesn't like the attention, and tells Alyssa.

Before she gets any response the ground starts to shake and undulate, cracking the concrete and asphalt. People all around are flung to the ground and those still standing start to run in all directions. There is a rolling rumble that gathers momentum. Earthquake?

Alyssa seems calm, and the homunculus takes its cue from her. The cracks run around, forking like lightning, and Aminat jumps from one island to another, shouting at Alyssa, trying to get her into a building.

The ground yawns wide, and a roll-up emerges, scattering rocks and debris in all directions. Aminat shields herself. It is half out of the ground and it waves its many legs about, like a giant centipede. With elongated, segmented, armoured bodies that sometimes reach twenty-five feet in length, roll-ups are so named because despite their fearsome looks, compared to other xenofauna, they are gentle and startle easily. When afraid they curl up into a spiral and become immobile until they think the threat has passed. Unfortunately, they often cause damage by their habits and by virtue of being massive. This is the first one Aminat has seen outside the S45 teaching videos and nature documentaries on Nimbus, which did not prepare her for the feeling of mixed attraction to the attitude of the animal and fear of being crushed. The street clears quickly, and some COB hawks hover, documenting. Aminat does not wish to be seen by them. This roll-up's directional organ points at Alyssa, and it stops moving when it locates her. It lays down on the broken tarmac, its limbs unmoving.

Slowly, Aminat moves along the length of the roll-up, towards Alyssa. The creature does not react.

"Okay, it seems you're some kind of Alien Jesus to these things, but this drama is drawing attention. We have to leave, now. Is Godzilla here going to keep following you around like that poison bag?"

Alyssa talks to the roll-up in a language Aminat does not recognise, then she walks away. Aminat cannot decide whether this is a good or bad development, and if perhaps killing the alien should still be on the table. It does disturb her how easily she thinks of murder, but on the other hand, she does not think of killing aliens as murder. Does that mean aliens feel the same way about humans? She remembers Femi showing her the security footage of the people who blew up her office the year before, masked men splashing fuel and planting charges around the office. Aminat remembers wondering how anyone human could do that. At times she has nightmares where she is caught in the explosion and not lifted free by her angelic brother.

The roll-up reverses back into the ground, accompanied by thunder and shifting rubble and dust. Burst mains fountain water and create rainbows in the sun. Puzzled about her role, Aminat catches up and overtakes Alyssa, taking the lead, trying to get ahead of the problem, and failing to come up with any solutions.

Chapter Twenty-Three

Anthony

Anthony sits under the Ibeji statue. There are scattered statues of twins all over Rosewater, although this bronze is the major one. Commissioned by the twin gangsters who operated organised crime from the foundations of the city, the statue reflects the quasi-divine status of twins to the Yoruba, or so the old man tells Anthony as they share burukutu.

"Twins come from abiku," says the old man. Anthony cannot remember his name, but finds him pleasant enough. "The monkey gods punished a farmer with twin abiku because he wouldn't let monkeys eat his crops."

"What are abiku?"

"You've never heard of abiku? Where are you from, Anthony?"

"Not around here."

"Abiku are children who die young and keep coming back as different children in an endless cycle. You have to perform rituals to get them to stay. That, or you disfigure them so that the unborn spirits reject them and they are not queued up to live again. Either way, a pair of abiku were the first twins in Yoruba legend, and the farmer went to the diviners for

190

guidance. The diviners said you had to appease twins, and do whatever they want, so as to avoid the wrath of their patron orisa, Ibeji. If a twin dies, a wooden carving of it is made, and the mother has to treat the carving like a live twin, with birthday parties and milk. The carving is seen as a repository of the spirit of the twin."

Anthony looks at the eight-foot bronze twins above him. "So, the spirits of the gangsters are in these two?"

"They aren't dead yet, my friend."

They drink some more and the alcohol has such a kick that Anthony finds himself in the xenosphere. There is more black, which is less fragmented than the last time he was there.

I should be concerned about this. I should be worried.

Wormwood is still silent, and Home just wants Anthony to find the host, which is proving impossible. There are spectators, people watching the black cloud as it spreads over the psychoscape, humans. They do nothing, just stay a healthy distance away and observe. It is not uniform black, this cloud. If Anthony strains he can see variation and movement other than the billowing. There are people in there, just like in the xenosphere. Would he die if he dived in?

Fuck it.

He thinks it, then he is in the blackness. He cannot see anything at first, and he feels pain as if he is swimming in acid. Since his corporal self is not really present, he adjusts his mind and the pain stops. Anthony cycles through several styles of seeing and experiments with his perception until he can see the heart of the blackness. There is a man there, so Anthony aims for him. The man's movements are slow, and his facial expression is concentration verging on frustration.

"Hello," says Anthony.

As soon as the man becomes aware of the intruder the substance of the blackness changes and dozens of hands reach out and fix Anthony in place. They are impossibly strong, but Anthony does not try to break the grip. He is more curious than looking for conflict.

"Get out," says the man.

Anthony finds himself not just expelled from the blackness, he is flung out of the xenosphere as well. He falls off the lip of the concrete skirting and is on the ground looking up at the stylised genitalia of the twin statue.

The old man shakes his head at Anthony. "You have been drinking too much, I see. This burukutu is not for the weak, and you look kind of scrawny."

"Help me up," says Anthony. He metabolises the alcohol until he burps pure fishy aldehyde breath, then he finishes his drink. Who is the man in the centre of the blackness? He feels both repulsed and attracted, the feelings associated with highly specific prey for particular predators, which is concerning because the universe only sponsors such relationships for the doomed. Whether Anthony is truly alive or not is open for debate, but he does not wish to answer that question.

It is not a wasted exercise, though. He is able to map the approximate physical location of the anomaly, well, the edge of the anomaly. He found the host by finding the anomaly the last time. This time he will walk, not run, and he will be careful. He will not be surprised.

He thanks the old man for an entertaining afternoon, bowing, and he starts on his way.

The anomaly leads him here, to this bland block, residential, crowded, unremarkable, in a street full of similar dwellings.

The entire building is not just dead in terms of the xeno-sphere, it is a void. No mentation escapes, no feelings, no vague intuitions. This must be what it is like to be human, not quasi-human like the bodies Wormwood makes for Anthony, but really human. He stands across the road and watches. Caution. That's new, but he does not know how well Wormwood is doing, and who knows how long it will take to reconstruct the body if it gets destroyed? Best to be careful, to watch, and then to approach. He will be going in as a human, because that emptiness negates any chemical controls Anthony has.

The wait does bear some fruit. He sees two men giggling, holding hands and lugging art portfolios. Talking.

"He bristled at the fillip from Dade, and to prove he was a true artist he worked on a canvas for five years without letting anyone see the progress. When it was done, he invited thirteen people to a single viewing, with the proviso that they could take no pictures, and could not, in his lifetime, describe what they saw. After one hour he had the viewers escorted out, doused the painting with kerosene, and set it alight from the cigarette that hung constant at the left corner of his mouth."

"Then what did Dade think of him?"

Artists. This means something, something before this body. What is it? The memory is there, just needs sifting ... the studio. The studio where he saw the first plant, Earth artists work from studios, the plant is in the studio, maybe the artists took seeds home without knowing? Time to find out. He cuts down the adrenaline and takes hits of anandamide and low doses of endorphins. This may be the last time he can control it before he faces whatever is in there.

He walks around the building. There it is, the plant, the weed, growing out of a dustbin, tendrils in search of soil or water or both, using the fence as a trellis. He notes the flat number painted on the bin, and makes his way to the front.

From the surface thoughts of the artists he knows it is a four-storey building with several flats on each level. He walks in unchallenged, and makes his way to the back of the first floor where he knows the staircase that leads upstairs is. He feels unalive, with no connection even to Wormwood. Maybe he knows fear, or maybe he is too stoned to know the difference. He knocks on the flat door, then presses the doorbell, but nothing happens, as if the electricity is out. He tries the handle, but it is locked. He tries to boost his strength, but there is no corporeal manipulation in this field. He takes steps back and smashes into the door. It hurts his shoulder and down his arm. Huh. Pain that he can't banish. That's new.

He tries again. The impact takes the door off its hinges, but it does not fall. It just leans inwards, like a ship listing, weight borne by something on the other side. Anthony pushes against it, finds it springy, pushes harder and checks the gaps at the sides. Vegetation. Green and purple leaves, vines and wafts of pollen. As he puts pressure on the door, each tendril seems to actively make its way into the hallway. It can't be that fast, can it?

Slight dizziness, but otherwise Anthony feels able to continue. He puts all his weight against the door and leans in, and it falls sufficiently for him to step on it. It flattens the stems behind it, and Anthony gets a view of the rest of the apartment. Floor to ceiling, covered with the infernal plant. He tries to part stems, and registers sharp pain. Thorns on every stem, waxy spines on the leaves, his hands dripping blood and stinging from cuts. He stares bemused as rootlets grow around objects to get to the drops. As an experiment he spits, and they go for that glob as well. Used up all the moisture in the apartment?

The vines twist without warning, corralling the stems, parting the green sea until the body at the centre is exposed. It is emaciated, cadaverous, mottled light and dark green, punctured by roots and vines on most of its surface area. The milky eyes are open and it frowns.

"You." Its voice sounds like a crow speaking words.

"Me."

"Didn't I tell you to get out?"

"Not really. That was a different place."

"Go away."

"Not yet. What do you want? Why are you here?"

The man looks to his left a fraction, distracted for a moment. "I see. You're the footholder. Your blood just reached me. I am not impressed. Go away."

"I'm not the footholder any more than you are the plant. We're avatars, you and I, human shells. We reflect aspects of the humans we model."

"You asked what I want. I want to live. I want life, abundant life, everywhere. And the human, Bewon, is bitter at everything. We can both win."

"By harming me you are harming your own brother. We're on a mission to—"

"Go away."

There is movement in the woody portions, and the vines twist around each other, concentrating into a tightly coiled mass which takes on human proportions in less than a minute.

"I did warn you to leave, avatar."

The creature, the construct, is humanoid with six leafy wings, two covering its face, and two covering its legs. What

195

passes for skin is covered in thorns. The middle two wings flick forward and strike Anthony.

The force flings him back, his arm hitting the lintel of the doorway making his body spin so that he hits the wall opposite face-first. He feels nothing, but his nose and forehead seem wet. There are small lights dancing across his vision.

Before he can recover, he feels strong wooden hands grab hold of him, pinpricks of thorns puncturing his skin, and multiple wings enfold him. Anthony struggles, pushes, to no avail, and he feels them both leave the ground and fly forward along the corridor. The flight is haphazard, as if the creature has never used its wings before now, and they slam into the wall twice, zigzagging towards a window at the end of the corridor.

Now they crash through the window, jagged glass cutting them both, tinkling to the ground, laying open Anthony's skin. Outside, the creature corrects its pattern, and flies high, high, into the sky, powering through a kettle of idling COBs, who, after a brief appearance of disorientation, give chase. Anthony observes it all as if from a trance, bleeding, trying to determine which way is up.

The plant construct soars over the dome, with some COBs flying ahead, some behind like outriders, then folds its wings in, holding Anthony with arms and legs alone. This close it smells of wet earth and fermented food. It is stationary for a second, maybe two, and then it dives. They hit a COB that bursts apart in a flurry of feathers.

Anthony knows what is coming, but is helpless to stop it. At first he is impaled on a seven-foot spike on the dome, but the creature keeps pushing and both of them slam into the barrier, which reacts like rotting vegetables and holds only for a few seconds. The pain hasn't registered when Anthony and the plant creature breach the dome and fall inside.

Chapter Twenty-Four

Jacques

Jack knows he is about to be interrupted before it happens.

Lora comes in with a plasma image projected in front of her. "An object just punched a hole in the dome!"

Oh, fuck. "Missile?"

"Dahun says there was no detonation, no smoke trail. Unlikely."

"What then? That dome's been impenetrable since it emerged."

"All the COB footage goes federal, but some Script Kiddies on Nimbus intercepted some photos from the feed and . . . "

"Speak, Lora."

"They . . . er . . . they said it was an angel."

Jack massages his eyes. "Don't tell me the newsfeeds—"

"Yes."

"Great. Next they'll be saying how the hand of God came down and ruptured the dome so that the righteous Nigerian troops can prevail."

"Yes. Yes, that's exactly what they're saying."

Jack sucks his teeth. "Is that the image?"

The thing is multi-limbed and foliage green. If you squint, it does look like an angel, or several.

"Lora, how many wings do—"

"Cherubim can have six wings, sir."

"Right. Right."

He stares and stares until the image looks like green fuzz. But he sees something else now, a distinction between ...

"Those are two people," says Jack.

Lora squints. "Don't tell me you believe in the angel theory."

"Get someone to clean up the image, and get visual confirmation of the hole. Not instruments, actual soft eyes," says Jack. "And get that xenobiologist – what's his name? Cruz? Get him here sharpish. We need ... My whole strategy depends on that alien. I'll not have it fail now."

"Yes, sir. It's a she, and her name is Dr Bodard."

"Right, Dr Bodard, go. And leave me alone for an hour. I need to make a phone call."

"There's an organisation called the Citizens for a Free Rosewater whose reps are outside wanting to see you."

"Who are they?"

"Front for the president, sir. Thin disguise, rowdy, and here to berate you for your declaration."

"Are we going to start shooting these people at some point?"

Lora hesitates, opens her mouth to speak. Closes it.

"I'm kidding. Go. Jesus."

Alone again, and twice as nervous now. What the fuck is wrong with the dome? He steels himself, takes a deep breath, and calls the Tired Ones.

It rings once, and a brief silence before a man speaks. "I wondered how long it would take you to ring back, or if you would ring back at all."

Jack does not know what to say, and his heart bounds in his chest, so he does not speak. He would not trust his mouth or voice, at any rate.

"Child, have you betrayed us?"

"No."

"Are you still Tired?"

"Yes."

"Then explain to me the situation in Rosewater, child."

The situation in Rosewater is that we're fucked.

"Sir ... "

Sir.

Remember to say this every time. Prefix, suffix, mid-sentence. Sir.

He comes to visit and Jack brings him Gulder beer with a clean glass pre-cooled in the fridge. He stands outside the room, but within earshot so he can be on hand to wait on the visitor, but not close enough to eavesdrop on the conversation of adults.

You will never become remarkable by doing as you're told all the time. That's what the man told him on the last visit. Jack wrote it down.

Jack lives with his aunt, has done for two years since the accident that killed his parents and siblings. He has no memory of the accident. He just remembers the pain of recovery, the physio, the surgery. He remembers being in the car, and that his younger brother had farted at some point. He remembers the sun was shining, and the window ... something about the window.

After the funeral, his aunt takes him home. She has no children of her own, and the clan agrees that Jack should go to her.

This is fine the first year, but just after Christmas, she comes into his room at night, places a hand on his cock and strokes him, her other hand hard at work in the folds of her nightgown, her breathing wet and mouldy. When she is done, she says, *Clean yourself up.* She says the same thing each time. They do not talk about this in the daytime. Besides, Jack is too ashamed and does not have the words. He starts to plot how to get away, and he considers running.

Such a beautiful boy. You're so big now, so strong. She says this, as she grunts in the dark, graduating to straddling him and placing her stringy wetness on him.

It is an unending nightmare that follows him into the day, at school, where he withdraws and the teachers think it's because he has lost his family in a traumatic fashion. He'll snap out of it, of course. These things take time. To the teachers, his aunt nods sagely, and at night she nods faster when she climaxes. He showers whenever he can, and washes his hands until they are raw and bleeding.

The visitor takes an interest in him, asks him questions about what he is interested in. Jack has some good instincts about what other people want, and he tailors his answers. The visitor is looking for something, some potential to mould. Jack will play along, so far as it gets him away from his aunt.

He remembers being six. She visits and kisses him on the cheek. He wipes the spot off and all the adults laugh. There is nobody to laugh now.

The visitor has power. He works with the state governor in Lagos, and he gets things done so that the governor can look good. What can Jack do?

Countless Gulders and visits later, he asks, Do you want to come to Lagos?

His aunt hugs him when he leaves, and are those tears in her eyes? This entire part of his life is a slow dream, never precisely recalled, and buried deep.

Lagos, on the other hand, is fast and in full colour.

The traffic is faster, the people talk faster, *time* flows faster. He lives in the man's house, with his family, not a house boy, as he had expected, but as an equal to his children. They are clean, rich, polite, and soon Jack is faster, talks faster, flows faster, and is in full colour. Nobody comes to his room at night, but Jack still tenses whenever he hears footfalls after bedtime. He goes rigid with shame and sweats for hours after.

He attends St Finbarr's in the day, and in the evening the man teaches him. It is a strange mix of lessons, starting with the self and questioning whether the self truly exists or not, and where does the self fit with other people. There are talks about motivation, about group dynamics, about what it takes to shift large numbers of people from one way of thinking to another, about what exactly charisma is. This goes on for years, but does not bleed into the rest of his life at secondary school. The man teaches him chaos theory and chaos magick. Puts him in a chair and flings him backwards. At first Jack flails, but the man repeats it until there is no flailing, just acceptance. *Accept the lack of control. Let go. Leave it.*

And when Jack finally relaxes into the fall, he is caught and does not hit the ground. A third person Jack has not even been aware of. Jack does not see her, but a voice whispers in his ear.

Are you tired, Jack?

No, I can do more …

Are you tired, Jack?

What do you mean?

Are you tired, Jack?

She is gone and the man does not explain. Jack only understands when he is eighteen.

By his eighteenth birthday he is no longer working in the house. He assists in the office of the man. He has proximity to the governor. He knows things he has been taught, and the man has imbued the lessons with a sense of destiny.

The man drives him out to Badagry, to what used to be a staging accommodation for slaves to be sent across the Atlantic. There are other men and women there. He is made to sit on a bench where he is surrounded by people. A woman speaks up.

"Listen and do not interrupt. Answer only when you are asked a question.

"You are wondering why you are here and perhaps you have wondered for a long time why our brothers and sisters took you in. There are those of us in society, in black African society, who are tired. Our leaders have, through the decades, established a reputation for being incompetent, despotic and unsuited to power. Leadership is seen as ruling rather than serving. The people, the populace, are betrayed from the moment the election is won, or the cordite settles from the bloody coups. Campaign promises mean nothing in any country, but we have somehow perfected the art of pretending there was no manifesto. Swiss bank accounts swell with funds from our coffers, yet cannot be recovered even when we prove the money was stolen. The great powers – Russia, China, the EU – they laugh at us. Even England, isolated as it is, pretends not to know us as it slides to oblivion.

"What then is the thinking African to do when the Nkrumas and the Lumumbas are dead and gone? The past is past, the present is a mess, but the future is a ripe fruit waiting for harvest. We, the Tired, work on the future of leadership in Africa. The raw material of our project is you, the uncorrupted youth. The tools of our project are selection, education, mentoring and insertion. We will guide you to leadership positions after we have taught you. We want you to change not just Africa, but the world. Will you join us?"

Jack does.

He lives alone, now, helped by his sponsor. He works harder than anyone else supporting those Tired men and women designated to positions. He studies, he thinks, he writes his thoughts.

One day he receives a phone call and someone asks his sexual orientation.

"Why do you need to know?"

"We ask this of all single Tired. You see, a scandal, particularly a sexual scandal, can end your political career before it starts. We are realists, and we want to accommodate you."

Jack thinks of dark shadows after bedtime and moist genitals. He controls the timbre of his voice. "I'm heterosexual, but you needn't worry."

Nevertheless a package arrives for him the next day. It's a sex bot. The bots look and feels just like a real woman, supposedly, although Jacques isn't tempted to test that. He laughs to the empty room, then connects to Nimbus. He spends days accessing books on Artificial Intelligence. He cannot code, but it gives him a good idea about the specifics of what he needs to tell the person he hires. He thinks the bot has a kind face. She is the same height as he is, dark-skinned, athletic, not as physically obvious as he would have expected, and dressed in sportswear. Jack imagines some psychologist working on his profile in a dank room somewhere, deciding what features would be considered attractive. She does stir something in him, but it's a fraternal fondness.

"Are you kidding? It's a sex toy. You fuck it. You don't teach it Locke and Hobbes. Or, wait, are you one of those sapiosexual guys? You can't get hard unless a woman can quote long passages of *The Wealth of Nations*?"

"I'm paying you money, right? How's about you shut the fuck up and just do what I say? It's like repurposing the processor of a games console for a different function."

The tech guy continues to flip through the copious notes Jack provides. "Wait, you want to override the Agreeableness protocol?"

"Yes."

"You know that means it would be able to decide not to serve you?"

"Not 'it'; 'she'. I don't need a servant. I want an assistant. A ... deputy. Someone I can trust, but who will disagree with me if I'm wrong."

"Deputy what? You're a guy in a one-bedroom flat."

"Now. That's what I am now. Things change."

"Fine. What do you want to call it?"

"Her. And we're calling her 'Lora'."

Lora is not autonomous, but her reactions are not stereotyped. He finds her a surname (Asiko) and an identity chip with a fabricated life story based on Jack's deceased younger sister. She has to go for maintenance every year, and Jack pays for it. She lives with him as his sister in Lagos, and she quickly becomes his right hand.

"You have to exercise," says Jack.

"I don't need exercise," says Lora.

"Yes, but people will start to wonder why you don't get fat, why you don't age."

"And we care what people think?"

"Yes, we do."

Some direct instruction, some modification of code, and she gets the idea. They talk but she never initiates contact.

In '54, when the Lagos State governor is shot dead at a rally, Jack and Lora are there, and Jack survives because Lora drags him bleeding to the hospital. Five bullets passed through him, a paltry number compared to the thirty the governor got. The assassins shot Lora's face off, and in the hospital they know she is a construct, but it is not linked to her secret identity. It takes six months to restore Lora. The algorithm upgrade allows her to initiate conversation.

Jack is therefore unsurprised that she knocks on the shower one morning, saying she has to speak to him. It is 2055 and somewhere just south of Ilorin, an alien dome has risen. It's on the newsfeeds. When Jack finishes gathering information, he calls his Tired mentor.

"Pack a bag," he says to Lora. "We're going there."

It is chaos.

There are dead soldiers, smoking black helicopters and a pervasive smell of ozone. Jack sees lots of activity, but the people, the civilians, are calm and serene in a religious way, like they have seen something momentous. All the hardships involved in living around the dome in land that is arid and unyielding, the people are still happy. They have hope, and ultimately, this is the motivator that keeps people living in subhuman conditions.

"Thank you for saving my life," says Jack.

"I'm programmed to—"

"Thank you. And shut up about the programming."

"I can't allow you to die, darling, honey, sexgod."

Jack still has to tweak the code. At times the sex bot routines leak through, especially since the shooting, regardless of how many times he tells them to wipe the memory clean.

They are watching two men fight, and a crowd placing bets. "What do you see in this place, Lora?"

"Filth, excrement, wetness, government agents, pain, poverty, disorganisation."

"What do you not see?"

Lora looks puzzled, an amazing feat of engineering.

"Leadership."

He phones his mentor. "I'm staying here."

"Are you out of your mind?"

"This place is a mine. I've already organised meetings. The alien itself is unknowable, but there is an effect here . . . "

"You're wasting both your potential and the time and money invested in you. Are you still Tired?"

"I am Tired, but this, here, at Camp Rosewater, this is where I can fulfil that dream. I can feel it. It will need a local government."

"It'll be empty in a month."

"I respectfully disagree."

There are two phases of settling Rosewater. The initial bedraggled masses populate the southern areas near Yemaja. Later, there is an influx of the sick rich, people who have tried everything and need a miracle. These people have their own money and build the suburbs, and the early banks and the cathedral and central mosque. North-east and south-west grow towards each other and fuse at the meeting points. It is Jack's idea to divide the city into wards and have councillors for each. It is Lora's idea to use the twins for peace-keeping and crime regulation.

Jack brings in multinationals to build infrastructure though this does not go down well with the people to start with. In hoods, Jack and Lora watch the security bots dispel protesters from a construction site.

Jack says, "We need to modify the plans for the government house." The assassination of the governor is still fresh in his mind. "We need bunkers. In case they come for us while we're in the building."

"That will strain the funds," says Lora.

"I have no intention of dying at the hands of the baying mob. Contact the contractors."

"I suppose we can get it back with taxes."

Jack shakes his head. "Nineteen sixteen."

"Sir?"

"The first taxes in Yorubaland were in nineteen sixteen, imposed by the British using local rulers as stalking horses. It led to the Iseyin Riots. Rosewater has been tax-free so far. We need it to stay that way until we're in position."

"The Iseyin Riots were put down, sir."

"You miss the point. Taxes are a relatively new thing to the Yoruba. We don't even have a real word for it. The primal resentment is still there."

"Sir, everyone everywhere hates taxes."

"Just call the contractors."

Jack is right, and as the years go by, the protestations of the Tired reduce, and the rule of law prevails in Rosewater.

Until now.

"Sir, the president left me no choice," says Jack.

"That's interesting. He says the same about you."

"You've spoken to him?"

"Does this really surprise you?"

"No, sir. But he's—"

"He's Tired. Just like you."

"*The president?*"

"He's strayed from the path, but yes. He recently got back in touch. We forgive those who stray. Like you."

But the president, though. Really?

"Did you kill the president's candidate for the coming elections?"

207

"That was an accident, and I didn't—"

"You have never won an election, child. You are starting to look like the kind of leader we teach against, with the accidents and the declarations of independence."

"I know what it looks like, but it's not. Trust me."

"How do you plan to resolve the matter?"

"Does the president want to talk?"

"We are not go-betweens, Jack Jacques."

"Yes, you are. You act as facilitators all the time."

"Not this time, then."

"Why?"

"Because we don't think you are right. Surrender, publicly state that you made a mistake and leave Rosewater. We will provide you with shelter, child."

And re-education, no doubt.

It's tempting. This is not a shooting war yet and Jack is already exhausted. The alien, his one ace in the hole, is punctured by unknown means. Surrender, return to the bosom of the Tired, rest, find another mission. It would be the easiest course of action.

"Sir, I respectfully disagree."

A slow exhalation on the other side, as if he is smoking. "I will hear that as you wanting to take some time to think about how you will answer, child. Use the *time* wisely."

Click.

Was that a coded message about Lora? *Asiko* means "time".

Interlude 2067

Eric

There are three S45 men in my enclosure, one in military garb, none of whom introduce themselves. I'm reading *Kudi* by Walter Tanmola when they come in. I splay it open on the coffee table and give the visitors my full attention.

"There's a situation in Rosewater," says the military man.

"We want you to go in," says another. "Because of your experience."

"We want you to liquidate Jack Jacques," says the third. "A chance to redeem your earlier failure and save some lives at the same time."

"Where's Mrs Alaagomeji?" I ask.

"In Rosewater. Gone dark."

"What about Kaaro?"

"He's not in play," says the military man.

"Won't I die if I go out there?"

"We don't think so. We think the problem with the extinction of your kind has stopped since last year."

"You *think*? That's reassuring."

"If you need more time . . . "

"No, I don't. Let's go," I say.

*

The first step is surgery. They remove my ID chip and replace it with a generic population model, something that won't trigger any alarms. The deniability aspect goes without saying, but it is understood.

They make me sign and thumbprint a few documents, letters to the government, deranged rantings of a madman ultra-patriot who sees the secession of Rosewater as an insult to the country. I hope they have no intention of sending a missile to my ID chip location this time around.

I have a whole lot of material to get familiar with over the few days while my wound heals. I've been out of touch and where I'm going the wrong statement can kill me. It seems Jack Jacques has fulfilled his potential to be a fuckwit. If I had killed him back then would all of this be happening at all?

The déjà vu is startling. They say I have to go in without weapons, but they already have embedded people stirring up shit within the city. They feel sure I'll get weapons from the underground.

There's a hologram of Rosewater in front of me. I cannot believe how much it has grown. The dome is larger than ten years ago. It's thirty miles across, one-eighty feet high, and where it was smooth it now sports spikes, like a war mace or the ball of a morning star. There's a cathedral, mosques, stadium, cinemas, and high-rises. They have class distinctions and suburbs and school runs. They also have universal health and uninterrupted power from the alien, although intelligence shows that the extraterrestrial itself might not be faring so well.

I'm to go in through the south-west, by the Yemaja, come in through the marshes and slums of Ona-oko and meet my contact. I'm to report any instance of ill health to my handler, Eurohen, who happens to be in charge of S45. He has orders from the president to deal with this matter personally.

"Sir, what about Mrs Alaagomeji?"

"She's still in the field and out of contact. Don't worry about her." Eurohen's left eye twitches. Perhaps he hates being in her shadow. Perhaps he's lying.

"And if I encounter her?"

"Pretend not to know her."

"Sir ... " I hesitate.

"Speak freely, agent."

"What if she doesn't want me to kill Jacques?" Anyone who has been in the field will tell you the reality on the ground can change. What if Alaagomeji sees a different reality?

"Your service is at the pleasure of the office of the president. Your instructions are to liquidate Jacques. Anyone gets in your way, you liquidate them too. Is that clear?"

"Sir."

I wade through the marshland in the dark. My palm lights up with the compass phone app, directing me to Ona-oko. Mosquitoes alight on me, but I'm not worried because I have a dermal patch to prevent malaria. It's government issue, so probably unreliable, but I'm counting on the fact that they need me alive. Some asshole tried to cure malaria by gene-editing the plasmodium parasite that causes it. Worked for most strains, but a hardy, drug-resistant plasmodium emerged that just kills the few people who get it. So, prevalence is down but mortality is up. Way up.

There are ghost lights, and I can smell the methane as I slog along, and the gurgle of the Yemaja is distinct. There are droppers every few yards, faux-human bodies swaying in the night breeze, unblinking eyes watching me, imploring me to join their corrosive embrace.

I can hear a drum in the distance calling me in as the ground gets drier. I could swear to some seismic activity, but that might just be due to the difference between marsh and red sand.

I am inside the city limits and this is the key moment, the reason they had to find me, and not use another agent. The alien will kill anyone seen as an outsider with evil intent. S45's hope and mine is that Wormwood will recognise me and count me as a part of Rosewater. I realise I have slowed my pace and await, with ragged breath, a lightning strike from the south ganglion.

It does not come and I approach the first settlements. The drummer is a ten-year-old and I touch the back of his palm to transfer some money.

Welcome to Rosewater. It stinks less than it used to.

Chapter Twenty-Five

Aminat

The circuitous route has them in the slums of Ona-oko, where, given that it is dark, they will have to bed down for the night. Aminat can feel the distant vibration beneath her feet, the one that is not traffic, or the trains. She knows the roll-up is following Alyssa in a subterranean path, just like the homunculus is overground.

"We'll rest here," says Aminat. "Send that abomination away because nobody will rent us a room with it hanging around."

They find a single room that accepts what currency Aminat still has. Alyssa showers while Aminat waits. The window is sealed and the air conditioning works, but the abomination is on the roof and keens like a forlorn puppy.

Kaaro calls, and her belly flutters.

"I love you," she says, in lieu of "hello".

"I love you. I've got a solution for your ID chip problem, but I have to conference someone in. Did I ever tell you about a guy called Bad Fish?"

"I think I'd remember a name like that."

"Bad Fish is this tech-bandit from Lagos, a celestial."

"What's a celestial?"

"It's a church, but it's also a person who has skills with repurposed technology and post-hacking … it doesn't matter. The fact is he can adjust your implant remotely. I have to conference him in."

"Helloooo." Bad Fish sounds high.

"Baby, this doesn't sound like a good idea," says Aminat.

"It's fine. He won't steal any data because he knows that I'll know if he does, and that I know how to find him always, right, Bad Fish?"

"Of courseeeee."

"Bad Fish, are you drunk?" asks Kaaro.

"No, and I'm sssshocked you'd think so."

"You kind of sound like you are, Bad Fish," says Aminat.

"That's because I'm penetrating a space station at the ssss-same time as talking to you. Overclocking, overclocked. Too many brain cycles."

"We can call you later—" says Kaaro.

"Nonsense. I'm ready. Let'ssssss do this. *Ai m'asiko lo n'damu eda*." Aminat hears tapping from the other end, like a keyboard. "I'm sending a file to your phone. Execute it. I'll use the signal to do what I need to do. What I'll create is an overlay identity. You'll be able to switch back if you need to."

It takes half an hour to do, first Aminat, then Alyssa. Later, when all is quiet and she is trying to sleep, Aminat feels a weird turn, then she is in that field, that strange place where Kaaro takes their minds for privacy. It's night, with a full moon this time, and Bolo, the giant with dreadlocks, stands guard at the edge of the frontier as usual.

Kaaro stands in the ankle-high grass, waiting for her. That dog, Yaro, is beside him, wagging its tail maniacally.

"Lose the dog, Kaaro," says Aminat.

The dog dissipates and they sit in the grass.

"I didn't know you could bring animals in here."

"In theory, I could. A dog has a brain, neurons and sense organelles on its skin that the xenoforms can connect to. But that's not the dog. That's present because I've been spending all my hours with Yaro. It's a residual image, nothing more."

"Okay."

Kaaro points. "What's that?"

It's a discoloration in the air, a blackness, tendrils of concentrated night, alien, yet familiar to Aminat. "That's Alyssa."

Kaaro stares for some seconds, then grunts.

"She's not harmful," says Aminat.

"If you say so. Anyway, I have something to show you. Lie down."

She does, and the sky changes from darkness interrupted by stars to a scene.

In Lagos, within a massive rubbish dump, shielded by metal placements that look random but are carefully selected, Bad Fish stands in a white kaftan with a grey helmet on his head. Wires lead from the back of the helmet to several terminals about which acolytes fuss. There are sixteen high-performance fans cooling the hardware, yet everybody sweats. Bad Fish gives a thumbs-up and the acolytes switch the thing on. The helmet lights up on the inside, a view that Aminat sees because Kaaro has put her in Bad Fish's head. At first it seems like a profusion of numbers to Aminat, but she understands within seconds. Each person's ID chip has a unique hardware number which it broadcasts for a short distance. Bad Fish has acquired the number for every single one on the government database and used them to create a virtual map of Nigeria, or, rather, Nigerians. He sees everyone and it makes his heart swell with pride.

He points like the conductor of a grand symphony. "COB feeds and street cameras!"

In the background hard drives strain with the effort of keeping up with the processing required. He picks out one chip hardware number and he gets all the displays currently observing the person cross-referenced with a map. A stream of data about the person scrolls down one of the screens. Bad Fish is positively orgasmic. He picks a few other random numbers and has the same effect. Then one of the machines catches fire, triggering pandemonium.

Kaaro brings her out.

"In its own way it's like the xenosphere, or a crude facsimile. He has interesting ideas, that one."

"He'll get caught," says Aminat.

Kaaro shakes his dreamlike head. "He's too smart, too savvy, too hungry. Where are you, Aminat?"

"I'm making my way to you," says Aminat.

"Is that a reference to the Spinners' song?"

"Old man, you need new music."

"We both do. There hasn't been any good music since 1995."

Aminat runs her hands over the grass, marvelling at how it feels real, and how it smells like all the meadows she's ever been in. She moves closer to him and even Kaaro smells like he normally does. She brushes her lips against his neck and drops her hand in his lap.

"Are we going to—"

"We surely are."

*

216

Afterwards, lying back in the grass, Kaaro entertains her with Northern Light Simulations.

"Have you ever seen the aurora borealis?" she asks.

"No, but the planetarium has VR that's apparently better than the real thing. That's where my simulation comes from." He plays with her nipple. "What's Alyssa Sutcliffe like?"

"She's playing messiah to all the alien animals. I don't quite know what to make of her."

"Never turn your back on her."

"I'll be fine."

The illusion starts to break down and images flicker.

"Kaaro, what's—"

"There's a storm front coming your way, it's disrupting the xenosphere. I'll get ... and—"

Aminat finds herself back in the hotel room, in the dark, the cries of the homunculus keeping her company. Alyssa appears to be speaking to it from the window, but Aminat cannot figure this out, tired as she is, and falls into a tarry blackness.

She remembers. Or dreams, all is one.

Her first lab, where she does the first work on human–xenoform percentages, with her first crew, gathering the first batch of data. Femi sends a message: *Delete data, disband team, get out and I will be in touch.* Aminat follows the instructions, or is in the process of doing this, and she hesitates to delete the data because of how hard they worked to get it. Back then, the xenoforms could only be grown in a living being, the best being the liver of rats. The actual scientific team disperses fast, and Aminat goes back to work to ... Well, the work is finished, but she needs to get away from Kaaro. He has just told Aminat about some affair he had with some woman in the xenosphere, Molara. It sounds disgusting, and she should have walked away, but she loves him by then. He is stupid, a shabby dresser and clueless about most things, but under the surface there is pain and beneath that, a good soul. He's also really cute. Aminat does not need the xenosphere to tell her this. She is distracted when she goes to work, and boom.

The bomb does not cause pain at first, just a sense of disorientation and the shockwave to the ear. Instead of pain and torn flesh, Aminat feels warmth and crackling flames.

"Sister, I heard your scream," says Layi, her brother, surrounding them both in his own alien-hybrid flame.

Between Aminat and Femi, they find those responsible, people from within S45 who are collaborators with the invaders, and they purge them. The plotters are scattered to Enugu and Kirikiri prisons. The people who planted and detonated the bomb are dead. Femi shows Aminat images of the corpses.

"I didn't take it personally," says Aminat.

"Then *I will inflame thy noble liver and make thee rage,*" Femi says. "Nobody fucks with us."

She neglects to say who *us* is.

Her next assignment is to assemble a new team in a new lab, on the quiet, with as little documentation as can be managed.

She wakes with Alyssa standing over her, dressed.

"There is a problem," says Alyssa.

"What problem?" Aminat sees that the second bed has not been slept in.

"Look out of the window."

Aminat rubs her eyes and stumbles over to the window, even though her bladder is full and she would rather go to the toilet. Part of her brain notes that the homunculus has gone silent.

She gasps, and cannot believe what she is seeing.

There is brown water flowing through the streets, a flood, covering the first storey of most buildings. No cars in sight, probably all submerged. Some trees float by. How bad was that storm? There has never been a flood of the Yemaja in Rosewater since Aminat has lived there, and none that she has heard reported.

"Is this normal?" asks Alyssa.

"No," says Aminat. "No, this is not normal at all."

They access the news reports. After what is a trivial rainfall, barely an inch in some places, the Yemaja breaches its banks. Video footage pours in from people trapped in buildings, observers at a safe distance and drones. Mothers and fathers and children cling to improvised floatation devices. The fisher folk who live and work near the river use their boats and canoes to ferry the stranded. Slum-dwellers wave from rooftops. Some channels make a biblical connection, stating the timing of the flood does not augur well for the newly declared state, or that it is punishment.

"We need a boat," says Aminat.

Chapter Twenty-Six

Jacques

"It's a dam," says Lora. "They dammed Yemaja, downstream. We're in the river valley, and Ona-oko is in the floodplain, susceptible to flooding."

"Smart. Not a shot fired and they have our own people quoting the most apocalyptic parts of Exodus and saying, 'Let my people go.'" Jack kills the image of the flood. "What are we doing for those folks?"

"Evac is underway. Temporary shelter in the stadium, then we'll need better ideas."

"Start a database of second homes in the city. I want all the empty properties mapped and the owners contacted. They need to be on standby to take people in."

"Yes, sir."

He calls Dahun. "Let's go see our prisoner. Meet me at the cell."

The prisoner's clothes are different. She is more plainly dressed and Jack imagines someone got her something to sleep in. She is not surprised to see them. If anything, she seems amused, and her eyes glitter like those of a trickster demon.

She says, "Let me guess. Dam. Flood. Religious stories planted in the news. Stop me whenever you like."

Jack is surprised. "How do you—"

"I devised the strategy. I wrote the song, I dictated the tune. You really want us working together on this, Mr Mayor. You don't bench your striker in the World Cup final."

"What comes next?" says Jack.

She shakes her head. One of the strap muscles on her perfect neck stands out as she does. She is singular, this Femi Alaagomeji. "You give me my phone access, you let me check on my agents, and you remove me from this ridiculous room. We could have avoided this if you had listened to me yesterday."

Jack looks at Dahun who shrugs. "I can put a man on her."

He looks at Lora.

"We're in this situation because of her. She knows a lot more than anybody here. To enter into a deal with such a person is ill-advised, even if we're being told there is a wider perspective, a perspective to which only she has access."

"Your right-hand woman is smart," says Alaagomeji. "But she is operating under particular parameters that prevent her from seeing far enough."

Jack exhales. "We're setting you free within the mansion. You'll be under guard and if you step outside you will be shot. Your phone will be released for communication but it will be monitored."

"Thank you, Mr Mayor." Alaagomeji stands and is all business.

Dahun stands in her way. "Not so fast. What did they use to penetrate the dome?"

For the first time Alaagomeji seems stunned. "They what?"

*

She has spent fifteen minutes watching and rewatching footage. Her phone has been beeping with received messages, but she hasn't paid any attention to her wrist.

"So this wasn't part of your protocol?" asks Jack.

"No, this is something new." She leans back from the image and massages her lower back. "Did it self-repair?"

"A thin mesh has formed, but the wound is still there," says Dahun. "We have eyes on the ground."

"Which of you is in charge of security and murder and stuff?" asks Alaagomeji. "Don't waste time with emotional hand-wringing. Just tell me. That was my job."

"Why?" asks Jack.

"You're going to need your best people for what I'm about to say. You need to get a guy called Kaaro. He won't come willingly and he has the ability to ... neutralise inexperienced people."

"Why do we need him?"

"He can talk to the alien. He's a powerful sensitive. We need to know what went through the dome and why it's taking so long to heal."

"Can't we talk to him on the phone?"

"Bad idea. He doesn't like the government, he doesn't like me personally, and I already know from his file that he despises you, Mr Mayor. He'll soon have a second reason."

"What's that?"

She starts to access her phone. "You may have killed his girlfriend by declaring Rosewater independent, and I think he fancies himself a tragic lover who will avenge her death with prejudice. Excuse me, I need to make a call. Don't send the men after him before speaking to me. I have specific instructions on how to take him safely."

Lora stares at Jack like he has betrayed her.

"Don't," says Jack. "I'm not in the mood."

"Sir, I didn't say anything," says Lora.

"That's what I'm not in the mood for."

"What would you like me to do, sir?"

"I want you to arrange bank transfers. Money to all the ward councillors."

"For what service?"

"Bribes, Lora. We are bribing them for their support. We need to ratify the declaration."

"What if they take the money and still come out against you?"

"Bribes have a second function. Blackmail. We keep the records. Those who will not be bought will be blackmailed."

"And the ones who will not take the money?"

Jack smiles. "Keep a list. I also want you to pay the heads of the radio stations, and the freelancers with influence."

"I'll get to it. Anything else, sir?"

"Yes, I need a journalist, or a writer. Someone needs to write our account of this ... this thing."

"I'll drum up some names, sir."

"Thanks. Lora?"

"Sir?"

"I'm sorry. I think we need her."

"You are not required to agree with me, sir."

"When you start to use words like 'required' I know you're angry."

Lora is expressionless. "You have larger problems than my emotional state, sir. Focusing on them is an indulgence you can't afford at this time."

"Okay, to be continued. I want it noted that I apologised."

"Your wife wants you, sir," says Lora.

"Now? Is it important?"

She shrugs as she walks away. She never shrugs at him like that. Jack hates it when she is angry.

Coincidentally, when he returns to his office, one of his wife's advertisements is playing on the flatscreen.

She sits there with liquid eyes and perfect hair, staring soulfully at the viewer with a sincerity that some might think is an act, but Jack knows to be real. After all this while he still feels that tug on the heart when he sees her, even a 2D image like this.

"Hello. I am Hannah Jacques. As we speak there are over two hundred thousand alternatively animated individuals in the city, and this is a conservative estimate. A small percentage are cared for by relatives but the vast majority are left wandering the streets, sequestered in prisons or special wards in the hospitals, sold into sexual slavery, used for sport or allowed to roam the bushes on the outskirts. These people are our husbands, our wives, our fathers, our mothers, our people. We cannot forget them. We cannot throw them away. The charity Not Gone works to find suitable accommodation and placements for people like this. We provide food and shelter and a loving environment, but we can always do more. Call the number below and donate freely. You never know what will happen by the next Opening."

Alternatively animated? Is reanimate out of favour as a term? In some quarters Jack knows they are called undead, and in the most recent hate crime against them four teenagers had set one on fire, all the while singing the Fela Kuti song "Zombie".

He calls Hannah.

224

"Darling?"

"How's the day going?" she asks.

"Do not make me recount the horror. It's going to get worse. I had to make a bargain with a witch, and not the good kind."

"Poor baby. Have you eaten?"

"Yes." Lie.

"Jack, I need to know if you have a plan for the welfare of the reanimates."

"Not the alternatively animated?"

She sighs. "That stuff is scripted by Not Gone. I have to say what I'm told, you know that."

"Who came up with it?"

"I don't know, one of the Not Gone drones. Olu. I don't know. So, do you have a plan?"

"Can this wait?"

"With the flooding and who knows what else? They are dying now."

"They are already dead."

Silence. This is a long-standing discussion in their marriage and the country at large, with no real consensus predominating.

Jack sighs. "I'm sorry. I know, I know, they draw breath. I get it. But you need to understand my position."

"What is your position?"

"My first responsibility has to be to ... the conventionally animated. Then I'll get to the reanimates. Fair?"

"We will discuss this again, husband."

I cannot catch a break with the women in my life today.

After the call he washes his hands. On this occasion he uses a cream heavy in lanolin but with no fragrance. He still instinctively puts his hands to his nose just afterwards. They shake. His reflection has a beard, but he does not have the time or inclination to shave. What started as artifice has taken root as necessity.

The developments bother him. He hadn't expected the flood, even though after the fact it seems logical and the kind of thing he would do. The hole in the dome disturbs Jack the most. The alien is the largest part of his strategy. If the president has a weapon that can kill it, or harm it, then Rosewater might as well surrender. He starts to think of getting Hannah to safety, maybe send her to India or Dubai. The real problem is there's no way to surprise the enemy. The defence army is not attacking Nigeria, it's defending Rosewater, a reactive position, and in combat terms, weak. The alien would have kept the balance.

Jack hopes this Kaaro is as useful as Alaagomeji seems to think, but he now has to look at a situation where he depends exclusively on troops, drones and robots. Taiwo, the godfather, has been good to his word. He has complete control over the rest of the criminal class and is like a general in his own right. There have been ten murders attributable to criminals competing for control with Taiwo, according to Dahun. Not all villains take to organised crime, and will not obey anyone. They are accepting the military training, though.

"What are you going to do when the war is over and you have crooks with truncated special-forces training?" asks Dahun.

Jack has no answer. This is one of those situations where he will have to solve that problem at that time.

His phone reminds him to power-nap. He ignores it. He has the feeling everything is slipping from his control, and resists the urge to wash his hands again. Instead, he reads fragments of Suetonius and the writings of Cicero, which he contrives to paraphrase for a coming speech.

His office tells him someone is at the door, shows him it is Alaagomeji, and he permits the door to open. She is alone.

"Where is the man tasked with keeping an eye on you?" asks Jack.

"You keep forgetting who I am. *The hunting dog does not teach the leopard how to catch prey.* Let's stop wasting time discussing amateurs. You need to send a team to blow up the dam, otherwise the flooding will continue."

"I had thought of this."

"I've listened to my messages. My ... agent is caught in the flood. We need her for two reasons. One, she has something of value to the alien, and two, we'll have some leverage over Kaaro."

"Wait, doesn't he work for you?"

"If he did, I'd simply order him to come here and not send murderers after him. Don't be dim. How long do you plan to stay here?"

"'Here'?"

"Surely you know this mansion will be a target for bombing?"

"It's a siege situation," says Jack. "This isn't a shooting war."

"Not yet," says Alaagomeji. "Give it time."

Excerpt from *Kudi*
by Walter Tanmola

It was Sandrine, and even in the dim light Christopher could tell that her eyes were wide and there was a slight tremor in her hand.

"He's gone," she said. "He went out the window."

"Let me ... give me a minute." Christopher dressed and followed her outside, into the hotel next door, and to the room where Sulaiman was supposed to be sequestered.

"He kept saying 'ana araby, ana araby', over and over, and when he stopped I thought he had finally gone to sleep," she said.

The curtains flapped in the night breeze, the glass of the window absent. Christopher checked the floor and looked out. No fragments. It looked like someone had installed a window frame, but no actual window.

The wall was warm on that side.

"It's not my fault. Nobody said he was a flight risk." She had the hint of a whine in her voice.

Sulaiman used to be a slave. He was liberated, unlike most of the modern slaves who benefited from the mass-manumissions of 2032. He was set to give evidence and they were babysitting him. Nigeria loved to house at-risk individuals in Rosewater because it was not a legal entity, and therefore the usual human rights opposition to torture could be ... overlooked while any damage done could be healed in an Opening. They like to use local talent, which is how Christopher came to be part of the detail. Emeka had called him a traitor.

Christopher's watch had been uneventful and Sandrine had yawned and barely listened to the report.

"Do you know that language?" asked Sandrine.

"It's Arabic," said Christopher. "I quit."

He dropped his ID and backed out of the room.

"Wait." Sandrine had both hands on the door frame. "What was he saying? What does it mean?"

"It means 'I am an Arab'." But if the Arabs found Sulaiman or if they were the ones who took him, they would flay him alive.

Christopher lit a cigarette and sought out Kudi. Her bright coloured hair and her loud personality would make her easier to find. There would be crowds to fight through, but he could do that. Where Kudi was, Emeka would be.

And it was Emeka he wanted.

Chapter Twenty-Seven

Anthony

The plant creature is still alive and ignores all of Anthony's blows to its head and chest area. The fall damaged them both, but not enough. Two of the six wings are off, scattered inside the dome. Anthony bit a further one off and has torn his mouth on the spines. His teeth are exposed to the air and flaps of flesh dangle. His knuckles are exposed and bloody from punching, but that doesn't stop him. He directs pulses of dopamine to surge with every hit and endorphins to dull the pain. Adrenaline to keep him awake.

The head is a pulpy green mass, but it still moves energetically. Where the creature lies on the mossy ground it causes lesions. The leaves sink into Wormwood's flesh. Anthony calls on the electric elementals, and they come, flowing down the dome, along the ground and into the leaf-creature, electrocuting it. Anthony suffers too, but it doesn't matter. He fights, as his body breaks down. The creature does not stop, continues to sink, takes Anthony with it. As they descend, it becomes impossible to get leverage to strike. Anthony feels something rise psychically, and Wormwood responds with a mental scream that sonically ruptures eardrums and mentally drives everything sentient insane with pain. Anthony adjusts, repairs what he can of his eyes and sees that the plant is unaffected. The pit goes deeper still, and Anthony fears they will reach critical parts of Wormwood without stopping the plant angel.

He changes the composition of his gastric acid and stomach lining, then he belches it on to the creature. The corrosive works, and defoliates the creature, which unravels and rots. The acid burns Anthony from the inside and his heart stops, followed by his brain seconds later.

In that place where Anthony dwells before a new body is ready.

Longer here this time, longer than he has ever spent. This gives him time to examine where he is. He thinks it might be the original Anthony's body, still in the core, in the centre of Wormwood, which might account for the low perception.

He can feel Wormwood.

Rather, he can feel a delirious, suffering presence, no coherent thoughts, wounded, mentations spiralling off into the incomprehensible. Is Wormwood dying?

Are we dying?

He gets no answer from Wormwood. He has no impression that his new body has even progressed beyond the ten-cell stage. There is some access to the xenosphere and he finds that some of the people within the dome are dead, some from the initial impact scattering toxic spores, others by electrocution, a few from brain overload when Wormwood screamed. There is no healing just yet. Wormwood's functions all appear to have shut down and the people are panicked.

ARE WE DYING?

[faint response, unclear]

HOW CAN I LOOK AFTER YOU?

231

[not words, concepts, ideas, remove body of leaf-creature, purging spores already, kill weed/strain/antagonist, in sorrow, in agony]

Build me a body, brother. I know what to do.

[expletive equivalent]

That's the spirit.

The clean-up is sombre, and Wormwood completely vents the air and creates a new atmosphere within the dome. The healing is slow, and the barrier is weaker than it has ever been. The pit does not heal, and it looks like a cauterised gunshot injury. The people are uncertain, their worldview shaken, looking to Anthony for cues. For his part he knows that the weed has to be destroyed. Strain-516 has to be completely eradicated. It is time to involve the humans.

He will walk among them again.

As for the host, he cannot see that as a priority at this time. Survival first. The Homian transfer protocol will have to wait.

He enters the xenosphere fully. The dark patches are more pervasive and cohesive, while the xenosphere is more broken up, almost as if Strain-516 is absorbing or taking territory. Stupid to include this in the make-up of footholders, poor design. Or perhaps there is something about Earth's environment that promotes 516's growth. None of this is helped by it bonding with a complete lunatic who seems filled with hate. The humans in the xenosphere are unaware and simply absorbed into the blackness. From their perspective, there is no difference except in the quality of their occasional nightmares.

Molara is waiting for him.

"Ready to talk?" she asks. This time she is a giant butterfly with no humanoid characteristics.

"That is not what I had in mind, but I'm listening."

"Your footholder is done, mortally wounded. I can activate one of the others and commence transfer on another tectonic plate."

"If you could do that, you would have already."

She bats the wings faster. "Respect for you."

"Don't patronise me, Molara."

"All right, what comes up in the meetings with the Chief Scientist on Home is for us to allow you to fail, so we can know what does not work. When we shift focus to the next largest footholder, which is embedded on the Pacific Plate under Samoa, we'll not make the same mistakes."

"I see."

"You don't agree."

"Nothing wrong with the African Plate."

"This has nothing to do with plate tectonics."

"Then what? Yes, I need help. If we all put our heads together we could stop this strain. It's probably in the other footholders, dormant until you activate them. Besides, Wormwood still—"

"You're still using the name the humans gave it?"

"Just shut up and watch me fail, then," says Anthony. "You can chronicle my mistakes."

"You're angry. I'm surprised, little human avatar, because this is your function: to die for the greater good of Homians. This is your function and mine. Your footholder must have kept a lot more of the human in you than usual, which makes sense because they fuck everything up."

"You—"

"You shut up. My job will be over when the last Homian has transferred, then what do you think will happen? We are constructs, biological and psychic constructs, engineered to a purpose, after which we are deactivated. This is as it should be. Stop whining and set to."

"And the host?"

"The host is considered contaminated, lost. We'll start the process anew in the Pacific. Allow this … drama to play out, make sure all the information makes it to the engineers on the server farm moon, then shut everything down. And don't be a fucking baby about it."

She wafts off on the psychic thermals of broken relationships, flooding fallout and impending chemotherapy.

Anthony hates her, but what he hates most is that she's right. If he must fail, however, he will fail brightly, a supernova. But first, contact humans for help. He knows just the one.

He starts looking for Kaaro.

Chapter Twenty-Eight

Kaaro

Kaaro spoons the bespoke dog food from the saucepan into Yaro's bowl. The dog starts eating even before the first lumps stop moving.

"Slow down! Savour the taste, you ingrate. I spent hours on that."

Yaro continues to scoff down the food, eyes occasionally flicking up to his master, but generally looking at the food. Kaaro places the saucepan in the sink and runs some water into it, after which he squirts some washing-up liquid and stirs. He opens the fridge, selects a beer and closes the door.

"Penultimate bottle," says the fridge.

"Fuck you," says Kaaro. "I know. I can count to two."

When Yaro finishes the meal he laps from his water bowl, then pads over to Kaaro's feet and sits down, crossed paws, like he's waiting for instructions.

"Don't fart. I swear to God, I'll turn you into a rug."

His phone rings. Japhet Eurohen, his old new boss. This is his third call, so it must be important. Good. Ignoring it is so much more satisfying.

He scratches Yaro's back. The dog twists his neck and licks Kaaro's fingers. Sleep will follow and Kaaro will have to creep out of the kitchen.

Kaaro's forearm beeps and a voice screeches through.

"Kaaro, ah-ah, ore wa! Why don't you want to speak to me, now?" Eurohen. How the hell?

"How are you—"

"Overrides, Kaaro. You'd be surprised what we can do these days. Stop trying to hang up, it won't work."

"I wasn't trying to hang up." Kaaro tries to hang up. "What do you want?"

"I'm calling on behalf of the president."

"Get to the point, Japhet, what do you want?"

"The president wants to know if you will do your duty in the coming troubles between Nigeria and Rosewater."

"There is no duty. I don't work for S45 any more, Japhet. You know that."

"Your duty as a Nigerian, Kaaro."

"Hmmm. I don't know about that."

"What do you mean?"

"Well, was I really a Nigerian to start with? Just because I happened to be born within the arbitrary boundaries that the British set up, I'm supposed to take on a citizenship? That's just an accident of biology. Being here, in Rosewater, now, that's an accident as well."

"So you won't answer when your country calls?"

"Have you not been listening? I'm saying Rosewater's my country now."

There is the sound of swallowing on the other side. Kaaro tries every combination of buttons to shut the call down.

"We will remember, Kaaro."

"Yes, yes, whatever. Can you hang up or tell me how to hang up? It's my nap time and my dog needs his beauty sleep."

Eventually, after huffing and puffing, Eurohen disconnects. Kaaro sends a text to Bad Fish asking for a fortification to stop this kind of intrusion. He gets no response. Yaro is asleep on the kitchen floor. Kaaro steps off the stool and makes his way to the bathroom. When he comes out, Oyin Da is in the hallway. He hasn't seen the Bicycle Girl – fugitive, supposed terrorist, dome-dweller – in over a year and she looks harried, except for her eyes, which are calculating as usual.

"Kaaro, there are people coming for you. Run."

With that she disappears.

He whistles for Yaro, and opens a hidey-hole he had dug into the foundations of the property. Yaro squirrels away inside, and Kaaro closes the latch.

"Windows, one-inch gap," he tells the room. He waits for ten seconds, as the xenoforms infiltrate the filtered air of his flat, then he enters the xenosphere.

There are two of them, armed, a few yards away from the front door, wearing suits. Kaaro doesn't know who they are, but doesn't care. He locks every neural pathway in both of their brains in the on position. They drop to the ground and start convulsing. One of them yelps with each muscle contraction and the other wets his pants.

Kaaro comes out into the physical world. Feeling like a bad taste in the mouth, barking coming from Yaro's hole.

Too easy.

"Security cam," he asks the house. "All directions."

All the feeds are jammed.

Definitely too easy. I need eyes.

He sits on the floor, closes his eyes. Back in the xenosphere. He flies out, his consciousness split in many directions, looking for eyes he can borrow. He finds a child, a reanimate, and what the child sees Kaaro sees.

Not good. There are six soldiers creeping towards the house. They are wearing skin-tight assault suits and have gas masks with oxygen tanks. No part of their skin is exposed to the air, therefore they are invisible to the xenosphere. The first two were decoys, then, feints. This is the real thing. Prepared by someone who knows his talents.

"Kaaro!"

Shit, they're not even hiding any more. Simply yelling through the door.

"Kaaro, come out. Your government needs you."

No point lying. "Did Japhet send you?"

Kaaro is surprised at this show of strength. He thinks of Japhet as an invertebrate. He reaches but cannot find the soldiers in the xenosphere, not a single gap. Professionals. He turns on the juice. He finds more reanimates. They are like empty vessels, hollow men, voids begging to be filled by Kaaro. On instinct, he enters those wells and ...

And they open their eyes, flooding Kaaro with data from all directions, a panoramic 3D view of the tableau. The black-clad attackers stepping over their convulsing comrades, suppressed rifles pointed at the doors and windows. Kaaro makes the reanimates move closer so he can see better, but then he realises he can make them move, and if he can make them move, he can make them attack.

"Oh, you guys, watch this, *watch this*!" says Kaaro.

He makes himself a beacon for the reanimates, draws them to his door. The squad notice and start to shoot them, but they're spooked because it's unexpected. They are here to get a retired sensitive, not clean up after an Opening. They work as they are trained, shooting the centre mass of the reanimates, but this makes no difference. Thirty reanimates now. Thirty-five. Kaaro did not expect so many.

It is now close-quarters, a hand-to-hand and small-arms fight, with bayonets and daggers, too near to use rifles. One attacker goes down among a cloud of fists and headbutts. Sporadic gunfire before the others are engulfed. Kaaro can feel each and every one of them. He feels the bullet wounds as pinches. All of the reanimates he controls appear with him in the xenosphere. They're like drones. Those shot in the head blink out; brain destroyed, no other way to control them.

—but what if you—

Stick to the matter at hand. They have removed the weapons. Some perish when the chip synchronisation fails and the weapons explode. They rip off the armour piece by piece. Collectively, they rip off limbs, and the courtyard is a mess of blood. When there are no more enemies to kill, they stand still, waiting, facing the house like an altar at which they worship a god of reanimates. Yaro starts to howl. Kaaro lets him out of the cubbyhole and strokes him.

Yet more reanimates arrive, and Kaaro does not know how to shut off the signal he started. He feels no guilt in killing the soldiers. Fuck them. It's not that he doesn't understand remorse. He does. He just doesn't feel that people who come to kill him should be spared. He feels like phoning Japhet and screaming, *Fuck you I killed them all, ha ha*, down the phone.

Vultures gather overhead, and after two circuits of the killing field, five descend. Kaaro knows they are COBs and orders the reanimates to capture, kill and dismember them. The others overhead keep their distance. Kaaro hates not knowing who is watching, but he can assume that at least S45 is surveying his handiwork.

He searches the bodies for credentials, finds nothing, which is odd.

He pings Bad Fish.

Shortly after, his phone rings.

"What?" Bad Fish seems to be in a perpetual bad mood. Or maybe he just doesn't like Kaaro. Probably the latter.

"I have some soldiers here, dead soldiers. Can't find any ID chips."

"And you want ... ?"

"I want you to look at them and tell me who they are."

"You are an asshole. Give me a second."

Kaaro has a fix on certain minds, and Bad Fish is one of them. He knows what the hacker does with a bank of ID chips and tinkering with satellites and drones. It is amazing that nobody has executed Bad Fish yet, but then he probably covers his tracks better than anyone in the world. He has acolytes who worship him as the tech-god of the future.

"Beloved," says Bad Fish. "These little piggies are mercenaries."

Huh.

Still, the president could be using them as proxies to avoid culpability, but that's not his style. He doesn't do subtle.

"They have chips, they're just masked from muggle-tech like yours. Stripping back the layers, I can tell you where they're from."

"And?"

Silence. Bad Fish goes off for two minutes and Kaaro is confused. Should he wait? Then he hears breathing. "Bad Fish?"

"Hmm? Oh, you're still here."

"Motherfucker, I'm waiting for your answer."

"Why? Kaaro, I'm busy here. The world is larger than your problems, you know."

Kaaro counts to ten under his breath. "Where did my six mercenaries come from?"

"They've been here and there, but from the patterns, they've taken flight from the mayor's mansion. Jack Jacques sent them to kill you. Have a nice day and fuck you."

Kaaro pulls out of the xenosphere and calls Aminat. It bounces or doesn't connect or something. He tries through the xenosphere, but cannot find her, which could be anything or nothing. There's flooding. The connections between xenoforms disconnect in adverse weather conditions. Still. He has always hated Jack Jacques, but now … well, now he has reason to kill him.

He leaves the house, ignoring Yaro's whining. Outside, there are over a hundred reanimates, all seeming to stare at Kaaro.

"Troops, I have nothing inspiring to say. Go. Make me proud."

Kaaro feels a mild headache coming on, a tightness around the eyes, but otherwise he's fine. They run away, towards the mansion, while he takes his stripped-down jeep. One of the only hydrocarbon-driven vehicles in Rosewater, it is not vulnerable to someone in power reprogramming it while in motion, or fluctuations in the central power like those electric ones are. He fills the tank from his underground stash of fuel which Aminat always says will consume the house in a ball of flame one day.

He barely remembers how to drive an internal combustion engine, and the lack of an onboard navigational computer confuses him. Traffic is harmonised by each on-board computer being aware of that of other cars. He is an anomaly in the system and several times he either almost hits or is almost hit. After twenty minutes, he is smoother.

Motherfucking Danladi, his trainer when he was with S45, used to say fleeing is stupid. *Enemy at your back? No plan?* He'd shake his mighty head. *You can step back to create the desired striking distance, but you do not run.*

Which is bullshit. Kaaro has run many times and is still alive, which is more than he can say for his fellow sensitives. All dead. Kaaro is the last of them, the last of the humans with access to the xenosphere, or at least access to the information. There were other humans with different skills conferred by the xenosphere.

But Jacques is a capitulator, a ball of green snot, a gigantic asshole. Kaaro will run from many things, but he will never run from Jack Jacques, and if the man is stupid enough to come after him, well, this is one enemy he will not leave at his back.

Interlude: 2067

Eric

It's uncanny that I can still find my way around Ona-oko. There are paved roads for the most part, but it seems they are based on the footpaths that we established back in 2055. I'm standing on a street called Ronbi. I don't know who it's named after, but I can tell you that it was the first place in Rosewater to have a cement-block wall. You probably already know there were tents and shacks. The materials for those structures came from everywhere, being dragged in by individual people for their own use. There were no shops or stores, but a kind of barter thrived, what would later turn into eru, a primitive credit system. There was a lot of stealing as well, and I'm not talking food. If you had six-inch nails holding up your structure, a thief would extract one or two during the night, not enough to collapse your shack, but enough to make it wobble. The rampant theft of nails led a guy called Solo to build the first wall. It was a miserable thing, itself made of stolen cement blocks, but Solo's wall stands as the first permanent structure of Rosewater. Solo built a wooden shack using his wall as a stabiliser, but someone else used the other side of the wall. These two structures became the first street because people naturally aggregated where others already were.

Today, Ronbi Street has the least modern houses, partly because those who arrived first were the most deprived. The later arrivals were middle-class folk who already had money, or at least the potential for money. Places like Ubar got taken by the government and Atewo became a suburb. But it all started here. I'm trying to locate a rendezvous point and bump into two Rastas while not watching where I'm going. I apologise, but they may not even have noticed me.

The house I aim for is a bungalow, plastered but not painted, with a courtyard but no gate. The wind sweeps the yard, lifts dust towards the east. It's cold and maybe moist, going to rain at some point, I know it. There is Arabic pressed into the gable. A dog sleeps across the entrance, which is open. I step over it.

"*Salaam alekum*," I say. My words echo down a dark hall.

"*Alekum asalaam*," comes the reply, a man's voice, but I don't know from which room.

There's a smell, a residue of incense, but the air is still, in contrast to the rowdiness of the wind outside. The largest single human being I have ever seen walks towards me from the other end of the hall. The lights flick on as he comes, motion sensors activated. He's tall, with his head barely clearing the ceiling, and he's broad. He's Polynesian, Samoan from what I read in his head – but Nigerian through and through. The man stops right in front of me, and he says nothing. He's waiting.

"Your name is Timu," I say. "And the pass phrase is Malietoa Tanumafili II."

"You're amazing. Welcome to the resistance," he says. "Follow me."

They have been told that I will arrive and know their pass code without them supplying it to S45. Parlour tricks. I can't see where I'm going because Timu's back is so broad, but I pick up his impression of me, which is benign, and the fact that he is a decent man, gentle and lonely. At the far end of the hall there are steps leading down, and at the landing there is someone waiting. He's black and has his shirt off and is covered in linear scars of varying lengths, from a few centimetres to a foot.

"I'm Nurudeen Lala. Call me Nuru," says the scarred man.

"Eric."

Timu slouches away, and I can't help staring.

"He came here in 'sixty-four with uncontrolled diabetes. An imam sent him here, and once cured, he decided to spend the rest of his life memorising the Noble Quran and teaching in the Ile Keu down the road. Don't ask me the logic. Your packages are right this way."

"Packages?"

"They arrived a few days ago, keyed to your ID, I'm told. We didn't touch them."

I look inside and hide my shock. Someone must really hate Jacques.

"When and where?" I ask.

"Not tonight," he says. "Tonight, we boogie."

I think he means going to a club and dancing, which reminds me of the last time I was in Rosewater and would have been freaky, but, no, to Nuru, "boogie" means sexual intercourse. And when I find out the rest of the details, I almost kill the one man who has everything I need.

Nuru takes me to a building I think is a brothel, but even when I'm declining, I see ... something. So I read the girls one

245

after the other and . . . I blow up at Nuru. It's a rape camp, the girls – and they are girls, not women – have been rounded up by the resistance to "comfort" the fighters.

"If you don't wish to partake, don't," says Nuru.

"Release them," I say.

"You are not from here; you do not understand."

I draw a gun, or at least, he thinks I have a gun. It's manipulation of his visual cortex, but I can't keep it going for long. "Release all the women and children."

It happens too fast. His scars split open like mouths and tentacles emerge. There is a wetness, like lubrication, that makes their touch disgust me, but pain overcomes that. He takes my gun hand and throws me off my feet. His mind is messy while he controls the tentacles, and I could use my ability to predict where he will send them, but it will take time to get used to.

I'm still trying to decide where to take the confrontation when it starts to rain. Flood waters make the argument a moot point. We have to take the equipment to high ground to avoid water damage. While we work, I see Nuru's mind. He considers himself an artist, and he co-authored his current body with the alien over years of Openings. The cuts, the scaffolding for the tentacles, the healing, the failures and re-cutting, he is the uber-reconstructed. And he has made others.

But I manage to drop a seed of doubt into Nuru's head, and it blossoms into regret.

The rape camp is dismantled before the waters rise about two feet. I still plan to report it to my superiors.

After my business with Jack Jacques.

Chapter Twenty-Nine

Aminat

The flood water has not receded, but it hasn't got worse either, for which Aminat is grateful. She and Alyssa are in a canoe; she paid half of her eru for it, the owner navigating the new currents to the new bank. The homunculus drowned in the night. At least, they assumed so as it had not been seen or heard from in hours. Some of the poor folk cling to rooftops and wood, with improvised flotation devices like inflated inner tyre tubing. There is no rain, but it is cloudy and there is a fine mist that leaves the skin and clothing wet after a few minutes. All kinds of vessels mobilised by a community that has lost everything, ferrying people back and forth, meagre belongings clinging like fungus.

The news is dire. All over Nimbus, there is talk of the government puncturing the dome, and that fills Aminat with genuine fear.

Incoming call, from Femi. For a split second Aminat does not wish to answer, but she resists this. She uses her palm this time, to keep Alyssa from listening in.

"Hello?" That calm, assured voice. Bitch.

"You took your sweet time," says Aminat. "I take it you got my messages."

"Mind your tone, Aminat. Remember who you're talking to."

"Don't. You have no idea the kind of time I've had."

"Did you sleep in a cell? Because I did."

"I suppose we've both had interesting times."

"Report."

Training and habit brings it all out of Aminat, about the car chase, about Alyssa Sutcliffe, about the murder attempt on her, about the death of her friend Efe, about the roll-up and the homunculus and, finally, the flood.

"You've had a busy time."

"Really?"

"Don't vex my spirit, woman, I know it's hard being cut off, but you're an agent, not a soldier. A soldier has to function with orders, but for you, orders are like suggestions. You have to—"

"Are you apologising?"

"I am not. I wasn't in touch for good reason. What's the state of Mrs Sutcliffe?"

Alyssa is sunning herself in the rocking boat despite the cloudy weather, as if they are out for some fun on the river on a Saturday afternoon. Her skin is covered with xeno-arthropods.

"Satisfactory," says Aminat.

"Good. Bring her to the mayor's mansion."

"What? No. That's a bad idea. If this war heats up, federal forces will target it."

"Somewhere you got the impression that we are negotiating, or in conference."

"Ma'am, I'm just saying she will be safer in the sublevels at Ubar, plus there's a lab there with back-ups of my data."

"Understand something, Aminat, this conflict has afforded us opportunities to do what we need to: rid the Earth of this insinuating alien presence. Alyssa is an important player in this. I can send a team to get you."

"No, ma'am."

"What?"

"I don't want to get killed. My best friend is already dead."

"And there will be a reckoning for that, Aminat, but now, today, I need you in here with me."

"Are you and Jacques in league now?"

"Bedfellows, Aminat. Strange ones. You know how it goes."

"I don't trust him."

"I don't think anybody should trust him, but that's not your concern right now. I'll see if I can find a helicopter, a civilian one, don't worry. I'll send you coordinates for the LZ."

"Fine."

"What?"

"Yes, ma'am."

"Good. And Aminat, if for any reason you think you might lose Alyssa or that the enemy will take her, you need to kill her."

"Who is the enemy?"

"Right now? Anybody who is not me."

Before Aminat can say anything else, Femi hangs up. Alyssa is now staring at her from the other end of the boat. The oars hit the water with a hypnotic rhythm and Aminat can smell the sweat from the man behind her.

"This is not water," says Alyssa.

"What isn't water?"

"This mist in the air. It isn't water. I tasted it. It's a chemical."

Aminat sticks out her tongue and immediately feels the artificial bitterness. She hawks and spits over the side. "What the hell is this?"

"I don't know," says Alyssa.

Now that she thinks of it, Aminat sees the mist hanging low over everything. Chemical weapon? Nobody was writhing or dying. Nobody's skin was bubbling with blisters or coming off in sheets. Nobody having a seizure. Nobody coughing.

"We need to get out of this," says Aminat. She turns to the boatman. "Can you go faster?"

He shakes his head, not to refuse, but because he does not understand. She says it again in Yoruba. She makes him head for the nearest shore, which is a muddy bank close to a copse of trees. They get off and plash through until they reach firm land. The boatman stays still until he sees that they have good footing, then he eases back in the direction from which they came.

A hyena man stands watching them from the timberline, holding a leashed, muzzled hyena. The man is lanky and starved, dressed in a tattered dashiki. Aminat is not a fan of hyenas – that walk, the sounds they make, their diet. The man says something in a language Aminat does not understand, but the receding boatman yells, "He said something is coming, and that you are going in the wrong direction."

Yeah, wide berth when walking past him.

They have to find the nearest pump and wash the filth off their skin and hair, then see about getting it analysed. The coordinates for their pick-up arrive. Aminat activates the locator program, a reassuring pulse with a glowing arrowhead on her palm. They have to go through the woods.

"Are you all right?" asks Alyssa.

"Yes, why?" It seems like the first time she's seen Alyssa smile.

"You've been through a lot, done a lot. I just wanted to let you know that we can rest if you want."

"That's nice, and thank you, but we're not anywhere near a place where we can rest just yet. You just follow me and do what I say, Alien Jesus, then we'll be fine."

The forest is full of footpaths and Aminat tries to match their vector with the arrow.

Between the trees there are reanimates, covered in caked mud, moving with purpose, all in the same direction, as if towards a beacon. That never happens. They are probably just fleeing flood water like any other living creature. Aminat puts it out of her mind.

Her forearm glistens with the unknown chemical. She has an instinct to contact Olalekan, then experiences a sharp acid jolt in the heart when she remembers his death. She calls Kaaro, mission protocol be damned. One phone call does not mean S45 is running shit again. Kaaro's phone is out of service or switched off. She calls the house, no answer. She calls the house AI, gives her code and waits.

"Occupants, human," says Aminat.

"Zero vital signs."

"Occupants, human, deceased?"

"Nil."

"Security."

"Integrity intact. Nil house breaches. Multiple ground breaches."

The fear is back. "Number of breaches."

"Sixty-eight."

???

"Casualties."

"Six."

"Visual to my phone."

She can barely breathe while waiting for the feed. Alyssa

251

says something but Aminat ignores it. The feed shows six dead and dismembered ... special forces? They are in grotesque positions, unnatural, difficult to look at. Kaaro is not among them, but then where is he? *Oh, my baby.*

"Aminat."

"What do you want?"

"Look."

In the direction of her finger, looming slowly but surely, a line of seven automatons, loaded for war, aimed at the city. Aminat brings the rifle scope to her eye and examines the bots. Egg-shaped trunk, no treads, quadruped, each just over six feet, with no sign of embossed stars and stripes. China made, which means they have centralised software servers wirelessly transmitted to them. No chance of local disruption. The American ones at least had old firmware and on-board operating systems. You could paralyse the bot by disrupting the code, assuming it didn't riddle you with bullets or blow you up first. The bots in these woods only have enough RAM to run the transmitted software. It also means the Chinese signed off on this excursion, which isn't great for Rosewater.

Shit.

Aminat has trained to fight automatons, but has never used that skill, nor does she have the equipment she trained with. That was just one, and in a controlled environment. Right now, all she has is a conventional firearm, which cannot harm the bots. Short bursts of fire cut the random reanimates in half. The undergrowth may be slowing the bots down, but they're still clocking twenty miles per hour easy. Even if she and Alyssa try to run, the machines will catch up.

"Switch off your ID," says Aminat.

"How?"

"Use the file Bad Fish sent to the phone. It deactivates both the real chip and the cloned ghost chip. Those bots always start from locator chips, before they use motion detection or visual data. That's how they stay away from animals, and that's why they're killing the reanimates. These are extermination bots; they'll kill any humans in their path."

Aminat tests the laser guide from the rifle on her palm.

The bots are going to sense Aminat and Alyssa, no matter what their mission, at this range. Hiding would just be a shorter way to die. Running away would get them shot in the back or grenaded. And the bots' path intersects the route to the landing zone.

"Alyssa, I'm going to try something. If it doesn't work, we're screwed. If there's a manual override, we're screwed. I'm going to draw their attention away from you. If I fall, if I get shot or blown up, run in the opposite direction to the landing zone. I've sent coordinates to your phone." She hands her sidearm to Alyssa. "Don't worry, it won't explode. It'll weigh me down, and I need to sprint. Do you understand?"

"Yes."

"Good. Engage or die, Alyssa. No middle ground."

"Engage or die."

The points of articulation of the bots are vulnerable, but you need a rocket launcher for that. They are about fifty yards out, and there are no reanimates in between. The forest is silent but for the crushed leaves and twigs in their path.

Aminat breaks cover and the three bots closest to her turn antennae in her direction, but the heads still point to the city. The carpet of fallen leaves does not protect and the mud sucks at her feet, which changes the speed Aminat can run at compared with what her plan demands. *Run, run.* She remembers track and field and her coach. *It is not in your muscles or your trainers or the tarmac or the crowd. It is in your head.* Aminat pushes herself, and pushes further, but it is still like running in a dream. She hears the air displacement as the bot fires a ranging grenade that falls short, but still knocks her over. A shower of wet leaves and clumps of earth fall to the ground around her.

Lucky.

It wasn't aiming yet, dummy, it was finding you.

Aminat aims the laser at the bot and prays she has enough time to send the signal. Three short pulses, three long pulses, then three short ones again.

dot dot dot, dash dash dash, dot dot dot

At first nothing happens and Aminat is sure she has fucked it up. It splits apart three seconds later and she is able to duck before part of its forelimb swishes past and smashes into a tree. The blast takes out the bot next to it, but the other five start firing. From Aminat's left she hears gunfire. Alyssa shoots at the bots, bullets bouncing uselessly off their hulls, and a second or two later they decide to split forces. Aminat aims her laser and the one that stayed focused on her blows up, this time the head going high towards the canopy, while shrapnel embeds in trees. The others are heading for Alyssa. What the fuck is wrong with her? Aminat told her to go the other way.

Aminat tries to send the same self-destruct signal to the leading automaton, *dot dot dot, dash*— But it weaves, and the others block the beam, although it's impossible to tell if they do this being wise to the trick. When it looks like they might open fire, the ground rises and bursts open, flinging soil and rocks in every direction, and uprooting tress. Both Aminat and Alyssa cover their heads. A bough hits Aminat's arm, knocking away the laser sight.

The roll-up springs free, rears up to a height rivalling the trees, and shakes itself from side to side to remove debris. The bots do not hesitate, but redeploy around the new target, ignoring Aminat and Alyssa. They spread out, surrounding the alien. The roll-up directly falls on one, smashing it into spare parts. The others open fire, focusing on the same spot, and the roll-up twitches with pain and its mouth yawns open, though it does not scream.

"No, don't hurt it!" says Alyssa. She leaps up from the defensive crouch, narrowly missed by a tangle of flaming wires flying through the air.

What the fuck, we should be running. "Alyssa, get the fuck out of the way. We are leaving!"

But of course a part of Aminat feels that if Alyssa dies, a large part of the problem goes away. She feels along her path, searching for the laser sight. She finds her gun where Alyssa seems to have dropped it.

The roll-up turns on its axis and takes one of the robots into its open mouth. The jaws crash down and a flurry of sparks escapes before the sound of a muted explosion forces smoke and scrap metal out of its mouth. The roll-up writhes, its legs twitch.

"No," Alyssa says. There are tears streaming down her face.

The last bot releases what seems like all its ordnance at the roll-up, including machine guns and small explosives. The alien's movements are disorganised, and some of its limbs have been cut off by bullets. It bleeds a dark green fluid. It is curiously silent.

In all this the bot is relatively stationary. Aminat finds the laser and, from a prone position, flashes out the Morse code on its hull. It explodes in a fireball that singes the canopy and sends a heatwave in all directions.

The roll-up falls and is still, a pool of its blood growing underneath it and mixing with the mud and leaves.

Alyssa starts towards the alien.

Aminat grabs her hand and drags her away. "The people who sent these will send more. Come with me now."

The landing zone is the Funmilayo Ransome-Kuti Sports Centre, on the football field. Aminat doesn't know if it's Femi's joke about her past as a sports medallist, but she's past caring.

They flop on to the grass in the centre so that Aminat can see any attackers as long as they aren't snipers. Her muscles are rigid as she pushed both of them hard on the hike away from the battlefield.

Lying flat beside her, Alyssa says, "Who is Funmilayo Ransome-Kuti?"

"Was. She was the person who fought, advocated and pushed for the women's vote in Nigeria. We didn't have universal adult suffrage back in colonial times. She also fought the British authority's proxy ruler, the Alake of Egbaland, to abolish differential taxes for women and won. She got banned from travel during the Cold War because she used to visit the Eastern Bloc countries and was probably socialist. She won the Lenin Peace Prize, so that isn't conjecture. She was the first Nigerian woman to drive a car, and she was the mother of the famed musician, Fela."

"What was the Cold War?"

The sound of rotor blades cutting air interrupts, and a chopper arrives from the east.

Aminat won't get in at first. She insists that all guns be thrown out. Then she asks that hunting knives and other items that could be improvised weapons be jettisoned. When she is satisfied she checks the helicopter before bringing Alyssa on board. Too many near-death experiences in a few days come with paranoia.

As they soar above the city, through the head mic, Alyssa asks, "How did you use that pointer to kill the robots?"

"It's not a pointer, it's a laser sight," says Alyssa. "All the war bots have self-destruct sequences. The usual controllers don't want their tech falling into enemy hands. There's also on-board data that might implicate people in war crimes. There are sensors all over the bots. I sent them their sequence and they obeyed."

"So it would never have worked without the roll-up?"

"It was never supposed to work, not really. I thought I would be able to take out two of them at the most. One blew up just because of proximity. It was a stunt. It was supposed to buy you time to get away."

"You would die for me?"

"Don't get out your engagement ring and propose, sunshine, it was orders." Aminat looks out of the window. Yes, her orders are the opposite of what she just said, but it's not like S45 or Femi have been either forthcoming or trustworthy. And working with Jack now. What the fuck was that? Aminat would kill for self-defence, but she did not like being put in a position where she would have to kill Alyssa in cold blood. Besides, she likes her alien Jesus. If nothing else, the girl was useful as a fly trap. No, fuck S45, fuck Femi and fuck Jack Jacques. She would deliver Alyssa, go get Kaaro and get the hell out of Rosewater. She'll figure something out when she gets to Lagos.

"It was orders," she repeats, maybe to Alyssa, maybe to herself.

Chapter Thirty

Jacques

Jack wants her to leave, but believes her to be essential, therefore he swallows the bile in the back of his throat and forces himself to smile. Smiles are cheap, and he has peddled them for years. He partakes of the glass of water, savours the cold fluid going down his throat, and closes his eyes for a few seconds, needing the peace.

Femi does all her work standing up, on her phone, looking fabulous. He muses that she is different from his wife in that she lacks humanity. She could be a living doll, or a perfect statue, whereas Hannah is warm, with softer edges. Jack knows he can never love a person this ruthless, this calculating. Which is okay, because she would never prefer a person like him. Actually, it's unclear if she even prefers anybody.

"Mr Mayor."

He opens his eyes and she is standing right in front of him, one hand on the desk.

"She's on her way, and she has the Sutcliffe woman."

"We need her because . . . ?"

"Alyssa or Aminat?"

"Either. Both. Just tell me."

"I already did, Mr Mayor, try to keep up. We need Aminat to control Kaaro when he comes in. We need Kaaro to get the alien onside. And we need Alyssa to force the alien if that becomes necessary."

Jack points to some papers to his left. "The British High Commission has something to say about Alyssa Sutcliffe. Her husband is kicking up dust and they want assurances. Why should the alien give a fuck about her?"

"Because she is, I believe, the first of—"

Dahun barges in, right hand full of semiautomatic, face grim. At first Jack wonders if the man has taken money from the president and is here to kill, but Dahun's gaze is directed to Femi and she backs away from him, although her face shows no fear.

"Who is this Kaaro guy? You tell me now, or I swear to Ogun, I will fill you with metal."

"I already told you who he is."

"You said he was retired."

"He is."

"You said he was a coward."

"He is."

"You said he was harmless."

"I didn't say that. I said I'd tell you what to do to render him harmless."

"Skin-tight rubber suits, oxygen tanks, antifungal cream."

"Yes. He can't access any of his abilities that way."

"Then why are my men dead?"

Femi for the first time is speechless. "I ... he's ... how many—"

"All of them. All of them are dead, you fucking idiot. What did you do? What kind of mistake is this? I have to call their spouses and children. I have to promise the families that they died for something. What the hell is wrong with you?"

"I don't understand. Kaaro doesn't use deadly force. He can cause pain, but ... and he shouldn't have been able to get through the defences."

"He didn't."

"Then who—"

Dahun conjures a plasma video, the mission record from the cam of one of the men.

"Those are reanimates," says Jack.

"I know," says Dahun.

"I don't understand. Why are they attacking the men?"

"Because your guy – your retired, coward, harmless guy? – he controls them."

"Impossible."

An alarm goes off.

Jack has never seen this many reanimates in one place, not when they first appeared in '55, not after any of the yearly Openings since then, not even when he visited the sequestered ones in the prison. And yet, he is meant to believe the evidence of his own eyes: that the entire grounds of his mansion are full of reanimates, that they have surrounded the building and that, though they die at the extra defences Dahun has put up, they keep coming with that steady sacrifice, that stoic expression, that eternal indifference.

They have two feeds, one satellite and a second rotating feed from drones, both generated from plasma fields on Jack's desk. They only had a few minutes of the satellite picture, but played on a loop it shows tiny figures gathering outside the gates and walls, sparse at first, then dense, increasing at an alarming speed. The drone feed on the right shows the current time, first from straight up, then from drones flying the perimeter.

From far out it looks like a protest, a million-man, million-woman march, with seething crowds all facing the gate, hammering on it, or just standing still, waiting. Budding off from the main mass at the gate are two arms making their way around the walls in each direction, but also trying to scale the barriers. From above it looks like the crowd is trying to hug the mansion. When the drones get closer the feed shows that when a turret or sniper kills one of the reanimates, the others lift the body out of the way and immediately someone from behind fills the gap. They shove against the gate in numbers, and they clamber over each other.

A few dozen make it through the barriers and the fusillade of rifle fire, but so far the flame-throwers have been able to stop them from getting into the building, but fuel supplies are not infinite. Bodies are piling up and forming their own barrier.

Another thing Jack observes is that even when shot, they continue unless their head is completely destroyed.

More of them arrive from every direction, a trickle, but constant.

"Dahun's right," says Jack. "You have miscalculated, big time."

Femi cannot seem to come up with anything to say, which is just as well, because who knows how the tension in the room will break?

"Can we keep them at bay?" asks Jack.

"I don't know." Dahun holsters the weapon he came in with and strokes his chin.

"That's not the answer I pay you to give me."

"Hey, I'm doing my job. I'm fortifying the city with the bulk of my forces and the ragamuffins that form the Rosewater army. Defending this place wasn't in the script."

"Excuse me?"

"I'm working on it." Dahun leaves.

Blood and ordure start to accumulate and new reanimates skid and slip on the remnants of the old. Jack can hear gunfire now, and the odd crackle of electromagnetic protective shields shorting out. With every reanimate that dies, Jack thinks Hannah is going to kill him. He and his wife are going to argue over this, no matter what the outcome. "Die" may not be the right word for destroyed reanimates, but it's one Hannah likes.

Some little shit called Adeoye Alao has brought a civil case against Jack, arguing that the government of Rosewater is now null and void. Jack suspends the courts till after the war. Dahun has heard rumblings of protests. The local and national press are clamouring for interviews.

This is worse than the Chamber of Commerce meetings. But you have to deal with mundane shit as a leader.

If you live to lead.

A reanimate runs into the barrier and dies from a bullet to the brain.

Femi tries to get Kaaro on the phone. She does not appear to be having a good time.

What day is it? God, he's tired. He really just wants sleep, just a few hours, or days. *All the same to me.* He lets his eyes close, no intention of sleeping, but he has to rest ...

"We need one," says Femi.

Jack wakes with a start. "What do you mean?"

"We need one of the reanimates. He may be able to perceive life through them, through each and every one. If I can just talk to him."

"Talk to him? You already fucked up."

"Suck my labia." She switches to another camera. The most activity is among the reanimates closest to the mansion. The rest seem to be on standby, shifting from one foot to the other. Jack notices that some are lying on the ground, unconscious or dead.

Dahun's voice booms over the alarm. "Close your eyes, flash-bang, flash-bang, in three, two, one."

The detonation is successful in disorienting the reanimates, and is followed by Dahun's men, a flame-thrower unit covered by heavy guns. There are no screams, just twisted, blackened corpses. The advantage does not last as several waves of reanimates crawl over the burned ones and overwhelm the fighting men. Heads explode, and bodies are thrown back with bullet impact, but there are always more reanimates. Always more.

"Breach," says Dahun over the PA. "We have a breach. Go to defensive protocols. We have a breach."

Femi's pistol appears in her hand like a magician's trick. Jack doesn't even bother asking how she got it back. "See if you can capture one alive," she says into her phone.

Outside quadcopters fire rounds into the crowd from different directions. Jack can imagine the PR nightmare already, and this isn't even part of the war.

The national press will flay me alive.

Jack isn't worried that there are reanimates in the building. His office isn't vulnerable to them. He sees that Femi has disrobed and is rubbing hand cream on herself.

"Are you completely insane?" asks Jack.

She hands him a tube. "It's antifungal, Mr Mayor. I don't have time to explain, but this is why it's part of the security protocols. Believe me when I tell you this has to go all over your body."

Jack does as she says, hating the smell and wondering how many showers it will take to get this off. He doesn't have time to check the constituents of the formulation. He finds her staring at his body, though she quickly looks away.

Dahun comes back on the intercom. "I have one alive. Well, kind of alive. Where do you want him?"

"I'll come to you," says Femi. "Tell me where."

"Your old cell."

Jack goes with her, although his bodyguards are unhappy about this.

As they walk down the corridor of orisa, two reanimates run towards them. The statues come alive and the robots inside obstruct the reanimates and restrain them. The pair go limp, all violent intentions leached from them. As Jack and his people walk by, Femi shoots each reanimate in the head.

The captured reanimate is held with four plastic ties and covered by Dahun's machine gun and baleful glare. It's in a bloody school uniform, male, and muddy, as if it has been exhumed, like a murder victim. It strains against the bonds until Jack and Femi come in, then it stops and smiles.

"Mrs Alaagomeji," it says. Its voice sounds like air bubbled through ditch water, and its breath smells that way too.

"I thought you liked to call me 'Femi'". You don't work for me any more, remember?"

"And there's that invertebrate Jack Jacques. Just stay right where you are, Mr Mayor. I've heard dying can be a pleasurable experience towards the end. Euphoria and visions, and the like."

"Why would you want to kill me?" says Jack. "I don't know you."

"We've met, actually, but only one time, and I don't expect you to remember. Femi, unless you sent those soldiers to kill me, I have no quarrel with you. I'll let you leave."

"You killed my men, you abomination," says Dahun. He fires a burst into the thing's left foot, obliterating it.

"Stand the fuck down!" Femi is surprisingly effective and Dahun retreats. "Kaaro, can you see what I'm holding?"

"Looks like an old-style phone."

"It's a remote. If you look up at the sky wherever you're hiding, or use your proxies, I don't care, you'll see a helicopter circling the grounds. Can you see it?"

"Yes."

"Can you see inside it?"

"No."

"Then use your abilities, reach inside. Anything seem familiar to you?"

"—"

Femi smiles. "Aminat's in there."

"And what if that's true?"

"If you don't cease and desist I'm going to blow the helicopter up. You have three seconds."

"Oh, Femi, if Aminat's up there I'm going to—"

"One."

"Seriously—"

"Two."

"Get your—"

"Three."

"*Stop!*"

The reanimate goes limp and the eyes lose focus.

265

Dahun receives some radio reports. "They've stopped all purposeful activities. Some are wandering away. Should we detain them?"

"Why? They're empty of reason. The one we want is Kaaro, and I guarantee he's on his way here." She speaks into the phone. "Land the chopper and come straight up with both of your charges. Have your weapons out and be prepared to fight."

"This is the first thing you've done all day that impresses me," says Jack.

"Stay tuned," she says. *"Aimasiko lo n'damu eda."*

"Where are you going?" asks Dahun.

"To the helipad," says Femi.

"There's still movement out there."

"Is it organised? Showing singleness of purpose?"

"No, but—"

"Thanks for your concern. I'm going."

Jack moves to follow her, but Dahun blocks him. "No, Mr Mayor. You're not doing that."

Before he can respond, Lora comes in. "Sir, Nigeria is spraying rapid defoliants in the south and south-east. Twenty-four, forty-eight hours, our farms and forests will be denuded. They're trying to starve us out."

I would really like to catch a break right now.

That thing Femi said, aimasiko lo n'damu eda – *"the problem with people is not knowing what time it is". Do I know what time it is?*

"Food stores will hold?" asks Jack.

"Maybe a year? Eighteen months on the outside, unless the alien can recover from this. That hole is still in the dome, sir, partially repaired. More worrying is that it's not like the Opening. Nobody outside the dome is getting healed."

On the plasma monitor Femi approaches the helicopter, which has now set down. She leads two women, one black, one white, back to the mansion. The reanimates appear uninterested in them.

"According to our spy master, one of those ladies is the key to solving our problem."

"Oh, so we can all go home, then," said Lora.

"Don't make jokes."

"I wasn't, sir. I actually want to go home."

Jack doesn't know what Lora does at home. After he lobbied for her citizenship, celebrated when she got it, and gave her formal working hours with bonuses and overtime, he has kept firmly out of her personal life. He does know she lives alone, seems to like akpala and highlife music, and uses the gym, an activity that is superfluous, but Jack recognises that he started her on the fitness path. She is also able to self-modify, to rewrite her own code, a feature that Jack was warned against, but still approved.

At times, though, she used "going home" as a euphemism for needing maintenance.

"Want or need, Lora?" Jack asks.

"Want."

"Can it wait?"

"For now."

"Thank you. I need you here."

"What you need is a miracle, sir," says Dahun. "I have news."

What now?

Chapter Thirty-One

Aminat

The helipad has to be cleared of bodies before they can land, and the pilot asks her to be ready to fight if need be. Waiting for them, tiny revolver in her right hand, is Femi Alaagomeji.

The dead don't appear to be enemy combatants, or even trained fighters of any stripe.

"Who are these people?" asks Alyssa.

"I don't know," says Aminat. "Stay with me."

She does not say anything until she is a foot from Femi, then she slaps her superior officer hard across the face. Femi falls to the ground from the force of it, although she does not drop her gun. On her cheek there is an imprint of Aminat's palm.

"I've done a lot of strange things over the last few days, so I guess I deserved that. I have no idea what your particular problem is, Aminat, but that will be your only freebie. Touch me again and—"

Aminat kicks her in the ribs. It's half strength, but with her sporting background, Aminat knows how powerful her legs are. Femi winces.

"You were saying?" Aminat is ready to hit again.

"Baby, leave her alone." She looks around. It's not a voice she recognises, but it is clearly addressed at her. One of the "dead" is staring at her.

"Who ... ?"

"Your boyfriend," says Femi. "He's possessing people now."

"Just reanimates," says the body talking to Aminat. "I'm on my way. Stop beating on Femi. She's tricky."

"She almost got me killed."

"Yes, more than you know, but please stop kicking her. At least leave some for me."

"Kaaro, you asshole, those people weren't sent to kill you. They were sent to escort you," says Femi. "We need your help. Just stand down and come in to talk."

"We're talking now."

"You need to talk to the mayor. He calls the shots."

"You sent people with guns to my house, Femi."

"For your protection. We might not be the only ones looking for you."

"Fine, I'm on my way in. Just be sure that no harm comes to Aminat."

Alyssa says, "I thought the woman was your boss."

"She is," says Aminat. She wants to say she will quit, but she thinks of her brother and knows she will not. "She is."

The reanimate on the ground becomes limp again and Aminat can tell Kaaro's presence has left it. She helps Femi up, prepared for retaliation, but none comes. Femi can be like that, mind on the task, at times above human emotion. It is unclear to Aminat if this is an advantage or not.

She hopes there is running water.

Whatever violence was going on has finished, and armoured soldiers drag corpses to pile up and set fire to. They're well paid because their equipment is top-of-the-line and they don't search the bodies for valuables. They are not Nigerian Army, then.

The strip of the dome she can see is mottled grey and black, and aside from a variegation she has never seen before, there is no inner glow.

"Your skin tastes funny," whispers Kaaro.

"Then why aren't you laughing?" asks Aminat.

"Will you both keep it down? I swear, it's like I never trained either of you," says Femi.

They are in a meeting to which Aminat isn't invited, but Kaaro insists that where he goes, she goes. Jacques, his bodyguard, his military strategist, his assistant, Lora and Femi are present, but Alyssa is elsewhere.

"We'll keep this short. I have a city council crisis meeting."

"Kaaro, you are here because the dome is not functioning and we think the alien is sick. Your job is to find out what's wrong and enlist the creature to our cause."

"And what is that cause, again?" Kaaro asks.

"Survival. We need to survive what's coming. If the alien is dead, there is no point. We might as well surrender. If you don't succeed then we try to barter Alyssa. Which brings us to Femi. You take a team to your headquarters in Ubar, and you sequester Alyssa there, at the same time run the necessary experiments to separate her alien parts from her human parts.

"We have to do this fast. We've received word that high-altitude bombing will start within the next twenty-four hours. Robot border excursions have already occurred, and the ganglia did not fry them. We have to set up the defence of the city. Any questions? None? Okay, then. Begone."

270

Jacques gives orders in his silky voice with a face that is reassuring, despite his body language communicating high alarm to Aminat. She tugs on Kaaro's sleeve.

"You killed people," she says, *sotto voce*.

"So did you," he says. He sounds casual, but she can sense pain underneath it.

"I guess we're both going to hell."

Kaaro shakes his head. "Heaven loves those who defend themselves. If motherfuckers come to my house with guns, they get what they deserve. You know I hate guns."

Aminat has time to touch foreheads with Kaaro before the first bombs detonate.

Interlude: 2067

Eric

Nuru and I drill into the concrete of the alley with jackhammers. Two other guys stand guard because this noise might draw attention. I've never worked a pneumatic device before, so I'm clumsy and almost take my own foot off. Nuru drills like a pro. The holes are for the stabilisers of the plasma cannon and the sound cannon. I send people to evacuate the buildings directly across the street. We basically bribe them to move. I find the alleyway too bright so we staple plywood to block sunlight and it works. I want to ask Nuru if his intel is solid, but I read it from his mind instead. He has been surly since I broke up his rape camp. He has some concerns that I might speak to my superiors about what I've seen and, big surprise, he is of two minds as to whether he should shoot me in the head after we complete our task. I'll have to work out how to acquire a tactical advantage against a man with multiple tentacles. Even now, with Nuru facing away from me, two tentacles point in my direction with sensory organs at their tips. He does not trust me. It is slightly dizzying being in his mind and seeing myself through his extra senses.

We will not be able to test the weapons, at least not by firing. There's a subroutine, a self-check, that doesn't come back with any errors. The weapons are warm. The grapheme armour has some camo function, but I want to conserve the charge for now. I'm manning the plasma cannon since I have experience from the Desalination Wars. Nuru has the sonic. I stay in position, hands at the ready. Nuru is on the ground, sleeping.

"We have spotters, man," he tells me. "Relax. We'll have at least five minutes to get into position when the time comes." From his side a tentacle extends to the mouth of the alley and flips from one direction to the next. It's easily four feet long, the largest I've seen from him, and I wonder if that's the limit. I've only just noticed it, but each time one of his scars opens and a tentacle comes out, a sweetish smell, like honey, fills the air. That, combined with the squelching noise, makes me feel sick each time.

"The cannon is synced to me. If I sit it might drift and waste precious seconds resyncing." This sounds lame even to me. The ID sync is reliable up to a foot or so.

Nuru sucks his teeth. "When all this is over I must buy you a beer so we can have a clarification session or something."

"Or something," I say. I can read that he's serious about it in his forebrain. He has a begrudging respect for my forthrightness. Hmm. Maybe—

"They're here." He is up in seconds and the cannon warms up with a soft whine.

Here we go.

Chapter Thirty-Two

Walter

Rosewater has declared independence, and I've decided to keep this as a wartime diary until I can figure out the structure required. These will serve as my notes, source material for the ... work. I don't know if what I'll end up with will be a book or a series of articles, or a dry official document for the Jacques Administration. Jacques Administration. That felt strange to write.

You know me. My name is Walter Tanmola. Yes, I wrote *Banana Identity* and *The Tao of Black Motherhood* and *Kudi*. *Banana Identity* and *Motherhood* were critical successes, but *Kudi* made me financially secure. Yes, my last book was ten years ago. I've been coasting on the fame and fortune of *Kudi*, which was adapted into a stage play, a graphic novel and two movies. Fun fact: kudi means money. Some said I used witchcraft to enhance the sales and that the name was a condition for the ritual. I don't disabuse people of that because it sells books. I pontificate on Nimbus, on national television and web casts. I have opinions that are sometimes popular, sometimes populist.

I've been in Rosewater since 2064. Like many I came here for the healing and I got it. I suffered from PF-81, one of the myriad diseases unleashed when the world lost a lot of the permafrost. I was lucky, and here I am. I spend my days reading and rereading the non-fiction of Soyinka and smoking weed. My agent thinks I'm working on a book called *A is for Eternity* but she's not stupid and I've resisted sharing even a snippet of the first draft, mainly because the first draft only exists in my head.

Rosewater grows the best weed in the world.

I'm writing and recording this particular segment in a bomb shelter on Kuti Street. It is difficult to compose with the bombardment and dust dropping on my notepad every few minutes, but needs must. When I can't write, I use a voice recorder on my phone.

I got this particular assignment last week. I received a call from a contractor who identified himself as Fadahunsi.

"How did you get this number? It is unlisted," I asked.

"I work in security. I'm calling to know if you are interested in meeting an important person for the purpose of an assignment." He has a deep baritone, and I picture a large, muscular man, which is wrong. When I meet him, he's barely six feet, and wiry.

"I'm not in university any more, so I don't do assignments."

"Nevertheless, he'd like to meet you." He pronounces it "ne-vah-di-less", the Yoruba way, with poor exposure to pop-culture. I wonder where he's spent his life.

"There's a war on, in case you didn't know. We're being shelled. If I could get out of the city, I would, but I'm not going to travel around."

"I can guarantee your safe passage. I only require your discretion."

"I'm very discreet." Yes. I used the lives of all the people around me and a significant number of strangers to populate my novels and you expect discretion. Of course. I'm discreet until the next novel.

"Someone will be at your door in an hour."

"How do you know where I live?" But he has disconnected.

I dress up, by which I mean I change my boxer shorts and hunt down clean clothes to wear. I haven't worn a top for days now. I test my breath against my palm, but what bounces back is disgusting, and I have no mouthwash, so I gargle vodka, brush my teeth, and take an extra swig of the vodka for luck.

Two soldiers arrive to take me. They wear brown and beige desert camouflage and one of them has a plasma rifle. A quad bot follows them around, the kind with a truncated head and loping movements. They have a jeep with an internal combustion engine. All the cars in Rosewater are electric and since the power went out the roads have been empty. There is the small matter of bomb craters as well. There are sporadic generators, but the real problem is fuel.

There are checkpoints everywhere, but I'll get back to that later. I want to focus first on the people who are running this rebellion or revolution or whatever we're calling it these days.

The mayor's mansion is somewhat reduced from its former glory on approach. I think it was built in '60 or '61, and is the official residence and seat of government. A number of concrete barriers have been constructed, so our route in is zigzag. There's a tower pointing to the sky, about ten feet tall, repeated at intervals, which I suspect is meant to jam or interfere with satellite detection. I'll ask later. The building itself has suffered a direct hit or two, and while it's still standing, I wouldn't swear by the structural integrity. There is active reconstruction going on when I arrive and there are yellow signs directing us to safety, although I'm handed a hard hat.

I am surprised that the mayor is right there in the battered building waiting for me. He spreads his arms like he knows me, and I am absorbed into his gravitational field. He is a big fan of *Banana Identity* and can he call me Walter and have I ever been to the mansion before and he hopes we can work well together, but either way can I sign his copy and let's go downstairs where it's more comfortable and am I hungry or thirsty? Jacques smells good and he hugs like he means it. I know he's a politician and that getting me onside is his stock in trade, but damn, he picked the book that I thought expressed what I wanted to, and he's just friendly enough to be the right side of smarmy. His greatest weapon, I surmise, is that he seems genuine. Maybe he is genuine, who knows. He's definitely brave to be up where an errant bomb could take him out, but he knows this, and he knows that I know this, and that it will affect my impression of him.

He does not introduce his entourage, but there is one strikingly beautiful woman with dead eyes who looks at me like I'm a bug, and another woman who attends to Jacques's every word. She's like an administrator or something. She is precise and whispers things to Jacques every few seconds. I know neither of these is his wife Hannah, and none of their body language signals suggest sexual or even flirtatious relationships.

The stairs only go down one floor, then there's a lift system that goes an indeterminate distance down, then we go sideways, and I understand that we've moved beyond the boundaries of the mansion, which I think is wise. The noise of construction is so loud that there is no point even attempting speech.

We come to an anteroom, white walls, a side table with bottled water, glass containers, which is a nice touch considering the number of plastic garbage islands on the oceans. Jacques spends exactly five minutes discussing *Banana Identity* and asking me pointed questions. Well done to whoever primed him. Then he gets serious.

"Walter, I need your help. All wars are propaganda wars. I want you to write the story of our struggle. Rosewater needs an impartial chronicle of this injustice."

Do I detect a strange accent on the word "impartial"?

"Sir, I'm flattered, but I write personal pieces and my non-fiction is commentary. I don't do reportage. No offence, but I find it boring."

"Just do it in your own way. There is such a thing as historical fiction, right? Do that."

"But," I decide to be honest, here in this bunker, surrounded by the revolution itself, "I'm not sure I'm on board with the whole ... Rosewater as a city state thing."

"Excellent. That makes you a disinterested party. That will lend authority to your account." If Jacques is surprised, he doesn't show it.

"I don't know, sir. This is outside my area of expertise."

I relent, though. Not because Jacques is a convincing motherfucker, which he is, and not because I believe in their cause, which more on that later, or because I'll have access to all the information I want. No, the real reason I join the team is they have access to fuel and food, fast becoming problems in a city that suddenly finds itself needing generators and non-electric cars. The sprayed defoliants damaged the ecosystem and the local council dishes out food once a day, but it is obviously rationed. The flowering black market can't keep up with demand. I say I'll do it on a trial basis, for a week, to see if it fits me, and we agree on a fee for the week and a bonus if I decide to take the job on. My agent will kill me when she finds out.

Walter, never enter into any negotiations without me. Don't even discuss the possibility of negotiations.

Once I sign a non-disclosure, Jacques turns me over to his assistant, Lora Asiko. My first thought is that this woman is of the Machinery. At the time I did not know the position of the Machinery on the war. I do now, but we'll get to that.

Turns out hers is a story I want to know. The first few hours I spend with her are dizzying because she provides me with what she calls contextual facts. These amount to the tonnage of wheat used weekly in Rosewater, for example, and the amount of potable water left and estimates of survival rates to four decimal places with Confidence Intervals and P-values. She has an eidetic memory without a doubt. Her contextual facts are an inhuman amount of data which she simply recites. When I ask her to repeat something she does it in exactly the same way.

I demand a break, and while I sit on a sofa contemplating a painting of a housefly menacing a hibiscus, I doze off. Maybe it's the weed comedown or stimulus overload, I don't know. Either way, I'm standing in the courtyard, although this time bombs are falling all around me. I'm aware that I am dreaming, but I cannot wake myself up as incendiaries gulp the oxygen and eat everything in sight. Then I see a flying . . . thing, I know the name, but it's gone. It's an eagle and a lion. It lands in front of me. In its beak lie the remnants of some plant it has torn to pieces.

"Who are you?" asks the animal.

I don't say anything. Every Yoruba child is brought up early to be wary of creatures you meet in dreams. You don't speak to them, you don't tell them your name, and for Olodumare's sake, you do not tell them your mother's name. In the Yoruba spirit world your name combined with that of your mother is your unique identifier.

The creature skips forwards and drops the leaves at my feet. "Eat."

Definitely not doing that. Everybody knows that if you eat in dreams you die in real life.

"Fine, be like that," says the creature, and bites me on my left calf. As it tastes my blood, I am suddenly aware of my own nakedness. "Oh, right, you're the writer. Sorry. I'm kind of busy, it's taking longer than I thought to find Anthony. You can wake up now."

"What?"

"Walter," says Lora. I open my eyes.

"Hi."

"You were thrashing about in your sleep."

"I was just resting my eyes."

Gryphon. That's what it was. Why would I dream of a gryphon?

"How did you meet the mayor?" I ask.

"I'm not important. All you need to know is I came with him from Lagos because I believe in him and what he intends for Rosewater."

"So you're from Lagos?"

"I didn't say that."

She's attractive, but not in the same way as, say, Hannah Jacques who is discussed in the society pages every week. Lora, I decide, is perfectly symmetrical. Her left and right halves are perfect mirror images and, to me, pleasing. Her face is in constant enquiry, and her eyes are serious, intelligent, a lighter brown than usual. She parries all my questions about her, and in the end I just ask her for her phone number.

"Why?" She seems genuinely surprised.

"I'd like to phone you."

"Why would you want to phone me?"

"So we can take a walk and drink shots of vodka while we yet live. If you don't want to talk about yourself, we can talk about me. That's my specialist topic."

"I already know all about you. I did a background check."

I shake my head. "You don't know all about me. Do you dance?"

"I know how."

"Good. Good."

"Can we get back to the information you need?"

She scourges my brain with her data and when the day is over and distant explosions sound like thunder, I lie on the same sofa trying to sleep. It makes the night seem long and the darkness without moon or starlight makes me think I've descended into the land of the dead. I count sheep, literally imagining sheep being stalked by a screeching gryphon and running across my mind's eye. I count them. Then I lose count. I argue with myself about whether I should start again or just pick a number and continue from there.

Lora wakes me up. She says it's fortunate that I joined today because there's an important phone call which Jacques wants me to witness. It's all very hush-hush.

In case you've been living under a rock, here's how energy works in Rosewater: early on, before the area was incorporated, people had generators and a few people used illegal taps from the national grid, with mixed results. Cross stealing by stealth flex-wire was rife. The dome was up, and there are two projections from the alien called the north and south ganglions. Ganglia? Whatever. Both of them are nerve endings, or so we have been told. They regularly crackled with electric energy and were often the source of the defensive strikes the alien made against intruders. People died walking into or around the ganglia. When Jacques took over, he started a number of capital projects, but the first thing he succeeded with was the utilisation of the electricity that the alien used to think and defend itself as a power source for the city. The invention of the Ocampo Inverter made it possible. But.

The controller for the inverters lies in the hands of the federal government and the president switched off the lights hours before the first aerial bombardment of Rosewater. Now the ganglia just stand there like giant erections or the hand of Sango, electrocuting people with no rhyme or reason. Let's not talk about the death cults who encourage their members to prance around the ganglia. I never saw the ganglia before Ocampo's work, but those who were here tell me that they find the electrical activity somewhat attenuated. This might be so, but it might also be because the dome is degraded and they *expect* the ganglion to be less than it was.

We've been in darkness since.

So when I hear we're going to speak to Ocampo, I get excited.

It's a stand-up meeting, with a hologram generator in the centre. Lora silences me with an index finger to her closed lips. Jacques stands front and centre, the glow from the generator lighting up his features and doing the same to a lesser extent for his bodyguards and the other woman in his entourage. Who is she? Her eyes flick to me when I enter, and flick away in seconds. This seems to me like a séance more than the most modern form of communication.

The device beeps and Victor Ocampo stands before us, diminished, but jolly and bespectacled. For some reason he has the flag of the Philippines draped over his left shoulder and an old NASA logo from the 1960s sewn as a patch on his right. Someone speaks indistinctly from behind him, a female, which could be his wife, or his daughter, who knows. He comes to us from his private space station. Yes, he is that rich. The Chinese had a problem with it, wanting to regulate a Filipino in space, but he is rumoured to have pretended to only speak Tagalog and confounded the negotiators. I've heard all the documentation on the station is in Tagalog. He has a staff of forty keeping it running and comfortable for his family. Nobody knows how long he has been in space, and there are rumours of osteoporosis.

"Mr Mayor," says Ocampo.

"Please, Victor, call me Jack. How long have we known each other?"

"Yes, and you gave me that hundred-year-old Scotch, didn't you?"

"I did."

"I have to tell you, it's not the billions I made off the Rosewater deal that made me take your call. It's the memory of that Scotch going down my throat. It was smooth."

"I may have more," says Jack. I note the cadence of his voice. He is trying to manage Ocampo.

"I'm sorry, Jack. I know why you're calling me, and I wanted to tell you face to face that I cannot help you."

"Victor, do you have access to the inverters?"

Ocampo has a pained look.

"Can you remotely turn our lights back on?"

"I can, but my control access is only for the purpose of servicing or maintenance should that become necessary. That is how businesses work, that's how you sell technology. You and Miss Lora should know that."

283

"Victor, it has become necessary. The device is shut down. Isn't it your duty to turn it on again?"

"Jack, from my perspective, and from my consoles, I have a device voluntarily shut down. My hands are tied. I can only intervene in the event of a client request."

"I am requesting—"

"You're not the client, Jack. I reviewed the paperwork, or rather, my wife reviewed the papers and gave me the highlights. I did the work at Rosewater, but on behalf of the *Nigerian* government, and that isn't you. Like I said, I'm sorry."

Jacques must already know that. I can't imagine he'd take the meeting without having read everything pertinent. Lora would have prepared as well. Which means this is a gambit of some sort, a pose. Jack looks pained and rubs his left temple with the tips of his fingers. The impression he's trying to give is of deep thought, but I know he has known what he is about to say next for at least a day or two.

"What if ... what if the blueprints leaked?" Jack sounds uncertain, just enough to be charming.

"Of the inverter? Are you kidding? That's my livelihood. It's proprietary."

"No, I mean the switch. Just the switch."

"I suppose—"

Mrs Ocampo comes into the plasma field like a curtain dropping. "This communication is over."

The light goes dead.

"Your boy is good," I say to Lora.

Jacques is even better than I thought because an hour later a file "the size of Olumo Rock" is dropped into his private server from parts unknown. His tech experts begin to decode what is clearly the blueprints for the switch and instructions for construction. I don't know how long it will take, or even if the necessary expertise is available in battered Rosewater, but the entire team counts it as a win. They start to source the best 3D printers still functional in the city and a language expert to translate from Tagalog.

Sadly, there is no hundred-year-old Scotch to celebrate with.

The next day, after an abbreviated cleaning ritual which I have now perfected, I go out with Dahun and two of his soldiers. He talks to me about the different fronts in this war as we drive around. He starts with the dome, which we arrive at in short order.

The dome is under siege in a microcosm of what is happening to Rosewater. Ten or so flying creatures are at the dome, doing . . . trying to eat the dome? They are green and made of vegetation from where I'm sitting in the jeep. The dome itself, close up, looks mushroom grey, with black spots. From a distance it resembled a pimple, or a mouse-bitten piece of cheese. The soldiers and turret bots fire on the creatures, cutting each one to bits. While I watch, two fall, but from the west two new ones replace them.

When the bots run out of ammunition they safety their machine guns and trot to a makeshift depot. Humans fit them out and change coolant like high-performance engines in a Formula One race.

There are three ragged holes in the top of the dome, but all are partially fixed. The real problem is nothing is deterring the green things. As each one falls, humans in hazmat suits pick up the bodies and take them to a building.

"Autopsies. Analysis," Dahun says before I ask. "The results have been uniform. They're made of leaves, vines, stems, some wood, and that's it."

"Do they ever attack humans?"

"Not unless you attack them first, and only if the attack is a nuisance. They're single-minded, although mind is an exaggeration. They have no brains. The xenobiologists agree that they're drones of some kind, but natural enemies to the alien."

It's interesting that I've not heard of this but access to the dome has been restricted since the war began. Cordons are set up a mile in all directions for non-military personnel. You can still see the tip of the dome, and the uppermost perforation, but little else. There are other matters keeping the people of Rosewater busy, most to do with survival. There are ... new things, or perhaps old things that are emboldened by the sickness of the alien, of Wormwood. I have stayed in my home for most of this conflict, but I've heard rumours.

I ask Dahun where the green things come from and he says this is our next destination. These are, he says, the only two fronts within Rosewater, although there are protests and saboteurs undermining the war effort. He calls it that: the war effort.

Again, there is a cordon, then half a mile of demolished buildings, patrolled by irregulars, freemen and combat bots. Drones criss-cross the sky and we have our ID checked several times. What I'm looking at is akin to a tree bursting out of an apartment block. Some of the external walls are intact, but a complex trunk system and several stems exit through windows and cracks. There is no roof; a florid explosion of flowers occupies that space and even though it is mid-morning, even I can tell that there is bioluminescence. A root system has worked its way into the ground creating cracks that creeper vines grow towards.

"What the hell is this?" I say. It is hard to be understood from behind the mask, and I have to repeat myself.

"We don't know," says Dahun. "It's not terrestrial is all I can tell you."

"The green things come from this?"

He nods. "They come from the flowering part. It moves, too, so be careful."

This thing is mostly green, but there are red, mauve and brown parts, excluding the flowers, which are a mess of colours. There is pollen in the air, explaining why Dahun has me in a face mask. Hallucinogenic, maybe? Or poisonous. From time to time an organ pumps out the particles, but otherwise the plant looks docile.

I don't have to wait long for it to extrude one of its proxies. The roots and stems experience a tumult and start to agitate, then they part slowly to form an orifice with a vine-encrusted humanoid thing coming through. It has to snap connecting tendrils to finally be free, and it takes to the sky with flaps of its wings. It's not like a new animal, and nothing about its flight is tentative. I am not sure why it has six wings, but in less than a minute it has shrunk in the clouds and disappeared. The limbs and roots rearrange themselves until the hole that spawned the creature is closed.

It is difficult to breathe through the mask. "So, there is a new alien creature, growing to giant proportions, just like the old, and it's at war with Wormwood? Is this one of those "only room for one of us" scenarios? High Noon over Rosewater?"

In my notes I call this creature the Beynon, because I always did love *The Day of the Triffids*, but when I give my first review of the situation in Rosewater the name sticks and Jacques's people have called it that ever since. My first contribution to history?

*

We drive north. Here I am given a protective helmet where I did not need one before. I can hear gunfire and shelling. There are concrete barriers and short-span force fields that we have to weave around.

"What we have here," says Dahun, "is machine warfare. Our turrets and drones fighting the Nigerian government's turrets and drones. Our spotters think that so far they are evenly matched, but it becomes a matter of time. The feds can keep this up for ever, but we cannot continue to supply ammo or technicians for maintenance and repair. We can print parts, but we don't have limitless material. And there are snipers who pick off our technicians. In turn, our snipers try to pick off theirs. Like I said, we seem evenly matched."

"How long can we hold this line?"

"I can't say that out loud. Surveillance bugs."

The enemy has the high ground in the north as Rosewater occupies the river valley cut by the Yemaja through hill country. It forms a bowl with the dome at the centre, and the exhalations and extrusions of the alien provide a microclimate. When driving in that way you can look down to a vista that captures the entire city. Dahun concedes that it was a mistake early on, not fortifying and holding the area outside the city limits.

"The brief the mayor gave me forbade invading Nigeria, which, technically, holding those hills would be."

It is not exactly a stalemate. We're landlocked, we have no supply lines, and time is on their side. The sides of the roads are littered with discarded placards from yesterday's protest, most of which say NOT IN MY NAME or I AM A NIGERIAN. It's impossible to tell what percentage support the rebellion.

While observing food distribution I hear rumours and whispers of spontaneous human combustion.

Food is given away daily in various halls in different wards. The emaciated people of Rosewater have started to resemble the Africans you used to see on those infernal charity appeals back in the day, always begging for money that would ultimately go into the pockets of the local big men. All things considered, it's an orderly process and I drift among the people, trying to get a flavour of the opinions. There's a lot of verbiage about the hardships, which, to be fair, is normal for Nigerians. I mean, yeah, life outside Rosewater can be shitty, but even within, even when I started living here, people complained. It's a communication tic.

But this is specific. It's one thing for kids to complain that you can't find snails any more, which is true because the defoliants removed the food source and threw the entire ecosystem out of whack. It's quite another to talk of people bursting into flame.

"She burned to ashes. My brother came back from the market to see her corpse."

" . . . in the middle of the night, set the house on fire . . . "

"My husband was right there. The woman started sweating from heat, then collapsed, then just started burning, starting from the thigh."

I'm sceptical at first because the most likely explanation is some kind of mob justice for stealing or witchcraft. Necklacing is a common form of retribution or punishment. I don't want to observe sacks of rice or grateful crowds, so I decide to follow this thread.

I interview those with the most specific stories, those with detail. I question those from whom they heard the story. It convinces me that there is *something* strange happening. I convince Dahun to follow me. There are specific addresses and they have the pattern of an infection to me, but I'm not a doctor. I know they have one in the mayor's mansion, so I call Lora.

"I'll tell Dr Bodard, but if there's an infective agent I wish for you to leave the area immediately."

"Because you want me to be safe?" I ask.

"Yes," she says.

"Because you like me?" I say.

"No, because you are important to the cause."

"So you don't like me?"

"I didn't say that. I'm busy. Goodbye."

She's odd that one. I do not leave the area. Instead, Dahun and I go to each address. Sometimes kids throw rocks at us, mostly because of the uniform, but Dahun doesn't mind and I have a flak jacket and helmet. Dahun is not just babysitting me. He takes calls and gives instructions over the radio, and he is monitoring the conflict in real time.

There are no stray dogs; they have all been eaten or blown up.

We find one burned corpse in a house. The paint is scorched, but no evidence of petrol or any accelerant. The person also seems to have burned from the inside out, like she swallowed phosphorous or something. I take flesh samples.

"It's a xenodisease," says Dr Bodard later. The xenobiologist sounds harried and tired. "Wormwood must have served as a balance on the alien micro-flora, and with it incapacitated, organisms are becoming bolder and stronger. This one is an insect – no name yet, I'm calling it B718 – lays eggs on the skin, the larval forms burrow into the subdermal fat. As it feeds, its waste causes host cells to generate heat and combust."

As I write this no cure has been found, and people burn up every two days or so.

Jack Jacques is surprisingly upbeat and has taken to yelling "scribe!" at me when we pass in the corridors of the government building. Today, I am meant to sit in on a cabinet meeting but there's heavy shelling and we're all confined to the mansion. I have a sort of date with Lora. I bring coffee and chocolate rations. We stake out a corner of the canteen and the buzz of conversation seems normal, not wartime at all. I have never seen a woman eat in such a regular fashion. I watch her for a while, and the time between each bite, each swallow, is exactly the same. It does not seem strange to her that I am watching her, or that I am not eating. She does not make any small talk, and expects me to lead.

"How do you smell so clean?" I ask. Why, I don't know. I ask strange questions when I'm nervous. I get nervous when I like a woman.

"Because I am. You don't smell clean, though. You smell . . . of sweat and antimicrobial soap and gunpowder. Did you fire a gun?"

"No, but Five Yellow, one of my escorts, had to shoot at some people trying to rush the school convoy."

"Why were they attacking schoolchildren?"

"Nobody knows yet. They ran away. Dahun docked Five Yellow's pay for not hitting a single one."

She has no pimples. Her skin is this russet colour, and I'd have put her as coming from the East of Nigeria, but who knows? Her hair is pulled back with not a strand out of place. She has those Indian extensions that fluff out beyond the hair tie. Her eyebrows are precisely cut, her lashes businesslike and unenhanced, and she wears no jewellery. I suspect she can look a lot more glamorous if she wants to. She watches me watching her. The coffee and the chocolate are gone.

"Walter, you are spending time with me because you like me," she says.

"You have a strange way of talking, but yes."

"Why?"

"I don't know yet. That's what asking you to have coffee is about, isn't it? You definitely don't remind me of my mother."

"How so?"

"I never met her. She died giving birth to me and my twin brother, who also died, by the way."

"I'm sorry to hear that." She inclines her head towards me. "Does it make you sad?"

"Not really. I never knew her, like I said, so it's this vague . . . absence. I did have a surrogate, a step-mother who was really cool, if a bit stern. She was a widow, manufactured in bereavement counselling for my dad."

"She was manufactured?"

"No. Figure of speech." Now I'm wondering if she's one of those literal people. I struggle to remember if she's ever cracked a joke in my presence. She is always so serious.

"I sometimes struggle with symbolism," she says. She smooths her skirt. "Time for me to go. Thank you for the chocolate and coffee. I hope to reciprocate soon. I don't know if I like you, but I am happy that you choose to like me and demonstrate by inviting me here. Well."

She gets up and leaves with no backward glance. Decisive. I like that.

*

I don't want to talk about atrocities, but I have to.

I've procrastinated a number of times, but I can't get away from it. There are three types of soldiers in this conflict: automatons, mercenaries and freemen. As yet no government ground troops have entered the city. The automatons maintain the perimeter, with gaps plugged by the freemen. Most of the human soldiers are "freemen": incarcerated criminals serving in the makeshift army to earn freedom. The mercenaries are paid by Jacques, some say from his personal fortune and not the government coffers.

Freemen are less well trained and subservient to the mercenaries, but remember these are criminals, and not known for their obedience to authority. Fadahunsi, I found out, leads the mercenaries, and, of necessity, the war. There is no civil defence to speak of, and there are no military police. In some wards there are Rastas who have taken it upon themselves to defend their neighbourhood, seeing it as the honourable thing to do, but there are very few of them, like three, four hundred, and they have primitive weapons, often refusing to take ordnance from the government, who they consider to be "contaminated babylon". They won't accept food supplies. The Rastas have brief, bloody clashes with the freemen infrequently. A lot of the freemen are bored, hopped up on drugs and trying to amuse themselves. Drills won't quite cut it. They have hours to burn and we, the civilians, learn to avoid roving freemen.

There's a lot of interrogation of "saboteurs", some who can be found hanging from street lights next morning with placards around their necks. There's theft, although it doesn't get people anywhere because transactions are now by eru and the banks are shut. Lots of rumours of systematic rape in some wards. Dahun responds swiftly to these incidents, and I have heard from one of the grunts that he is brutal. Then there is the problem of the twins.

The twins are the heads of organised crime in Rosewater. What we've done, what Jacques has done in the last few weeks, is to train all the foot soldiers for the bosses. There is human trafficking and organ harvest. I don't know how they get past the blockade but they do. Drugs, of course. And they run the black and grey market.

People disappear all the time and nobody can say if they've been taken by a xeno-lifeform, murdered, vaporised in a bombing, trafficked, or what. Nobody knows who keeps attacking the school buses or why they want the children, so attendance has dropped. The good news is that no pupil has been successfully taken. That we know of.

There's a unit that goes on patrol with flame-throwers every day. Their job is to burn the droppers that have proliferated during this time. Dual organisms, perhaps plant-based, but we don't know. They have two parts, one that mimics human form and the other that drops or sprays digestive liquid on anyone curious or stupid enough to investigate. Few natives of Rosewater fall for this, but animals do, and sometimes they can catch you by surprise.

I think the flame-thrower unit burns humans sometimes, just for laughs. There is so much that I won't be able to unsee.

Whenever this war ends Rosewater will be a different place.

There is a direct hit on an ammo dump. It is beautiful and terrifying. It has to be allowed to burn out because the fire service is not functional. Fireworks, random metal fragments falling from the sky at odd times that smell of spent ordnance, that gigantic blue-black cloud in the sky for days, it's tiring.

The girlfriend of one of the soldiers told me it wasn't an enemy shell or a missile. She said one of the freemen set charges in the dump to cover up munitions they had stolen.

I believe this.

The night after the dump explosion, there is a bombardment for real and we cannot leave the bunker. I lie in my bunk writing. The door opens and Lora comes in, and locks the door.

"I didn't give you a key," I say, sounding stupid.

"I have all the keys," she says.

There's a lot of fucking going on in the wartime cabinet spaces, people being desperate or just looking for some comfort, a "for tomorrow we die" vibe that I have taken advantage of once or twice. When Lora disrobes, I am unsurprised. It lasts a long time, by which I mean, *she* lasts a long time, never gets tired or bored. I hold her afterwards and she never goes limp or changes her breathing. I fall asleep first. I wake up in the dark and she's sitting across from me. The bombardment has ceased and an eerie silence stalks the halls. We sneak into the kitchen and look for stray rations. Lora knows where there are sachets of honey and, though now it seems silly, sucking out of them seems hilarious. We act like we have a cannabis high, though the war is cramping my style.

"Walter," she says. I'm still giggling.

"Have some more honey," I say.

"I'm a construct."

"What do you mean?" At this stage I'm thinking it's too early in the morning for philosophical discussions.

"I'm a robot, Walter."

"I don't get the metaphor, girl. Is this about working for Jacques? You work all the time?"

"I am a woman manufactured, not born. I have personhood, and a passport, and autonomy, but I am not human in the conventional sense."

I finally understand what she is saying.

"Breathe, Walter. You have stopped."

I exhale.

I'll tell you one thing: a time will come in your life, at least one time, when you have to confront your own self, your own mind, your own prejudice. I don't know what is on my face, but my mind is racing and I imagine my speech centre is asking the other parts of my brain, *What the fuck do I say? Give me instructions, motherfucker.*

Say her name.

"Lora."

"I'll understand if you don't want to proceed."

Speak. Buy time.

"You're not playing with me, right?"

"I'm very serious."

Do not say, "You look so lifelike." Do not say, "I couldn't tell." Say something honest, dumbass.

"I have never been in this situation before."

"I have."

The words seem uninflected, but even at that moment I know it's untrue. My mind's eye has changed, that's all. In reality, those words are heavy with her personal history, with disappointment.

What if she malfunctions and kills you while you sleep?

What if something inside her, her power source or some chemical, gives you cancer?

What will your friends say?

Can a robot really be a person?

296

Speak, Walter, the silence has gone too long.

But no words come, so I place my hands on her cheeks, and I kiss her on the lips.

Religion is a problem here. The African Traditional Religion folks break curfew all the time, particularly the masquerades, especially oro. The Abrahamic ones, especially the more tradition-bound, just go the way they've always gone, ritual keeping them safe. Some of the evangelicals try to run retreats and those mass prayer meetings where they Jedi-push each other down en masse. They point-blank refuse the curfew at first, but one particular bombardment gives them a bloody demonstration of what God's will in the matter is. Since that time, evangelicals are more manageable.

The Machinery – are they even a religion? – can't make up their mind if they are Nigerians or from Rosewater, because each identity would require different duties. Their debates go on for weeks on end, and because their services are open to the public, I attend one.

In case you're not from here, the Machinery are people who seek tranquillity by removing emotion from their lives. I'll attempt an explanation, but I think they have to speak for themselves and don't deserve this slapdash explanation from an old reprobate like me. They posit that all of human-kind's problems stem from emotion. People of the Machinery act predictably, suppress any expression of emotion, act like machines as much as possible. They have meetings where they share "programming" and "re-synchronise" with each other. They are only found in Rosewater and sociologists have not been able to explain what it is about our microenvironment that breeds them.

They have names, but refer to each other by number. If someone not of the Machinery speaks to them, they answer to their names, not numbers. They make excellent employees, hardworking, loyal, dependable. All of them, male, female, trans and cis, sport the same short hairdo.

Hold your amateur psychology 101 bullshit about this section being due to Lora Asiko. Just shut the fuck up about that. I was always going to do this part.

A woman speaking – her name, 1638853 – says, "Transformation. When Rosewater was part of Nigeria, we were Nigerian citizens, bound to obey the laws of that country. The very moment Rosewater became a breakaway state, we became citizens of that city state. Our responsibility is to our new country. We build this country up. We fight at the front, those of us who are able-bodied. Those less able or less inclined to combat look after the vulnerable. This much is clear."

152381 says, "I disagree. Rosewater is neither country nor city state. Right now, it is in a state of rebellion. This is an insurrection. There is no real government, and the legitimate government of our country, *Nigeria*, is reasserting itself. We are Nigerians until the fate of this city is known. We have to go with the last or current passport."

It is a strange meeting for me, although Dahun notes down the people who insist on being Nigerians. There is none of that murmuring of dissent or assent. No hecklers. It's the most orderly gathering of humans I've ever seen.

Humans want to be machines; machines want to be human.

I can't help that thought. Unlike these motherfuckers, I have actual emotions.

*

298

Rough day.

The prototype replacement inverter is about to be tested when a high-altitude bomb obliterates it, causing electricity feedback. Forty dead, a hundred bystanders injured, and the idea of turning on the lights takes a massive setback. Jacques is superhuman and just says something like, "Let's get back to work reprinting the components." He gives solo applause to his people. "Well done, well done. You can do this. Go."

The engineers want a break, but it isn't going to happen. They lose a lot of good workers, but they go back to the grindstone.

Scant rumours of rats swarming like locusts, eating everything in their paths, including small children, although I doubt the last part.

I try to read an old copy of Achebe's *Things Fall Apart* but I can't get into it, can't get past the title, which is part of the Yeats poem "The Second Coming", a work that always freaks me the fuck out, especially the last line.

What slouches towards Rosewater?

I don't know which is more frightening, living in Rosewater without knowing what the leadership is thinking or living in the bosom of the mayor's team and knowing that we face the abyss here, propped up with a brutal detail of mercenaries and the charisma of the leader. Jacques takes setback after setback in his stride. He is a true leader in that sense, although if you ask me, his declaration of independence was a bit premature.

I get to spend some hours with him towards the end of my trial week, shadowing as it's called, which is what it says on the tin: I follow him everywhere. I don't know if it's for my benefit, but Jacques takes a lot of risks. He goes out of his safe bunker to speak to stitched-together crowds in a form of rally. The cheering is lacklustre, but he persists in that upbeat way he has about him. He spouts Yoruba proverbs. He promises a swift rebuild as soon as he can come to an accommodation with Nigeria. He says investors are lining up to work in Rosewater, that his phone is constantly ringing.

His beard is Castro lite, and he is not as dapper as he could be, but Jacques is canny. The bunker has ample opportunity and resource for him to groom. If he looks scruffy it is deliberate. He may even wish to channel revolutionaries dead and gone. Most people cannot fathom how Machiavellian Jacques can be because ... well, you feel at ease in his presence. He's handsome, everyone knows that, and he knows people. A bit weak on economics, but, as America once proved, that needn't stand in the way of becoming chief executive.

After the speech he steps off the podium, takes off his shoes and socks, rolls up his gabardine, and joins the street crews in repairing the craters. They like this more than all the words he throws at them, and it's on the internet within minutes.

Oh, and, yes, internet. So, before Nimbus, internet is how the world used to connect. I can't tell you much about it, except that it was slow, not much removed from tin cans and wire according to some historians. Well, Nigeria cut us off, didn't it? Some folks found out that the internet infrastructure wasn't taken down, it was abandoned. Well, abandoned by the mainstream. Unregulated, it's become the nesting place of extreme porn, paedophilia, alien trades and terrorist cells. Into this morass Rosewater carved out a space for its citizens. Because subdermal phones are powered by our own bodies, they still work in a local peer-to-peer cloud formation, as they are designed to, but signal problems abide. Lots of local solutions of which I'm proud. The spirit of Jugaad, alive and well in Rosewater.

Jacques takes off his shirt and I swear I hear a gasp go through the crowd. His body is sculpted, and with his lighter complexion he easily holds all the eyes. A detonation at this time would immortalise him for ever. He works, I sweat.

Later, back at the bunker, he takes a quick shower. I meet Hannah. I met her before at an event, but she doesn't remember, and I don't push the matter. If these two decided to have children, their offspring would be magical demi-gods of perfection. And yet, it's all a construction, part of the Jacques plan, the machine. Perfection meets perfection and presents itself to the world. This is a man destined to be a head of state, and I don't mean destined in a mystical "all hail, Macbeth and Banquo" way. He just has all the qualities and has studied the right philosophers. It makes me want to light a joint and take him apart one hair at a time.

I don't know if I can bring myself to tell Jacques that most people on the street see him as a tyrant. I don't know how to tell him. I don't even know how to tell Lora.

When he emerges I ask him if what he said about investors is true.

"It will be," he says. "Stop. I know what you're thinking."

"What am I thinking?"

"*Among the calamities of war may be justly numbered the diminution of the love of truth.* You're thinking that or a variant thereof."

I am not.

"Who said that?"

"Samuel Johnson. But I have a different saying for you. Truth is a tool of war. It must be treated as a scarce resource."

"You mean you're justifying lying to your public."

"As generations of radioactive Fukushima pigs will tell you, that means fuck all in the grand scheme of things."

What is he talking about? Is this an advanced form of verbal misdirection where I'll keep quiet because I don't understand his obscure allusion?

"Jack, what is your endgame here?"

But Lora comes in and urges us out because the sky is about to fall.

Later that day Jacques inspects the new farms. We're in a convoy of three cars, Dahun driving the front one with a mounted machine gun and a guy standing looking tense, Jack and I in the middle, his bodyguards behind. I forget what Jack is saying but a plasma bolt comes out of our left and slices off the upper torso of the gunner. A sonic weapon goes off and the jeep behind us tips over on to its side. Fucks up my middle ear. Shit. Shit. Shit. Dahun does a U-turn and comes alongside us, protecting us from the field of fire. He launches micro-drones, robotic insects, which fly off in a cloud towards the direction the attack originates from. The car is sprayed with conventional bullets, which Dahun's jeep can take. I think this is a good sign until Jack says that their plasma weapon is probably recharging. The insects mark several targets with red lines of laser and Dahun fires a rifle through the open window. Charges fly towards the targets which are still beyond view and there are six individual explosions. I'd like to say I was carefully noting everything down, but I concentrate on main-taining sphincter integrity. There is nothing glorious about facing death. I hear a sound, maybe, because memory is a funny thing. I push fucking Jacques down just as plasma cuts a superheated path through Dahun's jeep and crosses where the mayor used to be. There's a crack as air rushes back and my hearing finally goes. The car splits open, dropping both of us on the asphalt. I smell burning flesh. I see smoke rising and fluid leaking from the bodyguards' car.

"The fuel is dripping out," I say.

"Don't panic. That's not fuel," says Jacques. "That's the body fat of the . . . yes. Body fat. The guards."

I try to think of an exit, but it's not to be because I lose consciousness. I wake on a stretcher in one of the ambulances. Jack is lying parallel.

"Good job, scribe!" says a cheerful Jacques. He is making a thumbs-up sign. "You probably saved my life."

I feel a "but". It doesn't come, but hangs in the air swirling between us, only me. I say nothing and I don't try to get up because I'm still woozy.

"We rounded them all up, you'll be glad to know. Paid by the president, no doubt."

"Motherfucker, give it a rest," I say, before I can stop myself. "I can tell when you're lying now. You haven't rounded up shit and that wasn't the president. That was your own people crowdsourcing weapons to kill you hard."

"The president—"

"No, no, no. Not the president. The people of Rosewater rising up against a tyrant. They hate you, Jacques. You'd know this if you read the graffiti that your mercenaries clean up before you come round. You're beautiful and perfect and fucking patronising and paternalistic and my God, do they hate you."

He is silent and I'm breathing hard. I've gone way too far, but I've decided against the gig anyway.

"Thank you for your candour," he says. "*Memento homo.*" He is, for the first time, subdued and withdrawn. His screen is down.

"Mr Mayor—"

The ambulance stops and the doors open. Dahun is there, bearing enough arms to kit out a whole ocean of octopuses.

"You're not my paramedic," says Jacques. "Help me up."

They help him up and the sheet slips, revealing air where there should be a left leg. He looks back at me. "Not so perfect any more, eh, scribe?"

He winks and is gone.

Lora purses her lips, which is a thing she does when she's thinking, although I don't know exactly how constructs think. "*Memento homo*," she says. "*Remember you are human.* It's a call to humility in a successful person."

I know this, but I don't interrupt, although like many things we think we know about the Roman Empire, it has probably been exaggerated over time because it is striking.

"He showed you his amputated leg on purpose," she says. "You had attacked him, and he had to counter-attack, make you feel bad."

"The sheet fell."

"No. The mayor does not make mistakes, especially when it comes to impressions of him. How do you feel?"

"Guilty. Ashamed. A bit angry with myself."

"Exactly. And how do you think he felt when you told him Rosewater hates him?"

"I wonder what he'll think if he finds out about us."

"Oh, he already knows."

"Wait, what?"

"I'm an employee of the Office of the Mayor. So are you, even if it's temporary. There are policies. We have to disclose any fraternisation. I told him the day after we first became intimate."

"I'm not sure I'm okay with that."

"This is real life, Walter, not sitting at home all day, living off royalties and being whatever it is you were. In real life there are protocols to avoid conflicts of interest."

My boxers are bunched around my ankles. I start to pull them up at the same time as I rise from the bed. Lora sweats. Do you know how freaky it is that robots sweat?

"Why are you getting dressed?"

"This," I say, doing up the buttons on my trousers, "this is a big milestone. This is us having a quarrel."

The bombing stops and people start to stir. It's my last day and I'm mentally prepared to return to my cubbyhole, outside the protection of the bunker. I've been sweating since after sex with Lora.

I hear footfalls stop in front of me and I look up. A woman stands there with an eight-, nine-year-old girl. The girl has a perm; the woman has afro-puffs. The child tugs at her arm, and she bends down to listen to a whisper. The movement exposes some of her belly skin and I swear, the child has tattoos that move.

The woman straightens up and tells me, "I'm sorry. If it's any consolation, your work lives for ever. Or whatever passes for for ever in this part of spacetime."

"What do you mean? Who are you?"

They seem to fade, and I reach for where they are, but ... but my hand is burning. Both of my hands, arms, torso ... I'm cooking from the inside. I may be screaming, but I don't know, my head feels hot. I think that

Interlude: 2067

Eric

Holy *fucking* shit.

Nuru catches all six of the arthrobots with his tentacles, and coils one around my torso to push me out of harm's way, but the explosive fire that comes after rips him apart.

I am not sorry to see Nuru die.

The shockwave flings me through the plywood barrier we set up all the way to the next street. Armour absorbs most of the kinetic energy and stops shrapnel, but I'm winded. When my hearing returns I can hear shouting and the roar of flames. And footfalls.

Up. Nuru's tentacle is still wrapped around me, pulsating.

I check my sidearm on the run. I do not know if I succeeded in killing Jacques, but I know I hit his jeep, the part he sat in, full on. I heard a scream, so I hit *someone*. But then those insects, the explosions ... I hate not knowing, but I have no time. Small-arms fire, shots zinging past me. I look behind and see freemen irregulars, closer than I would like. I do not fear their marksmanship, but there is the element of luck, bad luck in my case. They might accidentally hit me, and while the armour can take your regular .45 round, it might have been weakened by the explosion. I stop, turn and calmly shoot the nearest in the chest. He goes down.

There are three others dressed and armed variously. I try to aim, but the tentacle starts to shift. It moves like it is still alive and unwraps itself from my chest. I grab hold of it to discard it, but the tip shoots out and stings one of my assailants. I can't stop it; even if I wanted to, I don't know how. It kills another with a whiplash action, and I shoot the last pursuer.

I keep the tentacle and I can finally understand why Nuru spent almost a decade cutting himself and perfecting the exact reconstruction he wanted.

I'm running towards the marshes, but someone in a robe stops me. The tentacle does not respond, so I'm guessing it does not sense danger, but I'm still careful and unholster my sidearm.

"I know where you think you're going: the house on Ronbi Street. Don't go there. They're rounding people up."

I look closer and I see her face tattoo in the dying light. She is one of the women of the rape camp. Taking her lead, I turn away and head north, the tentacle rhythmically peeling itself off, then slapping back across my shoulders.

Chapter Thirty-Three

Jacques

Jacques says, "Add to the sins of my administration the killing of Walter Tanmola. He was a good guy."

"He had an infection, Mr Mayor. You didn't kill him," says Femi. "Either that or your powers extend a considerable amount further than I gave you credit for."

"Oh, you give me credit?"

Femi waves her hands dismissively. "What do you want done with the document he wrote and the voice recordings?"

"Is it out of our network?"

"It was never on it. He worked offline. Nobody else has it."

"What's it called?"

"*Notes on the Insurrection.*" Femi says this with fake fanfare.

Jack rubs his temples. "That's terrible. Store it in a vault somewhere. If we win this war we'll get back to it. Where's Lora?"

"In her room. She said she is in mourning."

"For how long?"

"I didn't ask. She's hostile to me."

"So is everybody else. You're not nice, Femi."

"I make up for it in other ways. What are we doing?"

There is a hologram of Rosewater in front of them, updated live from arthrodrones sending data back constantly. The dome occupies its normal place in the centre, but diminished in dominion because of the perforations. The Beynon is a couple of miles to its west and arrows indicate the travel of the cherubim from plant to dome in a sustained action. The borders hold still with wobbles here and there. Civil unrest flickers in and out as transient green clouds.

"The way I see it, we need to kill the Beynon, then we need to heal Wormwood. We're holding against the Nigerians, so that can stay as is for now."

"Can we concentrate fire on the Beynon?"

"It's taking all we have to keep the invaders at bay. When we have fired at it or tried to burn it, it doesn't even acknowledge us as a threat. Dr Bodard is exhausted, and can't find a weakness. This is your area, Femi; tell me how to deploy our assets."

"Send Kaaro into the dome," she says. "Kaaro and Bodard. He's a coward ... no, really, despite the people he killed, he won't want to go, but Aminat obeys orders, and I'll ask her to be their guide. Where she goes, Kaaro follows. His job will be to find Anthony, the Wormwood human proxy, and Bodard can help heal the dome or find a weakness for the Beynon."

"Is it dangerous in there?"

"Kaaro has been there before."

"That's not what I asked you."

"I don't know. The attacks could have any kind of effects on the ... disposition of the alien. Plus the place has always swarmed with floaters, droppers, lanterns and renegade homunculi. The alien usually kept them docile. I'm not sure what the situation will be right now."

"Can't Kaaro just query the xenosphere?"

"Ordinarily, yes, but he said the dome now blocks anything from coming out, and the Beynon has a distortion field. Inside, the situation might be different."

"Why does it feel like I'm sending these people to die?"

"Because this is grasping at straws and there are too many unknowns. Sir."

He doesn't like it. He particularly hates sending Bodard, their only competent xenobiologist, into harm's way. Kaaro he doesn't give a fuck about and borderline despises, but both the sensitive and his paramour have had S45 training. Most of his soldiers have only had the slapdash courses that Dahun runs. He wants the properly trained personnel ready for war. But no drones can get into the dome, even through the holes, and that giant fucking plant has resisted everything.

"I'm not risking Dr Bodard. Send Kaaro and Aminat. Kit them out properly. I want a live feed and as much telemetry as possible so that the good doctor can work on it from here."

Her phone is up before he has finished his sentence.

"Where's Hannah?" Jack asks the guard.

"She went out, sir."

"Does she have a meeting?" Jack checks the time.

"She went outside the bunker, sir."

"Haba! When? Why?"

"I don't know, but she had her bodyguard detail with her."

Jack lifts his right crutch and points it at the guard. "So did I."

He wants to charge into the apartment, but he can't because of his crutches. He has fallen a number of times since the amputation, undignified and not a look he wants to repeat in public. As soon as he is inside, he says, "privacy" and a number of shields come down. Then he phones Hannah, full 3D.

"Yes, baby?" says Hannah. Her hair is ruffling in the wind, and she is either in a top-down jeep or has a window open.

"Where are you?"

"Out. I'm going to help the less fortunate."

"What does that mean?"

"It means there are starving people out here, and reanimates are being killed for target practice by the criminals you put in charge. Nobody thinks they are worth anything or important enough to save. I'm going to do what I can."

"Hannah, it's dangerous."

"I know, which means it's dangerous for all the citizens. I should not be ensconced in a tower making sympathetic noises. We should share the danger of the war."

"Haven't I shared enough of the danger for our family?" His missing leg itches.

"That's a craven use of emotional blackmail, Jack. Clearly, you need discipline. We will sort this out when I get back. Goodbye."

The plasma fizzes out.

Hannah was never a person Jack would be able to control.

Chapter Thirty-Four

Kaaro

When Kaaro wakes, Aminat is seated across the foot of the bed in full combat gear, watching him.

"Hi," he says.

Aminat smiles, tight-lipped, but she does not move. "I have orders."

There is a scratching sound from outside the door: Yaro hearing his master's voice, trying to get in. That dog is excitable.

"I know. It's in the xenosphere. I can read everyone here except Femi, because she takes precautions, and that Lora woman, who doesn't use antifungals but somehow I can't get through to her mind. Whatever. Yes. Orders. You and me. Into the dome. It's like a Stephen King book."

"Stop making jokes."

"I'm scared."

"I know. I will protect you," says Aminat. "I'm good at this. I promise you, I will look after you. I don't give a fuck about the mission, but you and I will make it out of there alive."

"How about Alyssa Sutcliffe?"

"She's safe in Ubar in a secure facility."

He dresses. It is not just the mission that frightens him. Every day fire falls from the sky, or assassination attempts miss by inches or electric elementals breach the ganglia and kill people. There is death everywhere, and being in the bunker doesn't guarantee safety. He wants to be where Aminat is if he must die.

"What if we just find our way through the lines and leave? We could go to Lagos, to your family," he says.

"My brother, Kaaro. Remember that I took this job to keep him safe from S45."

"But Femi isn't S45 any more, remember? She is, like us, a rebel."

"Do not think you know what game she is playing. She could be a spy for the federal government. She could be working for herself towards ends that we do not know. Matryoshka dolls have nothing on that woman, my love. Do not underestimate her. If I thought there was any other way, I would take it, believe me. Let's just get this over with."

"I'm taking the dog."

"What? No."

"Yaro's coming."

"Kaaro, why the fuck do you have to spoil everything? *Mo ro pe ori e o pe. Epe nja e. Aja? O fe gbe aja dani lo s'ogun? Iwo ati tani? Oya, gbono fu ara e, tori emi oni tele e, o. Sho gbo mi?*" I think you're daft, or you're burdened by a curse. A dog? You want to take a dog to war? You and who? All right, go by yourself, because I'm not going with you, you hear?

"*Fara bale.*" Calm down.

"*Gbenu soun.*" Shut up.

"What do you suggest I do with him? Leave him here with these godless fucks?"

313

"He is going to die, Kaaro."

"He might die here, too. We all might."

"If it gives away our position or jeopardises the mission in any way—"

"Yes, you'll kill him and mount his hide. I get it."

Nobody is happy that Kaaro possessed a reanimate and made it bring Yaro to the bunker, a mouth to feed, dog poop to keep clean, yapping to keep muffled. The reanimate control has improved and for Kaaro it is like having senses everywhere in the city, a whole new xenosphere.

"Should we take some reanimates along?"

"Jesus, Kaaro, this is not a block party, you know?"

"We might need some cannon fodder."

"First of all, from whom? The alien is sick. Second, the reanimates are people too. You can't just decide to use them as human shields."

"They aren't human any more."

"I think you're trying to pick a fight. This is really not the time to stir up matters that we both know we disagree on. Unless you're doing it on purpose."

They soft-sulk to the staging area and all the way to the dome in the back of the jeep there is studied silence and deep breathing. Yaro is quiet in the carrier, which Kaaro holds. They are taken up a high-rise and at the top there is a zip-line. It does lead to one of the larger gaps in the dome, but there are cherubs eating at the edges of the hole, and the spikes on the dome ... if they make a mistake, they might be impaled, not a future Kaaro wants for himself.

"We'll be fine," says Aminat, reading his mind.

"You don't know that. You've never done this."

"I'll go first."

"No, wait!"

Too late. She hooks her belt and jumps. Her figure recedes until it is at the opening, where the cherubs, thankfully, show no interest in her. She peers into the darkness, then gives Kaaro the thumbs-up. Behind him, the soldier who set everything up stares at Kaaro, as if to say, *What kind of wimp are you where you let your girlfriend go first?*

Kaaro is aware that some people zip-line for fun. He cannot understand this. He jumps. The shaking view gives him nausea, so he squeezes his eyes shut until he feels himself make impact, held from falling by strong arms.

"You can open your eyes now," says Aminat.

This is the closest Kaaro has ever been to the cherubs. It's like someone knitted them out of tree bark, vines and foliage. They don't all have eyes or nostrils. Some just have mouths with sharp, wooden teeth. Some of the ones with large, green eyes don't seem to use them for sight as they move randomly. Their wings beat slowly, peacefully, while they chew and swallow, chew and swallow. Yaro growls at them.

The dome feels bouncy underfoot, but what Kaaro isn't prepared for is the stench from the hole. Like a blocked sewer line. This is the smell of stagnation and rot, a smell that bodes evil.

"How do we get inside?" Kaaro notices that one of the cherubs is keeping a green and black eye on them while it eats.

"Parachutes. We jump."

The darkness prevails, as does the smell. Where are the electrical elementals? Where's the glow from the inside of the dome? Aminat snaps some flares and drops them through the hole. They put on helmets with oxygen masks just in case there are toxins. Aminat goes first. They use base-jump chutes for the short drop, pre-opened because they assume no breeze inside the biodome. After Aminat touches down, Kaaro follows, feet first.

Kaaro cannot believe what he sees to start with, but it soon becomes evident that there is no malfunction of the eyes.

All the dome-dwellers are dead. They lie about in clumps as if stacked for burning. In the bright, fizzling light they seem to be moving, but it's the flares causing the shadows to grow and shrink. Kaaro knows some of these people, or knows of them. They came to live here when he chickened out. This is going to hit him hard at some point, but for now, he has a job to do. Once the flares burn out there is pervasive darkness. Aminat activates light from her helmet and Kaaro follows suit. He examines the bodies.

"No trauma here. There's no blood or wounding," he says.

Aminat comes through on the radio. "There's some post-mortem biting here."

If not for the helmets, Kaaro would have smelled them. When the attack comes, he is unprepared, but it doesn't matter. Four floaters, attacking from different directions, silent, hungry, though not as hungry as Kaaro has seen before. Aminat has a rifle out and shoots three in quick succession. They die but they don't fall. The fourth soars away. Aminat puts further bullets in the dead ones, to be sure. Their gas bags rupture and hiss. Kaaro can hear Aminat's heavy breathing through the radio. He signals for her to open the channel.

"They don't like dead flesh," she says.

"Apparently not."

"Where do we go now?"

"I need to take my helmet off," says Kaaro.

"Negative. You have no idea what killed these people. There could be contagion, toxins, anything."

"And yet Yaro seems fine. Look at him. You're okay, boy, aren't you?" Yaro barks from a few yards away. "See? He's alive and well. If we don't do this, then we could spend the entire year searching. Underground, this creature is larger than the city, and that estimate is from over a decade ago. It may be even bigger now. I need to get an idea of what's happening, but I can't do that if I'm cut off from the xenosphere."

Kaaro can tell Aminat is thinking of it. The moss on the ground is sickly. How did it get so bad in here? He releases Yaro from the carrier and the dog sniffs about.

"For the record, it's a bad idea, but I can't think of anything else. You realise if you take off your helmet, I need to do the same, otherwise we won't be able to communicate. Which means we could both die."

"How about just watch me and keep guard? When I'm back from the xenosphere I'll signal, or put my helmet back on."

She pulls him close and they touch visors. He takes off his helmet and she mouths, *I love you. Don't do anything stupid in there.*

On this side of the dome there are folds in the membrane, and they form alcoves at ground level. Kaaro scoots over, sits, and rests the helmet in his lap. Aminat strokes his cheek, then holds her rifle across her chest, backing him. He resolves to write this woman a love letter if they survive, using a pen and sheet of paper and everything. Yaro comes over and sits nearby. The ground is cold, wet and soft against his buttocks, but the stench isn't so bad. He wishes he had a cigarette for his ritual, but he'll have to do without. Instead, he breathes deeply and imagines "I Heard it Through the Grapevine" playing in his head.

Getting into the wider xenosphere involves flowing outside his own mental defences. Kaaro has constructed a maze, along with certain attributes like wind, heat, smells, that must be negotiated in a particular sequence. He repeats seemingly random phrases, and after the maze, he is in a field. Yaro, he is surprised to find, follows him even here. It's the real dog, not a memory like before.

"Good dog," says Kaaro. He cannot understand why people think animals don't have awareness.

Normally, Kaaro would transform into a gryphon, but on this mission he wants to be recognised, which makes him more vulnerable. Bolo is there, patrolling the shallows of consciousness.

"Bolo, follow me."

What is meant to be the ground vibrates with the weight of the giant. What Kaaro perceives as the Drop Off is the edge of his mind and the entrance into the local shared consciousness. Usually, there would be representations of human minds scattered all over the place. This time, there is desolation. It is not exactly desert, but scrubland. The sky is devoid of clouds, but is the dark blue of gangrene. No birds, no insects, no wind.

"Well, fuck," says Kaaro.

This means everybody within the dome is either dead or immune to the xenosphere. Anthony was always immune, and Kaaro has never read his mind.

"It's going to be a long walk, boys."

He feels an unexpected surge of well-being and he thinks Aminat may have kissed him where he sits.

In this place, time can be meaningless, but it seems they have been walking for an hour when Yaro starts to growl. The sky darkens and Kaaro looks up. A sheet of black moves towards

318

them from the west. There's a dot of white in the centre of the curved leading edge which turns out to be a single large eye that comes to a stop over the trio. With a closer look the sheet is thin legs attached to the eye, packed tightly together and scattering off into infinity at the edges of the "fabric". Kaaro soothes Yaro, and Bolo follows his lead.

"Molara," says Kaaro.

The shape comes to Earth, shrinks and changes into the more familiar shape: a naked black woman with blue butterfly wings. Last year she had been a succubus engaging Kaaro in hidden liaisons. He found out too late that she is an embodiment of the xenosphere, an anthropomorphised planet-mind, both alien and working for the aliens to gather and transmit information about Earth.

"Kaaro. It's been a while." She does not smile.

Molara had once said she would like Kaaro as a pet when the last human had been converted to alien cells, which makes Yaro's presence meaningful in some way, but there is no time to unpack it.

"What do you want, Molara? I'm busy."

"You're looking for Anthony, aren't you? I knew you'd come sooner or later. I know where he is. Follow me."

Bolo stamps on her, but she dissipates into small blue butterflies, then reforms a hundred yards away.

"Sorry," says Kaaro. "He no doubt sensed that I hate you."

"Is there more posturing to come, or shall we proceed?"

"I think that's it for now. Lay on, Macduff."

She gestures, and they do not move, but the landscape runs under their feet and over their heads, as if the world rotates on its own axis faster, as if the destination comes to them. The flatness yields to a desert which waxes and wanes with dunes.

The world stops at the edge of a large depression which looks like one of the craters formed after an underground nuclear weapon test. In the sand, someone has written "S.O.S." in large wobbly letters.

There are monkeys all around the banks of the crater, about a hundred of them, hanging on, silent, all types. Howlers, marmosets, spiders, gibbons, macaques, and many whose names Kaaro does not know. Others he has never even seen, primates, but who knows what they are. How do you get monkeys to sit so still? They stare back, but do not react. They make way for Kaaro.

At the centre, Anthony. At closer look, he is curled into the foetal position around a small red plant. In his right hand, a teak statuette of an exaggerated woman, and in the left an exaggerated man.

"What is he—" Kaaro asks.

"He's dead, Kaaro. That was his last mental image."

Kaaro had saved Anthony's life once, and the alien had saved Kaaro's life in turn. Twice. But when Kaaro found that the friendliness from the alien was a patronising "kindness", similar to Molara's, similar to what humans show to animals, he had separated himself. Both Molara and Anthony are manifestations of the same thing: aliens who want our Earth. Kaaro makes his way down the incline and touches the body. Still and cold, no smell. He is about to touch the plant when a gust of wind stops him.

"Don't," says Molara.

"What is it?"

"That's all that remains of the footholder's life force. That's Wormwood."

Kaaro feels uneasy for the first time. He's here to communicate with Wormwood, after all. Anthony was a stepping stone to that. "Is it dying?"

"Yes. It cannot truly live without an avatar. We need a new one, and we need to suppress the weed, Kaaro. This has gone on long enough."

She looks at him with meaning.

"Forget it. I do not want to be a Wormwood avatar."

"It isn't so bad, Kaaro."

"What is it with you and things like this? You were better when all you wanted was to fuck me."

"I recall that you wanted it too."

"I'm not being an avatar."

"Well, we need a human to be a ... Wait, I sense something. You know where the host is."

Kaaro knows, intuits that she means Alyssa, and because of the nature of the xenosphere she knows that he knows.

"Give us the host, Kaaro."

"I don't have her."

"It's a female, then."

Shit.

"Kaaro, as the only living Homian on Earth, she is the only one with the authority to be the avatar to Wormwood, more so than Anthony."

"How do you figure that?"

"It's Homian technology. All of this – me, the xenosphere, even Wormwood itself – the Homians made possible, and she has overriding importance and authority."

"You're asking me to help the extinction of my race."

"You humans are doing a good enough job of extinctioning each other already. Rosewater is being bombed right now, and that's only one of thirty-three conflicts currently happening around the world. Shall I talk about hydrocarbon waste products? Shall I talk about surface water contamination? Nuclear

321

waste? Stop me when we get to a world-ending scenario that impresses you enough."

"What happens if there is no avatar?"

"It delays things, but we have other footholders in different continents in hibernation. One has to die before the next activates, but rest assured, we will take this planet. Either we get an avatar and Wormwood lives or we don't and Wormwood dies, but our mission will continue."

"I don't speak for humanity. I can't make this decision by myself."

Molara invades his space such that he can smell her musk. "Can you make the decision to fight the plant by yourself?"

"We've already tried to kill that thing."

"I didn't say we were going to kill it. The footholders have a tendency to take over entire planets, so you have to balance them out with one of these weeds. This got out of control and we need to slow it down, not exterminate it."

"And you know how?"

"Oh, no, I've never done this before. It's never been needed, but I've studied this one from a distance. It works along similar designs to Wormwood, meaning it has a human at its heart. I'm sure if we kill its avatar that will slow it."

Kaaro reasons. Without the alien, Rosewater will collapse and be exterminated by federal troops. That indestructible plant has to go either way. The Alyssa issue is separate. How is she disposed towards humans? Aminat didn't say much about it, just that the woman had a husband and daughter somewhere.

"All right, I'll help with the plant, but you have to guarantee that at least the people of Rosewater and their families will be safe when the time comes."

Those monkeys. Staring.

"We have an agreement."

At that moment Kaaro feels a sting which increases to red heat and he is dragged out of the xenosphere without warning. Aminat is crouched, facing him, staring in his face, her own helmet off, knife in her hand.

His hand is bleeding at the heel where she poked him to make him aware. "What the fuck, Aminat."

"Shhh. Look." She points.

Two, three hundred yards away, emerging from a tunnel, armed and cautious, Nigerian troops, four and counting.

Huh.

Chapter Thirty-Five

Jacques

Before Jack can invite the person in, the door is flung open and Dahun stands there, chest heaving.

"What is it?"

"We need privacy."

Jack talks to the room. "Go secure."

The door shuts itself, locks, seals, the windows go opaque and start gently humming, the room fills with electromagnetic chaff, which Jack knows about but neither of them can see.

"Done. What?"

"The map of the bunkers that we made? An operative of mine just pulled it off a Ministry of Defence Nimbus portal."

"So they know where our bunkers are ... "

"Mr Mayor, they can target each one with bunker busters. That we have a leak does not surprise me because so many in Rosewater are ideologically opposed to breaking away, but that does not minimise the danger of targeted missile use."

"Then you don't know."

"Know what, sir?"

"I was about to call you." Jack points to the livefeed coming from within the dome. He clicks his fingers and it rises to

3D: Nigerian commandos some yards away from Kaaro and Aminat.

"Those are 82nd boys. How did they get through our lines?"

"Good question, one that is yours to answer, but meanwhile, tell me how we are going to protect our two assets."

Jack notes astonishment on Dahun's face but not panic, and he knows he picked the right soldier of fortune. Dahun makes a call. "Rose-6, this is Rose-1, hit back ... Yes ... Deploy five, six and twelve, concentrate fire on location eighteen-B, plasma fire only, nothing with shockwaves, there are friendlies in there ... South-east quadrant ... damn straight. Go. Do it now."

It takes a minute or two, but the fire begins and the commandos turn towards the part of the dome that disintegrates. They see Aminat raise her rifle and shoot two in the head, impressive shots rendered with less grandeur due to the miniaturisation. She runs *towards* the others before they can react. Kaaro stays where he is.

The radio squawks and multiple alarms go off. Dahun listens and whispers into his phone.

"Sir, multiple boundary breaches and incoming."

"Incoming from where?"

"Everywhere, sir, it's like a sky armada. This is it."

Jack spares one last glance for the fight in the dome. *Good luck.*

He moves his wheelchair back to clear the desk, then he and Dahun leave.

Nigeria is all in. The sky is full of bombers and they drop bombs like seagulls dropping shit. Most are conventional weapons, but Dahun recognises bunker busters and the unerring accuracy with which at least four bunkers have been destroyed.

"This is some Second World War blitzkrieg shit, boss," he says.

Jack is quiet. He finds privacy and makes a phone call to the Tired Ones. It is time to negotiate, he thinks.

"I knew you'd call," says his erstwhile mentor.

"You knew about this air attack, didn't you?"

"What do you think? Some of us are still committed to the well-being of African states, and cooperate with each other."

"Do you know how many people he has killed? How many he is killing as we speak on the phone?"

"I taught you better than that, Jack. Never blame the other party for your woes. You and you alone are the architect of where you find yourself. That's one of the first lessons. You cannot be a leader otherwise."

"I guess all I need to do is wait. I won't have anybody left alive to lead."

"And self-pity is another thing I trained out of you. When did you become this pathetic?"

Jack slows his breathing, and says, "I want to talk to him."

"Oti. He won't do that any more. He has the upper hand, and he's looking to end this within the week."

"Then be a go-between. I haven't called you because I don't know how bad my position is. I've called you to help me start a conversation."

"My son, there is only one conversation the president wants to have: conditions of surrender. The question right now is whether he will let you live. Rosewater is finished. The alien is dead, and your little experiment with independent statehood is over. The Tired Ones will make sure you have a soft landing. I suspect teaching younger acolytes would be good for you, since you have learned the hard way."

Jack cannot speak. Everything he wants is falling away. His wife will probably die in this shelling. The president probably wants him alive, humiliated. Maybe they will video the whole thing, like President Samuel Doe in Liberia, in 1990. They killed his guards, shot him in the leg, took him prisoner, tortured him, dragged him through the streets naked, dactylectomised him, finally decapitated him, and desecrated his bones a year later. Of course Doe himself took power by bloody coup, so –

"Well?"

"I'm sorry, the bombardment affects the signal here. What were you saying?"

"Do you want me to make the call to the president? No Nigerian will follow a cripple."

The last sentence hurts more, it seems, than every other indignity.

"Sir, I will call you back."

He hangs up, places his phone hand over his stump, and he weeps. He does not think he has ever wept as an adult. When there are no more tears, he breathes in a hitching fashion, then it quietens. He dries his face on his shirt sleeve.

Back in the war room, Dahun, Femi and Lora wait for him.

Dahun says, "Boss, they are taking and holding ground. Not robots, not turrets, human troops."

"We are going to surrender," says Jack.

"Why?" says Femi.

"Look around you. We're finished."

"If we can just get Wormwood on side—"

327

"Wormwood is dead, Femi. The cherubs are eating what's left of the dome as we speak and the ganglia are giving no power."

"I'm still waiting to hear—"

"It's over. It's my decision."

Unperturbed, Dahun says, "Pay me what you owe, sir. I need to pull my people out."

Jack gestures to Lora. "Settle the accounts, please."

Dahun talks into the radio. "All points, this is Rose-1, stand down, stand down, stand down. Signal 73, signal 73, signal 73. Good luck, and see you on the outside. Rose-1 out."

"This is a mistake," says Femi. He thinks she is afraid at first, but then realises she is shaking with rage. "We need to be a hundred per cent sure the alien is dead."

"Which alien now? Wormwood or the plant?" asks Jack.

"The Beynon needs—"

"Either way, it's my mistake. You can leave any time you like."

Femi storms out.

"What now?" asks Lora.

"We make phone calls."

Chapter Thirty-Six

Aminat

"Run, Kaaro!" Aminat says.

Two soldiers left, but they are good. Aminat has been hit, but her armour holds. They are tough and agile, clearly worked together before. They seem to be everywhere, even though this should be close-quarters fighting, sidearms and bayonets only. She cannot get off a shot, but neither can they. There is little cover except cadavers, and she has to worry about her lover at the same time. She does not wish to fire at random in case she hits him. They have no such compunction, but risk hitting each other. It's a stalemate, but only for now. Aminat can feel the fatigue in her muscles and knows she can only keep this pace up for minutes at most.

Why the fuck is Kaaro just sitting there? The commandos know about him and are wearing skin-tight body suits under their armour and breathing helmets. One of them throws a flash-bang, but Aminat's helmet polarises the visor and noise-cancels. The dome is open behind them, and Aminat can see a way out, but Kaaro is being an asshole again. And the fucking dog is right beside him, tail tucked in, whimpering at the sporadic gunfire.

She takes a shot to the shoulder and it makes her drop her gun. She falls to the rotten ground to avoid fire. There are people crowding the opening in the dome. She squints. They are not cherubs, they are people. They rush the soldiers and hold them down. They get shot, but they ignore the wounds, even though they bleed.

They're reanimates.

"Okay, now we go," says Kaaro. "Are you okay?"

"I have to be. Jacques made us an exit. Let's use it."

The last they see of the soldiers is a hand struggling under a mound of reanimates lying on top of them.

Outside, the sky is full of war planes and drones not quite on bombing runs yet, but in formation, crawling, showing off the might of the Nigerian Air Force.

"We have to get to cover. We'll be spotted soon."

Kaaro grabs her arm. It hurts from the shot, but she bears it. "Anthony's dead. You have to get Alyssa. You need to bring her back here and she needs to bond with Wormwood. It's the only way any of us will survive this."

He explains the conversation with Molara to her, the death of Anthony, his agreement to fight the plant creature, and she nods. "Why do these things always end with you teaming up with a former girlfriend?"

He shrugs and starts running towards the Beynon plant, holding his stupid dog. He has to leap over a woman who is dragging the front end of a horse that has been blasted in two by God knows what powerful force. She pulls it like a reluctant child, back facing the direction she travels in, trailing a long streak of blood. Aminat has never eaten horseflesh. She watches Kaaro recede, knowing he isn't fit enough to sprint the two miles. Sedentary motherfucker, but she loves him.

Oh, how she loves him.

She heads for Ubar.

All the stations on the Rosewater train track are roughly a mile from the dome, and they circle it. The Ubar station is a further mile out, north-west, and if you keep going in that direction you'll hit the east bank of the Yemaja, but not in the flood zone. Aminat commandeers a jeep and its driver, so she's at the ministry of agriculture in fifteen minutes. She calls Femi throughout, but that bitch has gone dark again. In fact, she cannot reach Lora or Dahun or any of the people who should be "mission control".

The ministry looks quiet, ordinary, but Aminat knows how dangerous it is, and begins to sweat. She checks her phone, makes sure that the right implant is switched on. She does not know what happens to those misidentified at Ubar, but she does not want to find out. She knows the building will be functional because it has always had an independent power supply. The gate still stands, and she walks through. It's deserted, but the reception area looks like it's been looted. The president's portrait hangs askew, and someone has painted a black cross through his face and on to the wall. Broken glass on the floor and the smell of defecation. The lift stands amongst all of this, aloof, untouched. Aminat stands before it to be judged, and the doors shift open.

A disembodied voice says, "Drop your weapons, Agent."

Aminat unslings her rifle and carefully places it on the floor. She takes the magazine out of her sidearm and leaves it beside the rifle. After a moment's hesitation she drops the hunting knife beside the handgun.

The elevator takes her down the sublevels, down, down, until it slows and stops. She is in the lab level, and two soldiers await. One covers her while the other pats her down. They walk her to where Femi Alaagomeji waits.

"I'm glad you made it, Agent. I was worried you'd die of love." Femi holds a glass of red wine. Her hand is on the control panel, and behind the protective screen, in the chamber where Aminat had seen scientists puree a guy, sits Alyssa Sutcliffe.

"Why is she in there? We already know this device doesn't work," says Aminat.

"That depends on what you want it to do. If disintegration is your aim ... "

"Femi, you're not making sense."

"No, I'm making perfect sense. Think, Aminat. This, *she*, is the only leverage we have against the aliens."

"So you want to kill her?"

"Not unless someone tries to take her away."

"Why did you let me in?"

"Because you're my agent, and because this facility is hardened. It's the safest place to sit out the final phase of this ridiculous war."

Something occurs to Aminat. "You're the one who let the Nigerian troops in."

"Yes, I showed them how to use Wormwood's vents; and they know where each bunker is, thanks to me. Aminat, wake up; I trained you better than this. We walk in shadow and when the light between those shadows hits us, it is temporary until we can flit to the next shadow. I will stop this invasion and I'm willing to pay any price to get it done. Where's Kaaro?"

"Why do you care?"

"I need to know where my assets are."

"Asset? He hates you."

"Maybe, or maybe he just wants to fuck me so bad, but knows he can't. And maybe you need to learn that emotion isn't important. He may hate me, but he spends his time doing my will, even if he doesn't know that's what he's doing. Where is he, agent?"

"Killing the plant."

"He's going to get himself blown up," says Femi. "Didn't know he had that in him."

"At least he'll die on the right side of history," says Aminat.

Femi points to Aminat, stabbing the air with her words. "Love makes you stupid, Aminat. I don't mean you in particular. Love makes *us* stupid. Pull back and look at the whole picture. You are here to give the aliens what they want – Alyssa. Your boyfriend is going to try to destroy the only effective weapon against those aliens. And Jacques is about to surrender, saving thousands, maybe millions of lives. "Right side of history". Bitch, there is only *history* if humanity is here to write it. You have it the wrong way around, Aminat. You should kill Wormwood and save the Beynon plant. But don't worry. Auntie Femi is here to save the day.

"Despite all of that, I'm glad you're here. In spite of your insipid emotionality and your questionable choice of men, I quite like you. You'll survive all of this, and I'll give you a medal, and promote you. Your one job was to get this asset to me, and you did it. The president will be pleased. There is no way out of here without my authorisation and she's not getting out of that chamber without me releasing her, so sit down, get a glass and toast the end of the war."

Alyssa has seen Aminat and raises her hand in a weak wave. Aminat responds, but feels hopeless. There is no plan, no eventuality hack to get her out of this. She wonders if Kaaro is walking into some trap because Femi does not seem worried about his mission. The walls vibrate even all the way down here.

"Don't worry, nobody is sending bunker breakers to these coordinates," says Femi.

"Can I talk to her?" asks Aminat.

"Be my guest."

Aminat indicates to Alyssa the radio buttons.

"Are you okay? Do you need anything?" she asks.

Alyssa shakes her head.

"I can hear you if you speak," says Aminat.

"I don't have anything to say."

"I'm sorry," says Aminat.

The rumble seems closer and Aminat begins to doubt Femi's assurance. Even the soldiers seem uncertain.

"Are you sure—"

The far wall in the chamber cracks from floor to ceiling all at once, before buckling and breaking apart, flinging some debris with such force that one chunk of masonry bounces off the screen and spiderwebs it. The transmitted force flings Aminat to the ground and shatters the wine bottle with the glass. One of the rifles goes off, but probably by accident or from fear. With shock Aminat watches Femi activate the test. The view of the screen is broken into multiple fragments, functionally opaque, but whatever the attack is continues. Metal groans, plaster falls and everybody screams, including Alyssa on the other side of the screen. No sounds of explosions, though. There is a winding, tightening sound, high-pitched, as if something is stretching, which reaches a crescendo and everything shatters. Aminat keeps her head down, with her hands wrapped around it, trunk curled up, foetal. It's not a detonation, it's a demolition, and when the noise dies down, and there are no girders or beams groaning, and the dust no longer makes her cough, Aminat looks up.

It's not luck that has kept rubble from smashing her head open.

This roll-up is larger than the one that died in the woods. Its mouth alone is fifteen feet high when open, which it is. Alyssa stands at the entrance to that maw, hair flying back and forth with the breathing of the beast. It has curved itself to form a roof with its body, which saves not only Aminat, but Femi and the guards as well.

"I'm going to ask you to do something strange," says Alyssa.

"I've done strange things," says Aminat.

"You know the story of Jonah?"

"I am not getting inside that thing."

"It's a she, and getting in is the only way. She can take us all the way back to the surface. Here, there is only death and betrayal."

"What about them?" Aminat points to her unconscious superior.

"They can come too. The creature is a gentle soul and wouldn't leave without them anyway. I would have acted differently. Let's make haste, the tunnels may collapse."

"I have to tell you something," says Aminat. "You need to go inside the dome."

She tells the story to Alyssa as they both drag the soldiers and Femi into the roll-up's mouth. There are blunt teeth the size of traffic bollards at various points all around, and it is dry, and smells of dust and earth. Aminat had expected saliva, but roll-ups tunnel by passing the earth and rock through themselves.

"Is this safe?" Aminat asks.

"We'll soon find out."

"Does it know where to go?"

"We're communicating, Aminat. Have no fear."

Inside the roll-up is warm, and they stay in what corresponds to a pocket in the cheek. It's snug, but not exactly uncomfortable. Aminat is pressed against Alyssa in the dark. The unconscious ones lay at their feet.

"Did they hurt you?" asks Aminat.

"No. They took samples of everything, but none of it hurt. Your commander is committed."

The movement begins, and the dust fills the close air as a train of rock and debris passes them. Pebbles break off and hit the passengers. Sometimes it is larger stones and Aminat is sure she has been cut and bruised, though not seriously. The creature moves at maybe five miles an hour, and the pulsing movement of its wall is coupled with the passage of heavy earth, the kind Aminat has only encountered at construction sites. Every five minutes or so an explosion of sparks breaks the darkness apart as the creature swallows an inexplicably live power cable. Aminat is starting to feel a rising claustrophobia when the darkness starts to abate. She swallows to equalise the inner ear pressure and strains her eyes to see anything at all.

They breach and Aminat has never been so happy to see the light. They break out just outside the dome. The roll-up keeps her mouth open so they can exit. Alyssa exchanges a moment with her, then the roll-up backs away into the soil, twisting on her own axis, leaving a crater with burst water mains and generous mounds of rubble in her wake.

Alyssa faces the opening in the dome.

"Do you need me to go with you, girl?" asks Aminat.

"I really don't." She walks into the dome like she's been doing it all her life. She stops at the threshold. "Aminat, thank you for taking me to your friend's house. I'm happy to have seen that side of humanity, the warmth, the loyalty. I have a favour to ask of you. If I don't survive this will you find my husband and child and ... comfort them?"

"Of course," says Aminat. "But I thought you weren't Alyssa Sutcliffe."

"I am today."

When she is swallowed in that darkness, Aminat drags the unconscious three out of the open, lest they attract bombs. This done, she runs towards the Beynon to find her lover.

Chapter Thirty-Seven

Jacques

"He accepts the surrender in principle, but he will only officially accept it in person. Not a representative, Jack, he wants you." There is a hiss on the phone line for some reason. Jack changes to the other ear in case it's tinnitus, which a lot of people have these days, being common in combat zones.

"He's going to throw me in a prison somewhere, isn't he?" says Jack.

"I don't know."

"Safe passage for my people?"

"Your wife and immediate staff get a pass, but not combatants. Any war crimes will need to be accounted for. Heads always have to roll in this situation, you know that. If there are no atrocities, then, fine, they can walk free. But there are no polite wars, Jack. There are always people who go too far. Even regular people snap in wartime. We just don't include them in the documentaries or the history books unless they're systematised like the Nazis. And you have criminals as troops, Jack. You knew the risks."

Jack sighs. "Where do I have to do this?"

"Aso Rock."

The president is going to kill me in a very public place in a sensational manner because he needs to make an example of me, to discourage any other insurgents.

"Don't think I enjoy this. I've personally invested a lot in your potential. I know what this silence from you means."

I bet you do.

"I accept," says Jack. "Ask him to stop the bombing and give me a date and time to be in Abuja."

"He'll expect the green-white-green to be flying in your mansion by the end of today, and he'll send a transport for you."

"I'm sure we can find a flag somewhere."

"Jack, you're doing the right thing. I—"

Jack hangs up.

"Lora," he says.

"Sir." She has been outside the room. She is wearing all black, in mourning for her writer.

"I'd like to ask a favour," says Jack.

"Yes?"

"I'd like to use a small part of your memory to store some documents, to be released under certain conditions."

"What conditions?"

"Death by unnatural causes, even if those causes are legal."

"Like an execution?"

"Precisely that."

Something is wrong with the air behind Lora, like a sped-up gathering storm, the reverse of thrown confetti, a gap that forms a human shape, then detail fills in.

"What's that?" asks Jack.

Lora turns around, but apparently sees nothing. "What's what?"

It is a woman, black, in a dark green body suit, head bare, hair in an afro. No weapons.

"Mr Jacques, you don't know me and have no reason to listen to me."

"But you're going to tell me something anyway, right?"

She stays absolutely still. "It's short and simple: wait."

"For what?"

"You'll know it when you see it. Don't do anything just yet. Instead, I advise you to wait. Goodbye."

Her form dissipates.

Lora says, "Who were you talking to?"

"You didn't see her?"

"No."

Jack pulls the room surveillance and it shows Lora, and it shows him talking to air. This time there is no distortion like with the Alaagomeji woman.

"Mr Mayor, are you well? Mentally, I mean?"

"I'm fine. Let's just back this data up, shall we?"

Who the fuck was that? Or rather, what was that? Neither Lora nor the cameras could pick her up, which means it could just be in Jack's head. Great. Hallucinations are just what he needs right now. Or. Or maybe his mind is trying to tell him something in a roundabout way. Maybe he's rushing to surrender. But he cannot see any other way out. He is outnumbered and outplayed, the people of Rosewater hate him. And he has already agreed to surrender. In principle.

What if it isn't just in his mind? Some kind of implant hack? A secure message tunnel? But who is she, then? What's her affiliation? She's not with the feds because they only want one thing. Antithetical. The Hausa people say, *The dance changes when the drumbeat does.* Jack is not sure what drumbeat he hears.

Lora's phone rings and she takes the call, then looks at him. "Sir, something's happening to the plant."

Chapter Thirty-Eight

Kaaro

The plant has all but consumed the apartment block that contained it. It now wears remnants of brick walls, cabling, tortured water pipes and segments of roof like reminders of lost loves. Kaaro watches through a window from an abandoned building a block away. It's moving, too, and not seismonastic movements in response to touch, like fly traps or touch-me-nots. It is initiating movements with its tendrils and whatever projections it has. Several feet above, the cherubs fly in random patterns.

In the darkened room with him there are sixteen reanimates, whom he brought along to be shields, to protect his body when he goes into the xenosphere. The room smells of desperate, unwashed humanity, and it is at times difficult to breathe, but there is a price to pay for everything.

He cannot feel Aminat any more and imagines she has descended the sublevels of the Ubar facility. He feels a pang, but he cannot entertain it.

In the sky he sees the bombers disengage, but the drones keep formation. He does not know why, and Dahun is not answering his phone. The guards around the plant seem to have walked away as well.

There is a portrait of Nelson Mandela on the wall. Kaaro toasts it and drains the glass of ogogoro he found in one gulp. He glances at the blank-eyed reanimates and they remind him of the monkeys that surrounded Anthony's ghost. Yaro whimpers and falls asleep again. Time.

He closes his eyes and disables his routine defences, finding himself beside Bolo, with Yaro in front. A churning pillar of darkness is yards ahead, and between Kaaro and the enemy, Molara. Blobs of dark miasma break off the main mass, drift around, then rejoin it.

"That's our target?" Kaaro asks.

"Yes. The host?"

"It's being done. Let's go."

"Aren't you a little underdressed?"

Kaaro allows himself to transform into the gryphon and fluffs up his feathers.

"That makes me so horny for you. Did I ever tell you that you are my favourite human?"

"Shut up, Molara."

The gryphon screeches, a combination of a lion's roar and the call of a raptor. A light spot forms in the middle of the darkness and a face forms.

"What do you things want? What are you?" it asks.

Molara speaks. "You've grown too—"

"You know what? I don't care. I'll just kill you."

The face disappears and dark, shadow versions of cherubs separate out and fly towards them. Kaaro doesn't like the floating so he grounds the environment. Scrubland for miles. Works for now. The cherubs surround him. *Where is Yaro?* It hurts when they touch him, and they gouge at his mindbody and tear. He flaps his wings to dislodge the cherubs, swipes

with his claws and bites the head off one. It is bitter to his soul
and he starts to feel dizzy, as if poisoned, and he begins to flash
between the xenosphere and Rosewater where his body is. He
falls and darkness overwhelms him as the cherubs swarm over
him. The pain stops him from thinking of a defence.

A roar brings him back. The darkness parts and the cherubs
screech as they are caught in the jaws of a slavering canine with
five heads. Six heads. Yaro? Why not out-Cerberus Cerberus.
Each time a cherub comes close he buds a new head with a
longer neck and bites hard. He's a fucking hydra now.

Molara is a fire-breathing butterfly, changing size with the
exigencies of battle, spreading devastation everywhere.

Bolo jumps into the main black pillar cloud, swallowed up,
pummelling as he goes. Kaaro feels cold in his heart at the
same time, and though he senses Bolo fighting in there, he
thinks it might have been a mistake.

"Oh shit, Kaaro, you're dying," says Molara. She seems
more curious than distressed.

Kaaro looks down and sees that he is bleeding from his
heart all over his fur. It's not so bad, the cherub attacks don't
hurt any more and the cold can be ... can be ...

Fuck.

Everything splinters he knows the battle

Continues ...

But ...

Shit, where the fuck ...

It comes back together all at once. He is in a chair, but cannot
move, ordinary chair, wooden, uncomfortable against his
backside, the room itself large, he cannot see the walls they
are so far away. A foot from him, a boxer stands working

Tade Thompson

a heavy bag, spraying sweat droplets with every punch, and ignoring Kaaro.

"Hey," says Kaaro. "Where am I?"

The boxer stops punching and seems to just notice Kaaro, chest rising and falling.

He says, "*Cilvēka, nevis paša kultūras attēlojums vienmēr būs subjektīvs, lai cik objektīvs būtu autors vai novērotājs. Pat antropoloģijā ikdienas lasītājs atzīmē pakāpenisku objektivitātes pieaugumu gadu desmitiem. Paraugu un metožu izaicinājums un pretprasība ir norma. Margaret Meads darbs Samoā (agrāk Rietumsamoas salā) kādreiz tika uzskatīts par sēklu. Esmu šeit dzīvojis un, lasījis citas etnogrāfijas, vislabāk esmu teikusi, ka laiks ir laiks. Napoleons Chagnons uzskata, ka Yanomamö ir kara vārds, ir vienlīdz atvērts izaicinājumam. Eriksens sacīja, ka sociālās / kultūras sistēmas apraksta veidam jābūt atkarīgam no savas interesēm.*"

"I have no idea what you—"

The environment fragments again.

Hold   on

Try to

Control

                                        The   fall is

344

He grips the tree branch and hangs by the arm. All around the arboreal environment ... monkeys of all kinds ... silent, staring. Where has he seen this before? Why is he thinking of it now? He almost has it when

Gone again

It

It is

This is how dying is done in the xenosphere. Falling.

I don't want to die.

Chapter Thirty-Nine

Aminat

A shit ton of weapons that Aminat doesn't know how to use and all the soldiers have gone home, that's what she has to work with. The plant is bigger, and the weapons didn't work on it, according to her briefings. Standing helpless. Thinking. Okay, not thinking, just being helpless and wallowing in pity. She fires off a few rounds from her rifle and they bounce off the vines without scratching the integument. She tries explosive rounds, a burst of plasma, a chemical shot, nothing. Zero.

Four reanimates are on the street just standing there, without will, nobody home, and cherubs swoop down and crush them in grips, then take them into the plant. They don't struggle. It makes sense, if it grows, it needs material to grow from.

Then two cherubs come for Aminat. She fires at them, incendiary. They both keep coming without heads. She fires again, slices them in half. They fall, but still writhe.

More. They have noticed Aminat.

This won't end well. *What was I thinking? A solo assault on this ... whatever it is?*

Drones and COBs draw closer, hover, for better shots at her demise, no doubt. Some analyst in six months' time will come across the footage and release it on to Nimbus as a snuff film for degenerates to jack off over. Beyond the machines, a skein of geese make their way across the sky, but stop and hang there.

The drones aren't hovering; they are stationary. The quadcopter blades are not moving, yet the drones do not fall. Nothing moves, everything is still, even the air.

"Don't panic," says Kaaro from behind her.

He is in gryphon form, and he is moulting, feathers floating everywhere.

"Baby," says Aminat. "Aren't you supposed to be—"

"I'm not really here, and nothing has stopped, it's just reeeeeally slow while you become aware of this. I placed a small tangle of xenoforms in your nervous system to be activated in the event of a certain combination of thoughts and emotions. Okay. In a minute you're going to see Bad Fish—"

"Wait, when did—"

"My love, you have to listen. I'm sorry, but there's no time. Bad Fish knows some esoteric stuff and he owes me a favour. Well, no, he doesn't. I'm kind of blackmailing him, but the point is he will do this for me. As soon as I sense him—"

"Kaaro, this is invasive," says Bad Fish. He appears in a white gown, bulging at the belly, as bewildered as Aminat.

"Aminat's in a tight spot. Do something about it and you'll never hear from me again." Kaaro goes quiet and starts scratching his forepaws.

"What ails you, my lady?" asks Bad Fish.

Aminat points. "Giant potted plant, eats flesh, kills aliens, and impervious to everything we have, probably about to kill me."

Bad Fish turns around, looks at every aspect of the scene in front of him, strokes his chin. "You still have that ID hack I did for you?" he asks.

"Yes."

"All right. I need five minutes, and I don't know if what I plan will work, but you'll need to stay alive for a bit. Can you run?"

"I can, but I won't. I'm not going to spend my last hours on Earth running from anyone or anything. I can fight for five minutes."

"That'll have to do. Good luck, Aminat. Kaaro, fuck you as usual."

"You have done a good kind thing, Bad Fish. I'll buy you a present, with wrapping and a bow and everything." The gryphon seems to purr. "Aminat—"

"I'm not talking to you," says Aminat. "Let's go. Crank this baby up again."

"I love you," says Kaaro.

"Shut up. Crank."

Time speeds up again.

Right.

Aminat builds a fort of supplies, using only what she can understand or is trained to use. The rest she uses as crude mechanical barriers, praying that nothing explodes or sprays noxious chemicals in her face. She works steadily, hearing the beating of wings and noting how far away the sounds are. She turns and lifts a gun at the same time. This cherub is lacking a head, but has all six wings and thorny limbs flailing towards her as if falling rather than flying. She fires at it, and the super-dense bola tangles up the wings, bringing it down to the ground in a dead drop.

It struggles against the cable, and seems to be tearing off parts of itself in order to still come at Aminat. She switches guns and shoots white phosphorus. She does not have the time to see if it was effective as two more cherubs descend, too fast

348

for her to draw a bead. She waits, and when the first is within a foot, she slams the rifle stock against it, which seems to stun it into disorganised movement. The second one is on her before she can swing back.

Its embrace is like fire, latching on to Aminat and tearing her skin where the armour is absent. She does not scream. She breathes away the panic as she has been taught. It is like being surrounded by a rainforest, and there seem to be leaves, vines and thorns everywhere, trying to kill her. She draws her hunting knife and begins to slash, range limited at first, and the wood-like parts do not sever, but slowly, she gets freer, enough to grab a sidearm with a Magnum load. Covered in sap and blood, she slashes and blasts her way free. Still they writhe at her feet. Still more come.

She drops remote-control charges at intervals and backs away. When the cherubs descend she activates the charges and flattens herself. Limbs of grass and bough scatter in all directions.

Still they come, spawning from the Beynon, smelling of rot.

Damn it, there are turrets, but she doesn't know how to use them. Where the fuck is that miracle from Bad Fish?

The mind behind the plant is aware of Aminat now, as the sporadic spawning stops and a concentrated front of cherubs advances on her. Dozens. Absolutely no way to fight them in the open like this.

"Bad Fish, you asshole, what the fuck are you waiting for?" But she fires at the wall of green anyway, realising that there is a narrow window of survival here, but not knowing if she can fit herself in it. "Shit, I'm going to die here. Shit."

The change in the air is pleasurable at first. It becomes warmer, and an electromagnetic change tugs at the body hair.

There is gooseflesh, a feeling of an angel tickling the front of the brain, an impulse to laugh, a bubbling of the urine in the bladder. Or maybe Aminat imagines all of this while fighting homicidal plant proxies.

The plant, its leaves, vines, stems and flying cherubs, the drones and COBs above it, all glow golden yellow, then turn black, then fly apart in the wind, an ash shower being all that remains.

The cherubs Aminat is holding at bay stop fighting, become confused, and move without purpose, enlivened but mindless. She leaves them where they writhe and scuttles forward to get a closer look at the place where the plant was, to be sure it is indeed dead and gone. Her phone rings.

"Are you still alive?" asks Bad Fish.

"What the hell was that?"

"Ha-ha, I'm so glad you're here. Kaaro would have killed me. That, darling, is a particle weapon from the *Nautilus*. Did it work, or do I need to fire again? It'll take longer to charge, like thirty minutes or so."

Aminat brushes ash off the tip of her nose. "No, we're good here."

"Glad to hear that. If you're ever in Lagos ..."

Aminat sits cross-legged at the edge of the destruction zone. She is silent, but it is a loud silence, deafening. Her heart feels bald, shorn of all emotion, useful only for pumping cold blood through her exhaustion. She is unsure of where her body is, or where the Earth is moving her to, or why she is.

How long she stays she does not know, or recall later during debrief, but she does know that it ends with the cracks of lightning coming from the remnants of the biodome.

"Alyssa."

Chapter Forty

Alyssa

I know who I am. My name is Alyssa.

Alyssa knows everything.

This is her walking on her street to her home. This is her walking into the dome, stepping over corpses of fools and innocents, slipping, regaining her footing, slipping again.

This is high, high, above the clouds, on board the space station, opening hatches, preparing and charging weapons to strike down enemies.

This is a homeless man called Anthony Salerno in London being dissected by an entity he will never comprehend.

This is Alyssa cold inside the dome, unperturbed, looking for the paths to the deeper parts of the alien.

This is Rosewater full of people like her, Homians with human skins, happy, fulfilled, living again, contemplating renaming Earth.

This is the roll-up coiled in the ground, pining after her dead mate. She will be dead in a month from the grief, worms will eat her, and her stench will cause genteel noses to protest, but such magnificence deserves a last unsubtle hurrah, and the people must endure and even celebrate her putrefaction.

351

This is Alyssa fucking a surprised Mark.

This is Alyssa being told to dial the power down, to be more circumspect, to avoid alarming the humans, to be measured in her implementations. She says, "I refuse."

This is Alyssa walking down a dark hole inside Wormwood, climbing, stumbling, skinning her knees.

On a rowboat, on muddy brown water, Aminat says, "The reason we get floods is the sky god, Olorun, did not take permission from the god of the waters, Olokun, before letting Obatala create land. In her anger she tries to wash all the land away."

Inside Wormwood, there is a level of dead floaters, all hanging in the air by their bladders, looking like seahorses. Alyssa goes deeper still, where everything is moist and rotten, and the miasma is not breathable, and darkness prevails.

This is Alyssa irritated at the inequality of life.

This is Alyssa in the regeneration chamber, with the dead and half-formed Anthonys. Here is the penultimate Anthony, where he came to die. Here is the last Anthony, dead aborning. He has no skin. All of him is a skeleton embedded in the flesh of Wormwood, a few ligaments stringing one bone to another, and some drying mucus. Beyond this chamber is the place for the first Anthony. Withered, shrunken in flexion like a burn victim, with an open skull and nervous tissue stretching from his brain to the walls and beyond. A few of the connections have detached. Alyssa knows that this connection is not functional, but is more symbolic of the bond between man and alien. All the connections needed can be made through the xenosphere.

"Here I am," says Alyssa. "More Homian than human. Let's do this thing."

Here is Alyssa on Home, before it died, cataloguing empty cities and villages on her home continent. It is interesting to her that she now identifies as female, an adjustment to Earth, and that she now identifies as Alyssa, an adjustment to humanity. On Home she did not wish to live in space and was one of the last. She likes to think she *was* the last, but there is no way of knowing.

This is Alyssa receiving the first neuro-tentacle from Wormwood. The pain is unlike anything she has ever experienced, except maybe childbirth. The electrocution pulls at her individual nerve fibres, flowing to her spine, then rising into her brain where it explodes. And yet it is brief, because as soon as it hits the brain, Wormwood switches off her sensory cortex, and she feels nothing. The alien remembers the last time it had to do this, knows it hurts, and does not wish to cause suffering.

I know you now, says Wormwood. **Welcome.**

"I'm happy to be here," says Alyssa. Her voice echoes in the chamber.

Do you want to rebuild the dome?

"There will be no dome, my friend. Follow my lead. I can see everything. Oh, this is good, this is fantastic."

Anthony would—

"I am not Anthony, my friend. I am different."

Alyssa sees the full xenosphere for the first time, and the battle at the heart of it. She sees a giant, a fairy, a dog and a gryphon fighting Wormwood's nemesis, and losing. Here is her friend Aminat, on the outside, contacting another. Here is salvation from space, striking down the evil plant in an instant.

This is Alyssa in an ecstasy of power, all the restraint removed with the plant.

"So much more ... it's impossible ... "

353

First, there are intruders in the sky and on land. She should warn them, but she chooses not to. She splits and expands the north and south ganglia, spreads them out all over the city, a network, then she protrudes new pylons, dozens, hundreds.

This is Alyssa playing with her child. Mark takes a plastic toy out of the oven where the child has deposited it. They laugh, all three of them.

This is the destruction of the invaders of Rosewater. She wants them out of her city, and they stand out, smelling like dead rats, running like cockroaches. She drops all of the drones and they fall like perverse rain, blackened. The planes fall harder, burn longer.

Chapter Forty-One

Jacques

Lora lowers Jack into the chair after his shower. He likes that she is neither disgusted nor impressed. He wonders if there's been a change in how she deals with him since Walter's death. She helps wheel him into the room where Hannah waits. Lora leaves and Hannah hands him cream to apply to his stump. Citric monohydrate, methyl hydroxybenzoate, some other shit, he no longer cares. She does not flinch, but he has seen the looks on her face at various times. It is quite an adjustment for her. They have not had sex since the attack. While he grooms, Lora comes back.

"Taiwo is here. He wants to talk."

Taiwo is in fatigues, but he has several bright medals pinned to his chest. Only God knows where he got them from since Jack didn't award them. He is considerably fatter than when Jack last saw him. He is also looking jolly. Behind him, there are four minions, armed with rifles and jacked on amphetamines.

"Mr Mayor," he says.

"Not for much longer. You look well."

"You do not."

"What do you want, Taiwo?"

"Courtesy call, really. I see there are barbarians at the gate."

"You don't seem worried."

"I'm not. Your little war has been good for me. I'm a decorated war hero *and* a free man. Rich, too, because business boomed."

"That won't make a difference when the Nigerian troops string you up." Most of Rosewater's soldiers had dumped their uniforms and slunk back to hidey-holes.

"Oh, I'm not going to get strung up."

"Taiwo, again, what do you want?"

"I have a way out. You were square and honourable with me. I'll be the same way. Come with me. I'll take you and your family along."

Jack is touched, in spite of everything. "Wow. I never expected this from you."

"Let's make haste. I'll get you new ID chips and passports."

"I'm not going," says Jack.

"Seriously?"

"Seriously. I told you when we started this journey, there is no life for me outside Rosewater. I wasn't kidding. I'm not going anywhere, but you will take Hannah and Lora for me."

Taiwo shrugs. "Okay, get the illustrious Mrs Jacques and let's go."

"I'm not leaving you, sir," says Lora.

"Do I have to give you an order?"

"My job is to assist you. It looks like you still need assistance."

"You will be assisting me by looking after my family, Lora." He does not know whether this will sway her.

"This loyalty is touching and I may shed a tear when I'm in

Majorca, but I am leaving. Now or never." Taiwo signals to his people.

"Give me twenty minutes to say goodbye to my wife," says Jack, and he swivels towards the quarters.

"You have five," shouts Taiwo, but it is without venom, and Jack knows he will wait thirty minutes if need be.

In the room, he starts to apply cream to his ulcers and broach the topic with Hannah, when he double takes. The ulcers seem ... smaller.

"Hannah ... " He can barely speak. He points.

As they both watch, the ulcers dry up, then the skin from the edges grows towards the centre of each one, leaving a small dot of scar tissue which is itself dissipated within minutes.

"What is ... ?" Hannah is as confused as he is.

"This, my darling wife, is us getting back in business. *Lora!* Get the motherfucking president on the phone. I have to tell him directly to fuck himself with a small yam or a large potato."

It is as he thought. The healing means the alien is back in play, and Jack can see from the hologram that those people have somehow killed the plant. The dome is not only open, but the edge of it appears to be spreading in real time. The vegetation springs back up, with shrubs, trees and creeper plants crawling out of any random collection of moist soil. Ivy grows over buildings, spouting flowers on its way. More ganglia have popped up all around the city and invaders retreat or are destroyed. Rosewater denizens are out on the street dancing, knowing healing like they have before, and celebrating.

They did it, those rag-tag assholes.

"Majorca can wait," says Taiwo. "I think we can build a tropical, tax-free paradise right here."

"Let's just call it tax-*friendly* for now," says Jack. "You should go home, or wherever you have decided to stay. I have people to disappoint."

The Tired are already calling, but Jack has no interest in talking to them just yet. He makes calls to Femi and tries to connect with her away team, but he cannot reach any of them. Dahun and his crew are out of contact. He starts to get multiple, enraged text messages from the president again, but strangely, no phone call.

Lora stares at him like this was his plan all along.

"What?" he asks.

"It's like you always say, Mr Mayor. Skill, hard work and competence will only take you so far. Luck is the final ingredient for success."

"Did I say that?"

"Multiple times."

"Fine. I'll take the credit, then."

"Good. Are you in the mood to speak with the president?"

"Can you reach him?"

"I've had him on hold for thirteen minutes."

Ah.

He looks at the last text from the president.

It's a photograph of a penis.

Jack says, "Let's keep him on hold for a little while longer."

Chapter Forty-Two

Aminat

Aminat can still run.

In spite of the upheaval and the crowds in the street, she follows a phantom, a transparent image of the hellhound who seems to want her to follow. As soon as she is almost on him, Yaro turns a corner and runs.

He stops at a building and disappears.

"Don't let him be dead, don't let him be dead," Aminat says or thinks.

She dashes up the stairs to get to Kaaro who she can feel in her mind. She breaks into the room and is confronted with a room full of reanimates, although she knows he is still in there. They are passive, so she pulls three out of the room to make space, then she starts pushing them out of her way. When they are too slow she uses a hip toss and over-arm throw to speed things up. She hears the dog yapping after a few moments.

"Kaaro!"

She finds him huddled in a corner, awake but weak, mumbling, alive. She crouches and covers him in kisses. He stinks of dried sweat and his clothes are crusty, but she clutches him all the same. She even pets the mongrel.

"What are we ... ? Hi ... " says Kaaro.

"Hi," says Aminat. "Send your drones away."

"Why?"

Aminat steps out of her fatigues. "Why do you think?"

Later, they walk hand in hand through the celebrating crowds. Aminat's injuries hurt more, but she doesn't mind. The dried blood can stay until she gets back to base. Wounds probably need suturing too. Discarded soldiers' uniforms line the streets, and there seem to be more reanimates than ever. There are no dead lying on the ground, and Aminat knows Alyssa has succeeded. People scramble for drones and COBs, maybe as souvenirs. In the air, flakes of ash from the Beynon float about. Soft mossy substance underfoot, not terrestrial, at least not originally. Femi was right: the real war is with the aliens. Some people, singing, come along and hug them both, then depart with joy. The very air seems sweeter, but that must be an illusion, surely.

Aminat says, "Baby, what now? We're the frontline of a concerted alien invasion. What do we do?"

Kaaro shrugs. "I don't know. To be fair, they don't want to kill us. Just ... occupy us."

Kaaro had related the death of Anthony, and in the remix of the knowledge, something occurs to Aminat. Monkeys and statuettes of twins ... then it comes to her.

"I have an idea, but we have to go back to the mayor's bunker, or wherever he is right now." Aminat drags Kaaro through the people drunk with happiness, towards the mansion.

The mayor's office seems to be kitsch and trying too hard to Aminat, easily the ugliest office she has ever visited.

"You're sure this will work?" asks Jack Jacques.

"It's better than what you have right now," says Kaaro, "which is just the threat of annihilation. This gives us some control. Anthony figured it out and tried to tell me, and Aminat made sense of it."

"It'll work," says Aminat.

"They're here," says Lora.

Alyssa has changed. She is taller, for one thing, well over six feet, and with a higher muscle-to-fat ratio than before. She has also changed her skin colour. Anthony also did this, but his were various comical shades of brown, to blend in. Alyssa has no pretensions about fitting in, and is now various shades of green, with seaweed hair and her skin varying between chartreuse and olive about the folds. There are organelles on her body, crystalline, like embedded diamonds, placed randomly, even on her face. Her eyes are black and large enough to obscure the white, which is only visible when Alyssa side-eyes. The air around her is charged, literally. Aminat can feel her body hair rising with the static. She wears a flowing gown, probably made of something degradable. *She knows she can wear whatever the fuck she wants and still be taken seriously.*

"I speak for Wormwood," says Alyssa. "I have decision-making proxy for both of us."

"I speak for humanity," says Jack, without a hint of embarrassment or humility. "We would like to offer you something in exchange for the protection and care you have always provided for us."

"What would we need from you?"

"A place for your people," says Jack. "A home for the Homians."

361

I told him not to say that. How do we know if they appreciate poetry or if it's an insult on their planet?

"Jack Jacques, we are already taking the home we want. We do not need you to give this to us."

"You'll have to wait for years doing it your way. I'm offering you something now."

"We are patient, Jack Jacques. We have different understandings and experience of time and entropy."

"Your way will kill us, just like you killed Alyssa Sutcliffe to take her body. I don't believe it's what you want, or at least, what you all want."

"No, the death of your kind is regrettable, but it's no different from you killing cattle and swine to survive. Many of you may regret animal death, but if it came between you and survival ... " Alyssa spreads out her arms, then lets them fall to her sides.

"There is another way. Aminat?"

Aminat takes the floor, and tries not to think of how much the future of humanity rests on what she's about to say. "Your predecessor, Anthony, left a message before dying, but we couldn't figure it out for a while. Monkeys and a wooden statue of a twin. The monkeys have to do with the origin of twins in Yoruba mythology, and the wooden statues are receptacles of the souls of dead twins, which the mother carries around and treats as if still alive."

"Interesting. Actually, not really interesting, but what does this have to do with my people?"

"The reanimates," says Aminat. "They are empty of souls, like the wooden carving. They are so devoid of will even Kaaro can control them. Your people can transmit their consciousness into them and live here, with us, side by side. And when our people die, you can simply transmit into that body. Your culture, your civilisation can start a new chapter living with humans in harmony."

"Since when have humans lived in harmony with anybody? Even with each other?"

"Since now. You know it's a good idea because you're still in the room," says Jack, and he has his signature smile now. Odd to see him in a wheelchair.

"I need to consult on this," says Alyssa.

"I thought you had proxy?" says Aminat.

"For Wormwood, yes, because we are one, but not for the entire Home population. You're asking me to alter a fundamental plan agreed aeons ago. I need to consult."

With that she sits where she is, gown pooling around her, eyes closed.

"How long will this take?" Jack asks Kaaro.

"Who knows? I'm hungry."

In the day room Kaaro eats a tower of crackers with ground nuts because that's all there is. There are crumbs all over his shirt front, and when he speaks, bits fly out of his mouth. He is uncouth and Aminat loves him.

"Can't you eavesdrop on the conversation in the xenosphere?" she asks.

"I tried. Got kicked out."

Through the bay windows, two guards walk a prisoner past. Femi Alaagomeji. She glances at them, but then looks straight ahead.

"She's going to a deep, dark hole like for ever," says Kaaro.

Aminat rises, races after. "Wait."

"Are you happy? You saved your little city," says Femi.

"I am, kind of, yes."

"That's because you're simple. But then, I only ever employed you because of what was between your legs."

Aminat's first assignment. Her ex-husband. "That would hurt my feelings if I thought it was true."

"You should have just followed my orders, Aminat. Now you have the dubious honour of having doomed humanity."

"And you'll have the dubious honour of being right, if not compassionate."

"Baby, it's time. They're calling us in," says Kaaro.

"I'll visit you in prison," Aminat says.

"We'll see," says Femi. "The president and Jacques will make a deal. I'll be out in days. I want you to spend time thinking of what I'll be doing on the other side of the inevitable border, what my focus will be."

Aminat wants to hit her then, but turns to attend the meeting instead. Time enough for Femi afterwards.

"We accept your offer. We will begin transmitting into the reanimates as soon as is practicable. I expect arrangements for housing and welfare of my people to begin just as swiftly."

"It will be done," says Jack. He stretches out his right hand. "Welcome to Earth."

On their way out they run into Taiwo, who knows Aminat as the ex-wife of his criminal associate, and Kaaro as an undercover cop. She feels Kaaro cower and she subtly steps between them.

"Well, well. One traitorous wife and one traitor," says Taiwo. "How's your husband?"

364

"Ex-husband. Rotting somewhere, for all I care," says Aminat.

"And this is your man, now? This amebo?"

Aminat moves closer to the gangster. "Go away, Taiwo. We want no trouble."

Taiwo smiles with his eyes and teeth, a slow predator's smile. "It's going to be interesting living in Rosewater from now. I mean, look at me, a free man, all sins forgiven, and a war hero."

"That sounds well rehearsed," says Aminat. "How many times have you repeated the war hero bit?"

Taiwo leans in, talking to Aminat, but aiming the words at Kaaro. "In this new future of mine I'll have nothing else to do but look up old friends. Exciting times ahead. Boys, let's go. I feel the need for an expensive hooker, Viagra, and some ketamine."

"Assholes come thick and fast here," says Aminat. She holds Kaaro's shoulder. "I won't let him hurt you, my love."

"I'm tired of all this, Aminat, I'm tired of fighting. Taiwo almost killed me one time. He should be in prison, not venerated."

She holds his gaze. "I will not let him harm you."

Her phone rings. It's Lora. "He wants you." She transfers the call to Jacques.

"Where are you going?"

Aminat shrugs, knowing he can't see her. "Home, with one man and his dog."

"Do you want a job?"

"I'm sorry?"

"I've just got off the phone with the president. We had an arbitration by ... an interested third party. Anyway, we've

365

been granted city state status, in principle, although there are many constitutional bits to work out. I need a head of security, Aminat."

"What makes you think I'm qualified to lead?"

"If I can do a job I'm unqualified for, surely you can? Besides, I saw you in action. I want you."

Aminat looks at Kaaro. "I'll have to think on it."

"Take all the time you need. I'm kidding. You have twenty-four hours."

And with that he is gone. She is about to tell Kaaro when she notices his eyes have gone glassy. She follows his gaze and there's Oyin Da, the Bicycle Girl herself, thinker, anarchist, time-traveller and former crush of Kaaro's. She always brings trouble.

"What the fuck are you doing here?" Aminat spits.

"I want to speak with Kaaro," says Oyin Da.

"You can't," says Aminat. "We've been through a lot, and he wants to go home. He literally just said that to me."

She nods, twice, seems about to say something, then turns to leave. "Do not let Femi die in custody, Aminat. It would be bad for everyone."

She seems to walk into the air, there now, gone in a second.

Aminat relays the information to Lora, then takes Kaaro home where she is uncharacteristically domestic to tease him out of his funk.

She even feeds the hellhound.

Interlude: 2067

Eric

I can't leave the way I came, the celebrations and the crowd density are insane in the south-west, so I break even further north, hoping to work my way through the ruins of what was the financial district, and hike up the hills, make contact with S45 when I'm beyond the waste processing plant. The bombing has been uneven here, with some high-rises broken to the foundation and others oddly intact. I walk through concrete canyons paved with broken glass, holding Nuru's tentacle as a weapon. The suckers stick to my forearm sometimes, but the tip always points outward. I can feel a pulse in it, like it's developed a heart. I'm plagued by phantoms as I walk, ruin-dwellers afraid of my confidence and scampering like cockroaches. Someone takes a potshot at me, but the grapheme absorbs it. I don't even bother to chase the person down.

I avoid roads where there are new ganglions, but it's hard. They are everywhere now, which is good for Rosewater, but bad for me.

I see a crater with a downed drone, and seven skeletons around it. I'm guessing it had an incendiary payload that went off after a delay. These poor scavengers got caught in the blast.

I'm starving and running out of drinking water, but I'll be out of town by nightfall, so I'm not worried about that. I do look in some of the buildings, but the taps aren't on yet. The new mossy green layer on the ground absorbs sound and sticks to the boot. I try to eat it, or squeeze moisture out, but it's bitter, and that might mean toxic. I take ten-minute breaks every half an hour during which time I try to search the xenosphere, but it's full of what I can only call neuro-static, all flashing lights and incoherence. In the quiet moments I still remember the ambush, and the fear at the moment I thought I was going to be killed, the scattering of Nuru's body parts in the blasts. When I think this the tentacle twitches, as if it remembers, at which point I wonder if it's accessing my thoughts in some way, but then I see three people coming towards me. They are armed with cudgels and maybe a gun.

I rise to them, but the tentacle does all the work. Of its own volition it streaks out at the first person's face and drives a spike through. She drops. It detaches and wraps around the arm of the one with a gun then it reverses its track, coming away with clothing, skin and muscle, desleeving the bones. The screams of its owner echo all around us. The third is changing his mind, but the tentacle, sensing only a fraction of my movement or intent, whips across the neck and tears out a handful of flesh from the side of his neck. Blood fountains as he staggers for three steps, then stops.

The tentacle becomes inert again.

I search them, and come away with one locust bar, and two unspecified protein sachets, which usually means blended cockroach and ant. No water. I chew two squares of the locust, and keep moving.

I soon come to three topless boys taking turns to drink out of a tubular plant shoot. They say it's their plant and I have to pay. I give them the unspecified protein, then I drink. The water is sweet with a hint of chalkiness. After a bit of suction it flows, and rushes abundantly, so I rub some on my head. Then I see her standing where I was. The tentacle is not reactive. She is tall, with variegated green skin and black studs here and there, which are either piercings or growing out of her. She's wearing a flowing gown that the wind is trying to take away from her. She does not look pleased to see me.

"You're Eric. The assassin."

And, just as suddenly, I know. "You're the new proxy for Wormwood."

"Even so."

"What do you want from me?"

"You have crimes to answer for."

"First of all, they're not crimes. I am an agent of the legitimate government of Nigeria, which includes Rosewater, although I don't yet know what's happened with this armistice. I'm an agent on orders. Secondly, why do you care? You're an alien. This does not concern you."

"I need to keep this area safe because my people are coming."

"And you can do that. I'm walking away, so even if you consider me dangerous, letting me go would be the thing to improve the safety of Rosewater."

"Or I could kill you and be sure."

At this point, though, I see hesitation, and I gamble that she is torn. With all my will-power I turn my back on her and take another gulp of the fresh water. "You could, but I'll tell you what: kill me quick. I have no patience for listening to words from an alien in league with someone as evil as Jack Jacques. I wish I had succeeded."

I fill the canteen I found on my trek, and walk away from her, expecting to be disintegrated or crushed or given a stroke any minute. It doesn't happen, although I sweat for a mile despite the sun going down. Once it is nightfall, I no longer sense her around me, although she is everywhere in Rosewater. I start to wonder about the speech I gave her, and the words do not seem like my own at all. In fact . . .

"Kaaro," I say.

The gryphon appears to me in the xenosphere. "*Bawo ni?*"

"What else have you left in my head?" He sounds a lot cheerier than I would have expected.

"Nothing, nothing, I swear. This is all in real time. I didn't puppetmaster you, Eric."

"And yet."

"And yet I may have given you a nudge or two, for old times' sake. The rest was all you, I swear. Some intercollegiate stuff, agent to ex-agent."

"What do you want?"

"Just making sure you're really gone. And Eric?"

"Yes?"

"Don't ever come back here. Gryphons are territorial."

I walk past the processing plant, the marker of city limits. I don't know exactly everything that happened here, but I am glad to be out. I look back and there is a large area of darkness where the dome used to be. All the dozens of new ganglia glitter like stars. A breeze carries the smell of waste from the plant.

I give Rosewater the middle finger. "Fuck you."

I hold it up for some minutes, then I signal for a pick-up.

Chapter Forty-Three

The Sutcliffes

It has been four hours since Mark and Pat Sutcliffe returned home. They work in silence, solemn, unresponsive to the noise and jubilation outside. Their war is not over because Alyssa is missing still.

In their absence the house has been looted, stripped clean of possessions and vandalised, but not burned down like some on the street, and not hit by bombs. Mark is one to count his blessings. Pat is alive, well, if a little thin, and more grown up than he would have liked. She sweeps, he carries the heavy stuff. The plan for today is to clear a simple sleeping space for the two of them, then tomorrow, they will continue to work. There is some food, meagre, but hunger-breaking. The things Mark fears are the roving rats, the swarms, but since the new incarnation of the alien, they seem to have retreated, as have the droppers, and nobody has spotted a cherub in a long while.

He glances at Pat, pained by her shorn hair and her thin look. He knows he himself is much thinner, and his hair is just as short. Lice.

He'll have to find a way to secure the property. The last few weeks have been spent on the move, keeping himself and his daughter safe, sometimes by hiding, sometimes by alliances and joining groups. Mark has done violence for the first time in his life, finding a vein of savagery he did not know possible, and at times his dreams are full of blood and choking. He does not know if he will ever pick up a brush to paint without pain spilling out, but maybe that's a good thing.

How will his daughter learn to be a child again? Will she smile? Will she laugh?

"Hey, Pat, on what side does a chicken have the most feathers?" he asks.

"On the outside," says a voice from the door, the last thing either Mark or Pat is expecting.

Alyssa.

Alyssa.

From the xenosphere, Alyssa watches the family reunited, watches them hug each other and cry, watches them close the door on the outside world and start living their lives again.

The Alyssa in there is as real as she can get. All the memories she could scavenge are in her. Alyssa's ID chip is in her. They will think her traumatised or just confused, and they will make excuses for her lapses.

She does not know why she has done this. Guilt? A sense of justice? Over-identification with Aminat and Kaaro?

It matters little. This is the simplest solution to the simplest problem, and that niggling thought, that feeling of unease is gone.

Now she can focus on her work, on Rosewater, the first new Homian city in centuries.

She makes herself visible outside the prison, just as Jack Jacques opens the door. He smiles, standing a little awkwardly on his new prosthesis.

"I can fix that leg for you," says Alyssa. "Grow you a new one in less than an hour."

"Thank you, but no thanks," says Jack. Then he thinks, *You'll fuck it up and my knee will bend backwards or something.*

"That was Anthony, not me," says Alyssa, but she lets it pass.

"Would you like to come with me?"

Aminat is on his entourage and she winks to Alyssa. The rest are armed personnel wearing opaque visors. Alyssa is aware they are connected to a high-altitude drone that bears explosive weapons.

Jacques keeps up a monologue. "Most sections of the prison are empty because the prisoners were released to fight in the insurrection, but J-wing was always special."

On the walkway, standing arms akimbo, is Hannah Jacques.

Jack says, "Honey, what are you doing?"

"I'll get to you later. For now, I have words for this person."

Alyssa seems patient. "Speak."

"You haven't saved your planet or your people. Those of you who survived should have stayed in the space stations. What you've done instead is commit mass suicide. The mind is an illusion, a hologram generated by the body. What you've encoded is memory, and personhood is not just memories. Personhood is embodied.

"Your billions are dead and what you have, what you are, is a new type of human. This exercise of yours is an expensive memory project, and all you've saved is your culture."

"We're just trying to stay alive, Mrs Jacques. Any kind of life will do. You would act the same if our positions were reversed."

"I can't convince you to withdraw?"

"Not a chance."

"Then *kara o le*. We will meet again." Hannah strides off.

Alyssa continues along the walkway.

There are thousands of reanimates, some still, some milling, all with that empty-vessel feel in the xenosphere. Alyssa walks to the centre of the catwalk and enters the xenosphere. First she finds the exact number of reanimates, which turns out to be twenty-one thousand and sixteen. She queries for Lua and waits till she receives a response.

[transmission commences . . .]

[error checking . . .]

[stand by]

Alyssa loses contact with Lua for a minute, then the contact is restored, but different. It is now down among the reanimates. Alyssa jumps from the walkway to the floor. The reanimates all have awareness and self-consciousness now.

"Welcome to Earth; welcome to Rosewater," says Jack Jacques, arms spread out in welcome. Alyssa is annoyed – she had wanted to say that, had wanted the first voice they heard to be a Homian one.

"I am Alyssa, the first, the footholder. We have much to discuss. Come."

Scores of prison workers guide the newcomers to medical, for registration and a check-up.

Alyssa's work is just beginning, but it is the beginning of the end.

Look out for the final book in the Wormwood trilogy,
The Rosewater Redemption . . .

Acknowledgements

Ashley Jacobs, Chikodili Emelumadu, Aliette deBodard and Kate Elliot for miscellaneous encouragement and reading.

My agent, Alexander Cochran, excellent as always.

The Orbit superteam: Jenni Hill, Sarah Guan, Nazia Khatun (Queen of the Universe and everything!!!) and Joanna Kramer for making me look good in more ways than one.

My SFF massive: Zen Cho, Victor Ocampo, Vida Cruz, Likhain, Rochita Loenen-ruiz, Alessa Hinlo.

My family, for putting up with my nerd-rage and general madman-in-the-attic histrionics.

Thanks!

extras

www.orbitbooks.net

about the author

Tade Thompson is the author of *Rosewater*, a John W. Campbell Award finalist and winner of the 2017 NOMMO Award for Best Novel. His novella, *The Murders of Molly Southbourne*, has recently been optioned for screen adaptation. He also writes short stories, notably "The Apologists", which was nominated for a British Science Fiction Association Award. Born in London to Yoruba parents, he lives and works on the south coast of England where he battles an addiction to books.

Find out more about Tade Thompson and other Orbit authors by registering for the free monthly newsletter at www.orbitbooks.net.

about the author

if you enjoyed

THE ROSEWATER INSURRECTION

look out for

BLACKFISH CITY

by

Sam J. Miller

EVERY CITY IS A WAR.

*After the climate wars, a floating city was constructed
in the Arctic Circle. Once a remarkable feat of
mechanical and social engineering, it is now rife with
corruption and the population simmers with unrest.
Into this turmoil comes a strange new visitor – a woman
accompanied by an orca and a chained polar bear.
She disappears into the crowds looking for someone
she lost thirty years ago, followed by whispers of a
vanished people who could bond with animals. Her
arrival draws together four people and sparks a chain
of events that will change Blackfish City for ever.*

People Would Say

People would say she came to Qaanaaq in a skiff towed by a killer whale harnessed to the front like a horse. In these stories, which grew astonishingly elaborate in the days and weeks after her arrival, the polar bear paced beside her on the flat bloody deck of the boat. Her face was clenched and angry. She wore battle armor built from thick scavenged plastic.

At her feet, in heaps, were the kind of weird weapons and machines that refugee-camp ingenuity had been producing; strange tools fashioned from the wreckage of Manhattan or Mumbai. Her fingers twitched along the walrus-ivory handle of her blade. She had come to do something horrific in Qaanaaq, and she could not wait to start.

You have heard these stories. You may even have told them. Stories are valuable here. They are what we brought when we came here; they are what cannot be taken away from us.

The truth of her arrival was almost certainly less dramatic. The skiff was your standard tri-power rig, with a sail and oars and a gas engine, and for the last few miles of her journey to the floating city it was the engine that she used. The killer whale swam beside her. The polar bear was in chains, a metal cage over its head and two smaller ones boxing in its forepaws. She wore simple clothes, the skins and furs preferred by the people who had fled to the north when the cities of the south began to burn or sink. She did not pace. Her weapon lay at her feet. She brought nothing else with her. Whatever she had come to Qaanaaq to accomplish, her face gave no hint of whether it would be bloody or beautiful or both.

Fill

After the crying, and the throwing up, and the scrolling through his entire contacts list and realizing there wasn't a single person he could tell, and the drafting and then deleting five separate long graphic messages to *all* his contacts, and the deciding to kill himself, and the deciding not to, Fill went out for a walk.

Qaanaaq's windscreen had been shifted to the north, and as soon as Fill stepped out onto Arm One he felt the full force of the subarctic wind. His face was unprotected and the pain of it felt good. For five minutes, maybe more, he stood there. Breathing. Eyes shut, and then eyes open. Smelling the slight methane stink of the nightlamps; letting his teeth chatter in the city's relentless, dependable cold. Taking in the sights he'd been seeing all his life.

I'm going to die, he thought.

I'm going to die soon.

The cold helped distract him from how much his stomach hurt. His stomach and his throat, for that matter, where he was pretty sure he had torn something in the half hour he'd spent retching. A speaker droned from a storefront: a news broadcast, the latest American government had fallen, pundits predicting it'd be the last, the flotilla disbanded after the latest bombing, and he didn't care, because why should he, why should he care about anything?

People walked past him. Bundled up expensively. Carrying polyglass cages in which sea otters or baby red pandas paced, unhappy lucky animals saved from extinction by Qaanaaq's elite. All of whom were focused on getting somewhere, doing something, the normal self-important bustle of ultra-wealthy Arm One. Something he despised, or did on every other day. Deaf to the sea that surged directly beneath their feet and stretched on into infinity on either side of Qaanaaq's narrow metal arms. He'd been so proud of his indolent life, his ability to stop and stand on a street corner for no reason at all. Today he didn't hate them, these people passing him by. He didn't pity them.

Fill wondered: *How many of them have it?*

A child tapped his hip. "Orca, mister!" A pic tout, selling blurry shots of the lady with the killer whale and the polar bear. Fill bought one from the girl on obscure impulse—part pity, part boredom. Something else, too. A glimmer of buoyant wanting. Remembered joy, his childhood fascination with the stories of people emotionally melded with animals thanks to tiny machines in their blood. Collecting pedia entries and plastiprinted figures ... and scowls, from his grandfather, who said nanobonding was a stupid, naive myth. His plastic figures gone one morning. Grandfather was sweet and kind, but Grandfather tolerated no impracticality.

On some level, the diagnosis hadn't been a surprise. Of course he had the breaks. No one in any of the grid cities could have as much sex as he had, and be as uncareful as he was, without getting it. And he'd lived in fear for so long. Spent so much time imagining his grisly fate. He was shocked, really, to have such a visceral reaction.

Tapping his jaw bug, Fill whispered, "Play *City Without a Map,* file six."

A woman's voice filled his ears, old and strange and soothing, the wobble in her Swedish precise enough to mark her as someone who'd come to Qaanaaq decades ago.

> You are new here. It is overwhelming, terrifying. Don't be afraid.
>
> Shut your eyes. I'm here.
>
> Pinch your nose shut. Its smell is not the smell of your city. You can listen, because every city sounds like chaos. You will even hear your language, if you listen long enough.
>
> There is no map here. No map is needed. No manual. Only stories. Which is why I'm here.

A different kind of terror gripped Fill now. The horror of joy, of bliss, of union with something bigger and more magnificent than he could ever hope to be.

For months he'd been obsessing over the mysterious broadcasts. An elliptical, incongruent guidebook for new arrivals, passed from person to person by the tens of thousands. He switched to the next one, a male voice, adolescent, in Slavic-accented English.

> Qaanaaq is an eight-armed asterisk. East of Greenland, north of Iceland. Built by an unruly alignment of Thai-Chinese-Swedish corporations and government entities, part of the second wave of grid city construction, learning from the spectacular failures of several early efforts. Almost

a million people call it home, though many are migrant workers who spend much of their time on boats harvesting glaciers for freshwater ice—fewer and fewer of these as the price of desalinization crystals plummets—or working Russian petroleum rigs in the far Arctic. Arm One points due south and Arm Eight to the north; Four is west and Five is east. Arms Two and Three are southwest and southeast; Arms Six and Seven are northwest and northeast. The central Hub is built upon a deep-sea geothermal vent, which provides most of the city's heat and electricity.

Submerged tanks, each one the size of an old-world city block, process the city's waste into the methane that lights it up at night. Periodic controlled ventilations of treated methane and ammonia send parabolas of bright green fire into the sky. Multicolored pipes vein the outside of every building in a dense varicose web: crimson chrome for heat, dark olive for potable water, mirror black for sewage. And then the bootleg ones, the off-color reds for hijacked heat, the green plastics for stolen water.

Whole communities had sprung up of *City* devotees. Camps, factions, subcults. Some people believed that the Author was a machine, a bot, one of the ghost malware programs that haunted the Qaanaaq net. Such software had become astonishingly sophisticated in the final years before the Sys Wars. Poet bots spun free-verse sonnets that fooled critics, made award winners weep. Scam bots wove intricate, compellingly argued appeals for cash. Not hard to imagine a lonely binary bard wandering through the forever twilight of Qaanaaq's digital dreamscape, possibly glommed on unwillingly to a voice-generation software that constantly conjured up new combinations of synthesized age and gender and language and class and ethnic and national vocal tics. Its insistence on providing a physical description of itself would not be out of character, since most had been coded to try their best to persuade people that they were real—Nigerian princes, refugee relatives, distressed friends trapped in foreign lands.

Other theorists believed in a secret collective, a group of writers for whom the broadcasts were simultaneously a recruitment tool and a soapbox. Possibly an underground forbidden political party with the nefarious endgame of uniting the unwashed hordes of the Upper Arms and slaughtering the wealthier innocents who ruled the city.

On Arms One and Two and Three, glass tunnels connect buildings twenty stories up. Archways support promenades. Massive gardens on hydraulic lifts can carry a delighted garden party up into the sky. Spherical pods on struts can descend into the sea, for underwater privacy, or extend to the sky, to look down on the crowds below.

The architecture of the other Arms is less impressive. Tight floating tenements; boats with stacked boxes. The uppermost Arms boggle the mind. Boxes heaped on boxes; illicit steel stilts holding up overcrowded crates. Slums are always a marvel; how human desperation can seem to warp the very laws of physics.

Fill subscribed to the single-author theory. *City Without a Map* was the work of one person—one human, corporeal person. He went through phases, periods when he was convinced the Author was male and times when he knew she was female—old, young, dark-skinned, light-skinned, poor, rich ... whoever they were, they somehow managed to get hundreds of different people to record their gorgeous, elliptical instructions for how to make one's way through the tangled labyrinth of his city.

Not how to survive. Mere survival wasn't the issue for the Author. The audience he or she wrote for, spoke to—they knew how to survive. They had been through so much, before they came to Qaanaaq. What the Author wanted was for them to find happiness, joy, bliss, community. The Author's love for their listeners was palpable, beautiful, oozing out of every word. When Fill listened, even though he knew he was not part of the Author's intended audience, he felt loved. He felt like he was part of something.

Nations burned, and people came to Qaanaaq. Arctic melt opened the interior for resource exploitation, and people came. Some of us came willingly. Some of us did not.

Qaanaaq was not a blank slate. People brought their ghosts with them. Soil and stories and stones from homelands swallowed up by the sea. Ancestral grudges. Incongruent superstitions.

Fill wiped tears from his eyes. Some were from the words, the hungry hopeful tone of voice of the last Reader, but some were still from the pain of his diagnosis. God, he was an idiot. Snow fell, wet and heavy. Projectors hidden below the grid he walked on beamed gorgeous writhing fractal shapes onto the wind-blown flurry. A child jumped, swatted at the snow, laughed at how a fish or bird imploded only to reappear as new flakes fell.

A startling, uncontrollable reaction: Fill giggled. The snow projections could still make his chest swell with childish wonder. He waved his hand through a manta ray as it soared past. And all at once—the pain went away. His throat, his stomach. His heart. The fear and the nightmare images of twisted bodies in refugee camp hospital beds; the memory of broken-minded breaks victims wandering the streets of the Upper Arms, the songs they sang, the things they shrieked, the things they did to themselves with fingers or knives without feeling it. Every time he followed a man down a dark alley, or met one at a lavish apartment, or dropped to his knees in a filthy Arm Eight public restroom, this was the ice-shard blade that scraped at his heart. This was what he'd been afraid of.

Fill laughed softly.

When the worst thing that can possibly happen to you finally happens, you find that you are not afraid of anything.